Anonymous

A treatise on physiology and hygiene for educational institutions

and general readers

Anonymous

A treatise on physiology and hygiene for educational institutions and general readers

ISBN/EAN: 9783742832849

Manufactured in Europe, USA, Canada, Australia, Japa

Cover: Foto ©Andreas Hilbeck / pixelio.de

Manufactured and distributed by brebook publishing software (www.brebook.com)

Anonymous

A treatise on physiology and hygiene for educational institutions

and general readers

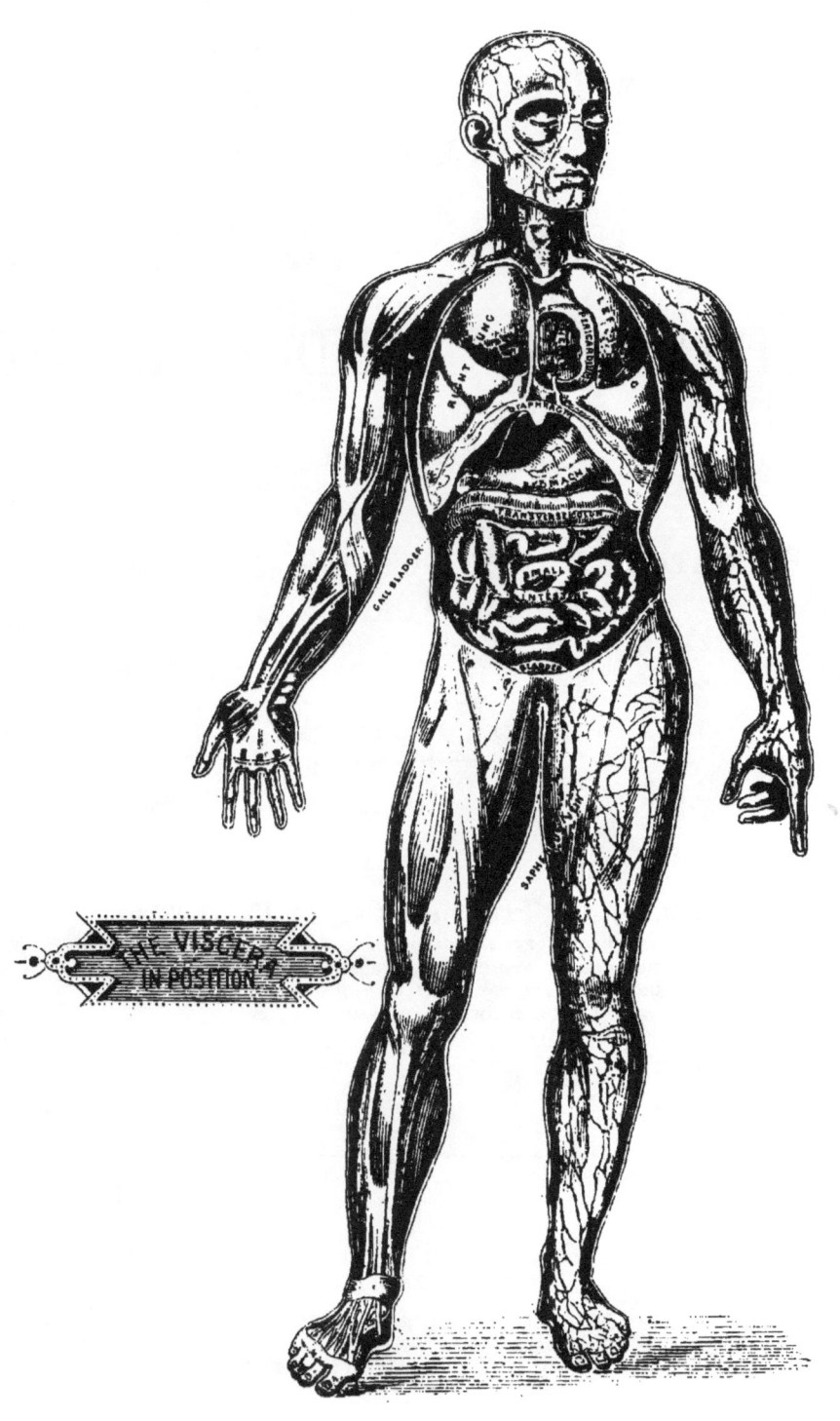

THE VISCERA
IN POSITION

A

TREATISE

ON

PHYSIOLOGY AND HYGIENE

FOR

EDUCATIONAL INSTITUTIONS AND GENERAL READERS.

FULLY ILLUSTRATED.

BY

JOSEPH C. HUTCHISON, M.D., LL.D.,

EX-PRESIDENT OF THE NEW YORK PATHOLOGICAL SOCIETY, EX-VICE PRESIDENT OF THE
NEW YORK ACADEMY OF MEDICINE, SURGEON TO THE BROOKLYN CITY
HOSPITAL, LATE PRESIDENT OF THE MEDICAL SOCIETY
OF THE STATE OF NEW YORK, ETC., ETC.

NEW YORK:

MAYNARD, MERRILL, & CO.,

43, 45 AND 47 EAST TENTH STREET.

1893.

PREFACE.

THIS work is designed to present the leading facts and principles of human Physiology and Hygiene in clear and concise language, so that pupils in schools and colleges, and readers not familiar with the subjects, may readily comprehend them. Anatomy, or a description of the structure of an organ, is of course necessary to the understanding of its Physiology, or its uses. Enough of the former study has, therefore, been introduced to enable the pupil to enter intelligently upon the latter.

Familiar language, as far as practicable, has been employed, rather than that of a technical character. With a view, however, to supply what might seem to some a deficiency in this regard, a Pronouncing Glossary has been added, which will enable the inquirer to understand the meaning of many scientific terms not in common use.

In the preparation of the work the writer has carefully examined all the best material at his command, and freely used it; the special object being to have it abreast of the present knowledge on the subjects treated, as far as such is possible in a work so elementary as this. The discussion of disputed points has been avoided, it being manifestly inappropriate in a work of this kind.

Instruction in the rudiments of Physiology in schools does not necessitate the general practice of dissection, or of experiments upon animals. The most important subjects may be illustrated by drawings, such as are contained in this work. Models, especially those constructed by Auzoux of Paris, dried preparations of the human body, and the organs of the lower animals, may also be used with advantage.

The writer desires to acknowledge his indebtedness to R. M. WYCKOFF, M.D., for valuable aid in the preparation of the manuscript for the press ; and to R. CRESSON STILES, M.D., a skillful microscopist and physician, for the chapter "On the Use of the Microscope in the Study of Physiology."

PREFACE TO THE REVISED EDITION.

IN the preparation of this edition, each paragraph has been carefully revised, but the changes that have been made relate chiefly to verbal alterations and errors of typography. Several new illustrations have, however, been introduced, and wherever practicable, the names of the organs have been printed on them, instead of under them with letters and lines pointing them out. This arrangement the pupil will find to be a great improvement. Considerable new material has also been added on the influence of alcohol and narcotics on health.

The favor with which the book has been received is the most conclusive evidence of its adaptation to the needs of the pupil.

CONTENTS.

CHAPTER V.

FOOD AND DRINK.

CHAPTER VI.

DIGESTION.

CHAPTER VII.

THE CIRCULATION.

CHAPTER VIII.

RESPIRATION.

CHAPTER IX.

THE NERVOUS SYSTEM.

CHAPTER X.

THE SPECIAL SENSES.

CHAPTER XI.

THE VOICE.

CHAPTER XII.

THE USE OF THE MICROSCOPE IN THE STUDY OF PHYSIOLOGY.

LIST OF ILLUSTRATIONS.

INTRODUCTION.

THE Human Body is the abode of an immortal spirit, and is the most complete and perfect specimen of the Creator's handiwork. To examine its structure, to ascertain the uses and modes of action of its various parts, how to protect it from injury, and maintain it in a healthy condition, is the design of this work.

The departments of knowledge which are concerned in these investigations, are the science of Human Physiology and the art of Hygiene.

PHYSIOLOGY treats of the vital actions and uses of the various parts of living bodies, whether vegetable or animal. Each living thing, therefore, has a Physiology. We have a *Vegetable* Physiology, which relates to plants; and an *Animal* Physiology, relating to the animal kingdom. The latter is also divided into *Comparative* Physiology, which treats of the inferior races of animals, and *Human* Physiology, which teaches the uses of the various parts of the human body.

HYGIENE, or the art of preserving health, is the practical use of Physiology. It teaches us how to cultivate our bodily and mental powers, so as to increase our strength, and to fit us for a higher enjoyment of life. It also shows us how to prevent some of the accidents which may befall the body, and to avoid disease. It is proper that we should understand the construction and power of our bodies; but it is our duty, as rational beings, to know the laws by which health and strength may be maintained and disease warded off.

There are various means by which we gain important information respecting the Physiology of man. Plants aid us in understanding the minute structure of the human body, its circulation, and absorption. From inferior animals we learn much in respect to the workings of the different *organs,* as we call those parts of the system which have a particular duty to perform. In one of them, as in the foot of the frog, we can study the circulation of the blood; in another, we can study the action of the brain.

By *vivisection,* or the laying bare of some organ of a living animal, we are able to investigate certain vital processes which are too deeply hidden in the human body to be studied directly. This is not necessarily a cruel procedure, as we can, by the use of anæsthetics, so blunt the sensibility of the animal under operation, that he need not suffer while the experiment is being performed. There are other means by which we gather our information. There are occasionally men, who, from some accident, present certain parts, naturally out of view, in exposed positions. In these cases, our knowledge is of much greater value than when obtained from creatures lower in the scale of being than man.

We are greatly aided, also, by the use of various instruments of modern invention. Chief among these is the microscope, which is, as we shall learn hereafter, an arrangement and combination of lenses in such a way as greatly to magnify the objects we wish to examine.

We have much to say of Life, or vital activity, in the course of our study of Physiology; but the most that we know of it is seen in its results. What Life is, or where its precise position is, we are not able to determine. We discover one thing, however, that all the parts of the body are united together with wonderful sympathy, so that one part cannot be injured and other parts not suffer damage. It is further evident that all organs are not equally important in carrying on the work of Life; for some may temporarily suspend their action, without serious results to the system, while others must never cease from acting. Yet there is nothing superfluous or without aim in our frames, and no part or organ can suffer harm without actual loss to the general bodily health. On this point Science and Holy Writ strictly agree.

PHYSIOLOGY AND HYGIENE.

CHAPTER I.

THE FRAMEWORK OF THE BODY.

The Bones — Their Form and Composition — The Properties of Bone — The Skeleton — The Joints — The Spinal Column — The Growth of Bone — The Repair of Bone — Changes in the Skeleton — Erect Posture.

1. The Bones.—The framework which sustains the human body is composed of the *Bones.* The superstructure consists of the various organs on which the processes of life depend. These organs are soft and delicately formed, and, if unprotected, would, in most cases, rapidly be destroyed when subjected to violence, however slight. The bones, having great strength and power of resistance, afford the protection required. (*Read Note* 1.)

2. The more delicate the organ, the more completely does Nature shield it. For example : the brain, which is soft in structure, is

---

1. Self-Knowledge.—" It has been said with truth that the human mind, which can survey the heavens and calculate the motion and density of the stars, finds itself confounded when, returning from these distant journeyings, it enters its own dwelling-place—the body. Man's own organization is still among those mysteries of nature which he is least able to penetrate, in spite of his incessant efforts to lift the veil which hides it. In all ages he has sought to *know himself.* In all times he has studied the relations between his own existence and that of the world, and those universal influences which, though evident to him, are nearly all inexplicable in their action upon living beings." —*Le Pileur on the Human Body.*

---

1. The framework of the body? The superstructure? Softness and delicacy of the organs? How protected?
2. The more delicate the organ? Example in relation to the brain? The eye? The lungs? The services performed by the bones?

enclosed on all sides by a spherical box of bone ; the eye, though it must be near the surface of the body to command an extensive view, is sheltered from injury within a deep recess of bone ; the lungs, requiring freedom of motion as well as protection, are surrounded by a large " chest " of bone and muscle. The bones serve other useful purposes. They give permanence of form to the body, by holding the softer parts in their proper places. They assist in movement, by affording points of attachment to those organs which have power of motion—the muscles.

3. The Form and Composition of the Bones. — The shape and size of the bones vary greatly in different parts of the body, but generally they are arranged in pairs, one for each side of the body. They are composed of both mineral and animal substances, united in the proportion of two parts of the former to one of the latter ; and we may separate each of these substances from the other for examination. First, if we expose a bone to the action of fire, the animal substance is driven off, or "burned out." We now find that, though the shape of the bone is perfectly retained, what is left is no longer tough, and does not sustain weight as before. Again, we may remove the mineral portion, which is a form of lime, by placing a bone into a dilute acid. The lime will be dissolved out, and the shape of the bone remain as before ; but now its firmness has disappeared, and it may be bent without breaking.

4. If, for any reason, either of these ingredients is disproportionate in the bone during life, the body is in danger. The mineral substance is useful in giving rigidity of form, while the animal substance insures toughness and elasticity, so that by their union, we are able to withstand greater shocks and heavier falls than would be possible with either alone. In youth, the period of greatest activity, the animal portion is in excess ; a bone then does not break so readily, but, when broken, unites with great rapidity and strength. On the other hand, the bones of old persons are more easily broken, and in some cases fail to unite. The mineral matter

---

3. Their shape and size? Of what composed? Possibility of being separated? Effect of fire? Of dilute acid?
4. Effect of deficiency of ingredient? Usefulness of the lime? Of the animal substance? Effect of their union? Condition, in youth? Old age?

being then in excess, indicates that the period of active exertion is drawing to a close. (*Read Note* 2).

5. The Structure of the Bones.—If we examine one of the long bones, which has been sawed through lengthwise, we observe

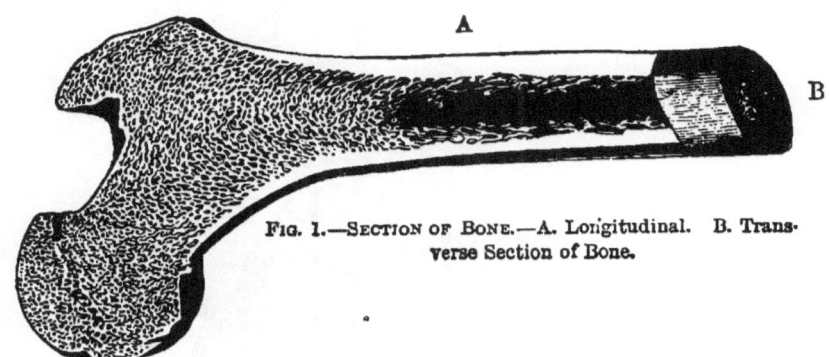

Fig. 1.—Section of Bone.—A. Longitudinal. B. Transverse Section of Bone.

that it is admirably fashioned for affording lightness as well as strength (Fig. 1). Its exterior is hard and resisting, but it is porous at the broad extremities, while through the central portion

---

2. Some Properties of Bone.—"The power of bone to resist decay is remarkable. Fossil bones deposited in the ground long before the appearance of man upon the earth have been found by Cuvier, exhibiting a considerable portion of cartilage. The jaw of the Cambridge Mastodon contained over forty per cent. of animal matter—enough to make a good glue—and others about the same. From this we see that a nutritious soup might be made from the bones of animals that lived before the creation of man. The teeth resemble bone in their structure, but resist decay longer ; they are brought up by deep-sea dredging, when all other parts of the animal have wasted away. The bones differ at different ages, and under different social conditions. In the disease called 'rickets,' quite common among the ill-fed children of the poor in Europe, but somewhat rare in America, there is an inadequate deposit of the mineral substance, rendering the bones so flexible that they may be bent almost like wax. In females and weak men the bones are light and thin, while in a powerful frame they are dense and heavy. Exercise is as necessary to the strength of bone as to the strength of muscle ; if a limb be disused, from paralysis or long sickness, the bones lose in weight and strength as well as the soft parts. Bone is said to be twice as strong as oak, and, to crush a cubic inch of it, a pressure equal to 5,000 pounds is requisite."

---

5. In what respect admirably fashioned? Its formation? Microscopic examination? The inference? "Line of beauty?"

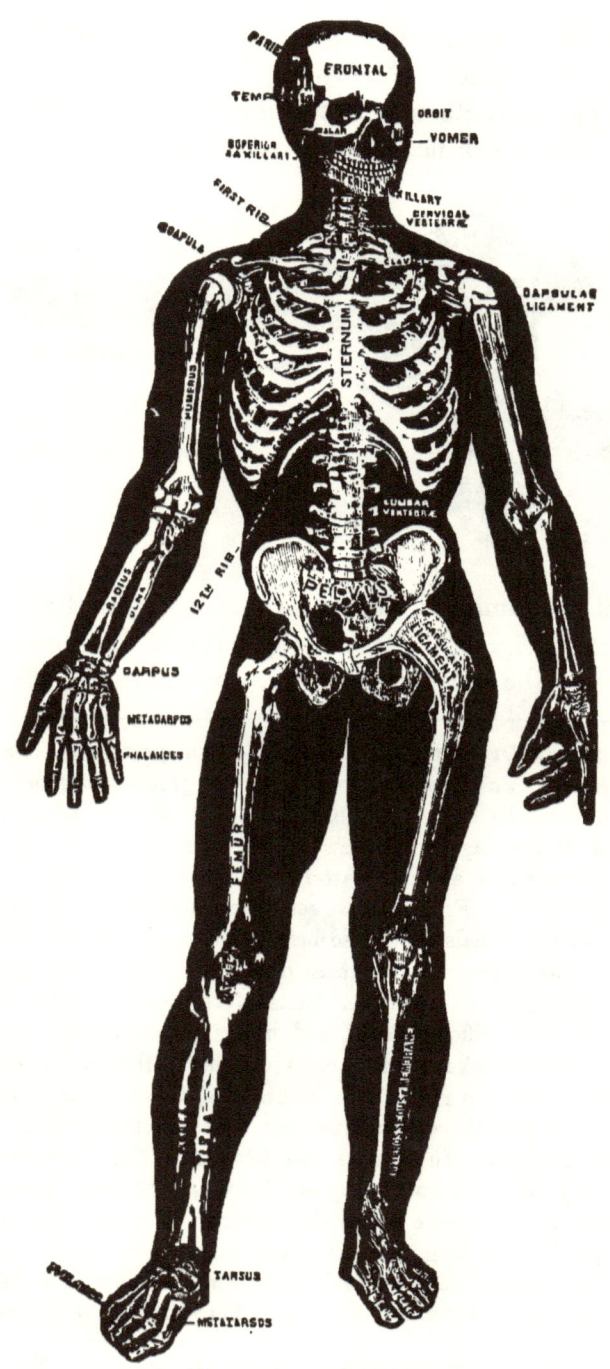

FIG. 2.—THE SKELETON.

there is a cavity or canal which contains an oily substance, called *marrow*. If a thin section of bone be examined under the microscope, we discover that it is pierced by numerous fine tubes (Fig. 3), about which layers of bone-substance are arranged. So that, although a bone be as hard as stone externally, it is by no means as heavy, by reason of its light interior texture. Another element of power is found in the curved outline of the bones. The curved line is said to be "the line of beauty," as it certainly is the line of strength, and is uniformly present in the bones whose position exposes them to accident.

FIG. 3.—STRUCTURE OF BONE ENLARGED.

6. The Skeleton.—The number of bones in the human body exceeds two hundred, and when joined together in their proper places, they form what is termed the *Skeleton* (Fig. 2). It embraces three important cavities. The first of these, surmounting the frame, is a box of bone, called the *skull;* below this, is a bony case, or "chest;" and lower down is a bony basin, called the *pelvis*. The two latter compose the trunk. The trunk and skull are maintained in their proper relations by the "spinal column." Branching from the trunk are two sets of limbs: the arms, which are attached to the chest by means of the "collar-bone" and "shoulder-blade;" and the legs, directly joined to the lower part of the trunk. (*Read Note 3.*)

---

3. Two Forms of Skeleton among Animals.—"The solid basis on which all the soft organs of the body rest is the skeleton. In the human body the skeleton is composed of a number of bones, each of which has a distinct name. In the animal kingdom there are two distinct forms of skeletons ; the one which is found chiefly in the lower animals is outside, and covers the soft parts, and is called an exo-skeleton. Examples of this kind of skeleton are seen in crabs, lobsters, insects, and the shells of mollusca, as oysters, mussels, and whelks. The shells of these animals are mostly composed of carbonate of lime. Fishes possess an internal skeleton ; and all the classes of animals above them, as reptiles, birds, and mammals, possess internal or endo-skeletons."— *Lankester's Manual of Health.*

---

6. Number of bones? Skeleton? The skull? Chest? The trunk? The trunk and skull, how maintained? What of the arms? Legs?

7. The cavities, three of which we have mentioned, are designed for the lodgment and protection of the more delicate and perishable parts of the system. Thus, the skull, together with the bones of the face, shelters the brain and the organs of four senses—sight, hearing, smell, and taste. The chest contains the heart, lungs, and great blood-vessels, while the lower part of the trunk sustains the liver, stomach, and other organs.

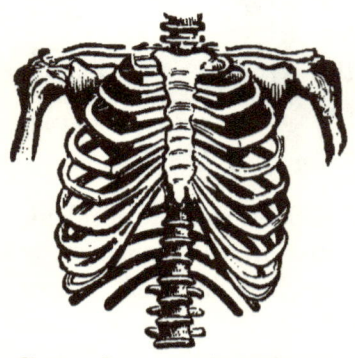

FIG. 4.—RIBS IN A NATURAL AND HEALTHY STATE.

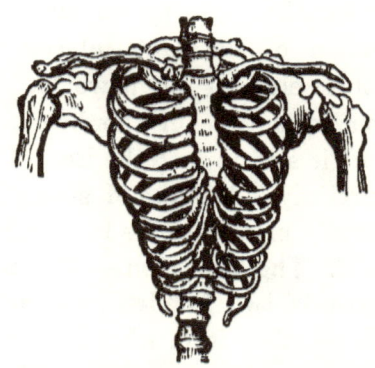

FIG. 5.—RIBS SHOWING THE EFFECTS OF TIGHT LACING.

8. The Joints.—The point of union of two or more bones forms a joint or *articulation*, the connection being made in various ways according to the kind and amount of motion desired. The movable joints are connected by strong fibrous bands, called ligaments. These ligaments are of a silvery whiteness, and very unyielding; so much so, that when sudden violence is brought to bear in the vicinity of a joint, the bone to which a ligament is attached may be broken, while the ligament itself remains uninjured. When this connecting material of the joints is strained or lacerated by an accident, a "sprain" is the consequence. An injury of this sort may be, and frequently is, quite as serious as the breaking of a bone. (*Read Note* 4.)

---

4. How Joints may be Injured.—"All the joints are liable to dislocation—that is, being 'put out' of their place. Owing to the shallowness of the cavity at the shoulder, this joint is frequently dislocated; and this some-

7. Design of the cavities? Give the examples.
8. Joint or articulation? Movable joints, how compacted? The ligaments of the movable joints? What is a sprain? Consequence of a serious sprain?

9. The ligament, then, secures firmness to the joint; it must also have flexibility and smoothness of motion.. This is accomplished by a beautiful mechanism, the perfection of which is only feebly imitated by the most ingenious contrivance of man. The ends of the bones are covered by a thin layer of *cartilage*, which, being smooth and elastic, renders all the movements of the joint very easy. In addition to this, there is an arrangement introduced for "lubricating" the joint, by means of a delicate sac containing fluid. This fluid is constantly supplied in small quantities, but only so fast as it is used up in exercise. In appearance, it is not unlike the white of an egg, and hence its name *synovia*, or egglike.

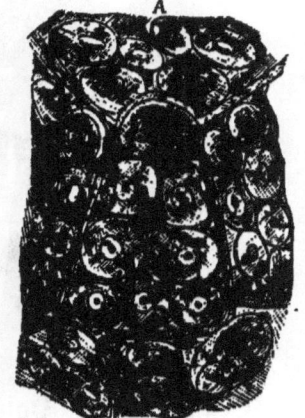

FIG. 6.—CELLS OF CARTILAGE.

10. Thus, we observe that two very different substances enter into the composition of a joint. The ligament, very unyielding, affords strength, while the cartilage, elastic and moist, gives ease and smoothness of motion. The amount of motion provided for varies greatly in different joints. In some there is none at all, as in the skull, where one bone is dove-tailed into another by what are termed *sutures*. Others have a hinge-like motion, such as those of the elbow, wrist, ankle, and knee; the most complete of these being the elbow-joint (Fig. 7). Belonging to another class,

---

times happens with the thigh, but not so often, as the cup in which the femur moves is much deeper. Joints which have been dislocated should at once be 'set'; but now that you have seen how liable you are to accident, I hope you will be careful not to indulge in too violent or rough exercise, by which you might not only dislocate the joints, and so in time weaken them, but might also break the bones, and perhaps become crippled for life. Many children have the habit of pulling their fingers so as to make them 'crack. This is exceedingly wrong, for it is to a certain extent pulling the joints out of their sockets, and this may so loosen the parts as to cause permanent injury."—*Davidson's "Our Bodies."*

9. Office of the ligament? What must it have? How accomplished? Describe it. Synovia?
10. What do we observe as regards the composition of a joint? The ligament and cartilage? What varies? Example of the skull? Other examples? The ball-and-socket joint?

the ball-and-socket joint, is that at the shoulder, possessing a freedom of motion greater than any other in the body.

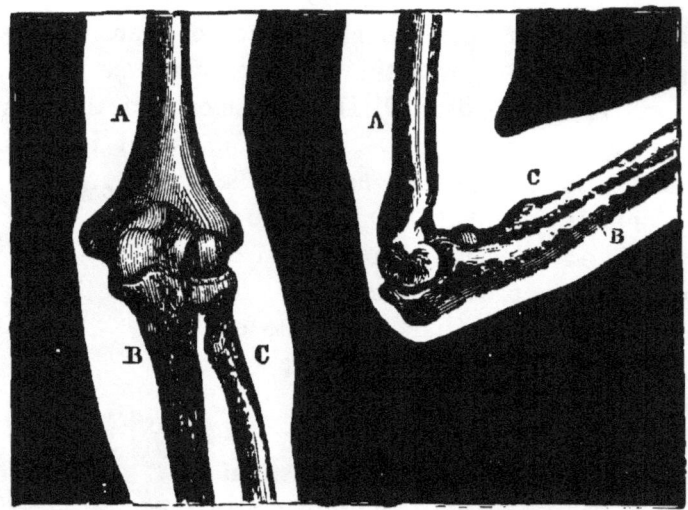

Fig. 7.—ELBOW-JOINT.   A, Bone of the arm; B, C, Bones of the fore-arm.

II. The Spinal Column.—The spinal column is often spoken of as the "back-bone," as if it were a single bone, while, in reality, it is composed of a chain of twenty-six small bones, called *vertebræ.* The spinal column is a wonderful piece of mechanism.   It not only connects the important cavities of the body, as has already been shown, but also, itself forms a canal, which contains the spinal cord.   The joints of the vertebræ are remarkable for the thick layers of cartilage which separate the adjacent surfaces of bone. The amount of motion between any two of these bones is not great ; but these little movements, taken together, admit of very considerable flexibility, in several directions, without endangering the supporting power of the column.

12. The abundant supply of intervertebral cartilage has another important use, namely, it adds greatly to the elasticity of the frame. It is due, in part, to this elastic material, and in part to the frequent curves of the spine, that the brain and other delicate organs

11. What is the spinal column? What does it connect and form? Joints of the vertebræ? Amount of motion? Result?
12. Elasticity of the frame? Protection of the brain from shocks? Tallness of persons? Effects of reclining?

are not more frequently injured by the shock of sudden falls or missteps. During the day, the constant pressure upon these joints, while the body is erect, diminishes the thickness of the cartilages; so that a person is not so tall in the evening as in the morning. The effects of this compression pass away when the body is in a reclining posture. (*Read Note* 5.)

---

5. Some Causes of Curvature of the Spine.—"Much as horse-riding is valued on account of the healthful character of its exercise, yet an over-indulgence by young ladies—owing to the oblique position in which the female form rests in the side-saddle—will cause the spine to become curved." To avoid this, it is important for young ladies to ride occasionally on the opposite side of the horse. Another frequent cause of curvature of the spine is the use of the sewing-machine, especially among needy seamstresses, whose bread frequently depends on the almost unceasing labor of their hands and feet, while sitting in a constrained position. Soon after croquet became a favorite amusement among the fashionable young ladies of England, it was noticed that the bent position assumed during the time the mallet is used caused a certain deformity, to which was given the name of the "croquet curvature." The use of high heels on boots and shoes of children, by throwing the weight of the body too far forward, on the front of the foot, and destroying the natural poise of the body, acts an important part in causing the spine to become crooked. By many this crooked position is considered to be largely a school-room disease, for the reason that children often are compelled to sit, and write or study, in a bent posture; but there must be other causes for it, since it has been found that it is almost exclusively a female deformity. Over eighty-four per cent. of the cases is stated by one writer to be among girls. But inasmuch as the majority of these cases begin during the years of schooling—from the ages of six to fourteen—great attention should be paid to the position of the body during school hours, and ample opportunity should be offered, by a regular system of gymnastics, to counteract all the evil influences of the school-room posture.—*Heather-Bigg on Deformities (in part).*

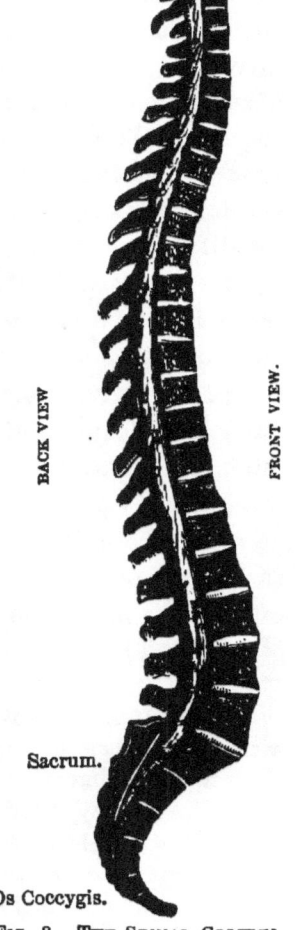

BACK VIEW

FRONT VIEW.

Sacrum.

Os Coccygis.

FIG. 8.—THE SPINAL COLUMN.

13. The Growth of Bone.

—Bone, like all the other tissues of the body, is constantly undergoing change, old material being withdrawn, to make room for a fresh supply. This change has been shown conclusively by experiments. If an animal be fed with madder—a red coloring matter—for a day or two, the bones soon become tinged; then, if the madder be discontinued for a few days, the original color returns. If, however, this material be alternately given and withheld, at short intervals, the bone will be marked by a succession of red and white rings. In very young animals, all the bones become colored in a single day; in older ones, a longer time is required. The process of waste and repair, therefore, is constantly taking place in this hard substance, and with astonishing rapidity.

14. The Repair of Bone.

—Nature's provision for uniting broken bones is very complete. At first, blood is poured out around the ends of the bone, as a result of the injury. This is gradually absorbed, and gives place to a watery fluid, which, thickening from day to day, acquires, at the end of about two weeks, the consistency of jelly. This continues to harden, by the deposit of new bone-substance, until, usually at the end of five or six weeks, the broken bone may be said to be united. It is, however, still fragile, and must be used carefully a few weeks longer. The process of hardening continues, but months must pass before the union can be said to be complete. (*Read Note* 6.)

---

6. The Management of a Broken Limb.—"Fractures are usually met with when the person is dressed. Therefore, unless there is bleeding, or something to call for immediate exposure and examination of the damaged part, do not be in a hurry to remove the clothes. If the arm be hurt, extemporize a sling from a neck-handkerchief or some other article of dress, and support the arm from elbow to wrist, tying the ends of the handkerchief in a knot over the coat-collar behind. If the thigh or leg be in pain, fasten the injured limb to its fellow by a cravat bandage or two, and take care that they lie side by side, and on the same level ; or fasten outside the clothes some temporary support— a piece or two of straight stick, with a bandage—and then remove the sufferer quietly and carefully to some house near at hand. If medical aid be available,

---

13. Change in bone? Example—animal and madder. Rapidity of change in color? Waste and repair?
14. How is a broken bone united? What becomes of the blood caused by the injury? What takes its place? How long does it usually take for a broken bone to unite?

15. Changes in the Skeleton.—Man does not reach his full height until he is about twenty-five years old; and even after that age, the bones continue to increase in strength and hardness. Before that age they are comparatively soft and flexible, by reason of the gelatin they contain. This is especially true in childhood; and it is fortunate that it is so, since that condition is much more favorable to the steady and rapid growth of the bones than if they contained more of the lime, as is the case in old age, when there is no occasion for change in the size or shape of the skeleton. The skull, however, is said to increase slightly in size, even in advanced life, in those persons in whom the brain is continually employed in thought or study. However, this very flexibility of the bones, in early life, which favors their steady growth and prevents their breaking easily, is sometimes the source of serious deformity. A young child may be allowed to stand and walk too early, and, as a consequence, the lower limbs become permanently bent inward, in the distortion called "knock-knees," or outward, as in "bow-legs." For the same reason, a bent position of the spinal column, permitted to exist habitually in childhood, may result in a life-long deformity.

16. The Erect Posture.—Youth is, in a great measure, the forming as well as the growing period of the frame. Bad habits of posture, early formed, become fixed in later life, and their results—

---

send for it without any delay; and be careful, if in the country, and so at some distance from the doctor's house, to forward a clear statement as to the apparent nature of the accident, which limb is hurt, and where and how it happened. Let this statement, too, be in writing, if possible. It may well happen, however, that skilled assistance cannot be had, and in this case the patient should be undressed quietly and cautiously. It will be far better to slit up the dress on the arm or leg with a pair of scissors than to pull it off; but however the covering of the injury may be managed, it must be done very slowly and gently, and the limb should be supported so as to prevent jarring and shaking to the damaged part. It must be carefully kept, too, in a right direction, for otherwise some sharp splinter of bone may penetrate the hitherto unwounded skin."—*First Help in Accidents and Sickness.*

---

15. When does a man get his growth? What changes then take place? What difference in the bones of a child and those of a man? What exception in case of the skull? Benefit in flexibility of bones? Cause of knock-knees? Bow-legs?

16. What is the forming period? Effects of bad habits of posture? Directions for correct posture?

as seen in contracted chests and round shoulders—are with difficulty remedied. Right habits, on the other hand, tend to produce an erectness of posture which is favorable, not alone to strength and health, but also to grace and ease. The following directions should be learned and practiced: hold the head erect with the chin somewhat near the neck; expand the chest in front; throw the shoulders back, keeping them of the same height on both sides; maintain the natural curves of the spine, as shown in the last figure. Man alone, of all the animals, has the power to stand and move in the erect posture.

QUESTIONS FOR TOPICAL REVIEW.

TABLE OF THE SKELETON.

(See Fig. 2, Page 18.)

The Skeleton Contains 206 Bones.

I. THE HEAD (28 Bones).

1. THE SKULL (8 Bones).

1 Fron'tal (forehead).

1 Oc-cip'i-tal (back of head).

2 Pa-ri'e-tals (side of head).

2 Tem'po-rals (temples).

1 Sphe'noid ("wedge-shaped").

1 Eth'moid ("sieve-like," through which filaments of the olfactory nerve pass to the nose).

II. THE TRUNK (54 Bones).

1. THE SPINAL COLUMN (26 Bones).

7 Cer'vi-cal (or neck) ver'te-brae.

12 Dor'sal (or back) vertebrae.

5 Lum'bar (or loin) vertebra.

Sa'crum (the "sacred" bone, because used in sacrifices).

Coc'cyx (the "cuckoo" bone, because of its likeness to the bill of that bird).

III. THE LIMBS (124 Bones).

1. THE UPPER LIMBS (64 Bones).

Clav'i-cle, or Collar-bone (from "clavis," a key).

Scap'u-la, or Shoulder-blade.

Hu'mer-us (arm).

Ul'na (forearm), from the Greek word meaning "Elbow."

Ra'di-us (forearm), from the Latin word meaning "Spoke."

8 Car'pals, or Wrist-bones.

5 Met-a-car'pals (in the palm); meta "beyond," and carpus "the wrist."

14 Pha-lan'ges (3 in each finger, 2 in the thumb).

TABLE OF THE SKELETON.—CONTINUED.

THE HEAD.—Continued.

2. THE FACE (14 Bones).

2 Na'sal Bones (they form the "bridge" of the nose).

2 Ma'lar (or cheek) Bones.

2 Lach'ry-mals (from a Latin word meaning "tear"; small thin bones which form a part of the inner wall of the orbits).

2 Pal'ate Bones.

2 Tur'bin-ated ("cone-shaped," one on each side of the outer wall of the nasal cavities).

2 Upper and 1 Lower Max'il-la-ry (or jaw) Bones.

1 Vo'mer ("plough-share," a thin bone which separates the nostrils).

3. THE EAR (6 Bones).

Mal'le-us, or "mallet."

In'cus, or "anvil."

Sta'pes, or "stirrup."

THE TRUNK.—Continued.

2. THE RIBS (24 Bones).

12 on each side; the upper seven are called "true" ribs, the five lower ones are "false," or "floating" ribs.

3. THE HY'OID.

A small "U-shaped" Bone in the upper part of the neck, and supports the base of the tongue.

4. THE STERNUM (Breast-Bone).

5. THE TWO HIP-BONES.

THE LIMBS.—Continued.

2. LOWER LIMBS (60 Bones).

Fe'mur (thigh-bone).

Pa-tel'la, or Knee-pan.

Tib'i-a (leg-bone), a Latin word meaning "flute."

Fib'u-la (leg-bone), a Latin word for "pin."

7 Tar'sals (forming the instep).

5 Met-a-tar'sals.

14 Phalanges (2 in the great toe, 3 in each of the others).

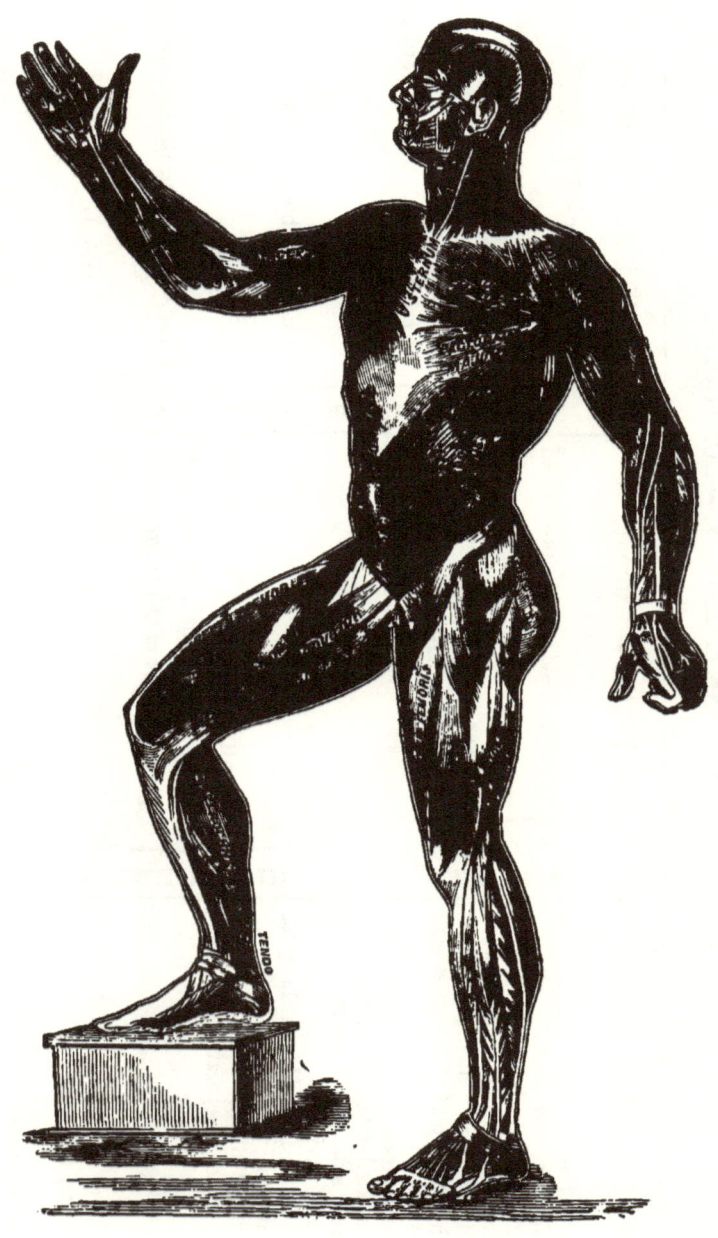

FIG. 9.—THE MUSCLES.

CHAPTER II

THE MUSCLES.

The Muscles—Flexion and Extension—The Tendons—Contraction—Physical Strength—Necessity for Exercise—Its Effects—Forms of Exercise—Walking —Riding—Gymnastics—Open-air Exercise—Effects of Exercise—Excessive Exercise—Sleep—Recreation.

1. The Muscles.—The great mass of the body external to the skeleton is composed of the flesh, or *Muscles*, which largely determines its outline and weight. The muscles are the organs of motion. Their number is about four hundred, and to each of them is assigned a separate and distinct office. They have all been studied, one by one, and a name given to each, by the anatomist. Each is attached to bones which it is designed to move. A few are circular in form, and enclose cavities, the size of which they diminish by contraction.

2. If we examine a piece of flesh, we observe that it is soft, and of a deep red color. Its structure appears to be composed of layers and bundles of small fibres. Let us further examine these fibres under the microscope. We discover that these in turn are made up of still finer fibres, or *fibrillæ*, as shown in Fig. 10. The fibres are beautifully marked by parallel wavy lines, about ten thousand to an inch, which give the fibre its name of

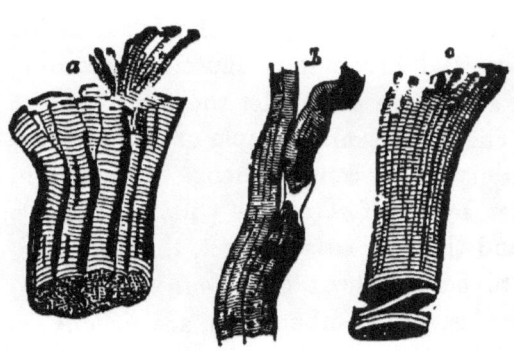

FIG. 10.—MUSCULAR TISSUE.

a, b, Striped muscular fibres; *c,* The same more highly magnified.

1. What are the muscles? Their number? The design of most of them? Of a few?
2. The structure of flesh? Its color, etc.? The composition of the fibres? How marked?

the *striped* muscular fibre. All of the voluntary muscles present this appearance.

3. Flexion and Extension.—The muscles are, for the most part, so arranged in pairs, or corresponding sets, that when motion is produced in one direction by one set, there is, opposite to it, another muscle, or group of muscles, which brings the limb back to its place. When they act alternately, a to-and-fro movement results. When a joint is bent, the motion is called *flexion ;* and when it is made straight again, it is called *extension.* When both sets act equally, and at the same moment, no motion is produced, but the body or limb is maintained in a fixed position : this occurs when we stand erect. The muscles which produce extension are more powerful than those opposite to them.

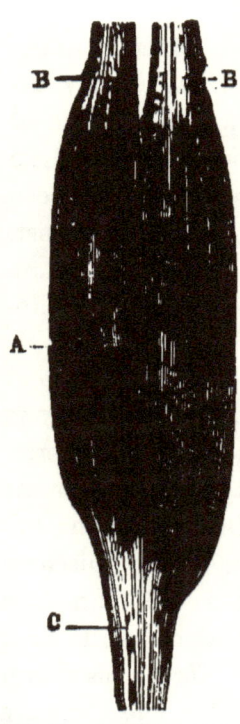

FIG. 11.—A, Biceps muscle of the arm ; B, C, Its tendons.

4. The muscles are also distinguished as the voluntary and involuntary muscles, according as they are, or are not, under the control of the will. The heart is an example of the involuntary variety. We cannot change its action in the least by an effort of the will. When we sleep, and the will ceases to act, the heart continues to beat without cessation. The voluntary muscles, on the other hand, are such as are used only when we wish or *will* to use them— as the muscles of the hand or arm (Figs. 11 and 12). (*Read Note* 1.)

---

1. The Perfection of the Human Hand.—"Gordy counts thirty-four distinct movements of the hand, and if we include the combinations of these different movements, we shall reach a much higher number. Properly speaking, the hand belongs to man alone, and its form does not permit us to consider it an organ of locomotion, as is the case with certain animals most closely resembling man. Nothing gives a more complete idea of the perfection of the

---

3. Arrangement of the muscles? Their action? Flexion and extension? Action of the muscles when we stand erect?
4. Kinds of muscles? The voluntary? Involuntary? The heart? Give the example. The hand? Arm?

5. The Tendons.—Tendons, or sinews, are the extremities of muscles, and are firmly fastened upon the bone. They are very

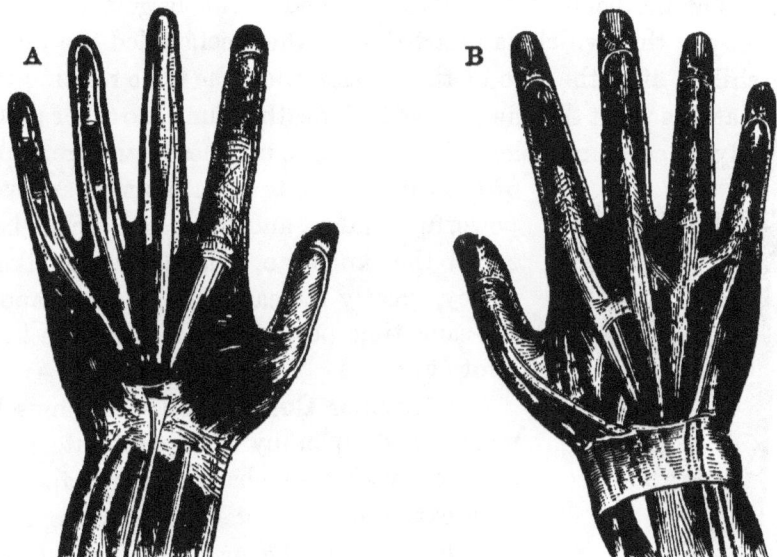

FIG. 12 shows the muscles and tendons of the hand; A showing the palm, B the back of the hand. These numerous muscles and tendons form a very complicated piece of mechanism, and help to give to the hand its marvellous dexterity and flexibility.

mechanism of the hand than the execution of instrumental music. Examine an artist while he plays the violin. His fingers rest upon the strings so as to leave them exactly of the length necessary for the tones they are to give. The half of a millimetre, more or less, greatly changes the accuracy of the note; and a chord a millimetre out of place produces a note which even the unpractised ear can recognize as false. But the fingers fall upon the strings at precisely the point required. They run over them, succeeding each other with giddy rapidity, following every imaginable combination, and yet the hand gliding over the instrument incessantly changes its position. Sometimes a single finger produces an isolated note; sometimes two or three act simultaneously to produce a concord; while a fourth, striking a string with increasing rapidity, produces a trill which rivals the nightingale. Add to all these the modifications necessary to swell the sound or let it die away—all, in a word, that constitutes musical expression, and it will be admitted that this mechanism is allied to the wonderful, and that it surpasses the most perfect productions of human art." A further idea of the rapidity of the hand's movements is given in the playing of a skilful pianist, whose hands, oftenest occupied together, produce on an average six to eight notes at a time, or about 640 notes in a minute in medium time, and 960 notes in extremely quick time.—*The Wonders of the Human Body.*

strong, and of a silvery whiteness. They may be felt just beneath the skin, in certain parts of the body, when the muscles are being used, as at the bend of the elbow or knee. The largest tendon of the body is that which is inserted into the heel, called the tendon of Achilles, after the hero of the Grecian poet, the fable relating that it was at this point that he received his death-wound, no other part of his body being vulnerable. (Fig. 13). The muscles in the front part

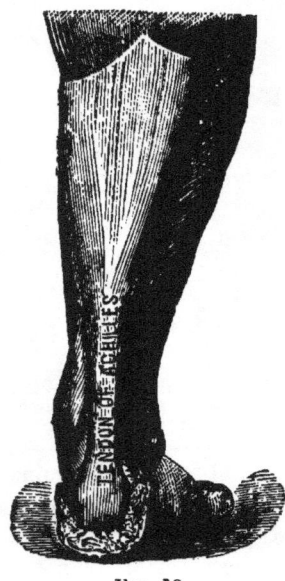

FIG. 13.
LOWER PORTION OF THE LEG.

of the thigh unite to form a single and very powerful tendon, and enclose a small bone called the knee-pan, which, acting like a pulley, greatly increases their power, and at the same time protects the front of the knee-joint (Fig. 14).

6. Muscular Contraction.—The muscles, when acted upon by the appropriate stimulus, contract, or so change their shape, that their extremities are brought nearer together. The bending of the arm, or of a finger, is effected in this manner, by the will; but the will is not the only means of producing this effect. Electricity, a sharp blow over a muscle, and other stimuli, also cause it. Contraction does not always cease with life. In man, after death from cholera automatic movements of hands and feet have been observed, lasting not less than an hour. In certain cold-blooded animals, as the turtle, contraction has been known to take place for several days after the head has been cut off.

7. The property which, in muscle, enables these movements to take place is called *contractility*. If we grasp a muscle while in exercise (for example, the large muscle in the front of the arm), we notice the alternate swelling and decrease of the muscle, as we move the forearm to and fro. It was at one time supposed that the

5. What are the tendons or sinews? Their strength? Color? Location? Tendon of Achilles? The fable? Muscles of the leg?

6. Contraction of the muscles? Bending of the arm or finger? Other agencies? Automatic movements? In cold-blooded animals?

7. Contractility? Give the illustration. What was supposed? What is the case?

muscle actually increased in volume during contraction. This, however, is not the case; for the muscle, while gaining in thickness, loses in length in the same proportion; and thus the volume remains the same in action and at rest.

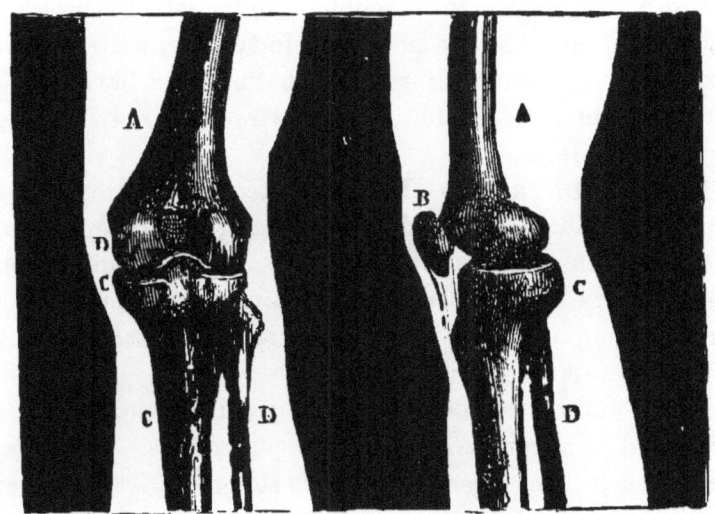

FIG. 14.—VIEW OF KNEE-JOINT. A, Thigh bone; B, Knee-pan; C, D, Leg bones.

8. Contraction is not the permanent, or normal, state of a muscle. It cannot long remain contracted, but after a time it wearies, and is obliged to relax. After a short rest, it can then again contract. It is for this reason that the heart can beat all through life, night and day, by having, as we shall hereafter see, a brief interval of rest between successive contractions. For the same reason, it is more fatiguing to stand for any great length of time in one position, than to be walking for the same period.

9. Relative Strength of Animals.—The amount of muscular power which different animals can exert, has been tested by experiment. By determining the number of pounds which an animal can drag upon a level surface, and afterward comparing that with its own weight, we can judge of its muscular force. It is found that man is able to drag a little less than his own weight. A draught-horse can exert a force equal to about two-thirds of his weight.

8. What further in relation to contraction? Weariness of a muscle? Beating of the heart? Standing and walking?
9. Muscular power of animals? How tested? Man's power? Horse's? The comparison?

The horse, therefore, though much heavier than man, is relatively not so powerful.

10. Insects are remarkable for their power of carrying objects larger and heavier than themselves. Many of them can drag ten, and even twenty times their weight. Some of the beetles have been known to move bodies more than forty times their own weight. So far, therefore, from it being a fact that animals have strength in proportion to their weight and bulk, the reverse of that statement seems to be the law.

11. Physical Strength.—The difference in strength, as seen in different individuals, is not due to any original difference in their muscles. Nature gives essentially the same kind and amount of muscles to every healthy person, and the power of one, or the weakness of another, arises, in great part, from the manner in which these organs are used or disused.

12. Many authors complain of the physical degeneracy of men at the present day, as compared with past generations. There is room for doubt as to the correctness of this statement. Certain experiments have recently been made with the metallic armor worn seven hundred years ago, by which it is found that any man, of ordinary height and muscular development, can carry the armor and wield the weapons of an age supposed to be greatly our superior in strength. When we consider that in those days only very strong men could endure the hardships of soldier-life, it is fair to suppose that our age has not so greatly degenerated in respect to physical strength.

13. Importance of Exercise.—Action is the law of the living body. Every organ demands use to preserve it in full vigor, and to obtain from it its best services. The value of that training of the mind, which we call education, is everywhere recognized. The child is early put to school, and for many years continues to study, in order that his brain, which is the great centre of mental power, may act healthfully and powerfully. It is important that the muscles, also, should receive their education by exercise. This is true,

---

10. Power of insects? Beetles? Give the conclusion.
11. Difference in strength of individuals? How caused?
12. Complaint in relation to degeneracy? How true? How determined by armor? The fair supposition?
13. Action? Use of organs? Training of the mind? The child's brain? Education of the body?

not only in respect to children, but also of adults whose occupation confines them within doors, and requires chiefly brain-work.

14. Persons who are engaged in manual labor in the open air obtain all the exercise necessary for bodily health in their regular business: their need is more likely to be a discipline or exercise of the mind. A perfect business of life, therefore, would be one which would combine both physical and mental labor in their proper proportions. If such a business were possible for all the human race, life would thereby be vastly prolonged. Such, in fact, is to a large extent the occupation pertaining to one period of life— childhood. One part of the time is given to study, and another to muscular education by means of games and sports. The restlessness and playfulness of children is not only natural but beneficial.

15. The Effects of Exercise.—Exercise consists in a well-regulated use of the voluntary muscular system. The effects, however, are not limited to the parts used. Other organs, which are not under the control of the will, are indirectly influenced by it. The heart beats more rapidly, the skin acts more freely, the temperature rises, the brain is invigorated, and the appetite and power of digestion are increased. An increased exhalation from the lungs and skin purifies the current of the circulation, and the body as a whole thrives under its influence. (*Read Note 2.*)

---

2. Health in Athletic Exercise.—"Health is perpetual youth—that is, a state of positive health. Merely negative health, the mere keeping out of the hospital for a number of years, is not health. Health is to feel the body a luxury, as every vigorous child does ; as the bird does when it shoots and quivers through the air, not flying for the sake of the goal, but for the sake of flight ; as the dog does when he scours madly across the meadows, or plunges into the muddy blissfulness of the stream ; but neither bird, nor dog, nor child enjoys his cup of physical happiness—let the dull or the worldly say what they will—with a felicity so cordial as the educated palate of conscious manhood. To 'feel one's life in every limb,' this is the secret bliss of which all forms of athletic exercise are merely varying disguises ; and it is absurd to say that we cannot possess this when character is mature, but only when it is half developed. As the flower is better than the bud, so should the fruit be better than the flower."

---

14. Work in the open air? A perfect business? The consequence of universal perfect business? Occupation of children?
15. In what does exercise consist? Effects of it?

16. The first effects of exercise, however, are upon the muscles themselves; for by use they become rounded out and firm, and increase in power. If we examine a muscle thus improved by exercise, we find that its fibres have become larger and more closely blended together, that its color is of a darker red, and that the supply of blood-vessels has increased. Without exercise the muscle appears thin, flabby, and pale. On the other hand, excessive exercise, without sufficient relaxation, produces in the muscle a condition not very different from that which follows disuse. The muscle is worn out faster than nature builds it up, and it becomes flabby, pale, and weak.

17. Violent exercise is not beneficial; and spasmodic efforts to increase the muscular strength are not calculated to secure such a result. Strength is the result of a gradual growth, and is most surely acquired if the exercise be carried to a point short of fatigue, and after an adequate interval of rest. To gain the most beneficial results, the exercise should be at regular hours and during a regular period, the activity and the time varying with the strength of the individual, and carefully measured by it. (*Read Note* 3.)

---

3. **The Ill-effects of Over-exertion.**—"It should be recollected that the action of the muscles has limits, as well as that of every other organ of the body. The muscles and the heart may be taxed too severely, and permanent derangements may be produced by overtaxing the human body. The ancient gymnasts among the Greeks are said to have become prematurely old, and the clowns (or acrobats) and athletes of our own days suffer from the severe strain put upon their muscular systems." The effects of boat-racing in England have been thus described by Dr. Skey, an eminent surgeon: "The men look utterly exhausted. Their white and sunken features and pallid lips show serious congestion of the heart and lungs, and the air of weakness and lassitude makes it a marvel how such great exertion should have been so nobly undergone. We have repeatedly seen the after ill-effects—spitting of blood, congested lungs, and weakness of the heart from over-distension." "Persons should neither walk, run, leap, or play at any game, to the extent of producing permanent or painful exhaustion. All exercise should be attended with pleasurable feelings; and when pain is produced by proper exercise, those who suffer should rather seek medical advice than persevere in exercise."—*Lankester's Manual of Health.*

---

16. General effect upon the muscles? Special effect? Effects of inaction? Of excessive exercise?
17. Of violent and spasmodic efforts? Strength, how attained? Give the particulars.

18. Different Modes of Exercise.—There are very few who have not the power to walk. There is required for it no expensive apparatus, nor does it demand a period of preliminary training. *Walking may be called the universal exercise.* With certain foreign nations, the English especially, it is a very popular exercise, and is practised habitually by almost every class of society; by the wealthy who have carriages, as well as by those who have none; by women as well as by men.

19. Running, leaping, and certain other more rapid and violent movements, are the forms of exercise that are most enjoyed in childhood. For the child, they are not too severe, but they may be so prolonged as to become injurious. Instances have been recorded where sudden death has resulted after violent playing, from overtaxing the heart : for example, we have the case of a young girl who, while skipping the rope, and endeavoring to excel her playmates by jumping the greatest number of times, fell dead from rupture of the heart.

20. Carriage-riding is particularly well suited to invalids and persons advanced in life. Horseback exercise brings into use a greater number of muscles than any other one exercise, and with it there is an exhilaration of feeling which refreshes the mind at the same time. It is one of the manliest of exercises, but not less suitable for women than for men. To be skilful in riding, it should be begun in youth.

21. For those who live near streams or bodies of water, there are the delightful recreations of boating, swimming, and skating. Certain of these exercises have a practical importance aside from and above their use in increasing the physical vigor. This is especially true of boating and swimming, since they are often the means of saving life. Practice in these exercises also teaches self-reliance, courage, and presence of mind. Persons who have become proficient in these vigorous exercises are generally the ones who, in times of danger, are the quickest to act and the most certain to do so with judgment.

---

18. What may walking be called? What further is said of walking?
19. What is said of running, and other like movements? What, as related to childhood? What instances are alluded to? Example?
20. Carriage-riding? Horseback-riding?
21. Boating, swimming, and skating?

22. Physical Culture.—That form of exercise which interests and excites the mind, will yield the best results; but to some persons no kind of exertion whatever is, at first, agreeable. They should, nevertheless, make a trial of some exercise, in the expectation that, as they become proficient in it, it will become more pleasant. In exercise, as many sets of muscles should be employed as possible, open-air exercise being the best. Parlor gymnastics, and the discipline of the gymnasium are desirable, but they should not be the sole reliance for physical culture. No in-door exercise, however excellent in itself, can fill the place of hearty and vigorous activity in the open air. (*Read Note* 4.)

23. Excessive Exercises.—If neglect of exercise is injurious, so also is the excess of it. Violent exertions do harm; they often cause undue strain, and even lasting injury to some part of the body. For this reason the spirit of rivalry which leads to tests of endurance and feats of strength should be discouraged. Those trials of the muscles, especially, which are supposed to demand " training," should not be encouraged. Training, it is true, can produce a remarkable muscular development, so that nearly every muscle of the limbs is as large and corded as the arm of a blacksmith; but it is too often at the expense of some internal, vital organ. Large muscles are not a certain index of good health. It was well known by the ancients that athletes of their day were short-lived, notwithstanding the perfection of the physical training then employed.

---

4. Exercise should be Pleasurable.—"The world seldom attaches much value to things which are plain and easily understood. The dervish in the Eastern allegory, well aware of this weakness, knew that it would be in vain to recommend the sultan, for the cure of his disease, simply to take exercise. He knew that mankind in general required to be cheated, gulled, cajoled, even into doing that which is to benefit themselves. He did not, therefore, tell the sultan, who consulted him, to take exercise, but he said to him : 'Here is a ball, which I have stuffed with certain rare, costly, and precious medicinal herbs. Your highness must take this bat, and with it beat about this ball until you perspire very freely. You must do this every day.' His highness did so, and in a short time the exercise of playing at bat and ball with the dervish cured his malady."—*First Help.*

---

22. What kind of exercise yields the best results? What advice is given?
23. Physical culture among the ancients? In Greece? In schools and colleges at the present time? Result to the body and mind?

When a person overtasks the heart, or, in other words, "gets out of breath," he should regard it as a signal to take rest. It is well known that both horses and men, after having been brought into "condition" for competitive trials, soon lose the advantages of their training after the occasion for it has passed.

24. Gymnastic Exercises for Schools and Colleges.—In the system of education among the ancients, physical culture predominated. In ancient Greece, physical exercises in schools were prescribed and regulated by law, and hence these schools were called *gymnasia.* At the present time, on the contrary, this culture is almost wholly unknown, as a part of the course of education, in our schools, and but to a limited extent in colleges. In a few of our schools, however, physical exercises have been introduced, with manifest advantage to the students, and they form a part of the regular curriculum of exercises,—as much so as the recitations in geography, grammar or Greek. The good effect of the experiments, as shown in improved scholarship as well as increased bodily vigor, in the institutions where the plan has been tried, will, it is hoped, lead to its universal adoption. We should then hear less frequently of parents being obliged to withdraw their children from school, because they become exhausted or, perchance, have lost their health from intense and protracted mental application.

25. Were gymnastics more common in our educational institutions we should not so often witness the sad spectacle of young men and women leaving our colleges and seminaries, with finished educations it may be, but with constitutions so impaired that the life which should be devoted to the accomplishment of noble purposes must be spent in search of health. Spinal curvatures, which, according to the experience of physicians, are now extremely frequent, especially among women, would give place to the steady gait and erect carriage which God designed his human creatures should maintain. (*Read Notes* 5 *and* 6.)

---

5. Health and Strength are not always Identical.—"Health and strength are not synonymous terms. A person may have great strength in his limbs, or in certain muscles about the body, but really not have good health. It is altogether a mistaken idea to suppose that physical exercises have for

24. The result of gymnastics in our colleges and other institutions of learning?
25. Were gymnastics more common? To what are spinal curvatures due?

26. All the exercises necessary for the proper development of the body may be obtained from the use of a few simple contrivances, that every one can have at home at little cost—less by far than that of useless toys. Many of these may be made available in the parlor or chamber, though all exercises are far more useful in the open air. A small portion of the day thus spent will afford agreeable recreation, as well as useful exercise. The Indian club, the wand, the ring and the light wooden dumb-bell are among the articles devised to assist in the smooth performance of class drill. Pleasant music timed to the movements of the drill is a further aid, just as martial music by a good band is a great help to soldiers on the march.

their sole object the attainment of strength. There are other tissues and organs in the human system besides the muscular; and the healthy action of the lungs and the stomach is far more important than great strength in the arms, legs, or the back. It is here, in this general exercise of all the muscles and parts of the body, that a well-regulated system of gymnastics has its great excellence. It aims to produce just that development of the human system upon which good health is permanently based, described by a distinguished writer as follows:—'Health is the uniform and regular performance of all the functions of the body, arising from the harmonious action of all its parts,'—a physical condition implying that all are sound, well-fitting, and well-matched. Some minds do not look far enough into life to see this distinction, or to value it if seen; they fix their eyes longingly upon *strength*—upon strength *now*, and seemingly care not for the power to work long, to work well, to work successfully hereafter, which is *health*."—*Dr. Nathan Allen on Physical Culture.*

6. On Recreation.—"Our whole method of amusements, especially for the young, should be reformed. Gas-light should yield to daylight, night vapors in heated and close rooms should give way to fresh air under the open heavens, and our young people should be brought up to work and play under the ministry of that great solar force which is the most benign and god-like agent known to men. Ardent spirits and tobacco should be given up, and in their stead genial exercise of riding, gymnastics, and the dance, with music and all beautiful arts, should be employed to stir the languid powers and soothe the troubled affections. The old Greeks taught music and gymnastics as parts of education, and Plato, in urging the importance of these, still maintains that the soul is superior to the body, and religion is the crown of all true culture. Why may not Christian people take as broad a position on higher ground, and with a generous and genial culture associate a faith that is no dreamy sentiment or ideal abstraction, but the best power of man and the supreme grace of God."
—*Rev. Dr. Osgood on " The Skeleton in Modern Society."*

27. Home Gymnastics.—This is perhaps a better name than parlor gymnastics for those exercises which may be practiced by individuals at home. Apparatus of various forms, and generally simple in construction, has been devised, and may be had at small cost. It can be set up in almost any room in the house. In some of these appliances cords or bands of rubber and pulleys are used; in others, simply weights with cords and pulleys, without elastic material. The latter kind is better, inasmuch as the movement is even and the action of the muscle steady, while with rubber bands the farther they are stretched the greater is the exertion. No apparatus yet invented answers its purpose so well as the " chest weight" (see Fig. 15). By its use all the prominent muscles of the body are easily exercised. No instruction is necessary and the space occupied is easily spared. A person is obliged only to grasp the handles and then follow the simple directions given to bring into action whatever muscles or groups of muscles he wishes to exercise. The weight can be changed to suit the strength of the one exercising. Illustrations showing a few of the positions and movements that are recommended with one of the chest weights, are given in the Appendix, page 304.

FIG. 15.

THE " CHEST WEIGHT."

28. In addition to the movements mentioned many others might be employed, varying with the particular muscles or parts that require to be exercised. Combinations of cords and pulleys suitable for particular cases can be made, and the resistance of the weights adjusted to the needs of the weakly and the young, as well as to the most robust. These exercises are by no means limited to those

27. What kind of apparatus is recommended for home gymnastics? Why? Describe advantages of the "chest weight."

who are in health and who resort to them as a relaxation from long study or sedentary occupations. Persons who are not strong, who cannot take advantage of school drill, or who are convalescing from sickness, may, under suitable conditions, be especially benefited by them. Not all the movements should be tried at first, but, on the contrary, there should be a careful selection of two or three that seem to be best suited to the needs of the patient. These exercises must also be undertaken gradually and increased in proportion to the ability of each individual. There should be some degree of uniformity as to the time of day as well as to the form and duration of the gymnastic effort engaged in. Remember always to stop short of the point where manifest fatigue begins to be felt, regardless of the shortness or the length of the time. The key-note to beneficial home exercise is to put into use as many muscles as is proper and safe, without bringing about a feeling of exhaustion. If exhaustion is produced, the exercise passes into violence, and as we have formerly learned, violence is harmful. It must be remembered that these movements not only develop the parts named, but each movement exercises many other muscles at the same time. In Figs. 9 and 10 (App.) always take a deep breath before each motion. Then the pressure of the filled lungs, together with the action of the muscles, will more quickly widen and deepen the thorax.

29. Rest.—We cannot always be active : after labor we must rest. We obtain this rest partly by suspending all exertion, as in sleep, and partly by a change of employment. It is said that Alfred the Great recommended that each day should be divided in the following manner : " Eight hours for work, eight hours for recreation, and eight hours for sleep." This division of time is as good as any that could now be made, if it be borne in mind that, when the work is physical, the time of recreation should be devoted to the improvement of the mind ; and when mental, we should then recreate by means of physical exercise.

30. During sleep, all voluntary activity ceases, the rapidity of the circulation and breathing diminishes, and the temperature of

---

29. Need of repose? How do we obtain rest? Alfred the Great? The eight hour division of time?
30. Cessation of voluntary activity? Temperature of the body? Consequence? Body and mind during sleep? Nutrition? Describe it. Consequence of insufficient sleep?

the body falls one or two degrees. In consequence, the body needs warmer coverings than during the hours of wakefulness. During sleep, the body seems wholly at rest, and the mind is also inactive, if we except those involuntary mental wanderings which we call dreams. Nevertheless a very active and important physical process is going on. Nutrition, or the nourishing of the tissues, now takes place. While the body is in action, the process of pulling down predominates, but in sleep, that of building up takes place more actively. In this way we are refreshed each night, and prepared for the work and pleasures of another day. If sleep is insufficient, the effects are seen in the lassitude and weakness which follow. Wakefulness is very frequently the forerunner of insanity, especially among those who perform excessive mental labor.

31. All persons do not require the same amount of sleep, but the average of men need from seven to nine hours. There are well-authenticated cases where individuals have remained without sleep for many days without apparent injury. Frederick the Great required only five hours of sleep daily, and Bonaparte could pass days with only a few hours of rest. But this long-continued absence of sleep is attended with danger. After loss of sleep for a long period, in some instances, stupor has come on so profoundly, that there has been no awaking.

32. There are instances related of sailors falling asleep on the gun-deck of their ships while in action. On the retreat from Moscow, the French soldiers would fall asleep on the march, and could only be aroused by the cry, " The Cossacks are coming ! " Tortured persons are said to have slept upon the rack in the intervals of their torture. In early life, while engaged in a laborious country practice, the writer not unfrequently slept soundly on horseback. These instances, and others, show the imperative demand which nature makes for rest in sleep.

33. Alcohol and Strength.—Alcohol, a substance to be fully described in our subsequent chapter on Food and Drink, merits

---

31. Amount of sleep for different persons? Cases? Frederick the Great? Bonaparte? Instances of long deprivation of sleep?
32. Instances of sailors? French soldiers? During torture?

consideration at this point by reason of the mistaken views held by many as to its beneficial effects upon the muscles when they are put into vigorous use, and especially into daily manual labor. It is well known that for generations it was thought to be essential to every army and navy of the civilized world that "grog"—which contains alcohol—should be regularly issued to the hard-worked soldier and sailor, especially when they were in the actual service of war.   To the slaves, also, on many plantations, during the days of slavery in this country, a daily ration of rum was given out in the busy seasons, in the belief that thus better results, in regard to the amount of muscular labor, were secured.   So too, in nearly every walk of life where hard muscular labor was demanded, a similar belief and practice commonly prevailed, and some form of alcohol was resorted to as a trusty servant whenever any great or unusual amount of labor was to be called forth.

34. How Alcohol affects the Muscles.—The scientific progress of recent years, however, has put the question in a different light, and it is now the commonly received view of scientific men that the benefits to labor derived from alcohol were apparent and not real.   Alcohol adds nothing to our bodily energy; it may spur up the muscles to a temporary and extraordinary exertion, but it does not strengthen the muscles any more than does the whip or the spur, that is applied to a hard-laboring horse to make him go faster, add to his strength.

35. Experiments have been made with instruments constructed for the purpose, and the results carefully recorded, and these show that a less degree of muscular power is possessed by the same person when he is under the influence of alcohol than when he has not taken it (see foot-note on p. 213).   This is no secret to men who go into training to bring about the best possible development of their muscular strength ; men who intend to engage in contests, such as boat-racing, foot-racing, and a great variety of other athletic sports, are taught to abstain entirely from all forms of drink that contain alcohol, if they would bring their powers to the highest point.

---

33. The former use of grog.
34. Present belief as to its use.
35. What experiments have been tried ?   Training of athletes ?   What experience of soldiers ?

The endurance of severe and prolonged bodily labor is not favored by the use of alcohol. The test recently made upon the British troops during the war in the Soudan, showed that the exhausting work, privation and the burning heat of the desert can be better endured by those who have not, than by those who have the ration of grog. The time is coming when this ration will be a thing of the past, and that, too, for good scientific reasons.

36. Abnormal Movements due to Alcohol.—The amount of disturbance in the muscular system that is produced by alcohol varies greatly under different circumstances. It may be very great or very slight according as a great or small dose of liquor is taken. The tongue, the organ of speech, is a muscle that early betrays the presence of drink. This is the cause of what is called the "thick" speech of the drunken man, whose words are not correctly uttered but are dropped, cut short or run together in an unusual and oftentimes unintelligible manner. "Seeing double" is another muscular disturbance observed in drunkenness. At a certain stage of the drunken fit every single object appears to the victim to be double. In this case the muscles that move the eyeballs are at fault; they are temporarily deranged, so that the two eyeballs cease to move harmoniously and are no longer brought to bear upon the objects before them, as in health, and the images of two objects are reported to the brain, while in reality there is only one. Then, too, objects that are at rest appear to be in motion, because the eyeballs are affected by an unsteady, rolling motion. This is one reason why, at a certain stage, the drunken man who tries to walk abroad, begins to stagger from side to side over the sidewalk, to stumble and perhaps to fall, and sober men appear to him to stagger and be drunken. The muscles of his limbs also, in their turn, becoming weakened, or not being properly controlled, may refuse to sustain the forlorn pedestrian, and he may be seen clinging for support to some friendly lamp-post, or, later on, sinking powerless into the gutter.

---

36. Does alcohol derange the muscles? What effect upon the tongue? The eyes and limbs?

TABLE OF THE PRINCIPAL MUSCLES.

(See Plate 9, Page 30.)

The Head.

Oc-cip'i-to—fron-ta'lis, moves the scalp and eyebrows.
Or-bic-u-la'ris pal'pe-bræ, closes the eye.
Le-va'tor pal'pe-bræ, opens the eye.
The Recti muscles (four in number) move the eye-ball.
Tem'po-ral, }
Mas-se'ter, } raise the lower jaw.

The Neck.

Pla-tys'ma My-oi'des, } move the head forwards.
Ster'no Mas'toid, }
Sca-le'ni muscles move the neck from side to side.

The Trunk.

Pec-to-ra'lis, moves the arm forwards.
La-tis'si-mus dor'si, moves the arm backwards.
Tra-pe'zi-us, }
Ser-ra'tus mag'nus, } move shoulder-blade.
Rhom-boi-de'us, }
In-ter-cos'tals, move the ribs in respiration.
External Oblique, } move the trunk forwards.
Internal Oblique, }
E-rec'tor spi'næ, move the trunk backwards.

The Upper Limb.

Del'toid, raises the arm.
Te'res ma'jor, lowers the arm.
Sub-scap-u-la'ris, } rotate the arm.
Spi-na'tus, }
Bi'ceps, bends forearm.
Tri'ceps, straightens forearm.
Pro-na'tor, } rotate forearm.
Su-pi-na'tor, }
Flex'or car'pi ra-di-a'lis, }
    "   " ul-na'ris, } move the hand.
Ex-ten'sor car'pi ra-di-a'lis, }
    "   " ul-na'ris, }
More than thirty muscles take part in moving the fingers.

The Lower Limb.

Il-i'a-cus, }
Pso'as mag'nus, } move the thigh forwards.
Pec-tin-e'us, }
Ad-duc'tor, }
Glu-te'us, } move the thigh backwards.
Pyr-i-form'is, }
Sar-to'ri-us (from Sar'tor, a tailor), crosses one thigh over the other.
Rec'tus, } move the leg forwards.
Vas'tus, }
Bi'ceps, } move the leg backwards.
Grac'i-lis, }
Tib-i-a'lis, }
Per-o-ne'us, }
Gas-troc-ne'mi-us, } move the foot.
So-le'us, }
Twenty muscles take part in moving the toes.

THE MUSCLES.

QUESTIONS FOR TOPICAL REVIEW.

The Integument—Its Structure—The Nails and Hair—The Complexion—The Sebaceous Glands—The Perspiratory Glands—Perspiration and its Uses—Importance of Bathing—Different kinds of Baths—Manner of Bathing—The Benefits of the Sun—Importance of Warm Clothing—Poisonous Cosmetics.

1. The Skin.—The skin is the outer covering of the body. The parts directly beneath it are very sensitive, and without its protection life would be an agony, as is shown whenever by accident the skin is broken or torn off, the bared surface being very tender, and sensitive even to exposure to the air. Nature has provided the body with a garment that is soft, pliable, close-fitting, and very thin; and yet sufficiently strong to enable us to come in contact with the objects that surround us, without inconvenience or suffering.

2. The Structure of the Skin.—When examined under the microscope, the skin is found to be made up of two layers—the outer and the inner. The inner one is called the *cutis*, or true skin; the outer one is the *epidermis*, or scarf-skin. The latter is also known as the *cuticle.* These two layers are closely united, but they may be separated from each other. This separation takes place whenever, from a burn, or other cause, a blister is formed; a watery fluid is poured out between the two layers, and lifts the epidermis from the true skin. Of the two layers, the cuticle is the thinner in most parts of the body, and has the appearance of a whitish membrane. It is tough and elastic, is without feeling, and does not bleed when cut. Examine it more closely, and we

---

1. What is the skin? Parts directly beneath? What is shown?
2. Microscopic examination? What is the cutis? The cuticle? Their union? How separated? What further is said of the cuticle?

observe that it is composed of minute flat cells, closely compacted, and arranged layer upon layer.

3. The outer layer, the *epidermis*, is constantly being worn out, and falls from the body in the form of very fine scales. It is, also, continually forming anew on the surface of the inner layer. Its thickness varies in different parts of the body.* Where exposed to use, it is thick and horn-like, as may be seen on the soles of the feet, or on the palms of the hands of those who are accustomed to perform much manual labor. This is an admirable provision for the increased protection of the sensitive parts below the skin against all extraordinary exposure. Even the *liabilities* of these parts to injury, are thus kindly provided for by "the Hand that made us." (*Read Note* 1.)

4. The cutis, or true skin, lies beneath the epidermis, and is its origin and support. It is firm, elastic, very sensitive, and is freely supplied with blood-vessels. Hence, a needle entering it not only produces pain, but draws blood. It is closely connected with the tissues below it, but may be separated by means of a sharp instru-

---

* Like all other parts of the body, the scarf-skin is constantly being worn out; it dries, shrivels, and falls from the body in the form of fine flakes, or scales. In the scalp, these scales form the "dandruff." As fast as it wears away it is renewed from beneath. This seemingly simple process is very important, for by it a uniform thickness is secured to the covering of the body. If it were otherwise, this covering would grow thicker as it grew older, like the bark of a tree, until it became unwieldy; it would prevent perspiration also, and this, as we shall see, would be fatal to life. The growth of the true skin is provided for in the blood-vessels which abound in it.

1. The Renewal of the Cuticle.—The skin is not a permanent sheath, but is, as it were, always wearing out and rubbing off, and new skin is always rising up from underneath. A snake leaves off his whole skin at once, as we leave off a suit of clothes or a dress, and sometimes we may find his whole cast-off covering turned inside out, just as he crept out of it. In man, generally, we do not notice the dead particles of the skin as it wears off; but where the cuticle is pretty thick, as on the soles of the feet, we can see it peel off in little rolls whenever we wash the feet in hot water. After scarlet fever, too, sometimes the dead skin comes off in great flakes, and from the hands almost like the fingers of a glove.—*Berners.*

---

3. Wearing out of the cuticle? What then? Variety in thickness of cuticle? How accounted for?
4. Location and office of the cutis? What further is said of it? Papillæ? Touch?

3

ment. The surface of the cutis is not smooth, but covered here and there with minute elevations, called *papillæ*. These are arranged in rows, or ridges, such as those which mark the palm and thumb; their number is about 80 to the square line (a line being one-twelfth of an inch). These *papillæ* contain blood-vessels and nerves also, and are largely concerned in the sense of touch; hence they are abundant where the touch is most delicate, as at the ends of the fingers.

5. The Nails and Hair.—These are modified forms of the cuticle. The nail grows from a fold of the cuticle at the root, and from the under surface. As fast as it is formed, it is constantly being pushed outward.* The rapidity of its growth can be ascertained by filing a slight groove on its surface, and noticing how the space between it and the root of the nail increases, in the course of a few weeks. When the nail is removed by any accident, it will be replaced by a new one, if the root be not injured. (*Notes* 2 *and* 6.)

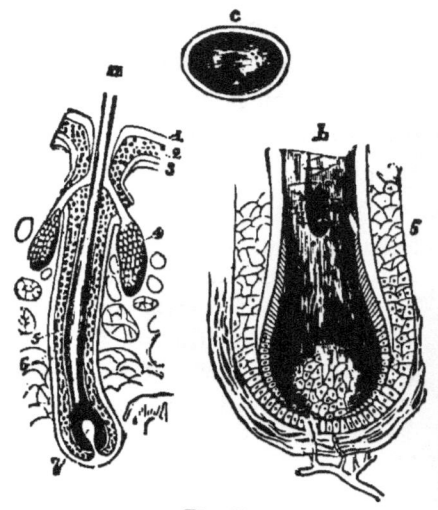

6. The hairs are produced in a similar manner; the skin forming depressions, or hair sacs, from the bottom of which they grow and are nourished (Fig. 17). They are found, of greater or

Fig. 17.

a, b. THE ROOT OF A HAIR HIGHLY MAGNIFIED. 1, 2, 3. The skin forming the hair sac. 4. Sebaceous glands. 5. The hair sac. *c.* TRANSVERSE SECTION OF A HAIR HIGHLY MAGNIFIED.

less length, on almost all parts of the surface, except the palms of the hands and soles of the feet. On certain parts of the body, they

---

* The practice of biting the nails should be avoided not only because of the ugly shape which is produced, but because it impairs the sense of touch in the ends of the fingers. In paring the nails, let them remain long enough

---

5. What are the nails and hair? The growth of the nail? The rapidity of its growth? Accident to the nail?
6. How are the hairs produced? Difference in their length?

grow to great length; on other parts they are so short, that they do not rise beyond the hair-sac from which they grow.

7. The bulb, or root, from which the hair arises, is lodged in a small pouch, or depression in the skin. The shaft is the part which grows out beyond the level of the skin. Its growth is altogether in one direction, in length alone. The outer part of the hair is quite firm, while its interior is softer, and supplies the nutriment by which it grows. The hair is more glossy in health than at other times.

8. The nail serves as a protection to the end of the finger, and also enables us to grasp more firmly, and to pick up small objects. The hair, too, is a protection to the parts it covers. On the head, it shields the brain from extremes of heat and cold, and moderates the force of blows upon the scalp. On the body, it is useful in affording a more extensive surface for carrying off the perspiration.

---

to nearly cover the pulp of the finger. Avoid scraping either surface of the nail; do not injure the "quick."

2. The Life of the Cells of the Body.—"The life of the body is long under fortunate circumstances; that of our cells is short. We all know that the surface of the body is covered by layers of cells. The superficial layers are in loose connection; they are cells in old age. The friction of our clothing daily removes an immense number of them. A cleanly person who uses sponge and towel energetically every day rubs off a still greater quantity.

"We swallow; our tongue acts in speaking; drink and food pass this way. Now, the mucous membrane of the mouth is covered with layers of cells. Here, also, many thousand senile cells are rubbed off daily. And so on through the entire digestive tract. An immense number of cells—these living corner-stones of the body—is thus lost daily.

"To show the duration of life in one kind of cell, let us turn to the human nail. The latter, growing from a furrow of the skin, is made up of skin-cells. In the depth of the furrow, youth prevails; at the upper margin—which we trim—old age. Berthold proved that a nail-cell lives four months in summer and five in winter. A person dying in his 80th year, has changed his nail 200 times, at least—and the nail appeared such an inanimate, unvarying thing! No other cells, we believe, have a life nearly so long as that of the nail."—*Compendium of Histology by Heinrich Frey.*

---

7. Root of the hair? Shaft? Firmness and softness of the hair?
8. Office of the nail? Of the hair? Give the illustrations.

9. Complexion.—In the deeper cells of the cuticle lies a pigment, or coloring-matter, consisting of minute colored grains. On this pigment *complexion* depends; and its presence, in less or greater amount, occasions the difference of hue that exists between the light and the dark races of men, and between the blonde and the brunette of the white races. Freckles are due to an irregular increase of this coloring matter.

10. The sun has a powerful influence over the development of this pigment, as is shown by the swarthy hue of those of the white race who have colonized in tropical climates. It is also well illustrated by the fact, that among the Jews who have settled in northern Europe, there are many who are fair-complexioned, while those residing in India are as dark as the Hindoos around them.

11. An Albino is a person who may be said to have no complexion; that is, there is an entire absence of coloring matter from the skin, hair, and *iris* of the eye. This condition exists from birth, and more frequently occurs among the dark-races, and in hot climates, although it has been observed in almost every race and clime.

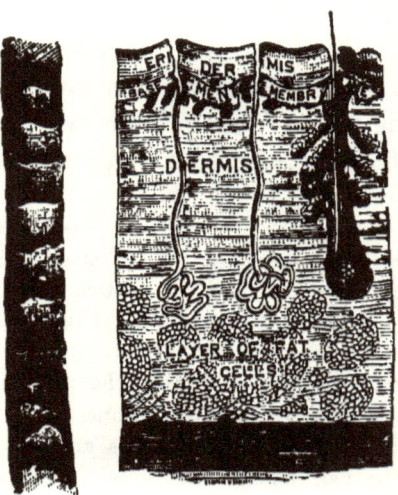

Fig. 18.—Showing a Hair and Section of Skin highly magnified.

12. Sebaceous Glands.—In all parts of the surface where the hairs grow, are to be found the *sebaceous*, or oil-producing glands. These glands are little rounded sacs, usually connected with the hair-bulbs; and upon these bulbs they empty their product of oil, which acts as a natural dressing for the hair (4, Fig. 17). A portion of the sebaceous matter passes out upon the surface, and prevents the cuticle from becoming dry and hard. The glands situated upon the

9. On what does the complexion depend? Light and dark races? Freckles?
10. Influence of the sun? How illustrated? Jews?
11. What is an Albino? Where are Albinos found?
12. What are sebaceous glands? How do they act? Sebaceous glands of the face? How do they act?

face and forehead open directly upon the skin. In these, the sebaceous matter is liable to collect, and become too hard to flow off naturally.

13. These glands on the face and forehead frequently appear on the faces of the young as small, black points, which are incorrectly called " worms." It is true, that occasionally living animalcules are found in this thickened sebaceous matter, but they can only be detected by the aid of the microscope. This sebaceous matter acts not only to keep the skin flexible, and furnish for the hair an oily dressing, but it especially serves to protect the skin and hair from the acridity arising from the perspiration.

14. The Perspiratory Glands.—The chief product of the skin's action is the perspiration. For the formation of this, there are furnished countless numbers of little sweat-glands in the true skin. They consist of fine tubes, with globe-like coils at their deeper extremity. Their mouths or openings may be seen with an ordinary magnifying-glass, upon the fine ridges which mark the fingers. These tubes, if uncoiled, measure about one-tenth of an inch in length. In diameter they are about one three-hundredth of an inch, and upon parts of the body there are not far from three thousand of these glands to the square inch. Their whole number in the body is, therefore, very great; and it is computed, if they were all united, end to end, their combined measurement would exceed three miles.

15. The Sensible and Insensible Perspiration.—The pores of the skin are constantly exhaling a watery fluid; but, under ordinary circumstances, there is no moisture apparent upon the surface, for it evaporates as rapidly as it is formed. This is called insensible perspiration. Under the influence of heat or exercise, however, this fluid is formed more abundantly, and appears on the surface in minute, colorless drops. It is then termed sensible perspiration.

16. Water is the chief component of this fluid, there being about ninety-eight parts of water to two parts of solid matter. The quantity escaping from the body varies greatly, according to the temperature

---

13. Black points, called worms? Animalcules? Service performed by sebaceous matter?
14. Perspiration? Sweet glands? Of what do they consist? Dimension of the tubes?
15. What is sensible perspiration? Insensible perspiration?
16. Components of perspiration? Upon what does perspiration depend? Amount of perspiration daily?

of the air, the occupation of the individual, and other circumstances. The average daily amount of perspiration in the adult is not far from two pints, or more than nine grains each minute.

17. The Uses of the Perspiration.—Besides liberating from the blood this large amount of water, with the worn-out matter it contains, the perspiration serves to regulate the temperature of the body. That is to say, as evaporation always diminishes temperature, so the perspiration, as it passes off in the form of fine vapor, cools the surface. Accordingly, in hot weather this function is much more active, and the cooling influence increases in proportion. When the air is already charged with moisture, and does not readily receive the vapor of the body, the heat of the atmosphere apparently increases, and the discomfort therefrom is relatively greater.

18. The importance of perspiration is shown by the effects that often follow its temporary interruption, namely, headache, fever, and the other symptoms that accompany "taking cold." When the perspiration is completely checked, the consequences are very serious. Experiments have been performed upon certain smaller animals, as rabbits, to ascertain the results of closing the pores of the skin. When they are covered by a coating of varnish impervious to water and gases, death ensues in from six to twelve hours—the attendant symptoms resembling those of suffocation. (*Read Note* **3.**)

---

3. On Taking Cold.—"Of all the things to which humanity is liable, there is none which recurs more frequently, and whose consequences are more troublesome and often dangerous, than '*taking cold.*' Some persons have quite a faculty for taking cold, while others do so but rarely. And yet the one does not argue delicacy of constitution, or the other strength. The body of man has a constant and agreeable temperature in health, the variation being slight. In fact, any great variation is incompatible with health, and constitutes disease. Clothes, by preventing the radiation away of heat from the surface, retain it, and so the feeling of cold is not so great—that is, the surface does not become so cold. Clothes are non-conductors of heat when dry; but let them be saturated with water, and unless the loss of heat be met by increased production, there is a lowering of the body temperature—'taking cold.' Thus, if exertion be continued, and more heat is produced to meet the

---

19. It is related that, at the coronation of one of the Popes, about three hundred years ago, a little boy was chosen to act the part of an angel; and, in order that his appearance might be as gorgeous as possible, he was covered from head to foot with a coating of gold-foil. He was soon taken sick, and although every known means were employed for his recovery, except the removal of his fatal golden covering, he died in a few hours.*

20. The Importance of Bathing.—From these considerations, it is evident that health must greatly depend upon keeping the skin clean. "He who keeps the skin ruddy and soft, shuts many gates against disease." For as the watery portion of the perspiration evaporates, the solid matter is left behind. There, also, remain the scales of the worn-out cuticle, and the excess of sebaceous matter. In order to secure the natural action of the skin, these impurities require to be removed by the frequent application of water. (*Read Note 4.*)

---

loss until a change of dry clothing is procurable, no injury results. But let the wet clothes be worn without a corresponding heat production, as when children sit down in school in their wet clothes, or the shop-boy stands in his moist garments; then there is a rapid loss of heat, a lowering of the body temperature, and a cold is 'caught.' So is a cold caught by wet feet, when the heat is radiated away from the feet; if exercise be continued the cold is not experienced. A damp bed gives cold because the moist bedclothes conduct away the heat, and the body temperature is lowered."—*Fothergill on the Maintenance of Health.*

* A clogged action of the skin is disastrous in many diseases, but especially those attended by an eruption, or "breaking out." One of these—small-pox—is exceedingly fatal among the American Indians, whole tribes having been swept away by it. And this is explained by the fact that they habitually close their pores by covering their bodies with bears' grease, as a protection against the cold, and with earthy paints as a means of decoration.

4. Bathing.—"When the civilization of Egypt, Greece, and Rome faded, the world passed through dark ages of mental and physical barbarism. For a thousand years there was not a man or woman in Europe that ever took a bath, if the historian of those times, Michelet, is to be believed. No wonder that there came the wondrous epidemics of the middle ages, which cut off one-fourth of the population of Europe—the spotted plague, the black death, sweating sickness, and the terrible mental epidemics which followed in their train—

---

19. Give the story in relation to the boy covered with gold foil.
20. Give the quotation. Perspiration?

21. In warm climates, and during hot weather, bathing is especially necessary. For a person in good health, a daily cold bath is advisable. To this should be added occasionally a warm bath, with soap, water alone not being sufficient to remove impurities of a greasy nature. Soap facilitates this, by forming with such substances a chemical mixture, which is taken up by water, and by it removed from the body. (*Read Note* 5.)

---

the dancing mania, the mewing mania, and the biting mania. Not only their persons, but their houses were uncleanly, even in the classes that were well-to-do. Filth, instead of being abhorred, was almost sanctified."—*Lyon Playfair.*

5. An Imaginary Conversation on Baths and Bathing.—"I have often amused myself, by fancying one question which an old Roman emperor would ask, were he to rise from his grave and visit the sights of London under the guidance of some minister of state. The august shade would, doubtless, admire our railroads and bridges, our cathedrals and our public parks, and much more of which we need not be ashamed. But after a while, I think, he would look round, whether in London, or in most of our great cities, inquiringly and in vain, for one class of buildings, which in his empire were wont to be most conspicuous and splendid. 'And where,' he would ask, 'are your public baths?' And if the minister of state who was his guide should answer—'O great Cæsar, I really do not know. I believe there are some somewhere in some out-of-the-way place ; and I think there have been some meetings lately, and an amateur concert, for restoring, by private subscriptions, some baths and wash-houses which had fallen to decay. And there may be two or three more about the metropolis ; for parishes have power to establish such places, if they think fit, and choose to pay for them out of the rates :'—Then, I think, the august shade might well make answer—'We used to call you, in old Rome, northern barbarians. It seems that you have not lost all your barbarian habits. Are you aware that, in every city in the Roman empire, there were, as a matter of course, public baths open, not only to the poorest freeman, but to the slave, usually for the payment of the smallest current coin, and often gratuitously? Are you aware that in Rome itself, millionaire after millionaire, emperor after emperor, built baths, and yet more baths ; and connected with them gymnasia for exercise, libraries, and porticoes, wherein the people might have shade and shelter, and rest? Are you aware that these baths were of the most magnificent architecture, decorated with marbles, paintings, sculptures, fountains, what not? And yet I had heard, in Hades down below, that you prided yourselves here on the study of the learned languages."—*Rev. Charles Kingsley on the Air-mothers.*

---

22. There is a maxim by the chemist Liebig, to the effect, that the civilization of a nation is high, in proportion to the amount of soap that it consumes; and that it is low, in proportion to its use of perfumes. In some degree, we may apply the same test to the refinement of an individual. The soap removes impurity; the perfume covers, while retaining it. (*Read Notes 6 and 7.*)

23. The Different Kinds of Baths.—All persons are not alike able to use the cold bath. When the health is vigorous, a prompt reaction and glow upon the surface will show that it is beneficial. Where this pleasurable feeling is not experienced, but rather a chill and sense of weakness follows, we are warned that the system will not, with impunity, endure cold bathing. Most persons experience the best results when the water is about the temperature of the body—"blood-heat."

24. It should also be borne in mind, that the warm or hot bath

---

6. Care of the Skin and Nails.—Much ignorance prevails amongst the public as to the use of soap and water. Those who have very sensitive skins should use soft water, for the face at all events, and the best water, if it can be had, is rain-water with the cold taken off it. Nor is it every kind of soap which is tolerated by such persons; probably the safest soaps are, not those which are said to contain, but those which really do contain, a large portion of glycerine.

The culture of the nails, which when perfect constitute so great a beauty, is of much importance; but the tendency is to injure them by too much attention. The scissors should never be used, except to pare the free edges when they have become ragged or too long, and the folds of scarf skin which overlap the roots should not, as a rule, be touched. The upper surfaces of the nails should on no account be touched with the knife, as it is so often done, the nail brush being amply sufficient to keep them clean, without impairing their smooth and polished surfaces.—*People's Magazine.*

7. On Scents.—"They are the only resource of rude and dirty times against offensive emanations from decaying animal and vegetable substances, from undrained and untidy dwellings, from unclean clothes, from ill-washed skins, and from ill-used stomachs. The scented handkerchief, in these circumstances, takes the place of the sponge and the bath; the pastile hides the want of ventilation; the otto of roses seems to render the scavenger unnecessary; and a sprinkling of musk sets all other smells and stinks at defiance."— *Johnston.*

22. Liebig's maxim? What further is added?
23. What is said about cold bathing?
24. What is said about warm bathing?

cannot be continued so long, or repeated so frequently, as the cold, on account of the enervating effect of unusual heat so applied to the body.   For persons who are not in robust health, one warm bath each week is sufficient.   Such persons should be careful to avoid every extreme in reference to bathing, clothing, and whatever greatly affects the action of the skin.

25.   Sea-bathing is even more invigorating than fresh-water bathing.   Those who cannot endure the fresh water, are often benefited by the salt-water baths.   This may be accounted for, in part, by the stimulant action upon the surface, of the saline particles of the sea-water; but the exciting scenes and circumstances of sea-bathing also exert an important influence.   The open-air exercise, the rolling surf, the genial weather, and usually the cheerful company, add to its intrinsic benefits.   (*Read Note* 8.)

26. Time and Manner of Bathing.—A person in sound health may take a bath at almost any time, except directly after a full meal.   The most appropriate time is about three hours after a

---

8. The Proper Use of Sea-bathing.—"The length of time during which a person should remain in the water necessarily varies according to the age, sex, and constitutional strength of the bather.   Due regard should also be had to the state of the weather and season of the year.

"In the case of children, five, gradually extended to ten minutes ; of women, ten to fifteen minutes ; and of men, a quarter of an hour or more, is a fair average period.   There are some people, doubtless, to whom these periods will appear insufficient, and who insist on remaining so long in the water that their skin becomes cold and blue, their teeth begin to chatter, and a condition of general exhaustion comes on ; people, in short, who have the 'most' for their money, like the countryman who grumbled at having been conveyed thirty miles in about half-an hour by an express train, on the score that the length of time occupied in the journey was not proportionate to the fare that he had paid.   On entering the water, the bather should immerse the whole of the body two or three times, so as to get the action of the shock from the cold water distributed over its entire surface.   There should be no hesitancy, no dabbling about with the feet, but a good plunge at once into the next wave that washes in.   Upon coming out of the water the bather should dry the body with good rough towels, dress quickly, and take a brisk walk for a short distance.   If there be any feeling of exhaustion or nervous depression, a little food or drink should be taken."

---

25. What is said about sea-bathing ?
26. What is said as to the time and manner of bathing ?

meal, the noon-hour being probably the best. For the cold bath, taken rapidly, no time is better than immediately after rising. Those beginning the use of cold baths should first try them at 70° Fahrenheit, and gradually use those of a lower temperature. From five to twenty minutes may be considered the proper limit of time to remain in a bath; but a sensation of chilliness is a signal to withdraw instantly, whether at home, or at the sea-side. Two sea-baths may be taken daily; one of any other kind is sufficient.

27. The body should be warm, rather than cold, when stepping into the bath; and after it, the skin should be thoroughly dried with a coarse towel. It is best to continue friction until there is a sensation of warmth or "glow" throughout the entire surface. This reaction is the test of the good effects of the bath. If reaction is still incomplete, a short walk may be taken, especially in the sunshine. It is very congenial, however, both to health and comfort, to rest for a short time directly after bathing, or to take some light refreshment. This is better than severe exercise or a full meal.

28. Bathing among the Ancients. — The Romans and other nations of antiquity made great use of the vapor-bath as a means of preserving the health, but more particularly as a luxury. Their method was not unlike that employed in some parts of Europe at the present day. The public baths of Rome and other cities are among the grandest and most interesting monuments of ancient luxury and splendor; and from their ruins have been recovered some of the most beautiful works of art.

29. The Thermæ, as the baths of Rome were called, were of great extent, built very substantially, and ornamented at vast expense. They were practically free to all, the cost of a bath having been less than a cent. It is related that some persons bathed seven times a day. After the bath their bodies were anointed with perfumed oil. If the weather was fine, they passed directly from the Thermæ into the gymnasium, and engaged in some gentle exercise previous to taking the midday meal. Between two and three in the afternoon was the favorite hour for this ancient luxury. Swimming was a favorite exercise, and a knowledge of it was regarded as

27. Condition of the body when bathing? Direction, after bathing?
28. Bathing among the ancients? Baths of Rome?
29. After the bath? Swimming among the ancients?

necessary to every educated man. Their common expression, when speaking of an ignorant person, was, "He can neither read nor swim."

30. The Sun-Bath. — Some also were accustomed daily to anoint themselves, and lie or walk in apartments arranged for the purpose, with naked bodies exposed to the direct rays of the sun. There is an interesting allusion to this practice, in a letter of the younger Pliny to the historian Tacitus, describing the destruction of Pompeii by an eruption of Vesuvius. "My uncle" (Pliny the elder) "was at that time in command of the fleet at Misenum. On the 24th of August, about one in the afternoon, my mother desired him to notice a cloud which seemed of unusual shape and dimensions. He had just returned from *taking the benefit of the sun*, and after a cold bath, and a slight repast, had retired to his study." Then follows a description of the destruction of Pompeii, and the death of the elder Pliny.

31. We may judge somewhat of the benefits of the sun, by observing the unnatural and undeveloped condition of plants and animals which are deprived of light. Plants become blanched and tender; the fish of subterranean lakes, where the light of day never enters, are undersized, and have no eyes; tadpoles kept in the dark do not develop into frogs; men growing up in mines are sallow, pale, and deformed. Besides the well-known effect of solar light in tanning the skin, it also makes it thicker and better able to resist exposure; though the complexion may be thereby injured, the health gained more than compensates for the loss of beauty. "To make good the loss of the lily, where the sun has cast his ray, he seldom fails to plant the rose." (*Read Notes* 9 *and* 10.)

9. Light Influences Growth and Health.—"I have several times taken two potatoes which were as nearly as possible alike, and placed one under a bell-glass through which the light could pass, and the other under a similar cover rendered opaque by several coats of black paint. Sprouting went on unchecked under the translucent glass, while it was always notably retarded and sometimes prevented in the potato under the dark glass. Milne Edwards, a distinguished French physiologist, performed a series of experiments which showed that tadpoles when deprived of light did not develop

32. Clothing.*—In reference to clothing, we are far more apt, in our changeful climate, to use too little than too much. An aphorism of Boerhaave, worth remembering, if not of adopting, is, "We should put off our winter clothing on midsummer's day, and put it on again the day after." He also says, "Only fools and beggars suffer from the cold; the latter not being able to get sufficient clothes, the others not having the sense to wear them." The practice of exposing the limbs and necks of young children, for the alleged

into the frog. I have several times repeated his experiments, and always with confirmatory results. On one occasion I prevented for one hundred and twenty-five days the development of a tadpole, by confining it in a vessel to which the rays of light had no access. On placing it in a receptacle open to the light, the process of transformation was at once begun, and was completed in fifteen days. The practical application of these and similar observations is this, that care should be taken both in health and disease to insure a sufficient amount of sunlight to the inmates of houses, and that it is impossible to rear well-formed, strong, and robust children unless attention is paid to this requirement."—*Hammond on the Influence of Light.*

* Man is the only animal that requires clothing; and as he advances from barbarism to civilization, more and more attention is paid to dress as a means of protection against cold. As a rule, more harm arises from using too little clothing than too much, especially in a changeful climate like our own.

10. Light in the Sick-room.—"It is the unqualified result of all my experience with the sick, that second only to their need of fresh air is their need of light; that, after a close room, what hurts them most is a dark room; and that it is not only light, but direct sunlight they want. You had better carry your patient about after the sun, according to the aspect of the rooms, if circumstances permit, than let him linger in a room when the sun is off. People think that the effect is upon the spirits only. This is by no means the case. Who has not observed the purifying effect of light, and especially of direct sunlight, upon the air of a room? Here is an observation within everybody's experience. Go into a room where the shutters are always shut (in a sick-room or a bed-room there should never be shutters shut), and though the room be uninhabited—though the air has never been polluted by the breathing of human beings, you will observe a close, musty smell of corrupt air—of air unpurified by the effect of the sun's rays. The mustiness of dark rooms and corners, indeed, is proverbial. The cheerfulness of a room—the usefulness of light in treating disease—is all-important. It is a curious thing to observe how almost all patients lie with their faces turned to the light, exactly as plants always make their way toward the light."—*Florence Nightingale's Notes on Nursing.*

purpose of "hardening" them, is quite hazardous. It is not to be denied that some seem to be made tough by the process. But it is so only with the rugged children ; the delicate ones will invariably suffer under this fanciful treatment. As the skin is constantly acting, by night as well as by day, it is conducive both to cleanliness and comfort to entirely change the clothing on retiring for the night. The day-clothing should be aired during the night, and the bedding should be aired in the morning, for the same reason. (*Read Notes* 11 *and* 12.)

---

11. Under-clothing and Bedding.—All clothing worn during the day should be removed at night. A practice prevails in tropical countries of shaking thoroughly every article of apparel just before it is placed on the body. The motive which prompts this comes from the fear lest a centipede or other lively and virulent specimen of natural history has hid itself somewhere within the folds of the garment. Even without the danger of wearing one's shirt in conjunction with such an intruder, it is an excellent practice to shake it and every other article of clothing thoroughly before putting them on. The garments worn next to the skin should be changed before they become saturated with the secretions of the sebaceous glands. This can be accomplished by renewing them twice a week, though the majority of people only change them once in that period. Combe recommends to wear two sets of flannels, each being worn and aired by turns, on alternate days ; he likewise praises a practice common in Italy, namely, instead of beds being made up in the morning the moment they are vacated, and while still saturated with the nocturnal exhalations, the bed-clothes are thrown over the backs of chairs, the mattresses shaken up, and the window thrown open for the greater part of the day. This practice, so consonant with reason, imparts a freshness which is peculiarly grateful and conducive to sleep. Florence Nightingale, who never fails to speak plainly, says : " Feverishness is generally supposed to be a symptom of fever ; in nine cases out of ten it is a symptom of bedding. A real patient should have two beds, remaining only twelve hours in each ; on no account to carry his sheets with him."—*Draper (in Part)*.

12. Rules as to Clothing.—*Protection against Cold.*—For equal thicknesses, wool is much superior to either cotton or linen, and should be worn for all under clothing. In cases of extreme cold, besides wool, leather or waterproof clothing is useful. Cotton and linen are nearly equal.

Protection against Heat.—Texture has nothing to do with protection from the direct solar rays ; this depends entirely on color. White is the best color ; then gray, yellow, pink, blue, black. In hot countries, therefore, white or light-gray clothing should be chosen. In the shade the effect of color is not marked. The thickness and the conducting power of the material are the conditions (especially the former) which influence heat.

33. Poisonous Cosmetics.—The extensive use of *cosmetics* for the complexion is a fertile source of disease. The majority of these preparations contain certain poisonous mineral substances, chiefly lead. The skin rapidly absorbs the fine particles of lead, and the system experiences the same evil effects that are observed among the operatives in lead works and painters, namely, " painters' colic," and paralysis of the hands, called " wrist-drop."

34. Certain hair-dyes also contain lead, together with other noxious and filthy ingredients. These do not work as great harm as the cosmetics, since they are purposely kept away from the skin ; but they rob the hair of its vitality. Eye-washes, too, are made from solutions of lead, and many an eye has been ruined by their use. They deposit a white metallic scale on the surface of the eye, which, when in front, permanently blurs the sight.

The body should not only be so protected by its covering as to be kept from rain and damp, but the clothing must be so ventilated that the emanations from the skin shall not accumulate. The wearing of the unventilated beaver hat, or fur cap, is a ready method of suppressing the natural growth of the hair, and of causing the retention of that effete epithelial scale commonly called scurf, or dandruff. The wearing of tightly-fitting water-proof coats cannot be habitually practiced without danger to the wearer ; the very painful and troublesome ailment, rheumatism, has in many persons been produced by this manner of locking in the excretions of the surface.—*Dr. B. W. Richardson.*

---

33. Cosmetics ? Painters' colic ?

QUESTIONS FOR TOPICAL REVIEW.

CHAPTER IV.

THE CHEMISTRY OF FOOD.

The Source of Food—Inorganic Substances—Water—Salt—Lime—Iron—Organic Substances—Albumen, Fibrin, and Caseine—The Fats or Oils—The Sugars, Starch, and Gum—Stimulating Substances—Necessity of a Regulated Diet.

I. The Source of Food.—The term *food* includes all those substances, whether liquid or solid, which are necessary for the nourishment of the body. The original source of all food is the earth, which the poet has fitly styled the "Mother of all living." In her bosom, and in the atmosphere about her, are contained all the elements on which life depends. But man is unable to obtain nourishment directly from such crude chemical forms as he finds in the inorganic world. They must, with a few exceptions, be prepared for his use, by being transformed into new and higher combinations, more closely resembling the tissues of his own body.

2. This transformation is effected, first, by the vegetable world. But all plants are not alike useful to man, while some are absolutely hurtful. Accordingly, he must learn to discriminate between that which is poisonous and that which is life-supporting. Again, all parts of the same plant or tree are not alike beneficial : in some, the fruit ; in others, the leaves ; and in others, the seeds only are sufficiently refined for his use. These he must learn to select ; he must also learn the proper modes of preparing each kind for his table, whether by cooking or other processes. *(Read Note I.)*

---

1. The Circle of Organic Life.—Man, as an animal, is chemically an oxidizing agent, reducing again to primitive forms the principles built up by the vegetable world, and taken in by him either directly as vegetables, or indirectly in the shape of the material of other animals. Without vegetable life

---

1. The term food? Source of food? Need of preparing food?
2. Usefulness and hurtfulness of plants? What then must man do? Parts of the same plant or tree?

3. Again, certain forms of the vegetable creation which are unfit, in their crude state, for man's food, and which he rejects, are chosen as food by some of the lower animals, and are, by them, made ready for his use. Thus the bee takes the clover, that man cannot eat, and from it collects honey. The cattle eat the husks of corn and the dried grass, that are by far too coarse for man, and in their own flesh convert them into tissues closely resembling his muscular tissue. In this way, by the aid of the transforming processes of the vegetable and animal creations, the simple chemical elements of the mineral kingdom are elaborated into our choice articles of food. (*Read Note* 2.)

---

animals could not exist, and never could have existed ; side by side they grow and flourish, indispensable to each other's existence ; the tree breaking up the exhaled carbonic acid of the animal—the carbon being stored up in its increasing mass—while the oxygen is returned again, free and uncombined, to the atmosphere for the respiratory needs of the animal world. Round and round go the elementary bodies in ceaseless change of form, nevertheless never more than they were at first and will be at the last—the atomic material of this planetary sphere being ever absolutely the same in amount. The material of the bodies of Saul and his sons, when burnt by the men of Israel after their ignominous exposure at Bethshan, in consequence of their defeat on Mount Gilboa, are circulating amongst us still ; it served others before them, and has formed part of thousands since. It is quite within the bounds of chemical possibility that some of the atoms contained in the fated apple of Eve, may have lain in the material of the apple which revealed to Newton the law of gravitation."—*Fothergill on the Maintenance of Health.*

2. The Food Circle in Nature.—"There are the same ultimate elements in flesh as in flour, the same in animals as in vegetables. The vegetable draws food from the soil and from the air. and being fully matured, it or some part of it is eaten by the animal. But in completing the circle, the vegetable receives and thrives upon the animal itself, in whole or in part, or the refuse which it daily throws off. The very bones of an animal are by nature or man made to increase the growth of vegetables and really to enter into their structure ; and being again eaten, animals may be said to eat their own bones, and live on their own flesh. Hence there is not only an unbroken circle in the production of food from different sources, but even the same food may be shown to be produced from itself. Surely this is an illustration of the fable of the young Phœnix arising from the ashes of its parent."—*Edward Smith on Foods.*

---

3. Certain forms of vegetable creation? Example of the bee? Cattle? The inference?

4. Inorganic Substances.—The substances we use as food are classified as *organic* and *inorganic*. By organic substances are meant those derived from living forms, such as vegetables and animals. Inorganic substances are those simpler inanimate forms which belong to the mineral kingdom. The former alone are commonly spoken of as food; but the latter enter very largely into the constitution of the body, and must therefore be present in our food. With the exception of two articles—water and common salt—these substances enter the system only when blended with organic substances.

5. Water.—Water, from a physiological point of view, is the most important of all the articles of food. It is everywhere found in the body, even in the bones and the teeth. It has been computed that as large a proportion as two-thirds of the body is water. The teeth, the densest of the solids in the human system, contain ten per cent. of water. The muscles, tendons, and ligaments are more than half water; for it is found that they lose more than half their weight when dried with moderate heat. But it is in the *fluids* of the body that water is found most abundantly. It gives to them the power of holding a great variety of substances in solution, and is the great highway by which new supplies are conveyed to the point where they are required, and by which old particles of matter, that have served their uses, are brought to the outlets of the body to be thus removed from the system. (*Read Notes* 3 *and* 4.)

---

3. The Only Natural Drink.—"Water is the natural drink of man, as it is of all organized beings. It enters more largely into his composition than any other substance, giving liquidity to the blood, moisture to all the tissues," and serving as the great solvent of the body; not less than two-thirds of its weight being of that element. It seems as if all organic beings were so much "organized water." "Soft water is more wholesome than hard, though water moderately hard is not perceptibly injurious. When very hard, a part of the salts of lime can readily be precipitated by boiling. As a rule, spring and well-waters, if brought from deep fountains, are better and more wholesome than running streams. Well-water, in towns and cities, unless brought from a great depth, is wholly unfit for drinking and cooking. The immense quantity

---

4. What classification? Define organic substances. Inorganic. Organic, how spoken of? The inorganic? Water and salt?
5. Water in physiology? Where found? Computation? Water in the teeth? Muscles, tendons, and ligaments? How ascertained? Water in the fluids of the body? What is the advantage?

6. Man can remain a longer time without solid food than without water. He may be deprived of the former for ten or twelve hours without great suffering, but deprivation of water for the same length of time will produce both severe pain and great weakness. The food should contain not less than two parts of water to one of solid nutriment. Water constitutes the great bulk of all our drinks, and is also a large constituent of the meats, vegetables, and fruits which come upon the table. Fruits, especially, contain it in great abundance, and, in their proper season, furnish most agreeable and refreshing supplies of the needed fluid.

7. Common Salt.—Salt, or sodium chloride, as an article of food, is obtained chiefly from the mineral kingdom; although plants contain it in small quantities, and it is also found in the tissues of nearly all animals used as food. In the human body it is an ingredient of all the solids and fluids. The importance of salt to animal life in general, is shown by the great appetite for it manifested by domestic animals, and also by the habitual resort of herds of wild beasts to the "salt-licks" or springs. In those parts of the world

---

of organic matter which permeates *every inch* of the soil, for many feet in depth, precludes the possibility of water passing through it without being corrupted. River water, polluted by sewers, is as disgusting to the senses as it is destructive to health. The notion that impure water can be rendered more wholesome by icing it is an erroneous one. Ice-cold drinks in summer, while the body is heated, are capable of producing lifetime disease, and even instant death."—*J. R. Black on the Ten Laws of Health.*

4. The Sustaining Power of Water.—"Water is the most reliable and grateful drink for man. Nature has many admixtures in the juices of fruits, but none so satisfying to excessive thirst as pure water. It will even prolong life when nutritious food is not taken, as we have a well-known instance, recorded by Dr. McNaughton, in the transactions of the Albany Institute of New York for 1836. The case was that of a man who lived upon water alone for fifty-three days. This he did while laboring under some delusion which impelled him to abstain from all ordinary nourishment—water alone could he be induced to partake of. His strength was tolerably well sustained during the first six weeks; he was able, in fact, to go out of doors; and even on the day of his death he was able to sit up in bed."—*Dr. James Knight.*

---

6. Length of time man can do without food or water? Give the comparison? Bulk of drinks? Constituent of meats, etc.? Fruits?
7. Salt, how obtained? Where found? In the human body? Importance of salt? What else can you state of the value of salt?

where salt is obtained with difficulty, man places a very high price upon it.

8. Experiments upon domestic animals show that the withdrawal of salt from their food, not only makes their hides rough and causes the hair to fall out, but also interferes with the proper digestion of food. If it be withheld persistently, they become entirely unable to appropriate nourishment, and die of starvation. (*Read Note* 5.)

---

5. Of Salt.—

> " Salt-cellars ever should stand at the head
> Of dishes, wheresoe'er a table's spread.
> Salt will all poisons expurgate with haste,
> And to insipid things impart a taste.
> The richest food will be in great default
> Of taste, without a pinch of sav'ry salt.
> Yet of salt meats, the long-protracted use
> Will both our sight and manhood, too, reduce;
> On tables salt should stand both first and last,
> Since, in its absence, there is no repast."
> —*The Code of the School of Salernum.*

" Animals will travel long distances to obtain salt. Men will barter gold for it; indeed, among the Gallas and on the coast of Sierra Leone, brothers will sell their sisters, husbands their wives, and parents their children for salt. In the district of Accra, on the gold coast of Africa, a handful of salt is the most valuable thing upon earth after gold, and will purchase a slave or two. Mungo Park tells us that with the Mandingoes and Bambaras the use of salt is such a luxury that to say of a man, ' he flavors his food with salt,' it is to imply that he is rich; and children will suck a piece of rock-salt as if it were sugar. No stronger mark of respect or affection can be shown in Muscovy, than the sending of salt from the tables of the rich to their poorer friends. In the book of Leviticus it is expressly commanded as one of the ordinances of Moses, that every oblation of meat upon the altar shall be seasoned with salt, without lacking; and hence it is called the Salt of the Covenant of God. The Greeks and Romans also used salt in their sacrificial cakes; and it is still used in the services of the Latin church—the '*parva mica*,' or pinch of salt, being, in the ceremony of baptism, put into the child's mouth, while the priest says, ' Receive the salt of wisdom, and may it be a propitiation to thee for eternal life.' Everywhere, and almost always, indeed, it has been regarded as emblematical of wisdom, wit, and immortality. To taste a man's salt, was to be bound by the rites of hospitality; and no oath was more solemn than that which was sworn upon bread and salt. To sprinkle the meat with salt was to drive away the devil; and to this day, among the

---

9. Salt is usually taken into the system in sufficient quantities in our food. Even the water we drink often has traces of it. The habitual use of much salt in cooking, or as a seasoning at the table, is not wise; and while it may not lead to consumption, as some writers declare, it is a bad habit in itself, and leads to the desire for other and more injurious condiments.

10. Lime.—This is the mineral substance which we have spoken of before as entering very largely into the composition of the bones. It is the important element which gives solidity and permanence to the framework upon which the body is built. Calcium triphosphate, or " bone-earth," is the chief ingredient of the bones and teeth, but is found in the cartilages and other parts of the body in smaller quantities. (*Read Note* 6.)

---

superstitious, nothing is more unlucky than to spill the salt."—*Letheby on Food.*

6. Phosphate of Lime and other Inorganic Substances.—" All food contains certain saline substances. If we burn a portion of the flesh of any animal, we may drive off the carbon, oxygen, hydrogen, and nitrogen, and 'ashes' are left. These ashes are the saline and mineral (inorganic) constituents of the animal. They exist in the blood and tissues, and are as essential to the life of the animal as those other elements which were expelled by heat. Like the latter, they are constantly being used up and carried off from the body, and like them must be replaced by means of our food. Cooking, especially boiling, tends to dissolve away some of these salts, and care should be taken to supply them by means of uncooked food, as fresh vegetables and fruits; milk also contains them. One of the most important of these inorganic substances is phosphate of lime, or ' bone-earth,' as it is called, from the fact that about forty per cent. of healthy bone is made up of it. When it is deficient, the bones are soft and are liable to be bent by the actions of the muscles attached to them, and a permanent deformity may be the consequence. This form of lime is contained in wheat, barley, oats, and rye, and from these sources the chief supply of it is derived. These plants require phosphate of lime for their growth and the perfecting of their grains ; hence it is supplied artificially by the farmer. A diet deficient in substances yielding the phosphate of lime is injurious to man, and should be avoided. Its presence in wheat-flour accounts in part for the fact that our ordinary loaf of bread makes so good a 'staff of life.' and that it is, and has been, so widely used as an article of food by the strongest and most vigorous races of mankind."—*Lankester's Manual.*

---

9. Salt, how taken into the system ? Its use in cooking ? Consumption ?
10. Lime in the bones ? What does it impart ? Chief ingredient of the bones and teeth ? Where else found ?

11. How does this substance find its way into the body? Meat, milk, and other articles obtained from the animal kingdom contain it, and it is abundantly stored away also in the grains from which our bread is made—in wheat, rye, and Indian corn. In early life, while the body is growing, the supplies of this substance should be carefully provided. The evil effects of the deprivation of it are too often and painfully evident in the softening of the bones, and in the predisposition to curvature of the spine—deformities which are most deplorable and which continue through life.

12. Iron.—This substance is probably the most abundant and widely diffused of the metals. It is found in most of the vegetables, and is a very important component of animal tissues. It enters into the composition of human blood in about one part per thousand. Ordinarily, the food conveys to the system enough iron for its use, but it must sometimes be introduced separately as a remedy, especially after great loss of blood, or after some wasting disease. Under its influence the blood seems to be rapidly restored, and a natural color of the lips and skin replaces the pallor caused by disease.

13. Other Inorganic Substances.—In addition to the substances mentioned, the mineral kingdom supplies compounds of soda, potash, and magnesia, which are essential for the use of the body. They occur in small quantities in the body, and enter it in combination with the various articles of diet.

14. Organic Substances.—These substances are derived from the vegetable and animal creations. They comprise all those articles which are commonly spoken of as " food," and which are essential to sustain the body in life and strength. They are divided into three groups, namely : the Albuminoid substances, the Fats, and Sugars.

15. The Albuminoids.—This class includes three important nutritive substances—(1) *Albumen*, which gives it its name ; (2) *Fibrin*,

---

11. How does lime find its way into the body? Early life? Effect of its deprivation?
12. Iron, its abundance and diffusion? Where found? What part of the blood is it? How supplied to the system? In case of loss of blood or wasting disease?
13. Soda, potash, and magnesia? How do they occur?
14. Organic substances, whence derived? What do they comprise? Groups?
15. The Albuminoid class, includes what? These compounds constitute what? The food? Their importance? Their properties?

including *gluten;* and (3) *Caseine.* These compounds constitute a large part of the human body, and the food contains them in proportionally large quantities. Their importance is so great, and the system so promptly suffers from their absence, that they have been styled the "*nutritious* substances." The properties which they hold in common are, that they do not crystallize, and have a jelly-like form, except when heat is applied to them, when they harden, or *coagulate.*

16. They likewise decompose, or *putrefy*, under the influence of warmth and moisture. Hence the decay of all dead animal tissues. Cold arrests this process. It is well known that milk, eggs, and the like, "keep" much longer in winter than at other seasons. The bodies of elephants, caught in the ice many hundred years ago, are occasionally borne by the icebergs to the coast of Siberia, completely frozen, but preserved almost perfectly in form and limb.

17. Albumen exists in milk, meat, the grains, and the juices of many plants; but the purest form is obtained from the white of egg. When we consider that an egg is composed chiefly of albumen and water—namely, six parts in seven; and when we also consider the numerous, diverse, and complex tissues—the muscles, bones, internal organs, bill, claws, and feathers,—with which the chick is equipped on leaving his shell, we are impressed with the importance of these apparently simple constituents of the food and body. (*Read Note* 7.)

---

7. Weight and Health.—"The weight of the body is very generally assumed to be an infallible index or proof of the maintenance of a healthy condition of the body; and that food which keeps up the weight has been regarded as satisfactory and nutritious. But this is not always a safe judgment, owing to the property in water from innutritious food to make good the loss of weight caused by the withdrawal of albumen and fat. The weight may remain the same, while we are "losing flesh." Fat, also, may increase in badly nourished people, while the more essential element of albumen is diminishing; the fact being that the badly fed are not always lighter than those who are well nourished. And further, the feeling of satisfaction after eating is deceptive; the Irish peasant who consumes ten pounds of potatoes in

---

16. Decomposition? Effect of cold? Illustrations? Elephants?
17. In what substances does albumen exist? What further is said of the egg?

18. Fibrin is derived from meats, and exists in the blood both of man and the lower animals. *Gluten,* or vegetable fibrin, resembles closely true fibrin, and is abundantly furnished in wheat and other grains from which flour is commonly made. Animal fibrin coagulates spontaneously when it is removed from the body, and thus causes the "clotting" of the blood.

19. Caseine is the curdy ingredient of the milk, and a highly important food-substance. Its coagulation in milk takes place not from heat, but by the addition of an acid, and also when milk becomes sour from exposure to the air. It is commonly effected, however, by introducing a piece of *rennet,* a preparation made from a calf's stomach. The *curds,* or caseine, may then be separated from the *whey,* and made into cheese, by pressing it sufficiently to drive off the water.

20. The Fats or Oils.—This is the second group of organic foods. Those which are more solid are called *fats;* the more fluid ones are the *oils.* Oleaginous substances are supplied in both animal and vegetable food; but, from whatever source derived, they are chemically much alike. They are insoluble in water, and yet they unite readily with the watery fluids of the body, and are by them conveyed to its various parts for their nourishment. This is due to their property of "emulsifying;" that is, they are held in suspension, in a finely divided state, in water. Ordinary milk is an example of an *emulsion.* We know that it contains fat, for butter is obtained from it; and, under the microscope, the minute oil-globules may be distinctly seen.

21. In our country and climate, and also in colder climates, fatty articles of food are principally derived from the animal creation, such as meat or flesh, milk and butter. But most of the breadstuffs contain more or less fat or oil—Indian meal as much as nine parts in a hundred.

---

a day feels quite satisfied, but is in reality badly nourished by his diet containing three-fourths water."—*Prof. Voit, of Munich.*

---

18. Fibrin, gluten, clotting of the blood?
19. Caseine? Its coagulation? Effect of rennet? Making of cheese?
20. What are the fats? The oils? How supplied? How alike? Emulsifying? Example? How do we know it?
21. Whence are fatty articles of food derived?

22. Among persons living in cold climates, the appetite for oleaginous food is especially eager; and they require large quantities of it to enable them to resist the depressing influences of cold. Since vegetation is scanty and innutritious, and the waters of the frozen regions abound in animal life, they must rely wholly upon a diet derived from the latter source. The Esquimau consumes daily from ten to fifteen pounds of meat or blubber, a large proportion of which is fat. The Laplander will drink train-oil, and regards tallow-candles as a great delicacy. In hot clima;es, on the contrary, where flourish the olive and the palm, this kind of food may be obtained from vegetable sources in abundant quantities. (*Read Notes* 8 *and* 9.)

8. The Necessity of Fat in the Food of Children.—"Children who dislike fat cause much anxiety to parents, for they are almost always thin, and, if not diseased, are not healthy. If care be not taken, they fall into a scrofulous condition, in which diseased joints, enlarged glands, sore eyes, and even consumption occur; and every effort should be made to overcome this dislike. If attention be given to this matter of diet, there need be no anxiety about the possibility of increasing the quantity of food consumed; whilst the neglect, the dislike, will probably increase until disease is produced. The chief period of growth—viz., from seven to sixteen years of age—is the most important in this respect, for a store of fat in the body is then essential. Those who are inclined to be fat usually like fat in food, and then it may be desirable to limit its use. Some who cannot eat it when hot like it when cold, and all should select that kind which they prefer. Those living in Russia and Lapland devour very large quantities—as seven pounds daily—and eat it even raw, while those dwelling in hot countries use very little. It produces more heat than any other kind of food."—*Edward Smith on Health.*

9. The Effect of Climate on the Appetite.—"Climate has an important influence on the quantity of food demanded by the system; and every one has experienced in his own person a considerable difference at different seasons of the year. Travelers' accounts of the amount of food consumed by the natives of the frigid zone are almost incredible. They speak of men eating a hundred pounds of meat in a day; and a Russian admiral, Saritcheff, mentions an instance of a man who, in his presence, ate at a single meal a mess of boiled rice and butter weighing twenty-eight pounds. Although it is difficult to regard these statements with entire confidence, the general opinion is undoubtedly well founded that the appetite is greater in cold than in warm climates. Dr. Hayes, the Arctic explorer, states, from his own observation,

---

22. Appetite of persons in cold climates? What do they require? Upon what must they rely? Why? The Esquimau? Laplander? Olive and palm?

23. The Sugars, or the Saccharine Substances.—These constitute the third and last group of the organic substances which are employed as food. This group embraces, in addition to the different kinds of *Sugar*, the varieties of starch and gum, from whatever source derived. The two substances last named do not, at first sight, present many points of similarity to sugar; but they closely resemble it in respect to their ultimate chemical composition, being made up of the same elements, in nearly the same proportions. And their office in the system is the same, since they are all changed into sugar by the processes of digestion.

24. Sugar is chiefly of vegetable origin, the animal varieties being obtained from honey and milk. The most noticeable characteristic of this substance is its agreeable, sweet taste, which makes it everywhere a favorite article of food. But this quality of sweetness is not possessed by all the varieties of sugar in the same degree; that obtained from milk, for instance, has a comparatively feeble taste, but rather imparts a gritty feeling to the tongue. The other important properties of sugar are, its power to crystallize when evaporated from watery solutions, such as the juices of many plants; a tendency to ferment, by which process alcohol is produced; and a ready solubility in water. This latter quality renders it very easy of digestion, and more so than any other of the saccharine group. It is computed that the annual production of sugar, in all parts of the world, is more than one million of tons. The kind of sugar that is in ordinary use, in this country, is prepared from the juice of the sugar-cane, which contains eighteen per cent. of sugar. In France it is manufactured from the beet-root, which holds about

---

that the daily ration of the Esquimaux is from twelve to fifteen pounds of meat, about one-third of which is fat. He once saw an Esquimau consume ten pounds of walrus flesh and blubber at a single meal, which however lasted several hours, with the thermometer 60° or 70° below zero. Some members of his own party manifested a constant craving for fatty substances, and were in the habit of drinking the contents of the oil-kettle with evident relish."— *Flint's Physiology.*

---

23. Which are the third of the organic groups? What do they embrace? Points of resemblance?

24. Origin of the sugars? Ordinary sugar? Beet-root? Maple-sugar? Grape-sugar? Cane-sugar?

nine per cent.; the maple-tree of our climate yields a similar sugar. The sweet taste of fruits is due to the presence of grape-sugar : the white grains seen on raisins belong to this variety. Cane-sugar is more soluble than the latter, and has twice the sweetening power. (*Read Note* 10.)

25. Starch.—This is the most widely distributed of the vegetable principles. It is tasteless, inodorous, and does not crystallize. It consists of minute rounded granules, which, under the microscope, reveal a somewhat uniform structure (Fig. 19). Starch will not

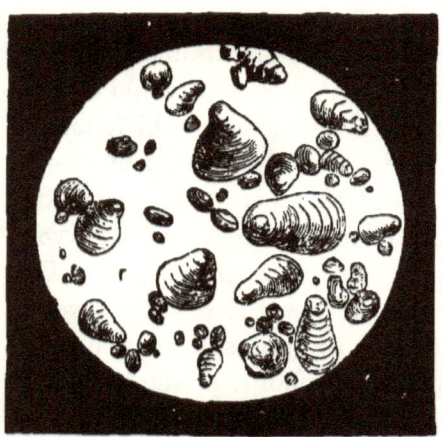

FIG. 19.—GRANULES OF POTATO STARCH MAGNIFIED.

dissolve in cold water, but in boiling water the small grains burst open, and may then be dissolved and digested.

26. The breadstuffs—wheat, corn, and rye flours—are more than one-half starch. Rice, which is the "staff of life" to one-third of the human family, contains eighty per cent. Unripe fruits have much starch in them, which renders them indigestible when eaten uncooked, for the grains of raw starch are

---

10. Why too much Sugar is Injurious.—"Sugar is very wholesome, and, as I told you, we want some in our diet. But children will often eat too much sugar, just as they will eat too little fat. The harm it does them is—first, it is very apt to spoil the teeth ; second, it takes away the appetite for other food. If you are always eating sweet cakes and sugar-plums, you will not care for plain, nourishing diet. Now, what is best for us all is, to have good appetites for wholesome food ; it will do more to keep us in health all our lives than anything else ; and there is a great deal in getting the right habit." Candies are frequently adulterated with plaster-of-paris, chalk, and certain forms of earth, that are indigestible ; but worse than that, the coloring matters and flavoring extracts that are used in the bright-tinted and fruity-flavored confectionery are absolute poisons in many instances, such as arsenic, copper, zinc, lead, prussic and sulphuric acid.—*Berner's Lessons on Health (in part).*

---

25. Starch, how widely distributed ? Its qualities ? Its constituents ? Its solubility ?
26. How much starch in bread-stuffs ? In rice ? Unripe fruits ? Ripe fruits ?

but slightly acted upon within the body. But, under the potent chemistry of the sun's ray, this crude material is converted into sugar. Thus are the fruits prepared by the careful hand of Nature, so that when ripe they may be freely used without further preparation.

27. Gum is commonly found in those articles which also contain starch, and has the same chemical composition as the latter, but is much less nutritious. In the East, gum-arabic and similar substances are largely employed as food. Persons who travel by caravan across vast, sandy deserts, find such substances well adapted to their wants, since they are not perishable, and are easily packed and carried.

28. Stimulating Substances.—The three classes of food-principles already considered—the Albuminoids, the Fats, and the Sugars —comprise all the more important organic ingredients of our food. There are, besides, a great variety of coloring and flavoring matters, that stimulate or increase the appetite for food by appealing to the eye and taste; but they are not nutritious, and· are quickly separated from the truly useful substances, and do not long remain in the body. Among these may be classed spices, flavors of fruits, tea, coffee, and vegetable acids.

29. Necessity of a Regulated Diet.—A great variety of experiments have been tried, in order to test the relative value of the different nutritive principles. They have been practiced to some extent upon man, but chiefly upon those inferior animals which require a similar diet to man.

30. By this means it has been demonstrated that—first, when any one of these substances is eaten exclusively, the body is imperfectly nourished, and life is shortened. Dogs fed exclusively upon either albumen, fat, or sugar, soon die of starvation. Second, a diet long deprived of either of these principles is a fertile cause of disease; for example, on ship-board, where fresh vegetables are not dealt out for a long period, *scurvy* becomes prevalent among the

---

27. Gum, where found? Its composition? Gum Arabic?
28. The three classes of food principles? What besides? What is said of them? Name the articles not nutritious.
29. What is said of experiments that have been tried?
30. What has been demonstrated in the first place? Example? Second demonstration? Example? Give the illustration in relation to convertibility.

sailors.   They are, however, to a certain extent mutually converti-
ble, and thus the missing article is indirectly supplied.   For instance, sugar changes to fat in the body; and hence, as is well
known, the "hands" on a sugar plantation grow fat during the
sugar season, by partaking freely of the ripened juices of the cane.
(*Read Note* II.)

31. That is the best diet, therefore, which contains some of each
of these principles, in due proportion; and that is the worst which
excludes the most of them.   The cravings and experience of man
had unerringly guided him to a correct regulation of his diet, long
before the chemistry of food was understood; so that his ordinary
meals long ago combined these various principles, the necessity and
value of which are now explained.   (*Read Notes* 12 *and* 13.)

---

11. The Effects of a Poor Diet.—"The food of the poor in olden
times was poor and scanty; so much so, in fact, that their powers of life were
depressed; and we believe this fact had much to do with the fearful mortality
of the plague throughout Europe during the middle ages.   The lower classes,
especially those living in crowded cities, and subsisting on the scanty and
monotonous diet that the historians of the period describe, were the principal
sufferers.   From 1296 to 1666, hundreds of thousands were carried off by the
most fearful pestilences the earth has ever known.   Rye in France and oats in
England were for generations the almost exclusive diet; wheat was a luxury,
which even the rich might only indulge in at Christmas.   Oats were known
in Germany 2,000 years ago, and were probably the original bread-grain for all
Europe."—*Dr. J. Knight.*

12. Variety in Diet and in its Preparation Beneficial.—"Every
dietary should contain fresh vegetables.   It is further necessary that certain
articles belonging to the same class be varied from day to day, otherwise the
appetite cloys.   Beef should alternate with mutton, for example; or variety
should be secured by different modes of cooking the same article.   Indeed, it is
not too much to say that the art of cookery is a matter of national importance,
not only because it renders food palatable, but because the more it is studied
and practiced, the greater is the economy which may be effected.   It is chiefly
in this relation, that beverages, condiments, etc., become such valuable dietetic
adjuncts."—*Wilson's Hand-book of Hygiene.*

13. Some Experiments as to Food.—"Magendie made numerous experiments on the inferior animals to test the value of different forms of nutriment.   He showed that a diet exclusively composed of starch and sugar would
not support life.   So, too, dogs confined to white bread and water died with
all the symptoms of starvation; but on the military brown-bread animals lived

pretty well, as this article contains a greater variety of the alimentary principles. Other experiments have given an account of geese limited to some one substance. All of them died—the animal fed upon gum, on the sixteenth day; that fed with sugar, on the twenty-first day; one fed with starch, on the twenty-fourth day; and one fed with white of egg, on the twenty-sixth day. In 1769, before these experiments were performed, Dr. Stark, a young English physiologist, fell a victim at an early age to ill-judged experiments on himself as to the effects of different foods. He lived for forty-four days on bread and water, for twenty-nine days on bread, sugar, and water, and for twenty-four days on bread, water, and olive oil; until finally, his constitution became broken, and he died from the effects of his experiments."—*Flint's Physiology.*

QUESTIONS FOR TOPICAL REVIEW.

CHAPTER V.

FOOD AND DRINK.

Necessity for Food—Waste and Repair—Hunger and Thirst—Amount of Food—Renovation of the Body—Mixed Diet—Milk—Eggs—Meat—Cooking—Vegetable Food—Bread—The Potato—Fruits—Purity of Water—Action of Water upon Lead—Coffee, Tea, and Chocolate—Effects of Alcohol.

1. Necessity for Food.—Activity is everywhere followed by waste. The engine uses up coal and water to produce motion, the stream wears away its bank, the growing corn-blade draws tribute from the soil. When the human body acts, and it is always in action during life, some of its particles are worn out and thrown off. This waste must constantly be repaired, or the body suffers. In this fact is seen the necessity for food. The particles, thus worn out, being henceforth useless, are removed from the body. Our *food* and *drink* are rapidly transformed into a new supply of living, useful material, to be in turn used up and replaced by a fresher supply.

2. Waste and Repair.—In this way the healthful body, though always wasting, is always building up, and does not greatly change in size, form, or weight. At two periods of life the processes of waste and repair are not exactly balanced. In early life the process of building up is more active, and in consequence the form is plump and the stature increases. Repair now exceeds waste. On the other hand, when old age comes on, the wasting process is more active, the flesh and weight diminish, the skin falls in wrinkles, and the senses become dull. Only during the prime of life—from about

---

1. What follows activity? Examples? Necessity for food?
2. Give the theory in relation to waste and repair.

twenty to sixty years of age—is the balance exact between loss and gain. (*Read Note* 1.)

3. Hunger and Thirst.—When the system is deprived of its supply of solid food during a longer time than usual, nature gives warning by the sensation of hunger, to repair the losses that have taken place. This sensation or pain appears to be located in the stomach, but it is really a distress of the system at large. Let a sufficient quantity of nourishment be introduced into the system in any other way than by the mouth, and it will appease hunger just as certainly as when taken in the usual manner.

4. The feeling of thirst, in like manner, is evidence that the system is suffering from the want of water. The apparent seat of the distress of thirst is in the throat; but the injection of water into the blood-vessels is found to quench thirst, and by the immersion of the body in water, the skin will absorb sufficient to satisfy the demands of the system. The length of time that man can exist without food or drink is estimated to be about seven days. If water alone be supplied, life will last much longer—there being cases

---

1. The Waste of the Body.—" In the physical life of man there is scarcely such a thing as rest—the numberless organs and tissues which compose his frame are undergoing perpetual change, and in the exercise of the function of each some part of it is destroyed. Thus, we cannot think, feel or move without wasting some proportion, great or small, according to the energy of the act, of the apparatuses concerned—such as brain, nerve or muscles. Now this waste-product cannot remain in its original situation, where it would not only be useless dross, but also obstructive and injurious. Such old material is being daily removed from our bodies to the average amount of three or more pounds ; and that an equal quantity of new shall take its place is the first principle of alimentation. To express it in commercial language, the income must be equal to the expenditure ; and in each of us the amount of this exchange must in a lifetime reach many tons. This tissue-change is so complete, that not a particle of our present body will be ours a short time hence ; and we will be, as I have lately seen it phrased, like the knife which, after having had several new blades, and at least one new handle, was still the same old knife to its owner. We are, in fact, constantly ' moulting.' "—*Mapother's Lectures on Public Health.*

---

3. System deprived of food? Warning? What is the pain? How proved?
4. Feeling of thirst? Seat of the pain? How proved? Time a person can exist without food?

recorded where men have lived twenty days and over without taking any solid food. (*Read Note 2.*)

5. Quantity of Food.—The quantity of food required varies greatly, according to the individual and his mode of life. The young, and others who lead active lives, or who live in the open air, require more food than the old, the inactive, or the sedentary. Those who live in cold regions require more than the inhabitants of hot climates. Habit, also, has much to do with the quantity of food required. Some habitually eat and drink more than they actually need, while a few eat less than they should.

6. The average daily quantity of food and drink for a healthy man of active habits is estimated at six pounds. This amount may be divided in about the following proportions: the mineral kingdom furnishes three and one-half pounds, including water and salt; the vegetable kingdom, one and one-half pounds, including bread, vegetables, and fruits; the animal kingdom, one pound, comprising meat, eggs, butter, and the like. This quantity is about one twenty-fourth the weight of the body, as it is generally computed; the average weight of an adult man being placed at 140 pounds. A

---

2. Hunger and Thirst.—"We none of us object to a sharp-set appetite; that is by no means unpleasant, especially when there is food at hand; but if this is not the case, it soon becomes a craving passion—a strong impelling power. The cravings of hunger have done much for this world; 'look where we may, we see it as the motive power which sets the vast array of human machinery in action.' Hunger is also the incentive which directs our attention to the system's need for food, and if it be sharp enough the most loathsome substances are greedily devoured. By it has man, and civilized man, too, been driven to feed upon the putrid corpse of his comrade. Hunger is one of the great forces in action in the preservation of the life of the individual; and the fear of it is one of the strongest incentives to action. But the pangs of hunger are tolerable in comparison with the tortures of raging thirst. In fact, so terrible are the latter that they form one of the cruelest tortures which man can inflict on man; so cruel a torture, indeed, that it has rarely been used, except in cases of bitter personal animosity, by others than brutal Eastern tyrants, or bigots under the influence of religious fanaticism."— *Fothergill on the Maintenance of Health.*

---

5. Amount of food required? The young and others? Those living in hot and cold climates? Habits?

6. Quantity of food daily? How divided? Compare with the weight of the body.

man, therefore, consumes an amount of solid and liquid nutriment every twenty-four days equal in weight to that of his body, a corresponding amount being *excreted*, or removed from the system in the same time. (*Read Notes* 3 *and* 4.)

3. A Lifetime Allowance of Food.—"M. Soyer, in his 'Modern Housewife,' makes a calculation as to how much food an epicure of 70 years of age has consumed. This imaginary epicure, who is supposed to be a wealthy personage, is placed by him on Primrose Hill at ten years old and told to look around him at the vast assemblage of animals and other objects he will in the course of a lifetime send down his throat—the sight of which is, of course, described as appalling. Among the other things, he is to devour 30 oxen, 200 sheep, 100 calves, 200 lambs, 50 pigs, 1,200 fowls, 300 turkeys, 263 pigeons, 120 turbot, 140 salmon, 30,000 oysters, 5,745 lbs. of vegetables, 243¾ lbs. of butter, 24,000 eggs, and 4½ tons of bread, besides fruits, sweetmeats, etc., and 49 hogsheads of wine, 548 gals. of spirits, and about 3,000 gals. of tea and coffee. This is a mere outline of what we are told is destined to be consumed. To show there is no exaggeration, Soyer assures us that he has from experience made up a scale of food for the day for a period of 60 years, and it amounts to 33¾ tons of meat, farinaceous food, and vegetables, etc."—*Journal of Chemistry.*

4. A Daily Ration for an Adult Man.—"We may arrive at something like an average daily diet by taking the case of the man in good health, weighing 154 lbs., and measuring 5 feet 8 inches in height. Simply to maintain his body, without loss or gain in weight, his ration of food should not contain less, during 24 hours, than the following proportions and quantities of the main ingredients :

THE AVERAGE DAILY DIET FOR AN ADULT.

FOOD SUBSTANCES.	PER CENTUM.	WEIGHT.		
		lbs.	oz.	grs
Water...	81.5	5	8	320
Albuminoids or flesh formers.	3.9		4	110
Starch, sugar, etc...........................	10.6		11	178
Fat....	3.0		3	337
Common salt	.7			325
Phosphates, potash, salts, etc....	.3			170
	100.	6	13	123

"Water, it will be remembered, enters into the composition of every article of food as well as in the liquids we drink. In reality, the weight of the dry

7. Renovation of the Body.—By this process, so far as weight is concerned, the body might be renewed every twenty-four days; but these pounds of food are not all real nutriment. A considerable portion of that which we eat is innutritious, and though useful in various ways, is not destined to repair the losses of the system. An opinion has prevailed that the body is renewed throughout once in seven years; how correct this may be, it is not easy to decide, but probably the renovation of the body takes place in a much shorter period. Some parts are very frequently renewed, the nutritive fluids changing more or less completely several times during the day. The muscles, and other parts in frequent exercise, change often during a year; the bones not so often, and the enamel of the teeth probably never changes after being once fully formed. (*Read Note* 5.)

8. Mixed Diet.—The habits of different nations in respect to diet exhibit the widest and strangest diversity. The civilized cook their food, while savages often eat it in a raw state. Some prefer it when fresh; others allow it to remain until it has become tainted with decay. Those dwelling in the far north subsist almost wholly on

---

food we take will exceed that given above ; chiefly for the reason that they do not come to us pure and unmixed with fibrous material and gelatine, whose use in nourishing the body is limited and uncertain."—*Kensington Museum Hand-Book on Food.*

    5. The Renewal of the Body.—"To meet these constant chemical changes, material is taken in, in the form of food and drink, which is being constantly assimilated, and so nutrition and repair are conducted. The rapidity with which these changes are carried on is much greater than is usually supposed. Paley, in his 'Natural Theology,' states that seven years are requisite for the perfect renewal of the body ; and this statement, owing partly to the mysticism associated with the number 7, is generally accepted and believed. The time really is rather months than years ; but it is absurd to fix a time which must necessarily vary in different individuals, being much less in the infant than in the aged, in the active than in the indolent ; widely different, too, in various tissues, from the epithelium lining of the glands of the stomach, renewed several times in each act of digestion, to the enamel of the tooth, which is probably never renewed during a lifetime."

---

    7. How often, then, might the body be renewed? Why is it not? Opinion? How correct? What further is stated?
    8. Habits of nations? Give the different cases.

animal food, while those living in hot climates have bountiful supplies of delicious fruits with which to satisfy all their bodily wants. One race subsists upon the banana, another upon the blubber of seals. In temperate climates, a diet composed partly of vegetable and partly of animal food is preferred. (*Read Note* 6.)

9. The important point to consider is, however, not one of origin, but whether the chemical principles (mentioned in the last chapter) enter into the composition of the diet. A purely vegetable diet may be selected which would contain all the principles necessary to sustain life. It is recorded of Louis Cornaro, a Venetian noble, that he supported himself comfortably for fifty-eight years on a daily allowance of twelve ounces of vegetable food, and about a pint of light wine. On the other hand, the food of John the Baptist, consisting of "locusts and wild honey," is an example of the sustaining power of a diet chiefly animal in its origin.

10. In our climate, those who lead active lives crave an allowance of animal food ; and it has been found by experience that with it they can accomplish more work and are less subject to fatigue, than without it. Among nations where an exclusively vegetable diet is employed, indigestion is a disorder especially prevalent. (*Read Note* 7.)

---

6. **Different Effects of Animal and Vegetable Food.**—"Raw meat gives fierceness to animals, and would do the same to man. This is so true that the English, who eat their meat underdone, seem to partake of this fierceness more or less, as shown in pride, hatred, and contempt of other nations."— *De La Mettrie.*

"The carnivora are, in general, stronger, bolder, and more pugnacious than the herbivora on which they prey ; in like manner, those nations who live on vegetable food differ in disposition from such as live on flesh."—*Liebig.*

7. **A Mixed Diet affords the best Results.**—"The mixed diet to which the inclination of man in temperate climates seems usually to lead him, when circumstances allow that inclination to develop itself freely, appears to be fully conformable to the construction of his dental and digestive apparatus, as well as to his instinctive cravings. And whilst on the one hand it may be freely conceded to the advocates of 'vegetarianism,' that a well-selected vegetable diet is capable of producing, in the greatest number of individuals, the highest *physical* development of which they are capable, it may, on the

II. The necessity for occasionally changing or varying the diet, is seen in the fact that no single article comprises all the necessary principles of food, and that the continuous use of any one diet, whether salt or fresh, is followed by defective nutrition and disease. There is one exception to this rule : in infancy, milk alone is best calculated to support life ; for then the digestive powers are incompletely developed, and the food must be presented in the simplest form possible. It should also be remembered that too rich diet is injurious, just as truly as one that is inadequate. When the food of horses is too nutritious, instinct leads them to gnaw the wood-work of their mangers.

12. Different Articles of Diet—Milk.—Milk is the earliest nutriment of the human race, and in the selection and arrangement of its constituents, may be regarded as a model food, no other single article being capable of sustaining life so long. Cows' milk holds caseine, one of the albuminoids, about five parts in one hundred ; a fatty principle, when separated, known as butter, about four parts ; sugar of milk four parts ; water and salts eighty-seven parts. The caseine and fatty substance are far more digestible in milk than after they have been separated from it in the form of cheese and butter.

13. Since milk, in itself, is so rich an article of food, the use of it as a beverage is unwise, unless the quantity of the other articles consumed be reduced at the same time. The milk sold in cities is apt to be diluted with water. The way to detect the cheat is by testing the specific gravity of the article. Good milk is about 1030 ;

---

other hand, be affirmed with equal certainty, that the substitution of a moderate proportion of animal flesh is in no way injurious ; but, so far as our evidence at present extends, this seems rather to favor the highest *mental* development. And we can scarcely avoid the conclusion that the Creator, by conferring on a man a remarkable range of choice, intended to qualify him for subsisting on those articles of diet, whether animal or vegetable, which he finds most suitable to his tastes and wants."—*W. B. Carpenter on the Principles of Physiology.*

---

11. Necessity for change in diet ? Continuous use of the same diet ? Exception ? Why ? Too rich diet ? Horses ?
12. Milk as a model food ? Cows' milk ? The constituents when separated ?
18. Milk as a beverage ? Milk sold in cities ? How to detect the cheat ?

skimmed milk, 1035 ; but milk diluted one-fifth is 1024.   An instrument called the lactometer is also used, by which the amount of cream present is ascertained.

14. Eggs.—The egg is about two-thirds water, the rest is pure albumen and fat in nearly equal portions.   The fat is in the yolk, and gives it its yellow color.   Eggs contain none of the sugar principles, and should be eaten with bread or vegetables that contain them.   Soft-boiled eggs are more wholesome than those which are hard-boiled or fried, as the latter require longer time to digest.

15. Meats.—The meats, so called, are derived from the muscular parts of various animals.   They are most important articles of food for adults, inasmuch as they are richly stored with albuminoid substances and contain more or less fat.   Such food is very nourishing, and easily digested if eaten when fresh,—veal and pork being exceptions.   The flesh of young animals is more tender and, in general, more digestible than that of older ones.   All meat is more tough immediately after the killing of the animal, but improves by being kept a certain length of time.

16. Some persons prefer flesh that has begun to show signs of decomposition, or is unmistakably putrid.   By some, venison is not considered to have its proper flavor until it is tainted.   In England, people prefer mutton that is in a similar condition, just as on the continent of Europe many delight in cheese that is in a state of decomposition.   In certain less civilized countries, flesh is not only eaten uncooked, but in a mouldy, rotten condition.   The use of such food is not always immediately injurious, but it predisposes to certain diseases, as indigestion and fevers.   (*Read Note* 8.)

---

8. A Summary Concerning Diet.—" The food on which the man who would be healthy should live, should be selected so as to insure a variety without excess.   Animal food should not be taken oftener than twice daily. The amount of animal and vegetable food combined should not exceed 30 ounces in the 24 hours; and for the majority of persons an average of 24 ounces of mixed solid food, a third only of which should be animal, is suffi-

14. Composition of eggs? Yolk? How should eggs be eaten? Why? How boiled? Why?
15. Meats, whence derived? Why important? Flesh of young animals?
16. Preference of persons? Venison? Mutton? Cheese? Uncooked flesh?

17. Cold is one means of preserving meat from decay. In the markets of northern Russia, the frozen carcases of animals stand exposed for sale in the winter air for a considerable time, and are sawed in pieces, like sticks of wood, as the purchases are made—such meat, when thawed, being entirely fit for food. Beef and pork are preserved by salting down in brine, and in this condition may be carried on long voyages, or kept for future use. Salted meat is not as nutritious as fresh, since the brine absorbs its rich juices and hardens its fibres. Long continued use of salt meats, without fresh vegetables, gives rise to the disease called scurvy, formerly very prevalent on ship-board and in prisons, but now scarcely known.

18. Cooking.—The preparation of food by the agency of fire is of almost universal practice, even among the rudest nations. The object of cooking is to render food more easy of digestion by softening it, to develop its flavor, and to raise its temperature more nearly to that of the body. A few articles of flesh-food are eaten uncooked in civilized lands, the oyster being an instance. Raw meat is occasionally eaten by invalids with weak digestive powers, and by men training for athletic contests.

19. In boiling meat, the water in which it is placed tends to dissolve its nutrient juices. In fact, the cooking may be so conducted as to rob the meat of its nourishment, its tenderness, and even of its flavor. The proper method, in order to preserve or promote these qualities, is to place the meat in boiling water, which, after a few minutes, should be reduced in temperature. In this way the intense heat, at first, coagulates the exterior layers of albumen, and imprisons the delicate juices; after that, moderate heat best

---

cient. All animal foods should be eaten while they are fresh, and after they have been well cooked. The habit of eating underdone flesh is an almost certain cause of parasitic disease. The amount of fluid taken, in any form, should not exceed the average of 24 ounces daily. Water is the only natural beverage."—*Dr. B. W. Richardson, The Diseases of Modern Life.*

17. Cold as a preserver? Meat in Russia? Beef and pork, how preserved? Salted meat as food? Scurvy?
18. The antiquity of the custom of cooking food? Object of cooking? The oyster? Raw meat as an occasional food?
19. Effect of boiling meat? How may the cooking be done? The proper method? Effect? Making of soup?

softens it throughout. When soup is to be made an opposite course should be pursued; for then the object is to extract the juices and reject the fibre. Meat, for such purpose, should be cut in small pieces and put into cold water, which should then be gradually raised to boiling heat. (*Read Note* 9.)

20. Roasting is probably the best method of cooking meat, especially "joints" or large pieces, as by this process the meat is cooked in its own juices. Roasting should begin with intense heat, and be continued at a moderate temperature, in order to prevent the drying out of the nutritious juices, as by this process an outer coating or crust of coagulated albumen is formed. During this process the meat loses one-fourth of its weight, but the loss is almost wholly water, evaporated by the heat. Too intense or prolonged heat will dry the meat, or burn it. Frying is the worst

---

9. Cooking Paves the Way for Easy Digestion.—The objects to be obtained by cooking meat are: 1. To coagulate the albumen and blood of the tissues, so as to render the meat agreeable to the sight. 2. To develop flavors, and to make the tissue crisp, as well as tender, and therefore more easy of mastication and digestion. 3. To secure a certain temperature, and thus to be a means of conveying warmth to the system. 4. To kill parasites in the tissues of the meat.

The action of heat should not be continued after these objects are accomplished, as the meat will thereby be rendered indigestible. If a piece of meat be placed in water which is briskly boiling, a crust, so to speak, is formed by the rapid coagulation of the albumen upon and near the surface; so that the juice of the meat cannot escape, nor the water penetrate its interior. If, on the other hand, the meat be put in cold water, and slowly heated, the albumen is gradually dissolved, and exudes into the water, making good soup, but leaving the meat poor and tasteless. Even in roasting meat the heat must be strongest at first, and it may then be much reduced. The juice which, as in boiling, flows out, evaporates, in careful roasting, from the surface of the meat, and gives to it the dark brown color, the lustre, and the strong aromatic taste of roast meat. All baked and roasted fatty foods are apt to disagree with delicate stomachs; and it is often remarked that, although bread and butter, boiled puddings, boiled fish, or boiled poultry can be eaten freely without discomfort, yet toast and butter, or meat pies and pastry, or fried fish, or roasted fowl will disagree with the stomach.—*Letheby on Food.*

---

possible method, as the heated fat, by penetrating the meat, or other article placed in it, dries and hardens it, and thus renders it indigestible.

21. Trichina.—It should be remembered that ham, sausages, and other forms of pork, should never be eaten in a raw or imperfectly cooked condition. The muscle of the pig is often infested by a minute animal parasite, or worm, called *trichina spiralis.* This worm may be introduced alive, in pork food, into the human body, where it multiplies with great rapidity, and gives rise to a painful and serious disease. This disease has been prevalent in Germany, and cases of it occur from time to time in this country.

22. Fish.—The part of fish that is eaten is the muscle, just as in the case of the meats and poultry. It closely resembles flesh in its composition, but is more watery. Some varieties are very easy of digestion, such as salmon, trout, and cod; others are quite indigestible, especially lobsters, clams, and shell-fish generally. A diet in which fish enters as the chief article, is ill adapted to strengthen mind or body, while its continued use is said to be the fertile source of nearly every form of disease of the skin. Some persons are so constituted that they can eat no kind of fish without experiencing unpleasant results.

23. Vegetable Food.—The list of vegetable articles of diet is a very long one, including the grains from which our breadstuffs are made, the vegetables from the garden, and the fruits. All the products of the vegetable kingdom are not alike useful. Some are positively hurtful; indeed the most virulent poisons, as strychnia and prussic acid, are obtained from certain vegetables. Again, of such articles as have been found good for food, some are more nourishing than others; some require very little preparation for use, while others are hard and indigestible, and can only be used after undergoing many preparatory processes. Great care must therefore be exercised, and many experiments made, before we can arrive at a complete knowledge in reference to these articles of diet.

---

21. What is "Trichina?" How guarded against?
22. What part of fish is eaten? What does it resemble? Fish as food for digestion? Fish as a diet?
23. List of vegetable articles? Usefulness of the different vegetables? Strychnia? What further is said in relation to the nourishing and other qualities of vegetables?

Tea, coffee, and other substances from which drinks are made are of vegetable origin.

24. Bread.—Wheat is the principal and most valuable kind of grain for the service of man. Bread made from wheat-flour has been in use for many hundreds of years, and on this account, as well as because of its highly nourishing properties, has been aptly called "the staff of life." We never become tired of good bread as an article of daily food. The white kinds of flour contain more starch and less gluten than the darker, and are therefore less nutritious. The hard-grain wheat yields the best flour. In grinding wheat, the chaff or bran is separated by a process called "bolting." Unbolted flour is used for making brown or Graham bread. (*Read Note* 10.)

25. The form of bread most easily digested is that which has been "leavened," or rendered porous by the use of yeast, or by some

---

10. Bread.—"The health and power of a nation, as of an army, depend greatly on its food. The quality of bread in any nation, community, or family is a pretty good measure of its civilization. No one can entirely dispense with it. Good or bad, in some form it must be had. So it is, and has been from the earliest records of the race, and so it will doubtless continue. Leavened or fermented bread is as old as the time of Moses, and its value has been fully tested. Whatever be the precise action of the leaven, it transforms the grain by partial decomposition of its original elements, and leaves as its resultant what all men in all ages have approved. Is the art of making good, honest, leavened, Bible bread lost in Massachusetts, as some of our friends declare? Baker's bread is almost universally adulterated. Bread hastily made in families is mixed in a variety of ways, with a variety of chemicals, and is generally imperfectly cooked. Very often the elements of wheat and fat which the body demands (a wise and witty clergyman of the last generation used to say, 'bread is the staff of life, but bread and butter is a gold-headed cane') are furnished in underdone pastry, made from flour and hog's lard. Any family who will take the pains can have good bread. It involves not more than ordinary skill and judgment. It is to be found on the continent of Europe, on all the great lines of travel, and is as common among the people of France and Germany as it is rare with us. The materials for an honest, wholesome loaf are simple and not expensive. The value of time and labor required for kneading the dough are the only difficulties, and these we would not undervalue; they are in many families very serious, and not easily overcome."—*Derby on the Food of Massachusetts.*

24. Wheat? "Staff of life? White flour? Hard-grain wheats? Bolting? Graham bread?
25. Leavened bread? Unleavened? Hot bread?

similar method. Unleavened bread requires much more mastication. Hot bread is unwholesome, because it is not firm enough to be thoroughly masticated, but is converted into a pasty, heavy mass, that is not easily digested.

26. Wheaten bread contains nearly every principle requisite for sustaining life, except fat. This is commonly added in other articles of diet, especially in butter,—"bread and butter," consequently, forming an almost perfect article of food. The following experiment is recorded : "A dog eating *ad libitum* of white bread, made of pure wheat, and freely supplied with water, did not live beyond fifty days. He died at the end of that time with all the signs of gradual exhaustion." Death took place, not because there was anything hurtful in the bread, but because of the absence of one or more of the food principles.

27. The Potato.—The common or Irish potato is the vegetable most extensively used in this country and Great Britain. Among the poorer classes in Ireland it is the main article of food. While it is not so rich in nutritious substances as many others, it has some very useful qualities. It keeps well from season to season, and men do not weary of its continuous use. It is more than two-thirds water, the rest being chiefly starch, with a little albumen.

28. The sweet potato differs from the white or common in containing more water and a small proportion of sugar. The common potato and the tomato belong to the same botanical order as the "nightshades," but do not possess their poisonous qualities, unless we except potatoes that are in the process of germination or sprouting, when they are found injurious as food.

29. Fruits.—These are produced, in this country, in great abundance, and are remarkable alike for their variety and delicious flavor; consequently they are consumed in large quantities, especially during the warmer months. The moderate use of ripe fruits, in their season, is beneficial, because they offer a pleasant substitute for the more concentrated diet that is used in cold

---

26. Wheaten bread ? Bread and butter ? Experiment on the dog ?
27. State what is said of the Irish potato?
28. Sweet potato ? Nightshades ? Potatoes when germinating ?
29. Fruits ? Use of ripe fruit ? Nutriment they contain ? Starch in unripe fruits ? Cooking of unripe fruits?

weather. The amount of solid nutriment they contain is, however, small. The percentage of water in cherries is seventy-five, in grapes eighty-one, in apples eighty-two. Unripe fruits contain starch, which, during the process of ripening, is converted into sugar. Such fruits are indigestible, and should be avoided; cooking, however, in part removes the objections to them.

30. Pure Water.—It is important that the water we drink and use in the preparation of food should be pure. It should be clear and colorless, with little or no taste or smell, and free from any great amount of foreign ingredients. Chemically pure water does not occur in nature; it is obtained only by the condensation of steam, carefully conducted, and is not as agreeable for drinking purposes as the water furnished by springs and streams. Rain-water is the purest occurring in nature; but even this contains certain impurities, especially the portion which falls in the early part of a shower; for in its descent from the clouds, the particles floating in the air are caught by the falling drops.

31. Water from springs and wells always contains more or less foreign matter of mineral origin. This imparts to the drink its pleasant taste—the sparkle, or "life," coming from the gases absorbed by the water during its passage under ground The ordinary supply of cities is from some pure stream or pond, conveyed from a distance through pipes, the limpid fluid containing generally only a small amount of impurity. Croton water, the supply of New York City, is very pure, and contains only four and a half grains to a gallon; the Ridgewood water, of Brooklyn, holds even less foreign matter.

32. Drinking-water may contain as large a proportion as sixty to seventy grains per gallon of impurity, but a much larger quantity renders it unwholesome. The mineral spring waters, used popularly as medicines, are highly charged with mineral substances. Some of them, such as the waters at Saratoga, contain three hundred grains and more to the gallon. (*Read Note* 11.)

11. Impure Water Spreads Disease.—"In the year 1867, three

30. How should drinking-water be as regards color and smell? Chemically pure water? How obtained? Agreeableness of perfectly pure water?
31. Spring and well water? Whence the sparkle, or life? The water supply of cities? Croton water? Ridgewood?
32. Impurities in drinking-water? Mineral springs?

33. Action of Water upon Lead.—The danger of using water that has been in contact with certain metals is well known. Lead is one of the most readily soluble, and probably the most poisonous of these substances in common use. When pure water and an untarnished surface of lead come in contact, the water gradually corrodes the metal, and soon holds an appreciable quantity of it in solution. When this takes place the water becomes highly injurious; the purer the water, and the more recent the use of the metal, the greater will be the danger. (*Read Note* 12.)

---

millions of pilgrims, of whom a handful had come from a cholera district, assembled at Hurdwar, a few miles from the spot where the Ganges escapes from the Himalayas. On the 12th of April the three millions resolved to bathe and drink. 'The bathing-place of the pilgrims was a space 650 feet long by 30 feet wide, shut off from the rest of the Ganges by rails. Into this long and narrow inclosure pilgrims from all parts of the encampment crowded as closely as possible from early morn to sunset; the water within this space, during the whole time, was thick and dirty—partly from the ashes of the dead, brought by surviving relatives to be deposited in the water of their river god, and partly from the washing of the clothes and bodies of the bathers. Now, pilgrims at the bathing ghaut, after entering the stream, dip themselves under the water three times or more, and then drink of the holy water, whilst saying their prayer. The drinking of the water is never omitted; and when two or more members of a family bathe together, each from his own hand gives to the other water to drink. On the evening of the next day, the 13th of April, eight cases of cholera were admitted into one of the hospitals at Hurdwar. By the 15th, the whole of this vast concourse of pilgrims had dispersed,' carrying the cholera in every direction over India; it attacked the British troops along the various routes, it passed the northern frontier, got into Persia, and so on into Europe, where it will work its wicked will for some time to come. That is a sample of the mischief water can do in the way of spreading disease."—*London Medical Press.*

12. **Lead in Drinking-Water.**—"The danger of using lead for pipes or cisterns is now well known, the case of the late royal family of France, at Claremont, having made the matter notorious. In this case there was one-tenth of a grain in the gallon, and one-third of the persons who drank the water were affected. But even one one-hundredth of a grain per gallon has produced palsy in those who drank this impurity habitually. It is remarkable that the Thames water will at one time dissolve lead, and not at another."—*Mapother's Health Lectures.*

---

83. What is stated of the action of water upon lead?

34. In cities, lead pipes are commonly used to convey water through the houses; lead being also used in the construction of roofs, cisterns, and vessels for keeping water and other liquids. After articles made of lead have been in use several months, the danger of lead-poisoning diminishes. An insoluble coating of the sulphate of lead forms upon the exposed surface, thus protecting it from further corrosion. It is, however, a wise precaution, at all times, to reject the water or other fluid that has been in contact with leaden vessels over night, or for a number of hours. Allow the water in pipes to run freely before using.

35. Coffee.—This is an important addition to diet, and, if moderately used, is beneficial to persons of adult age. As commonly employed, it consists of an infusion in boiling water of the roasted and ground berry. The water extracts certain flavoring and coloring matters, but that which gives it its peculiar stimulant qualities is the alkaloid *caffeine*. With most persons its action is that of a gentle stimulant, without any injurious reaction. It produces a restful feeling after exhausting efforts of mind or body; it tranquilizes, but does not disqualify for labor, and hence it is highly esteemed by persons of literary pursuits.

36. Another property of coffee is, that it diminishes the waste of the tissues, and consequently permits the performance of excessive labor upon an economical and inadequate diet. This has been tested among the miners of Belgium. Their allowance of solid food was below that found necessary in prisons and elsewhere; but, with the addition of about four pints of coffee daily, they were enabled to undergo severe labor without reducing their muscular strength. The caravans which traverse the deserts are supported by coffee during long journeys and lengthened privation of food. Among armies it is indispensable in supplementing their imperfect rations, and in relieving the sense of fatigue after great exposure and long marches. When taken with meals, coffee is also thought to promote digestion.

---

34. Lead in pipes and other things? Advice? What takes place after the articles of lead have been used much? What is wise?
35. Coffee as an article of diet? Of what does it consist? How does the water affect the coffee? The peculiar stimulant? How does it affect most persons?
36. Another property of coffee? Miners of Belgium? The Caravans? Among armies? Taken with meals?

37. Tea.—The effects of tea-drinking are very similar to those of coffee, and are due to a peculiar principle called *theine*. This principle is probably the same as that found in coffee—*caffeine*—since the chemical composition of both is precisely alike. Tea, as a beverage, is made from the dried leaves of the plant by the addition of hot water; if the tea be boiled, the oil which gives it its agreeable flavor is driven off with the steam. There are two kinds of tea—the black and the green; the latter is sometimes injurious, producing wakefulness and other nervous symptoms. The excessive use of either coffee or tea will cause wakefulness.

38. During Dr. Kane's expedition in the Arctic regions, the effects of these articles were compared. "After repeated trials, the men took most kindly to coffee in the morning, and tea in the evening. The coffee seemed to continue its influence throughout the day, and they seemed to grow hungry less rapidly than after drinking tea, while tea soothed them after a day's hard labor, and the better enabled them to sleep. They both operated upon fatigued men like a charm, and their superiority over alcoholic stimulants was very decided."

39. Chocolate is made from the seeds of the cocoa-tree, a native of tropical America. Its effects resemble somewhat those of tea and coffee, but it is very rich in nutriment. Linnæus, the botanist, was so fond of this beverage, that he gave to the cocoa-tree the name *Theobroma*—"the Food of the Gods." Its active principle is *theobromin*.

40. Alcohol.—The word alcohol is of doubtful origin. It is commonly supposed to be derived from the Arabic language, several words in that tongue resembling it in sound, but none of them or any other in the language have a meaning corresponding with that of the English term.

41. History.—Alcohol was distilled from rice many centuries before that seed was known in Europe. We hear of it in Bagdad about the year 900. It was known to the Moors of Spain, through

---

37. Effects of tea-drinking? Peculiar principle? The tea beverage, how made? Black and green tea? Excessive use of tea or coffee?
38. Experiments made during Kane's expedition?
39. State what is said of chocolate.
40. In what language has the word alcohol its origin?
41. Give its history.

whom the knowledge of its production spread into Western Europe. The first description of alcohol was given by a western writer about 1280, who wrote of a "burning or ardent water" that resulted from the distillation of wine. It may also have been known to the Romans, for Pliny, in the first century, wrote of a strong kind of wine that was inflammable—a quality that strongly suggests the knowledge of a product of distillation.

42. The Alcohols.—There are at least twelve members of the alcohol family, the oldest of which is common alcohol. This last is the only one that need be referred to here. *Common Alcohol* is sometimes known as spirit of wine, also as vinic alcohol. It is commonly obtained by the distillation of grains or of wine. The ardent spirits of commerce (brandy, whiskey, gin, and rum) contain about one-half water, the other half alcohol. Alcohol is also found in all the wines and malt liquors (beer, ale, and porter) in varying proportions. The juices of ripe, sweet fruits will, at seventy degrees of Fahrenheit, begin spontaneously to "work" or ferment; also wheat and other starch-grains, when sprouting, will have their starch changed into sugar, and this, in like manner, will undergo fermentation—alcohol being one of the results of this action in both cases.

43. Properties of Alcohol.—Alcohol is a clear, colorless, volatile, and inflammable liquid of penetrating odor and burning taste. It is lighter than water. As it cannot be frozen, it is used in thermometers for taking low or exceedingly cold temperatures. It is also used in spirit levels. It burns with a pale, bluish flame, without smoke, and with intense heat; hence its use in the spirit-lamp.

44. Is Alcohol Food?—Some authorities class alcohol among the food substances. Chemically it is allied to the sugars, but the effect of alcohol within the body is very unlike that of the sugars. The latter are nourishing, while the former tends to impair nutrition. It was on the mistaken theory that alcohol had sustaining power, that for two hundred years the armies and navies of certain countries were supplied with rations of rum or some other alcoholic

---

42. How is common alcohol obtained?
43. What are the properties of alcohol?
44. What can you say of alcohol as a food?

drink, under the name of "grog." During recent years, a systematic inquiry has been made to discover whether the grog-ration was really serviceable or the reverse. Tests have been tried upon considerable bodies of men, under military discipline, by withdrawing that ration; comparisons have been made at home and abroad, in hot climates and in cold, in active service and at rest. The results of these observations have, without exception, been favorable to the non-use of spirits. The proportion of ill-health, the number of sick days, and the incapacity for work have invariably been greater among the men to whom the spirit-ration has been issued, the quality of food and other circumstances being made as nearly equal as possible. Hence the conclusion that not only is alcohol not a food, but is injurious in itself, and a detriment to the food taken.

45. Does Alcohol Relieve Thirst?—One of the most striking properties of alcohol is its affinity for water. When swallowed, therefore, its tendency is to deprive the body of water, and to create thirst rather than to relieve it. It may then be stated that alcoholic drinks which appear to quench thirst do so by means of the water that, in greater or less quantities, dilutes the alcohol they contain. Water, the peerless beverage of nature, does its work better in proportion as it remains free from alcohol. To maintain normal action, the delicate organs of the body require a uniform supply of water. When alcohol is introduced, it draws the water to itself, and leaves the organs without their share of proper moisture; hence, after death from alcoholism, we find them affected in different degrees, being drier and harder than is natural.

46. Does Alcohol Enable its Consumers to Resist Extreme Cold?—If this could be proved to be a fact, some of its boasted usefulness would receive support. In extremely cold climates, the inhabitants are enabled to live comfortably by consuming vast quantities of animal food alone, especially if it is abundantly oily. Will alcohol act in a similar way or assist in maintaining heat? Experience and observation say no.

47. Before the thermometer was applied to the testing of the body's temperature, it was commonly supposed, by reason of the sensations of warmth, that alcohol increased bodily heat. When, however, this new test was applied, it became apparent that those sensations were deceptive, and that there had been an actual fall in temperature as the result of imbibing alcohol. The surface of the stomach is irritated by this powerful agent, causing the nerves of sensation to convey to the brain the impression that something has entered the stomach which is producing warmth. This is a delusive impression, as we know, by pouring a few drops of alcohol on the skin, that the tendency of alcohol is to cool the surface whenever evaporation can take place.

48. The sensation of warmth of the face and surface of the body is also deceptive. The flushing of the face, common to hard drinkers, does not indicate that they have a superabundance of animal heat, the temperature of their bodies being below normal. The true cause of the flush is a paralysis of one set of nerves governing the natural action of the hair-like vessels that course just below the skin. Nature has provided these infinitely fine vessels with minute controlling nerves, whose duty it is to regulate the flow of blood in exposed positions. Alcohol paralyzes this control; the blood flows at random, and the terminal vessels are overcharged with blood. Hence, the high color, which is so remarkable in habitual drinkers that it amounts to a disfigurement is Nature's signal of distress, showing that the circulation is deranged, and the blood is unduly brought into contact with the lower temperature of the outer air. Alcohol, therefore, is not a producer of heat, but a promoter of cold, and must be dangerous to any persons taking it when they are exposed to low temperatures. (*Read Note* 13.)

49. The testimony of those who have had experience in contact with the realms of snow and ice is unanimous against the cold-

---

13. Dr. Rae's Statement.—"The Arctic explorer, Dr. Rae, states that he found entire avoidance of alcohol necessary in the far North. The moment a man had swallowed a drink of spirits, it was certain that his day's work was nearly at an end. 'It was absolutely necessary that the rule of total abstinence should be rigidly enforced, if we would accomplish our day's task. Any use of liquor, as a beverage, when we had work on hand, in that terrific cold, was out of the question.' "

resisting property of alcohol. It is recorded of the men who served in Napoleon's campaign in Russia, under great exposure to cold, that death was hastened by the use of alcohol. The evidence of the Monks of St. Bernard is similar. Numerous Arctic explorers testify that not only is the temporary indulgence liable to result in most serious consequences, but that strong, able-bodied men in the habit of using alcoholic drinks are entirely unfitted to resist the cold to which they must be exposed. The natives and travelers alike rely upon fresh animal food, especially fatty food, and avoid alcohol as a danger to life.*

50. Alcohol Destructive to Life.—Instead of being a promoter of life, as the early alchemists who produced it hoped it would be, alcohol is hostile to life; it is a poison. Plant life is speedily destroyed when brought into close contact with it. The lower animals are poisoned by it. When applied directly to small insects and reptiles, death commonly occurs in a few seconds or minutes. It is hurtful to the larger animals, and the more intelligent of them appear to resent its use instinctively. This is seen when dogs have been forced to take brandy in small doses for some time. Instead of learning to like it, they gradually show a greater and greater dislike to it.

51. The Proper Use of Alcohol.—Like opium, chloral, arsenic, and many other poisons, alcohol may be rightly used, and that is as a medicine. For the relief of sickness and feebleness of body, or conditions of unusual fatigue, alcohol can be beneficially used under the advice of a physician. Like the other poisons, it should be definitely prescribed and the size and number of the doses precisely ordered by the physician.

---

* "Alcohol is not the warming cordial and invigorating stimulant that it is reputed to be, but there is a world-full of preconceived opinions in its favor that must be met and overcome before the true view can make its way. But the truth must prevail at last. Its true place is not along with the displays of wealth and luxury upon our sideboards, but in the medicine-chest along with hasheesh, henbane, opium, stramonium, and so forth, labeled as a Poison !"—*Dr. A. F. Kinne.*

---

50. What is the effect of alcohol upon life?
51. What is the proper use of alcohol?

52. Errors in the Use of Alcohol.—If this view of the question is the correct one, how utterly foolish is the practice of those who are continually prescribing for themselves doses of this poisonous substance for any trifling disturbance of their health. And how much worse is the practice of taking the various forms of alcohol when the person so taking them is in good health and merely indulges in drinking for the purpose of bringing about a temporary stimulation. And worse than all the others is the practice of those who not only indulge in these stimulants themselves, but who ask others to join in with them under the name of *good-fellowship*, when none of them are to be benefited by so doing, but rather all of them are in danger of being injured by the act.

53. This practice, last referred to, is often mistakenly spoken of as a sign of generosity, and is ordinarily called "treating." It is wholly indefensible from a physiological point of view, being harmful both to body and mind; and from a social point of view is without its equal for the evil that it has wrought and is capable of working. The "social glass" and the "treat at the bar" count a hundred victims to every other single one that can be traced to any other mistaken practice of human society. It is in regard to the evils that flow from this false show of generosity and geniality that the minds of the young should early be instructed. It will be seen from what has already been said about the physiological action of alcohol, that it conveys false sensations and leads to wrong judgments concerning its effects; in other words, it is misleading, it is a "mocker" even to the extent of enticing to dangerous personal and social habits; and "whosoever is deceived thereby is not wise."

54. Moderation Societies.—"Moderation societies" have been organized to check the evils of "treating," but they have not met with success, and it is not to be expected that they will, for there can be no moderation in the use of this dangerous drug except in the way mentioned at the beginning of this section, namely, as a prescribed medicine. As Dr. Alden has said, "There is no such

---

52. What three errors mentioned?
53. What is said of treating? Is alcohol deceptive?
54. What is said of moderation societies?

thing as a temperate use of spirits. In any quantity they are an enemy to the human constitution. Their influence upon the physical organs is unfavorable to health. They produce weakness, not strength; sickness, not health; death, not life."

55. Diminished Use of Alcohol as Medicine.—As a medicine, alcohol is far less freely used by physicians now than formerly. The dangers from its use are more generally recognized, and other remedies have been discovered and brought into use that are fully as efficient and active, but have not the tendency to habit-forming that is so peculiar to alcohol and other narcotics. There are able physicians who refuse to employ every form of alcohol as stimulant or medicine, in the belief that it can be safely and happily replaced by other remedies. In London and some other cities, hospitals have recently been organized and are now being operated on the basis of total abstinence from alcoholic treatment. In many parts of England the use of alcohol has greatly declined in the alms-houses and other public institutions, in which formerly the amount of stimulants annually consumed was very great.

56. It is well known that alcohol is an ingredient in many of the "Bitters" and other so-called patent medicines that have come into popular use through advertisement in the newspapers. Many persons have been deluded into the use of these, to them, doubly bitter substances; for, not only have they not found the curative results falsely proclaimed in the papers, but they have been beguiled into habits of drinking and into a liking for alcohol that the "bitters" soon fail to satisfy.

57. Concerning the Purity of Alcoholic Beverages.—It is well known that many makers and friends of wines and liquors claim that when these articles are pure they are not injurious, but that they become hurtful after they leave their place of manufacture by reason of the impurities that are added to them by unscrupulous dealers. "Pure and good liquor," they say, "does no harm." Is this correct? It cannot be denied that deadly additions have been, and may be, so made that these beverages will become more speedily

55. Is alcohol as highly valued in medicine now as formerly?
56. The effect of Bitters?
57. What do wine-dealers say? What is the harmful element?

and manifestly poisonous than they would otherwise be, but the teaching of modern physiology is this: that so long as the main element of danger—that same alcohol from which they get their stimulating and seductive properties—is present, the question of purity, or age, or smoothness of taste is one of little importance. The "unclean thing," as the Bible calls it, is present in all intoxicants, whether they be old and costly, or cheap and new and fiery to the taste. (*Read Note* 14.)

58. This so-called "purity" is commonly an accompaniment of high cost, especially as applied to wines, and represents money or capital that has been long lying idle in order that the commodities in question may acquire "age" and smoothness to the palate. "Purity" is therefore largely the cry of the seller, who is anxious to get back his invested capital, with interest, or perhaps with usury. It should be clearly understood that the best of these drinks, even though obtained from the vineyards or wine-cellars of princes, are injurious, and that the word "purity" is, in the light of science, a misnomer when applied to any beverage that contains alcohol. (*Read Note* 15.)

---

14. Adulteration in Liquors.—"It is not enough that alcoholic drinks are dangerous when purely made, but there is an added danger growing out of the almost universal practice of the manufacturers of these drinks to tamper with them and adulterate them with other harmful materials. Not many months ago the city government of Paris caused a testing of all the wines that were brought into the market during a month; there were 1,518 samples of French wine examined, and only 65 found absolutely free from injurious addition—that is, less than 5 per cent. was really pure."—*N. Y. Scientific Times.*

15. Adulteration of Wine.—The difficulty in the way of getting pure wine is nothing new. Pliny, who lived eighteen hundred years ago, wrote the following complaint: "Let us suppose that we all agree as to what wine is the best, how shall we get it? Our very princes do not drink pure wine; to such a point has the villainy of the producers and sellers of wine arrived that we can buy nothing more than the name of a vintage—from the very wine-vat it is all adulterated—and so, marvellous to tell, we may say of wine, the poorer, the purer."

---

58. What is said of purity as a commercial term?

QUESTIONS FOR TOPICAL REVIEW.

CHAPTER VI

DIGESTION.

The Principal Processes of Nutrition—The General Plan of Digestion—Mastication—The Teeth—Preservation of the Teeth—Action of the Saliva—The Stomach and the Gastric Juice—The Movements of the Stomach—Gastric Digestion—The Intestines—The Bile and Pancreatic Juice—Intestinal Digestion—Absorption by means of Blood-vessels and Lacteals—The Lymphatic or Absorbent System—The Lymph—Conditions which affect Digestion—The Quality, Quantity, and Temperature of the Food—The Influence of Exercise and Sleep—The Kidneys—The Spleen—Effect of Alchohol on Digestion, the Liver, and Kidneys.

1. Nutrition.—The great design of food is to give *nutriment* or nourishment to the body. But this is not accomplished directly, as the food must first pass through certain preparatory changes, as follows : (1), *Digestion*, by which the food is reduced to a soluble condition ; (2), *Absorption*, by which, when digested, it is taken into the blood ; (3), *Circulation*, which carries the enriched blood to the various parts of the system ; and (4), *Assimilation*, by which each tissue selects from the blood the materials necessary for its support.

2. By these four steps the sustaining power of food is gradually brought into exercise and the vital machinery kept in working order, somewhat after the manner of the steam-engine. To operate the latter, the force imprisoned within the coal and water is set free and converted into motion by the burning of the fuel and the vaporization of the water. It will be seen, however, when we come to study these operations in the human body, that they are conducted silently and harmoniously, with marvellous delicacy and completeness, and without that friction, and consequent loss of power, which attend the working of the most perfect machinery of man's invention.

---

1. Design of food ? How accomplished ?
2. Sustaining power of food ? Simile of the engine ? Operation in the human body ?

3. General Plan of Digestion.—The great change which food undergoes in digestion is essentially a refining process, reducing articles of diet, which are at first more or less solid, crude, and coarse, to a liquid and finely comminuted condition, suitable for absorption into the blood. The entire process of digestion takes place in what is called the "alimentary canal," a narrow, crooked tube, about thirty feet in its entire length. This canal begins in the mouth, extends thence downward through the gullet to the stomach (a receptacle in which the principal work of digestion is performed), and thence onward through the small and large intestines.

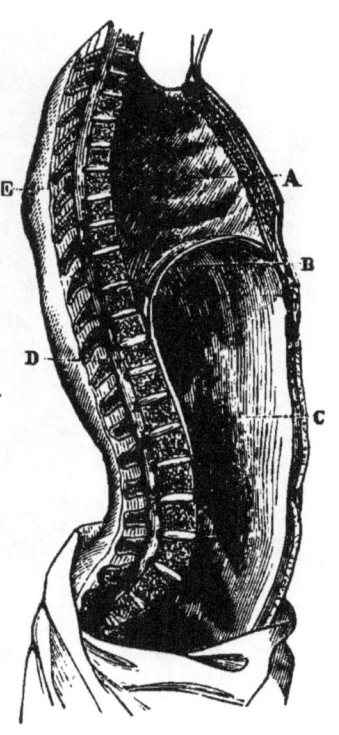

4. The stomach and intestines are situated in the cavity of the abdomen (Fig. 20, C, and Fig. 26), and occupy about two-thirds of its space. The action to which the food is subjected in these organs is of two kinds—mechanical and chemical. By the former it is softened, agitated, and carried onward from one point to another; by the latter it is changed in form through the solvent power of the various digestive fluids.

FIG. 20.—SECTION OF THE TRUNK, SHOWING THE CAVITIES OF THE CHEST AND ABDOMEN.

5. Mastication.—As soon as solid food is taken into the mouth, it undergoes mastication or chewing. It is caught between the opposite surfaces of the teeth, and by them is cut and crushed into very small fragments. In the movements of chewing, the lower jaw plays the chief part; the upper jaw, having almost no motion, acts simply as a point of resistance, to meet the action of the former. These movements of the lower jaw are

---

3. Change of food in digestion? Process of digestion? Describe the alimentary canal.
4. Situation of the stomach and intestines? Action of the food? Mechanical action? Chemical?
5. Describe the process of mastication. How many and what movements?

of three sorts: an up-and-down or cutting, a lateral or grinding, and a to-and-fro or gnawing motion.

6. The teeth are composed of a bone-like material, and are held in place by roots running deeply into the jaw. The exposed portion, or "crown," is protected by a thin layer of enamel (Fig. 21, *a*), the hardest substance in the body, and, like flint, is capable of striking fire with steel. In the interior of each tooth is a cavity, containing blood-vessels and a nerve, which enter it through a minute opening at the point of the root (Fig. 23).

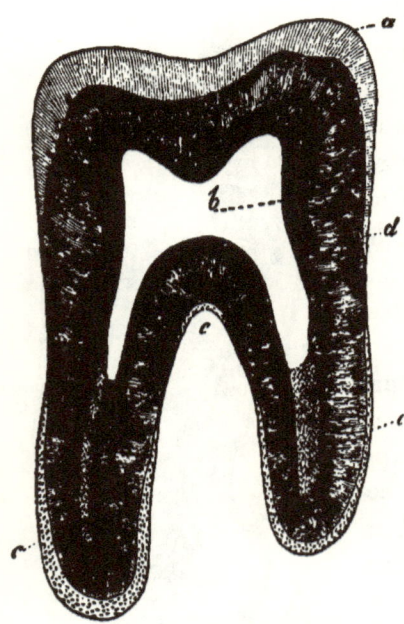

Fig. 21.—Section of a Tooth.
a, Enamel; *b*, Cavity; *c c*, Roots; *d*, Body of the Tooth.

7. There are two sets of teeth; first, those belonging to the earlier years of childhood, called the milk teeth, which are twenty in number and small. At six or eight years of age, when the jaw expands, and when the growing body requires a more powerful and numerous set, the roots of the milk teeth are absorbed, and the latter are "shed," or fall out, one after another (Fig. 22), to make room for the permanent set.

8. There are thirty-two teeth in the permanent set, an equal number in each jaw. Each half-jaw has eight teeth, similarly shaped and arranged in the same order; thus, two incisors, one canine, two bicuspids, and three molars. The front teeth are small, sharp, and chisel-edged, and are well adapted for cutting purposes; hence their name incisors. The canines stand next, one on each side of the jaw; these receive their name from their resemblance to the long, pointed tusks of the dog (Fig. 23).

6. Composition of the teeth? Enamel of the teeth? Interior of teeth?
7. The milk teeth? The permanent teeth?
8, 9. Number of teeth? How arranged?

9. The bicuspids, next in order, are larger and have a broader crown than the former; while behind them are the molars, the largest and most powerful of the entire set. These large back

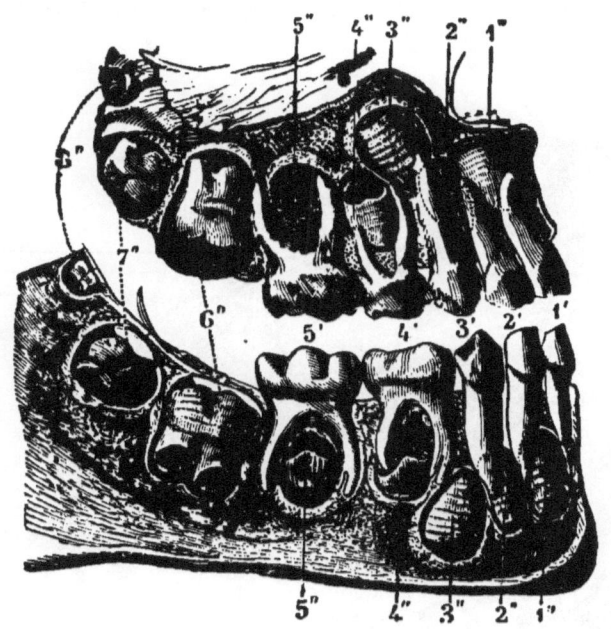

FIG. 22.—SECTION OF THE JAWS.
1′ 2′ 3′ 4′ 5′, The Milk Teeth ; 1″ to 8″, The Germs of the Permanent Set

teeth, or "grinders," present a broad, rough surface, suitable for holding and crushing the food. The third molar, or "wisdom tooth," is the last to be cut, and does not appear until about the twenty-first year. The arrangement of the teeth is indicated by the following dental formula :

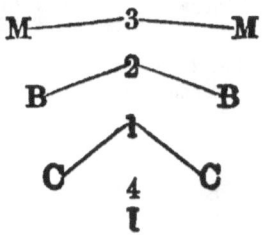

10. It is interesting, at this point, to notice the different forms of teeth in different animals, and observe how admirably their teeth are suited to the respective kinds of food upon which they feed. In the *carnivora*, or flesh-feeders, the teeth are sharp and pointed, enabling them both to seize their prey and tear it in pieces;

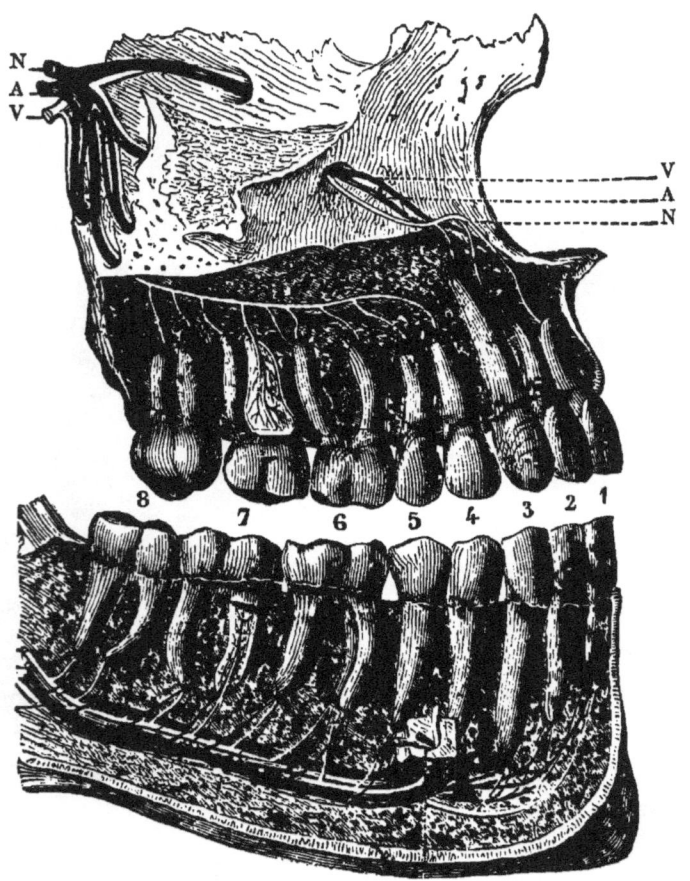

FIG. 23.—SECTION OF THE JAWS—RIGHT SIDE.

V, A, N, Veins, Arteries, and Nerves of the Teeth. The root of one tooth in each jaw is cut vertically to show the cavity and the blood-vessels, etc., within it. 1 to 8, Permanent Teeth.

while the *herbivora*, or vegetable-feeders, have broad, blunt teeth, with rough crowns, suitable for grinding the tough grasses and grains upon which they feed. Human teeth partake of both forms; some of them are sharp, and others are blunt; they are therefore well adapted for the mastication of both flesh and vegetables.

Hence we infer that, although man may live exclusively upon either vegetable or animal food, he should, when possible, choose a diet made up of both varieties.

II. Preservation of the Teeth.—In order that the teeth shall remain in a sound and serviceable condition, some care is of course requisite. In the first place, they require frequent cleansing; for every time we take food, some particles of it remain in the mouth, and these, on account of the heat and moisture present, soon begin to putrefy. This not only renders the breath very offensive, but promotes decay of the teeth.

12. The saliva, or moisture of the mouth, undergoes a putrefactive change, and becomes the fertile soil in which a certain minute fungus has its growth. This fluid, too, if allowed to dry in the mouth, collects upon the teeth in the form of an unsightly, yellow concretion, called tartar. To prevent this formation, and to remove other offensive substances, the teeth should be frequently cleaned with water, applied by means of a soft tooth-brush. The prevention of the tartar fungus is best effected by the use of a weak solution of carbolic acid. (*Read Note* I.)

---

1. The Proper Care of the Teeth.—"In the famous history of Don Quixote, the hero of La Mancha, it is related that at the end of one of his great battles, wherein he was as usual conquered, he found himself wounded in the face by a violent blow from a stone, and grieved to find that with it he had lost one of his teeth. Reflecting awhile on this unhappy accident, he sagely remarked that to lose a molar was very much like losing an old friend. And it is an important question, in view of this bit of wisdom, how to care for the molars, that they may become old friends. To this end, the cardinal maxim is cleanliness; and again cleanliness. One means of cleansing is the *natural* one—that is, by chewing food; for it is well known that if we have a tooth so situated in the jaw that it is seldom brought into use, that tooth early shows signs of decay. But more effectual is the *artificial* means—the brush. Children should early be taught to use this; and for them a softer brush should be selected than for adults. They should also early be taught to use no metallic substances, as pins, needles, etc., to remove substances from between the teeth. The teeth should always be thoroughly cleansed after taking acids into the mouth—for they are the great enemies to the teeth—and also after candies and other forms of sugar, for their particles that linger on the

---

11. Cleaning of teeth? Effects of not cleaning?
12. Effects of the saliva? Formation of tartar? How prevented? How destroyed?

13. It should be borne in mind that the enamel, Nature's protection for the teeth, when once destroyed, is never formed anew ; and the body of the tooth thus exposed is liable to rapid decay. On this account, certain articles are to be guarded against ; such as sharply acid substances that corrode the enamel, and hard substances that break or scratch it—as gritty tooth-powders, metal tooth-picks, and the shells of hard nuts. Sudden alternations from heat to cold, when eating or drinking, also tend to crack the enamel.

14. Action of the Saliva.—While the morsel of food is cut and ground by the teeth, it is at the same time intimately mixed with

the saliva, or fluids of the mouth. This constitutes the second step of digestion, and is called insalivation. The saliva, the first of the digestive solvents, is a colorless, watery, and frothy fluid. It is secreted (*i. e.*, separated from the blood) partly by the mucous membrane which lines the mouth,

FIG. 24.—STRUCTURE OF A SALIVARY GLAND.

but chiefly by the salivary glands, of which there are three pairs situated near the mouth.

15. These glands consist of clusters of very small pouches, around which a delicate network of blood-vessels is arranged ; they empty into the mouth by means of little tubes, or ducts. The flow from these glands is generally sufficient to maintain a soft and moist condition of the tongue and mouth ; but when they are excited by

teeth are changed by decomposition into lactic acid. Occasional examination of the teeth is prudent, in order that a commencing cavity may be promptly detected and remedied. Teeth that are decayed beyond remedy by filling should be immediately removed."—*Lane on the Hygiene of the Teeth.*

13. Destruction of the enamel ? How guarded against ?
14. Mixing of food with the saliva ? What is the saliva ? How secreted ? The salivary glands ?
15. The flow of saliva ? The thought of food ? Anxiety and grief ? Animals fed upon dry and coarse food ?

the presence and taste of food, they pour forth the saliva more freely. Even the mere thought of food will at times cause the saliva to flow, as when the appetite is stimulated by the sight or smell of some savory article; so that the common expression is correct that "the mouth waters" for the favorite articles of food. Anxiety and grief prevent its flow, and cause "the tongue to cleave to the roof of the mouth." In the horse, and other animals that feed upon dry and coarse fodder, and require an abundant supply of saliva, we find large salivary glands, as well as powerful muscles of mastication.

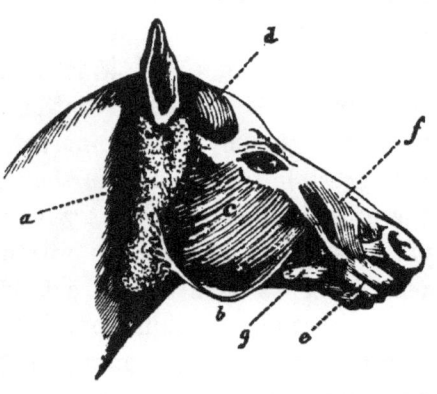

FIG. 25.—THE HEAD OF A HORSE, showing the large salivary gland (*a*), its duct (*b*), the muscles of mastication (*c, d, e, f,* and *g*).

16. The mingling of the saliva with the food seems a simple process, but it is one that plays an important part in digestion. In the first place, it facilitates the motions of mastication, by moistening the food and lubricating the various organs of the mouth. Secondly, it prepares the way for other digestive acts: by the action of the teeth, the saliva is forced into the solid food, softens the harder substances, and assists in converting the whole morsel into a semi-solid, pulpy mass, that can be easily swallowed, and readily acted upon by other digestive fluids. The saliva, also, by dissolving certain substances, as sugar and salt, develops the peculiar taste of each; whereas, if the tongue be dried and coated, they are tasteless. Hence, if substances are insoluble, they are devoid of taste.

17. Finally, the saliva has the property of acting chemically upon the food. As we have before stated (Chap. IV.), starch, as starch, cannot enter the tissues of the body; but, in order to become nutriment, must first be changed to grape-sugar. This change is, in part, effected by the saliva, and takes place almost instantly, whenever it comes in contact with cooked starch. This important func-

tion is due to an organic ingredient of the saliva called *ptyalin*. This substance has been extracted from the saliva by the chemist, and has been found, by experiment, to convert into sugar two thousand times its own weight of starch.   (*Read Note* 2.)

18. Importance of Mastication and Insalivation.—Each of these processes complements the other, and makes the entire work available; for, by their joint action, they prepare the food in the best possible manner for further digestive changes. The study of these preliminary functions will appear the more important, when we reflect that they are the only ones which we can regulate by the will. For, as soon as the act of swallowing begins, the food not only passes out of sight, but beyond control; and the subsequent acts of digestion are consequently involuntary and unconsciously performed.

19. It is generally known that rapid eating interferes with diges-

---

2. The First Step of Digestion.—"The digestive process begins in the mouth; among civilized people it begins in the plate, or even before. Undoubtedly mastication is the natural method of mincing meat, and not the least of its value lies in the fact that it takes time. A man who is eating a tough, and therefore not very digestible chop, will be slow in eating, if he is careful to masticate it well. There will be a long interval between each mouthful, and the stomach will run no risk of being hastily loaded.

"Now, a hastily-loaded stomach is as bad almost as, or rather, is the same thing as, an overloaded stomach; and there can be no doubt that artificial mastication becomes a snare when it leads any one to introduce a large quantity of finely-minced meat suddenly and rapidly into an unprepared stomach, especially into the feeble stomach of an invalid, under the idea that, because the meat is so nicely minced, and so very tender, it can be no possible burden to that sorely-tried organ. Natural mastication has, besides, another advantage over the artificial process, which is perhaps not always recognized. Whenever food enters the mouth, it gives rise to what is called a flow of saliva. This saliva is secreted by certain glands, which pour into the mouth the fluid they strain off from the blood, and which are excited or stimulated to action by the presence of food in the mouth, as well as by other causes. Saliva rapidly changes starch into sugar, and sugar is pre-eminently a soluble body, passing with the greatest ease from the alimentary canal into the blood."—*People's Magazine (London).*

---

18. Each of the processes? Why is a knowledge of the digestive functions important? How shown?
19. Rapid eating? Describe the process and effects.

tion. How does this occur? In the first place, in rapid eating, the flow of the saliva is insufficient to moisten the solid parts of the food, so that they remain too hard and dry to be easily swallowed. This leads to the free and frequent use of water, or some other beverage, at meals, to "wash down" the food—a most pernicious practice. For these fluids not only cannot take the place of the natural digestive juices, but, on the contrary, dilute and weaken them.

20. Secondly, the saliva being largely the medium of the sense of taste, the natural flavors of the food are not developed, and consequently it appears comparatively insipid. Hence the desire for highly-seasoned food, and pungent sauces, that both deprave the taste and over excite the digestive organs. Rapid eating also permits the entrance of injurious substances which may escape detection by the taste, and be unconsciously received into the system. In some instances, the most acrid and poisonous substances have frequently been swallowed "by mistake," before the sense of taste could act, and demand their rejection.

21. Thirdly, the food, being imperfectly broken up by the teeth, is hurried onward to the stomach, to be by it more thoroughly divided. But the stomach is not at all adapted to perform the task thus imposed upon it; and the crude masses of food remain a heavy burden within the stomach, and a source of distress to that organ, retarding the performance of its proper duty. Hence persons who habitually eat too rapidly, frequently fall victims to dyspepsia.* Rapid eating also conduces to overeating. The food is introduced so rapidly, that the system has not time to recognize that its real wants are met, and hence the appetite continues, although more nutriment has been swallowed than the system requires, or can healthfully appropriate.

22. The Stomach.—As soon as each separate portion of food is masticated and insalivated, it is swallowed; that is, it is caused to move downward to the stomach, through a narrow muscular tube

---

* For the same reason, persons who prematurely lose their teeth suffer from dyspepsia. For them a proper means of relief is the use of artificial teeth.

20. Loss of taste? Another effect of rapid eating? Mistakes?
21. Effect of imperfectly-broken food in the stomach? Dyspepsia? Over-eating?
22. Gullet? Describe the stomach and its location. Effects of gormandizing?

about nine inches in length, called the *œsophagus*, or gullet (Fig. 27). The stomach is the only large expansion of the digestive canal, and is a most important organ of digestion. It is a hollow, pear-shaped pouch, having a capacity of three pints, in the adult. Its walls are thin and yielding, and may become unnaturally distended, as in the case of those who subsist on a bulky, innutritious diet, and of those who habitually gormandize.

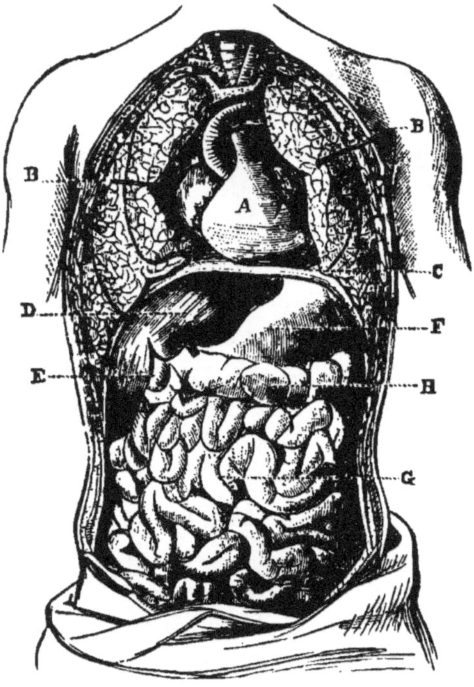

23. The stomach has also two openings; that by which food enters, being situated near the heart, is called the *cardiac*, or heart orifice; the other is the *pylorus*, or "gatekeeper," which guards the entrance to the intestines, and, under ordinary circumstances, permits only such matters to pass it as have first been properly acted upon in the stomach. Coins, buttons, and the like are, however, readily allowed

FIG. 26.—SECTION OF CHEST AND ABDOMEN.

A, Heart.
B, The Lungs.
C, Diaphragm.
D, The Liver.
E, Gall Bladder.
F, Stomach.
G, Small Intestine.
H, Large Intestine.

to pass, because they can be of no use if retained. The soft and yielding texture of this organ—the stomach—indicates that it is not designed to crush and break up solid articles of food.

24. The Gastric Juice.—We have seen how the presence of food in the mouth excites the salivary glands, causing the saliva quickly to flow. In the same manner, when food reaches the stomach, its inner lining, the mucous membrane, is at once excited to activity. At first, its surface, which while the stomach is empty

23. Heart-orifice? Gatekeeper? Coins, etc. ? Indication of the soft and yielding texture of the stomach?
24. What is meant by the gastric juice?

presents a pale pink hue, turns to a bright red color, for the minute blood-vessels which course through it are filled with blood.   Presently a clear, colorless, and acid fluid exudes, drop by drop, from millions of little tubes in the inner surface of the stomach, until finally the surface is moistened in every part, and the fluid begins to mingle with the food.   This fluid is termed the gastric juice.

25. The gastric juice dissolves certain articles of food, especially those belonging to the albuminoid class. This solvent power is due to its peculiar ingredient, *pepsin ;* in digestion, this substance acts like a ferment—that is, it induces changes in the food simply by its presence, but does not itself undergo change. The acidity of the gastric juice, which is due to *hydrochloric acid*, is not accidental ; for we find that the pepsin cannot act in an alkaline solution—that is, one which is not acid or neutral. The quantity of gastric juice secreted daily is very large, probably not less than three or four pints at each meal. Though this fluid is at once used in the digestion of the food, it is not lost ; since it is soon re-absorbed by the stomach, together with those parts of the food which it has digested and holds in solution.

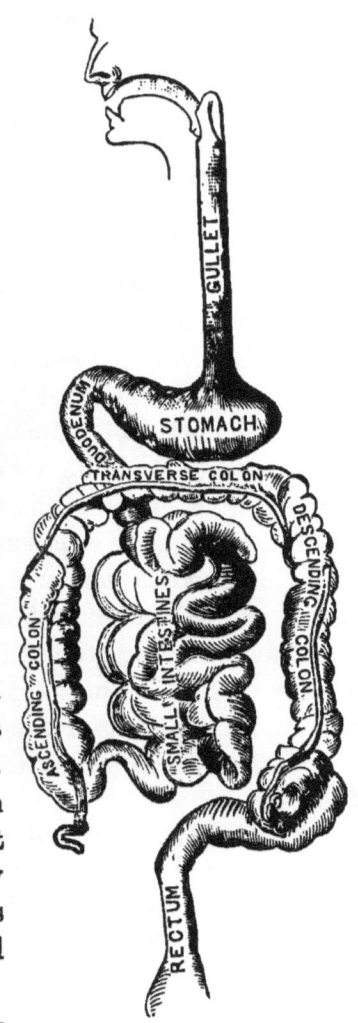

FIG. 27. ALIMENTARY CANAL—including Gullet, Stomach, Large and Small Intestines.

26.. **Movements of the Stomach.**— The inner coating of the stomach is the mucous membrane, which, as we have seen, furnishes the gastric juice.   Next to this coating lies

25. What is the office of the gastric juice? Acidity of the gastric juice? Quantity of gastric juice used?   What becomes of it?

26. Muscular coat of the stomach? Expansion and contraction of its fibres? Action of the fibres?

another, called the muscular coat, composed of involuntary muscular fibres, some of which run circularly, and others in a longitudinal direction. These expand to accomodate the food as it is introduced, and contract as it passes out. In addition, these fibres are in continual motion while food remains in the stomach, and they act in such manner that the contents are gently turned round from side to side, or from one end of it to the other.

27. By these incessant movements of the stomach, called the *peristaltic* movements, the gastric juice comes in contact with all parts of the food. We are, however, not conscious that these movements take place, nor have we the power to control them. When such portions of the food as are sufficiently digested approach the pylorus, it expands to allow them to pass out, and it closes again to confine the residue for further preparation.

28. The knowledge of these and other interesting and instructive facts has been obtained by actual observation; the workings of the stomach of a living human being have been laid open to view and examined—the result of a remarkable accident. Alexis St. Martin, a Canadian *voyageur*, received a gun-shot wound which laid open his stomach, and which, in healing, left a permanent orifice nearly an inch in diameter. Through this opening the observer could watch the progress of digestion, and experiment with different articles of food. Since that occurrence, artificial openings into the stomach of the inferior animals have been repeatedly made, so that the facts of stomach-digestion are very well ascertained and verified. (*Read Note 3.*)

29. Gastric Digestion.—What portions of the food are digested in the stomach? It was formerly thought that all the great changes of digestion were wrought here, but later investigation has taught us better. We now know that the first change in digestion takes

---

3. The Digestibility of Solid Foods.—"The accompanying table shows some of the results obtained from the experiments of Dr. Beaumont upon the stomach of Alexis St. Martin. It will surprise many to find that

---

27. Peristaltic movements? What is said of our consciousness of and power over these movements? Describe the movement of the pylorus.
28. How has the knowledge and the workings of the stomach been ascertained? St. Martin? How else?
29. What was formerly thought? What do we now know? What else do we now know? Water, salt, and sugar? Absorption?

place in the mouth, by the partial conversion of starch into sugar. We also know that, of the three organic food principles (considered in Chapter .IV.) two—the fats and the sugars—are but slightly affected by the stomach; but that its action is confined to that third and very important class from which the flesh is formed, the albuminoids. A few articles need no preparation before entering the system, as water, salt, and fruit-sugar. These are rapidly taken up by the blood-vessels of the stomach, which everywhere underlie its mucous membrane in an intricate and most delicate network. In this way the function of absorption begins.

30. The albuminoid substances are speedily attacked and digested by the gastric juice. From whatever source they are derived, vegetable or animal, they are all transformed into the same digestive product, called *albuminose*. This is very soluble in water, and is *in part* absorbed by the blood-vessels of the stomach. After a longer or shorter time, varying from one to five hours, according to the individual and the quantity and quality of his food, the stomach will be found empty. Not only the *unabsorbed* digested food, but also those substances which the stomach could not digest, have

vegetable foods—they are placed in the latter part of the table—require, as a rule, as much time for digestion as animal food.

Food.	Mode of Cooking.	Time required for digestion. h. m.	Food.	Mode of Cooking.	Time required for digestion. h. m.
Pork	roasted	5 15	Salmon Trout	boiled	1 30
Cartilage	boiled	4 15	Eggs (whipped)	raw	1 30
Ducks	roasted	4 0	Tripe (soused)	boiled	1 0
Fowls	do.	4 0	Pig's Feet (soused)	do.	1 0
Do.	boiled	4 0	Cabbage	boiled	4 0
Beef	fried	4 0	Beetroot	do.	3 45
Eggs	do.	3 30	Turnips	do.	3 30
Do.	hard boiled	3 30	Potatoes	do.	3 30
Cheese		3 30	Wheaten Bread	baked	3 30
Oysters	stewed	3 30	Carrot	boiled	3 15
Mutton	roasted	3 15	Indian Corn Bread	baked	3 15
Do.	boiled	3 0	Do. Cake	do.	3 0
Beef	roasted	3 0	Apple-dumpling	boiled	3 0
Do.	boiled	2 45	Potatoes	baked	2 33
Chicken	fricasseed	2 45	Do.	roasted	2 30
Lamb	broiled	2 30	Parsnips	boiled	2 30
Pig (suckling)	roasted	2 30	Sponge Cake	baked	2 30
Goose	do.	2 30	Beans	boiled	2 30
Gelatin	boiled	2 30	Apples (sour)	raw	2 0
Turkey	do.	2 25	Barley	boiled	2 0
Eggs	roasted	2 15	Tapioca	do.	2 0
Cod Fish (cured, dry)	boiled	2 0	Sago	do.	1 45
Ox Liver	broiled	2 0	Apples (sweet)	raw	1 30
Venison Steak	do.	1 30	Rice	boiled	1 0

30. Albuminose? The process? Chyme?

passed little by little through the pylorus, to undergo further action in the intestines. At the time of its exit the digested food is of a pulpy consistence, and dark color, and is then known as the *chyme*. (*Read Note* 4.)

31. The Intestines.—The intestines are continuous with the stomach, and consist of a fleshy tube, or canal, twenty-five feet in length. The small intestine, whose diameter is about one inch and a half, is twenty feet long, and very winding. The large intestine is much wider than the former, and five feet long (Fig. 27). The general structure of these organs resembles that of the stomach. Like it, they are provided with a mucous membrane, or inner lining, whence flow their digestive juices; and, just outside of this, a muscular coat, which propels the food onward from one point to another.

32. Moreover, both the intestines and stomach are enveloped in the folds of the same outer tunic or membrane, called the *peritoneum*. This is so smooth and so well lubricated, that the intestines have the utmost freedom of motion within the abdomen. In the small intestines the work of digestion is completed, the large intestine receiving from them the indigestible residue of the food, and in time expelling it from the body.

33. Intestinal Digestion.—As soon as the food passes the pylorus and begins to accumulate in the upper part of the intestines, it excites the flow of a new digestive fluid, which enters through a small tube, or *duct*, about three inches below the stomach. It is formed by the union of two distinct fluids—the *bile* and the *pancreatic* juice. The bile is secreted by the cells of the liver,

---

4. Indigestible Matters.—"Children sometimes *swallow coins, buttons, etc.*, and so cause great alarm. There is little real ground for apprehension under these circumstances, unless the coins are bronze. If the latter, there is some cause for fear that copper poisoning will ensue, and the ready passage of the coin is desirable. This is best effected by meals of figs or pudding, in which the coins are imbedded, and so passed harmlessly. As to bulk, whatever will go into the stomach will pass the various straits and emerge again."—*Fothergill.*

---

31. What are the intestines? The small intestines? The large intestines? Their structure?
32. Peritoneum? The work of digestion?
33. The presence of food in the intestines? Bile?

the largest gland of the body, situated on the right side and upper part of the abdomen (Fig. 26). The bile is constantly formed, but it flows most rapidly during digestion. During the intervals of digestion it is stored in the *gall-bladder*, a small membranous bag attached to the under side of the liver. This fluid is of a greenish-yellow color, having a peculiar smell, and a very bitter taste.

34. The pancreatic juice is the product of a gland called the *pancreas*, situated behind the stomach. This fluid is colorless, viscid, alkaline, and without odor. Like the digestive juices previously described, it owes its solvent power to its peculiar ferments. The most important of these ferments, called *pancreatin*, transforms starch into sugar. Another, *trypsin*, causes the solution of undissolved albuminoid substances; and a third ferment, which has not received a name, causes a partial acidification of the fats. By the joint action of these fluids, the food is prepared for absorption. There results from this action of the pancreatic juice a white and milky fluid, termed the *chyle*, which holds in solution the digestible portions of the food, and is spread over the extensive absorbent surface of the small intestines.

35. The mucous membrane of the intestines, also, secretes or produces a digestive fluid by means of numerous "follicles," or minute glands; this is called the intestinal juice. From experiments on the lower animals, it has been ascertained that this fluid exerts a solvent influence over each of the three organic food principles, and in this way completes the action of the fluids previously mentioned, viz.:—of the saliva in converting starch into sugar, of the gastric juice in digesting the albuminoids, and of the pancreatic juice and bile in emulsifying the fats.

36. Absorption.—With the preparation of the chyle, the work of digestion is completed; but it has not yet become a part of the blood, by means of which it is to reach the different parts of the body. The process by which the liquefied food passes out of the alimentary canal into the blood is called absorption. This is accomplished in two ways; first, by the *blood-vessels*. We have

34. The pancreatic juice? The joint action of these fluids?
85. The mucous membrane? Experiments on inferior animals?
36. How much thus far has been done with the food?

seen how the inner membrane of the stomach is underlaid by a tracery of minute and numerous vessels, and how some portions of the food are by them absorbed. The supply of blood-vessels to the intestines is even greater; particularly to the small intestines, where the work of absorption is most actively carried on.

37. The absorbing surface of the small intestines, if considered as a plane surface, amounts to not less than half a square yard. Besides, the mucous membrane is formed in folds with an immense number of thread-like prolongations, called *villi*, which indefinitely multiply its absorbing capacity. These villi give the surface the appearance and smoothness of velvet, and during digestion they dip

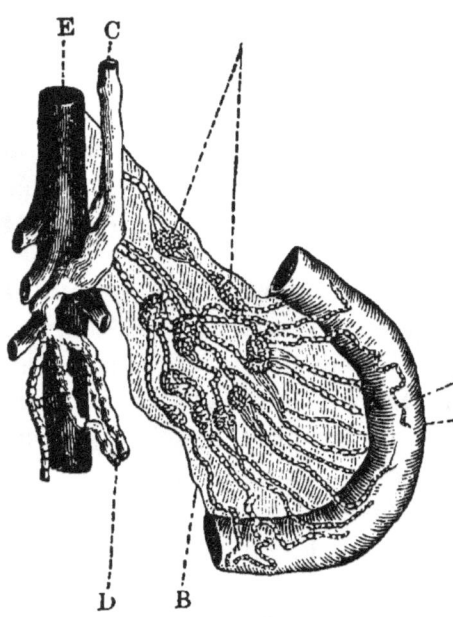

into the canal, and, by means of their blood-vessels, absorb its fluid contents, just as the *spongioles* which terminate the rootlets of plants, imbibe moisture from the surrounding soil.

38. Secondly, absorption is also effected by the *lacteals*, a set of vessels peculiar to the small intestines. These have their beginnings in the little villi just mentioned, side by side with the blood-vessels. These two sets of absorbents run in different courses, but their destination is the same, which is the right side of the heart. The lacteals receive their name from their milky-white appearance. After a meal containing a portion of fat, they are distended with chyle, which they are specially adapted to receive; at other times they are hardly discernible. The lacteals all unite to

FIG. 28.—THE LACTEALS.
A, Small Intestine.   B, Lacteals.
C, Thoracic Duct.   D, Absorbents.
E, Blood-vessel.

37. The next process? Give the first way?
38. How is absorption effected in another way? Describe it. Name of the lacteals? Thoracic duct?

form one tube, the *thoracic duct*, which passes upward through the *thorax*, or chest, and empties into a large vein, situated just beneath the left collar-bone.

39. The Absorbents.—The lacteals belong to a class of vessels known as absorbents, or lymphatics, which exist in nearly all parts of the body, except the brain and spinal cord. The fluid which circulates through the lymphatics of the limbs, and all the organs not concerned in digestion, is called *lymph*. This fluid is clear and colorless, like water, and thus differs from the milky chyle which the lacteals carry after digestion : it consists chiefly of the watery part of the blood, which was not required by the tissues, and is returned to the blood by the absorbents or lymphatics. (*Read Note* 5.)

40. Circumstances Affecting Digestion.—What length of time is required for the digestion of food? From observations made, in the case of St. Martin, the Canadian already referred to, it has been ascertained that, at the end of two hours after a meal,

---

5. Absorption of the Lacteals.—"The force by which the milky fluid moves upward through the lacteals is very considerable. This has been proved by the distension of the whole system of vessels, including the thoracic duct, even to the occurrence of rupture, when that duct has been tied in an animal a short time before it has been fed. The movement of the fluid thus, in some measure, resembles absorption by the spongioles at the extremities of the roots of trees, and the continuous rising of the sap. The thoracic duct may become diseased, and a serious derangement of nutrition take place. In the case of an unfortunate person, who was some years ago exhibited as a curiosity under the name of the 'living skeleton,' was illustrated the slow starvation that may thus be produced. Although he was able to take food in abundant supply, he was not nourished by it. Finally he died, and an examination of his body disclosed the fact that the thoracic duct had been obstructed by disease, and absorption by the lacteals was prevented. Hard work directly after a hearty meal is bad practice. Remember the story of the two hounds. They were both fed alike in the morning ; one of them was taken out to run on a hunt, the other was tied up at home. When the master came back from the hunt, both dogs were killed, and their stomachs examined. It was found that the hound that hunted still had the stomach full of food, while that of the stay-at-home was empty. When you have a hard piece of work on hand, do not eat much ; the more you eat the weaker you are for the purpose.-*Buckland* (*in part*).

---

39. The absorbents? Lymph? What further of the lymph?
40. What can you state as to the time required for digestion?

6

the stomach is ordinarily empty. How much time is needed to complete the digestion of food, within the small intestines, is not certain; but, from what we have learned respecting their methods of action, it must be evident that it largely depends upon the amount of starch and fat which the food contains.

41. In addition to the preparation which the food undergoes in cooking, which we have already considered, many circumstances affect the duration of digestion; such as the quality, quantity, and temperature of the food; the condition of the mind and body; sleep, exercise, and habit. Fresh food, except new bread and the flesh of animals recently slain, is more rapidly digested than that which is stale; and animal food more rapidly than that from the vegetable kingdom.

42. Food should not be taken in too concentrated a form, the action of the stomach being favored when it is somewhat bulky; but a large quantity in the stomach, especially if there is much liquid, often retards digestion. If the white of one egg be given to a dog, it will be digested in an hour, but if the white of eight eggs be given it will not disappear in four hours. A wine-glassful of ice-water causes the temperature of the stomach to fall thirty degrees; and it requires a half-hour before it will recover its natural warmth—about a hundred degrees—at which the operations of digestion are best conducted. A variety of articles, if not too large in amount, is more easily disposed of than a meal made of a single article; although a single indigestible article may interfere with the reduction of articles that are easily digested. (*Read Note* 6.)

---

6. **Digestibility of Warm Food.**—"It is very desirable that all cooked food should be taken hot. When it is eaten cold it reduces the temperature of the stomach, and both the nerves and vessels of the stomach are taxed in order to bring the temperature of the food thus taken up to that of the human body. Mankind in all ages seems to have discovered that it is desirable to prevent this tax upon the internal organs, and have taken their food hot in order to prevent it. It was death to the Roman slave to bring in his master's water tepid or cold—so much importance did they attach to hot water as drink." Many of our own beverages are taken hot even in summer weather; and it is an economy of the vital powers to take hot meals rather than cold ones.

---

41. Circumstances affecting duration of digestion? Fresh food?
42. Food in concentrated form? A large quantity of food? Experiment on the dog? Ice-water? Variety of articles?

43. Strong emotion, whether of excitement or depression, checks digestion, as do also a bad temper, anxiety, business cares, and bodily fatigue. The majority of these conditions make the mouth dry—that is, they restrain the flow of the saliva; and without doubt they render the stomach dry also, by preventing the flow of the gastric juice. And, as a general rule, we may decide, from a parched and coated tongue, that the condition of the stomach is not very dissimilar, and that it is unfit for the performance of digestive labor. This is one of the points which the physician bears in mind when he examines the tongue of his patient. (*Read Note* 7.)

44. The practice of eating at short intervals, or "between meals," as it is called, has its disadvantage, as well as rapid eating and over-eating, since it robs the stomach of its needed period of entire rest, and thus overtasks its power. With the exception of infants and the sick, no persons require food more frequently than once in four hours. Severe exercise, either directly before or directly after eating, retards digestion; a period of repose is most favorable to the proper action of the stomach. The natural inclination to rest after a hearty meal may be indulged, but it should not be carried to the extent of sleeping; since in that state the stomach, as well as the brain and the muscles, seeks release from labor. (*Read Notes* 8 *and* 9.)

As a rule, hot food is better than cold, in our climate, except in very hot weather; in tropical climates only can food be taken with advantage when cold, or ice and iced drinks be used with impunity."—*Lankester's Manual of Health.*

7. On the Demands of Digestion.—"The system never does two things well at the same time. No one can meditate a poem and drive a saw simultaneously without dividing his force; he may poetize fairly and saw poorly; or he may saw fairly and poetize poorly; or he may both saw and poetize indifferently. Brain-work and stomach-work interfere with each other if attempted together. The digestion of a dinner calls force to the stomach, and temporarily slows the brain: the experiment of trying to digest a hearty supper, and to sleep during the process, has sometimes cost the careless experimenter his life. The physiological principle is to do only one thing at a time, if you would do it well."—*Dr. E. H. Clarke: Sex in Education.*

8. Work or Exertion.—"The best time to make great exertion is about

---

43. Strong emotion? The tongue of the patient?
44. Eating between meals? Severe exercise? Sleep after meals?

45. The Kidneys.

45. The Kidneys.—Besides those already described, the abdominal cavity contains other important organs, viz., the *kidneys* and *spleen*.

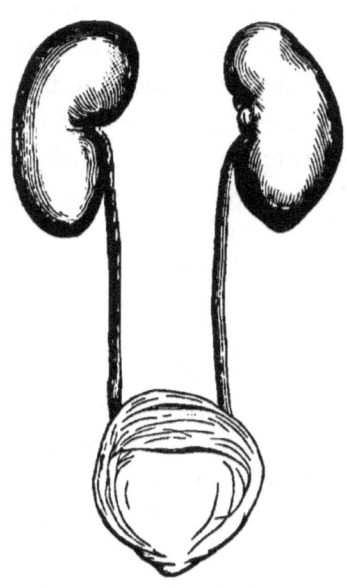

Fig.29.—The Kidneys and Bladder.

two hours after a meal. It is not a good time before breakfast, although moderate work may be then performed; and those who go to work before breakfast should first take a cup of hot milk, tea, or coffee, or other simple food. The body is weakest before breakfast.

"Violent or rapid exertion made by children, and also by stout and aged people, often injures, and sometimes causes disease of the heart, when the same taken in the ordinary way would do no harm. Rapidly running up stairs, or to meet a train, sometimes causes death. Hence, while exercise is of the utmost importance to health, it should be taken in a regulated and rational manner, and particularly by those who have passed the period of youth. But disease of the heart, even in youth, may often be traced to indiscretion in this particular, whether in rowing, running, or jumping."—*Edward Smith on Health.*

9. Tight Clothing interferes with Digestion.—"On one wet winter's day at Florence, some years ago, I had been spending the morning in the studio of a sculptor of world-wide reputation. We had discussed the perfections of female beauty, and I felt that I was sitting at the feet of a thinker, as well as an '*elegans formarum spectator.*' In the evening we met again at a hospitable palazzo, and, under cover of the waltz, from a quiet corner of observation, we saw whirling by in the flesh, much that we had been thinking of in the marble and the clay, and our eyes could not but follow one particular face, famous for the assistance its great natural beauty received from art. 'Face,' I said, but the mind of Hiram Powers was penetrating deeper, for he exclaimed, after a short silence: 'That is all very well, but I want to know where Lady —— puts her liver!' Where, indeed! for, calculating the circumference of the waist by the eye, allowing a minimum thickness for the walls of the chest, an area for the spine, œsophagus, and great blood-vessels, the section of the waist seemed to admit of no room for anything else. In such a body the liver must be squeezed down into the abdomen, stick into its hollow neighbors, and infringe upon all the organs. The organ which suffers most is the unresisting stomach, which is dragged and pushed out of all form during the continuance of this packing process."—*Dr. T. K. Chambers on the Indigestions.*

The kidneys are two in number, located in the loins behind the intestines, one on each side of the spinal column. They are shaped like a bean, being about four inches long, two inches wide, and one inch thick. The function of the kidneys is to purify the blood by removing from it a poisonous substance called *urea* and certain waste products. If their action is in any way interfered with, blood-poisoning takes place, on account of the accumulation of urea, and effete materials in the system, producing coma, which rapidly proves fatal unless it is relieved. The watery fluid secreted by the kidneys is carried by two tubes, called *ureters*, to the bladder.

46. The Spleen.—The spleen is situated on the left side of the abdomen behind the stomach. It is called the "milt" by the butcher. It has no duct, and its uses are not positively known. In malarial fevers, it is sometimes much enlarged, and the individual is said to have an "ague cake.'

47. Effect of Alcohol upon Digestion.—"The irritating effects of alcohol upon the lining of the stomach * are first seen in deranged digestive action, in loss of appetite, and at a later stage, in changes in the stomach's structure, principally by a thickening of the walls of that organ. (*Read Note* 10.)

---

* **Dyspepsia due to Alcohol**—"Many cases of dyspepsia are due to alcohol solely and wholly, and no reliance whatever can be placed upon the word, statement, or assertion under oath of a drunkard; for 'a drunkard is a liar.' And this holds good of both sexes, all ages, everywhere and ever."— *Dr. J. M. Fothergill.*

10. **Cordials, Bitters, etc.**—"In health, alcohol no wise plays a friendly part in regard to digestion. And it is just here that a mistake is made by many persons who have been deluded into the use of what are termed 'cordials'; these are very strong alcoholic liquors, and they are supposed by those who use them to be especially appropriate at the end of a hearty meal. Absinthe, the pet poison of the Parisian, is one of these falsely-named 'cordial' substances. These cordials are never less welcome than after a substantial meal. So many misleading names have been given to beverages (Cordials, Bitters, etc.), that many persons have used them without knowing the evil consequences which follow. It is made clear by recent proofs that the so-called cordials are the most rapidly poisonous of all the spirituous beverages."

---

46. What is the location of the spleen?
47. How is the digestion affected by alcohol?

Dr. Beaumont was able to observe the condition of the stomach of Alexis St. Martin (see paragraph 28, page 116) after alcoholic excesses. He states that the surface of the organ was overcharged with blood, at times drops of blood exuding from it; and that its secretions became thick, unnatural, and slightly tinged with blood.* It is a fact beyond dispute that other organs concerned in the act of digestion, particularly the liver, become diseased by the habitual use of spirituous liquors. (*Read Note* 11.)

48. Effects of Alcohol on the Liver.—When alcohol is taken into the stomach it is absorbed, and is carried by the portal vein directly into the liver. The blood in the liver is thus made more stimulating, and repeated stimulation produces over-action, which results in impairment or loss of power to secrete healthy bile. For the same reason, organic changes take place more frequently in the liver, from the use of alcohol, than in any other organ. It first becomes enlarged, owing to congestion from obstruction of the circulation and excessive growth of the connective tissue. One result of this overgrowth is compression and diminution in size of the cells which secrete the bile. Another result is a hindrance to the flow of blood through the liver. The organ is not only

---

* **Alcohol and Digestion.**—"The effects of alcohol upon digestion vary greatly according to the quantity imbibed; it may act as a temporary check, or in large doses it may completely arrest the digestive act: vomiting is frequently induced—the stomach thus freeing itself from the hurtful intruder. The habitual use of spirits often gives rise to a most distressing form of dyspepsia."

11. Effect upon the Appetite.—"At a Peace Congress held at Frankfort, Germany, the inn-keepers found it necessary to increase the price of board of the strangers attending the congress, the majority of whom were teetotalers, for the reason that their appetites required an amount of solid food in excess of that usually consumed by their own nationality, who are habitual drinkers of beer containing appreciable amounts of alcohol.

"By direct contact, alcohol acts upon the stomach and leads to a destruction of its secreting tubules. Nothing with such certainty impairs the appetite and the digestive power as the continued use of strong alcoholic liquids. From the stomach it is absorbed, and with its distribution through the system it interferes with nutrition and leads to a diseased state of the liver, kidneys, and other organs."—*Pavy.*

---

48. What effect produced on the liver by alcohol?

diminished in size, but it becomes hardened and roughened—an appearance which has given it the name of *hob-nailed liver* or drunkard's liver. This condition not only interferes with the proper formation of bile, but it obstructs the return of blood from the organs in the abdomen, and we have dropsy as a consequence.

49. The Effects of Alcohol on the Kidneys.—The action of alcohol on the kidneys is similar to that which takes place in the liver. The first effect of repeated stimulation by alcohol is an increase of the natural secretions of the organs, but this continued over-action, in obedience to a universal law, afterward results in a diminished secretion and in injury to the substance of the kidney. "Granular degeneration," one of the forms of Bright's disease, takes place. The kidneys are unable to perform efficiently the duty of removing impurities from the blood; urea, and other noxious materials accumulate, and the whole system is poisoned.

50. The Effect of Tobacco on Digestion.—Very few persons are able to take up the habit of smoking without first experiencing the sickening effect of tobacco upon the stomach. The use of tobacco has a perverting influence over the salivary glands, causing the secreted fluid to become so watery as to deprive it of its property of converting starch into sugar. In the case of some persons this amounts to a serious impairment of digestion, and can be relieved only by the abandonment of the offending substance.

The habitual use of tobacco has a tendency to leave the mouth and throat in a condition of unnatural dryness, and this has the effect of an artificially produced thirst which has, in many instances, led to the habit of taking alcoholic liquors. These two habits do not always co-exist in the same persons, but the danger that the one will lead up to the other is so great that they are frequently spoken of as the "twin vices."

The young should appreciate this danger, and should also remember that the habit of using tobacco is most commonly established early in life, if at all; very few persons, comparatively, who have passed twenty years of age without forming the habit, adopt it in their later years.

---

49. How are the kidneys affected by alcohol?
50. What effect of tobacco on digestion? Upon the mouth? What are the "twin vices"?

QUESTIONS FOR TOPICAL REVIEW.

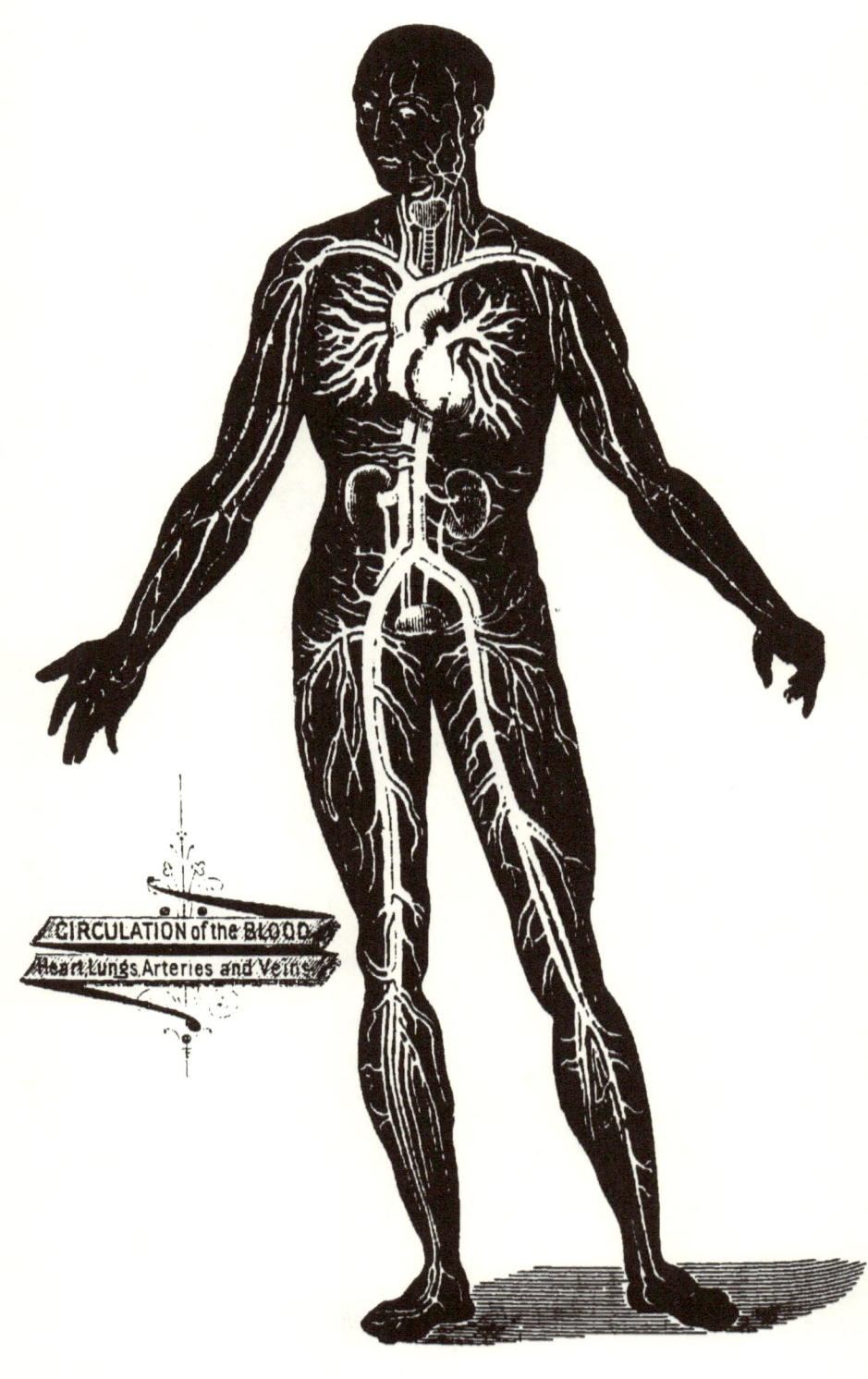

CIRCULATION of the BLOOD
Heart, Lungs, Arteries and Veins

CHAPTER VII

THE CIRCULATION.

The Blood—Its Plasma and Corpuscles—Coagulation of the Blood—The Uses of the Blood—Transfusion—Change of Color—The Organs of the Circulation —The Heart, Arteries, and Veins—The Cavities and Valves of the Heart —Its Vital Energy—Passage of the Blood through the Heart—The frequency and Activity of its Movements—The Pulse—The Spygmograph— The Capillary Blood-vessels—The Rate of the Circulation—Assimilation— Injuries to the Blood-vessels—Effects of Alcohol on Heart.

I. The Blood.—Every living organism of the higher sort, whether animal or vegetable, requires for the maintenance of life and activity, a circulatory fluid, by which nutriment is distributed to all its parts. In plants, this fluid is the sap; in insects, it is a watery and colorless blood; in reptiles and fishes, it is red but cold blood; while in the nobler animals and man, it is red and warm blood.

2. The blood is the most important, as it is the most abundant, fluid of the body; and upon its presence, under certain definite conditions, life depends. On this account it is frequently, and very properly, termed "the vital fluid." The importance of the blood, as essential to life, was recognized in the earliest writings. In the narration of the death of the murdered Abel, it is written, "the voice of his *blood* crieth from the ground." In the Mosaic law, proclaimed over thirty centuries ago, the Israelites were forbidden to eat food that contained blood, for the reason that "the life of the flesh is in the blood." With the exception of a few tissues, such as the hair, the nails, and the *cornea* of the eye, blood everywhere pervades the body, as may be proved by puncturing any part with

---

1. What is required by every living organism? In plants? Insects? Reptiles? Man?
2. Importance and abundance of blood? Dependence of life? Abel? Mosaic law? In what part of the body is blood not found? Quantity of blood in the body?

a needle.   The total quantity of blood in the body is estimated at about one-eighth of its weight, or eighteen pounds.

3. The color of the blood, in man and the higher animals, as is well known, is red; but it varies from a bright scarlet to a dark purple, according to the part whence it is taken.   " Blood is thicker than water," as the adage truly states, and has a glutinous quality. It has a faint odor, resembling that peculiar to the animal from which it is taken.

4. When examined under the microscope, the blood no longer appears a simple fluid, and its color is no longer red.   It is then seen to be made up of two distinct parts: first, a clear, colorless fluid, called the *plasma ;* and, secondly, of a multitude of minute solid bodies, or corpuscles, that float in the watery plasma.   The plasma, or nutritive liquid, is composed of water richly charged with materials derived from the food, viz., albumen, which gives it smoothness and swift motion ; fibrin; certain fats ; traces of sugar ; and various salts.

5. The Blood Corpuscles.—In man, these remarkable " little bodies," as the meaning of the word *corpuscles* signifies, are of a

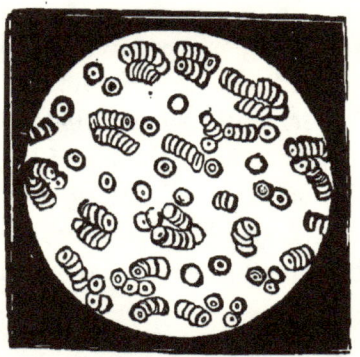

FIG. 30.—THE BLOOD CORPUSCLES, HIGHLY MAGNIFIED.

yellow color, but by their vast numbers impart a red hue to the blood. They are very small, having a diameter of about $\frac{1}{3500}$ of an inch, and being one-fourth of that fraction in thickness ; so that if 3,500 of them were placed in line, side by side, they would only extend one inch ; or, if piled one above another, it would take at least 14,000 of them to stand an inch high.   Although so small in size they are very regular in form.   As seen under the microscope, they are not globular or spherical, but flat, circular, and disc-like, with central depressions on each side, somewhat like a pearl button that has not been perforated.   In freshly-drawn blood they show a disposition to arrange themselves in little rolls like coins (Fig. 30).

3. Color of blood ?   Its consistence ?   Odor ?
4. What is stated of the blood as viewed under the microscope ?
5. State what you can of the little bodies called corpuscles.

6. The size and shape of the blood corpuscles vary in different animals, so that it is possible to discriminate between those of man and the lower animals (Fig. 31). This is a point of considerable practical importance. For example, it is sometimes desirable to decide in a court of justice the source, whether from man or an inferior animal, of blood stains upon the clothing of an accused person, or upon some deadly weapon. This may be done by a microscopical examination of a minute portion of the dried stain, previously refreshed by means of gum-water. Certain celebrated cases are recorded in which the guilt of criminals has been established, and they have been condemned and punished upon the evidence which science rendered on this single point, the detecting of the human from other blood.

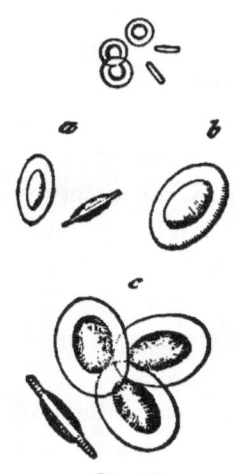

FIG. 31.

a, Oval Corpuscles of a fowl. b, Corpuscles of a frog. c, Those of a shark. The five small ones at the upper part of the figure, represent the human corpuscles magnified four hundred times.

7. The character of the blood of dead, extinct, and even fossil animals, such as the mastodon, has been ascertained by obtaining and examining traces of it which had been shut up, perhaps for ages, in the circulatory canals of bone. A means of detecting blood in minute quantities is found in the spectroscope, the same instrument by which the constitution of the heavenly bodies has been studied. If a solution containing not more than one one-thousandth part of a grain of the coloring matter of the corpuscle be examined, this instrument will detect it.

8. The corpuscles just described are known as the red-blood corpuscles. Besides these, and floating along in the same plasma, are the white corpuscles. These are fewer in number, but larger and globular in form. They are colorless, and their motion is less rapid than that of the other variety. The total number of both varieties of these little bodies in the blood is enormous. It is calculated that in a cubic inch of that fluid there are eighty-three

6. The size and shape of the corpuscles? Why is the fact important?
7. The character of the blood of dead animals? Means of detecting such blood?
8. White corpuscles? Total number of corpuscles in the body?

millions, and at least five hundred times that number in the whole body. (*Read Note* 1.)

9. Coagulation.—The blood, in its natural condition in the body, remains perfectly fluid; but within a few minutes after its removal from its proper vessels, a change takes place. It begins to coagulate, or assume a semi-solid consistence. If allowed to stand, after several hours it separates into two distinct parts, one of them being a dark red jelly, called the coagulum, or clot, which is heavy and sinks; and the other, a clear, straw-colored liquid, called serum, which covers the clot. This change is dependent upon the presence in the blood of fibrin, which possesses the property of solidifying under certain circumstances, one of them being the separation of the blood from living tissues. The color of the clot is due to the entanglement of the corpuscles with the fibrin.

10. In this law of the coagulation of the blood is our safeguard against death by hemorrhage, or undue loss of blood. If coagulation were impossible, the slightest injury in drawing blood would prove fatal. Whereas now, in many cases, bleeding ceases spontaneously, because the blood, as it coagulates, stops the mouths of the injured blood-vessels. In another class of cases, where larger vessels are cut or torn, it is ordinarily sufficient to close them by a temporary

---

1. The Blood—"You feel quite sure that blood is red, do you not? Well, it is no more red than the water of a stream would be if you were to fill it with little red fishes. Suppose the fishes to be very, very small—as small as a grain of sand—and closely crowded together through the whole depth of the stream, the water would look red, would it not? And this is the way in which the blood looks red: only observe one thing—a grain of sand is a mountain in comparison with the little red bodies that float in the blood, which we have likened to little fishes. If I were to tell you they measured about the 3200th part of an inch in diameter, you would not be much the wiser; but if I tell you that in a single drop of blood, such as might hang on the point of a needle, there are a million of these bodies, you will perceive that they are both very minute and very numerous. Not that any one has ever counted them, as you may suppose, but this is as close an estimate as can be made in view of what is known of their minute size."—*Macé's History of a Mouthful of Bread*

---

9. The blood in its natural condition in the body? Describe the process by which the coagulation of blood takes place?
10. If coagulation were impossible? How is it in fact?

pressure; for in a few minutes the clot will form and seal them up. In still more serious cases, where the blood-vessel is of large size, the surgeon is obliged to tie a *ligature* about it, thus preventing the force of the blood-current from washing away the clots, which, forming within and around the vessel, close it effectually.

11. It is worthy of remark that this peculiarity is early implanted in the blood, even before birth, and in advance of any existing necessity for it—thus anticipating and guarding against danger. But this is not all. Of most of the inferior animals, which, as compared with man, are quite helpless, the blood coagulates more rapidly, and in the case of the birds, almost instantly. The relative composition of fluid and coagulated blood may be thus represented:

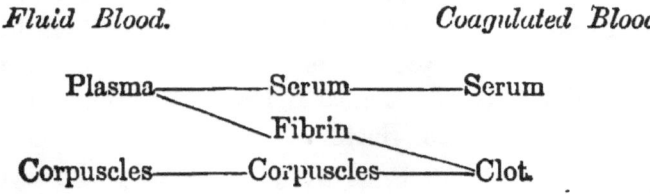

Fluid Blood.   *Coagulated Blood.*

Plasma — Serum — Serum

Fibrin

Corpuscles — Corpuscles — Clot.

12. The Uses of the Blood.—The blood is the great provider and purifier of the body. It both carries new materials to all the tissues, and removes the worn-out particles of matter. This is effected by the plasma. It both conveys oxygen and removes carbonic acid. This is done through the corpuscles. Some singular experiments have been tried to illustrate the life-giving power of the blood. An animal that has bled so freely as to be at the point of death, is promptly brought back to life by an operation called transfusion, by which fresh blood from a living animal is injected into the blood-vessels of his body. (*Read Note* 2.)

---

2. The Work of the Blood.—"The blood, which is our life, is a complex fluid. It contains the materials out of which the tissues are made, and also the *debris* which results from the destruction of the same tissues,—the worn-out cells of brain and muscle,—the cast-off clothes of emotion, thought, and power. It is the common carrier, conveying unceasingly to every gland and

---

11. What is worthy of remark? Coagulation of the blood of inferior animals? Of the blood of birds?
12. The blood, as a provider and purifier? What uses does the blood subserve? Experiments? Transfusion?

13. It is related that a dog, deaf and feeble from age, had hearing and activity restored to him by the introduction into his veins of blood taken from a young dog; and, that a horse, twenty-six years old, having received the blood of four lambs, acquired new vigor. And further, that a dog, just dead from an acute disease, was so far revived by transfusion, as to be able to stand and make a few movements.

14. Transfusion has been practiced upon man. At one time, shortly after Harvey's discovery of the "Circulation of the Blood," it became quite a fashionable remedy, it being thought possible by it to cure all forms of disease, and even to make the old young again. But these claims were soon found to be extravagant, and many unhappy accidents occurred in its practice; so that being forbidden by government and interdicted by the Pope, it rapidly fell into disuse. At the present time, however, it is sometimes resorted to in extreme cases, when there has been a great and rapid loss of blood; and there are upon record several instances where, other means having failed, life has been restored or prolonged by the operation of transfusion.

15. This reviving power of the blood seems to reside in the corpuscles; for transfusion, when performed with the serum alone, has, in every case, proved fruitless. Now, though so much depends upon the blood and its corpuscles, it is a mistake to suppose that in them alone is the seat of life, or that they are, in an exclusive manner, alive. All the organs and parts of the body are mutually dependent one upon the other, and the complete usefulness of any part results from the harmonious action of the whole.

---

organ, the fibrin and albumen which repair their constant waste, thus supplying their daily bread. Like the water flowing through the canals of Venice, that carries health and wealth to the portals of every house, and filth and disease from every doorway, the blood flowing through the canals of our organization carries nutriment to all tissues, and refuse from them."—*Clarke's Sex in Education.*

---

13. The case of the deaf and feeble dog? Horse? Dead dog?
14. Transfusion, as a fashionable remedy? What further of transfusion?
15. The seat of the reviving power of the blood? What further is related?

16. Change of Color.—The blood undergoes a variety of changes in its journey through the system. As it visits the different organs it both gives out and takes up materials. In one place it is enriched, in another it is impoverished. By reason of these alterations in its composition, the blood also changes its color. In one part of the body it is bright red, or arterial; in another it is dark blue, or venous. In the former case it is pure, and fit for the support of the tissues; in the latter, it is impure and charged with effete materials. (The details of the change from dark to bright will be given in the chapter on Respiration.) (*Read Notes* 3 *and* 4.)

---

3. On Purifying the Blood.—"By some the blood is regarded as the source of all diseases, and to 'purify the blood' is the object of their treatment. Quacks seize on this notion, and in sublime ignorance of the nature of the blood they profess to purify, and of the means by which their drugs could possibly purify it, make fortunes out of the credulity of the public. I would warn you against this notion of 'purifying' the blood. The blood is not like a river into which anything can be introduced from without. It gets rid of, or destroys, all substances which intrude—all which do not form part and parcel of its own structure; or, failing in that, it ceases to act as living blood."—*George Henry Lewes.*

4. By Means of the Blood, Exercise Benefits the Whole Body.—"The employment of the muscles in exercise not only benefits their especial structure, but it acts on the whole system. When the muscles are put in action, the capillary blood-vessels with which they are supplied become more rapidly charged with blood, and active changes take place, not only in the muscles, but in all the surrounding tissues. The heart is thus required to supply more blood, and accordingly beats more rapidly in order to supply the demand. A large quantity of blood is sent through the lungs, and larger supplies of oxygen are taken in and carried to the various tissues of the body." The oxygen engenders a large amount of heat, which produces an action on the skin whereby the increase of heat may be got rid of. By this means the skin is exercised, the perspiration is poured forth, the surface is caused to glow and is kept in health. "Not only are these organs benefited by the increased circulation of the blood, produced by exercise, but wherever the blood is sent, changes of a healthful character occur. The brain and the rest of the nervous system are invigorated; the stomach has its powers of digestion improved; and the liver, pancreas, and other organs perform their functions with more vigor."—*Lankester's Manual of Health.*

---

16. Changes in the blood? What further is stated?

17. Circulation.—The blood is in constant motion during life. From the heart, as a centre, a current is always setting toward the different organs ; and from these organs a current is constantly returning to the heart. In this way a ceaseless circular movement is kept up, which is called the Circulation of the Blood. This stream of the vital fluid is confined to certain fixed channels—the blood-vessels. Those branching from the heart are the arteries ; those converging to it are the veins. The true course of the blood was unknown before the beginning of the seventeenth century. In 1619 it was discovered by the illustrious William Harvey. Like many other great discoverers, he suffered persecution and loss, but unlike some of them, he was so fortunate as to conquer and survive opposition. He lived long enough to see his discovery universally accepted, and himself honored as a benefactor of mankind.

18. The Heart.—The heart is the central engine of the circulation. In this wonderful little organ, hardly larger than a man's fist, resides that sleepless force by which, during the whole of life, the current of the blood is kept in motion. It is placed in the middle and front part of the chest, inclining to the left side. The heart-beat may be felt and heard between the fifth and sixth ribs, near the breast bone. The shape of the heart is conical, with the apex or point downward and in front. The base, which is upward, is attached so as to hold it securely in its place, while the apex is freely movable. In order that loss of power from friction may be obviated, the heart is enclosed between two layers of serous membrane, which forms a kind of sac. This membrane, called the *pericardium*, is as smooth as satin, and itself secretes a fluid in sufficient quantities to keep it at all times well lubricated. The lining membrane of the heart, called the *endocardium*, is extremely delicate and smooth. (*Read Note* 5.)

---

5. A Poet's Summary of the Circulation:—

" The smooth, soft air with pulse-like waves
Flows murmuring through its hidden caves,

---

17. Motion of the blood ? What is meant by the circulation of the blood ? How confined? Discovery made by Harvey ?

18. Office of the heart ? Location of the heart ? Its beat ? Its shape? Protection to the heart ? What else is said in relation to the heart ?

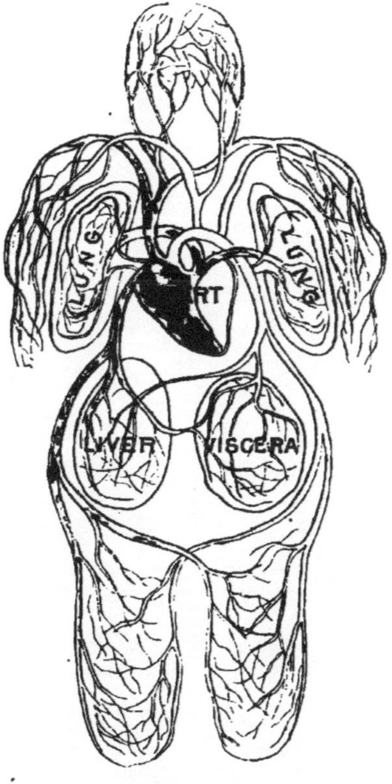

DIAGRAM SHOWING THE CIRCULATION OF THE BLOOD.

Fig. 32.

EXTERNAL VIEW OF HEART.

Fig. 33.

19. The Cavities of the Heart.—The heart is hollow, and so partitioned as to contain four chambers or cavities ; two at the base, known as the *auricles,* from a fancied resemblance to the ear of a dog, and two at the apex or point, called *ventricles.* An auricle and a ventricle on the same side communicate with each other, but there is no opening from side to side. It is customary to regard the heart as a double organ, and to speak of its division into the right and left heart. For while both halves act together in point of time, each half sustains an entirely distinct portion of the labor of the circulation. The right side always carries the dark or venous blood, and the left always circulates the bright or arterial blood.

20. If we examine the heart, we at once notice that, though its various chambers have about the same capacity, the walls of the ventricles are thicker and stronger than those of the auricles. This is a wise provision, for it is by the powerful action of the ventricles that the blood is forced to the most remote regions of the body. The auricles, on the contrary, need much less power, for they simply discharge their contents into the ventricles below them. (Figs. 32 and 33.)

21. Action of the Heart.—The substance of the heart is of a deep red color, and its fibres resemble those of the voluntary mus-

---

Whose streams of brightening purple rush,
Fired with a new and livelier blush ;
While all their burden of decay
The ebbing current steals away,
And, red with Nature's flame, they start
From the warm fountains of the heart.

" No rest that throbbing slave may ask,
Forever quivering o'er his task,
While far and wide a crimson jet
Leaps forth to fill the woven net,
Which, in unnumbered crossing tides,
The flood of burning life divides ;
Then, kindling each decaying part,
Creeps back to find the throbbing heart."

—*Dr. O. W. Holmes.*

---

19. Formation of the heart? Right and left heart?
20. Capacity of the chambers of the heart? What wise provision is mentioned? The auricles?
21. Substance of the heart? Its fibres? Its movements? The advantage of such movements? Action of the heart? Its period of repose?

cles by which we move our limbs. But the heart's movements are entirely involuntary. The advantage of this is evident; for if it depended upon us to will each movement, our entire attention would be thus engaged, and we would find no time for study, pleasure, or even sleep. The action of the heart consists in alternate contractions and expansions. During contraction the walls come forcibly together, and thus drive out the blood. They then expand and receive a renewed supply. These movements are called respectively *systole* and *diastole*. The latter may be called the heart's period of repose; and although it lasts only during two-fifths of a heart-beat, or about a

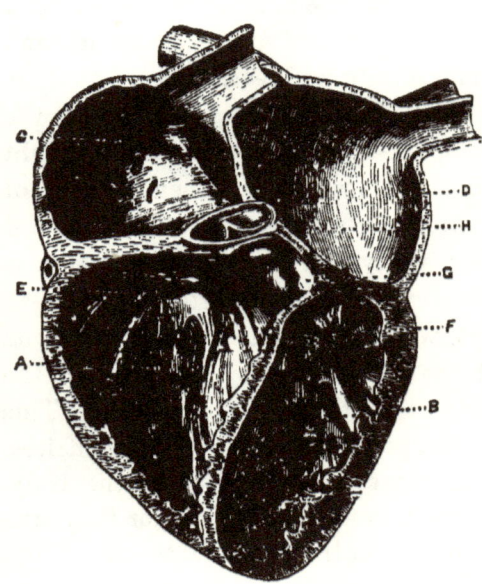

FIG. 34.—SECTION OF THE HEART.

A, Right Ventricle.   E, F, Inlets to the Ventricles.
B, Left   "   G, Pulmonary Artery.
C, Right Auricle.   H, Aorta.
D, Left Auricle.

third of a second, yet during the day it amounts to more than nine hours of total rest.

22. A remarkable property of the tissue of the heart is its intense vitality. For while it is more constantly active than any other organ of the body, it is the last to part with its vital energy. This is especially interesting in view of the fact that after life is apparently extinguished, as from drowning, or poisoning by chloroform, there yet lingers a spark of vitality in the heart, which, by continued effort, may be fanned into a flame so as to revivify the whole body. In cold-blooded animals, this irritability of the heart is especially remarkable. The heart of a turtle will pulsate, and the blood circulate for a week after its head has been cut off; and its heart will throb regularly many hours after being cut out. The heart of a frog or serpent, separated entirely from the body, will contract at the end of ten or twelve hours; that of an alligator has been known to beat twenty-eight hours after the death of the animal.

23. Passage of the Blood through the Heart.—Let us now trace the course of the blood through the several cavities of the heart. In the first place, the venous blood, rendered dark and impure by contact with the changing tissues of the body, returns to the right heart by the veins. It enters and fills the right auricle during its expansion; the auricle then contracts and fills the right ventricle. Almost instantly, the ventricle contracts forcibly and hurries the blood along the great artery of the lungs, to be purified in those organs. Secondly, having completed the circuit of the lungs, the pure and bright arterial blood enters the left auricle. This now contracts and fills the left ventricle, which cavity, in its turn, contracts and sends the blood forth on its journey again through the system. This general direction from right to left is the uniform and undeviating course of heart-currents.

24. The mechanism which compels this regularity is as simple as it is beautiful. Each ventricle has two openings, an inlet and an outlet, each of which is guarded by strong curtains, or valves. These valves open freely to admit the blood entering from the right, but close inflexibly against its return. Thus, when the auricle contracts, the inlet valve opens; but as soon as the ventricle begins to contract, it closes promptly. The contents are then, so to speak, cornered, and have but one avenue of escape—that through the outlet valve into the arteries beyond. As soon as the ventricle begins to expand again, this valve shuts tightly and obstructs the passage. The closing of these valves occasions the two heart-sounds, which we hear at the front of the chest. (Figs. 35 and 36.)

25. Frequency of the Heart's Action.—The alternation of contraction and expansion constitutes the heart-beats. These follow each other not only with great regularity, but with great rapidity. The average number in an adult man is about seventy-two in

23. Course of the blood through the heart? Course of heart-currents?
24. Openings of the ventricles? How guarded? How do the valves operate? The consequence? Heart-sounds?
25. Heart-beats? The heart as a susceptible organ? Heat, exercise, etc.? Posture?

a minute. But the heart is a susceptible organ, and many circumstances affect its rate of action. Heat, exercise, and food increase its action ; cold, fasting, and sleep diminish it. Posture, too, has a curious influence ; for if while sitting the beats of the heart number seventy-one, standing erect will increase them to eighty-one, and lying down will lower them to sixty-six. (*Read Note* 6.)

26. The modifying influence of mental emotions is very powerful. Sudden excitement of feeling will cause the heart to palpitate, or throb violently. Depressing emotions sometimes temporarily interrupt its movements, and the person faints in consequence. Extremes of joy, grief, or fear have occasionally suspended the heart's action entirely, and thus caused death. The rate of the heart-beat may be naturally above or below seventy-two. Thus it is stated that the pulse of the savage is always slower than that of the civilized man. Bonaparte and Wellington were very much alike in their heart pulsations, which were less than fifty in the case of each. (*Read Note* 7.)

---

6. The Heart is Injured by Over-exertion.—"During exertion, if the heart is not oppressed, its movements, though rapid and forcible, are regular and equal. But when it becomes embarrassed, the pulse-beats are quick, unequal, and at last become irregular, indicating injury to the organ. All great and sudden efforts are to be carefully avoided; excessive exercise often produces palpitation, and sometimes enlargement and valvular disease of the heart."—*Huxley.*

"No great intellectual thing was ever done by great effort; a great thing can only be done by a great man, and he does it without effort. The body's work and the head's work are to be done quietly, and comparatively without effort. Neither limbs or brain are ever to be strained to their utmost ; that is not the way in which the greatest quantity of work is to be got out of them; they are never to be worked furiously, but with tranquillity and constancy. We are to follow the plow from sunrise to sunset, but not to pull in race-boats at the twilight ; we shall get no fruit of that kind of work—only disease of the heart."—*Ruskin.*

7. Fainting.—"When the heart suddenly ceases to act, *fainting* or swooning is very apt to take place. This takes place for the reason that the brain feels most speedily the lack of its supply of blood. Many circumstances may cause a faint—such as a fright, joy, excitement, the sight of blood, or the breathing of foul air; or it may be due to disease of the heart. In some per-

26. Mental emotions? Sudden excitement? Excessive joy? The heart-beat rate? Bonaparte and Wellington?

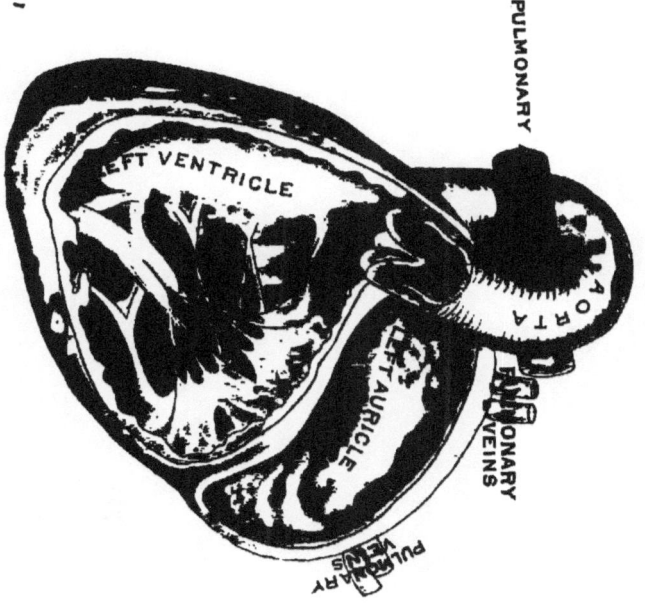

LEFT SECTION OF HEART

PULMONARY

AORTA

PULMONARY VEINS

LEFT VENTRICLE

LEFT AURICLE

PULMONARY VEINS

Fig 35.

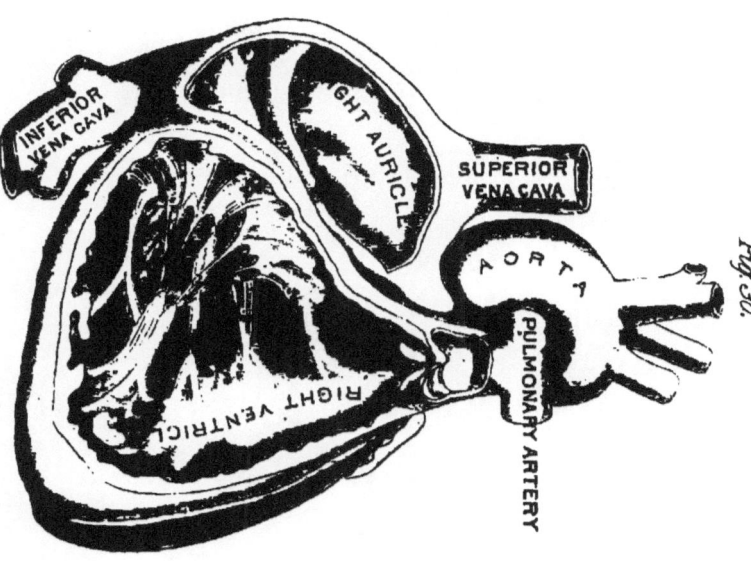

RIGHT SECTION OF HEART.

INFERIOR VENA CAVA

RIGHT AURICLE

SUPERIOR VENA CAVA

AORTA

PULMONARY ARTERY

RIGHT VENTRICLE

Fig 36.

27. Activity of the Heart.—The average number of heart-beats during a lifetime may be considered as at the rate of seventy-two per minute, although this estimate is somewhat low, for during several years of early life the rate is above one hundred a minute. In one hour, then, the heart pulsates four thousand times; in a day, one hundred thousand times; and in a year, nearly thirty-eight million times. If we compute the number during a lifetime—forty years being the present average longevity of civilized mankind—we obtain as the vast aggregate, fifteen hundred millions of pulsations. (*Read Note* 8.)·

---

sons, fainting becomes a kind of habit; they fall into a fainting fit on very slight agitation. In them the appearances are much worse than the reality, especially to those who are not familiar with the ailment. But persons who faint after exhaustion, fatigue, fasting, or anguish, require prompt attention. The ordinary signs are great pallor, loss of sensation, and trembling of the limbs and loss of power over the muscles ; the breathing and pulse go on imperfectly or stop. The first thing to do is to place the head low, thus favoring the supply of blood to the brain; the very act of falling is often sufficient to restore consciousness. Water may be sprinkled on the face, hartshorn held to the nose, or mustard over the heart. Pure air is a great restorative ; allow a current of fresh air to flow over the face, and loosen any tight bands that may confine the chest."—*Dr. J. Knight (in part).*

8. The Heart a Vital Machine.—"The heart is a machine. It is an organ constructed of muscular chambers and communicating· passages, and supplied with mechanical contrivances, adapted to guide the stream of blood passing through it, and to prevent a reflux in the backward direction. Does not this take away wonderfully from the character of fanciful mystery with which poets and sentimentalists have invested it? The heart that we have always heard of as the centre of the affections, the home of sensibility, the dwelling-place of courage, of faith, of hope, and all the rest of the virtues, is after all, nothing but an organ to serve for the impulsion of the blood—a mere force-pump, a machine. Does not this bring down our ideas, and show that no poetical mystery can escape the searching investigation of the anatomist? Not at all.

"For this machine that we carry about with us in our breasts is *alive.* There, at its post, at the central point of the circulation, with the soft lobes of the lungs folded round it like a curtain, it contracts and relaxes, and relaxes and contracts, with a steady and unremitting industry that by itself is something worthy of our admiration. No other muscle in the body can do this. By some incomprehensible vitality of its own, it keeps up its rhythmical con-

---

27. Average number of heart-beats? In one hour? Year? Lifetime?

28. Again, if we estimate the amount of blood expelled by each contraction of the ventricles at four ounces, then the weight of the blood moved during one minute will amount to eighteen pounds. In a day it will be about twelve tons; in a year, four thousand tons; and in the course of a lifetime over one hundred and fifty thousand tons. These large figures indicate, in some measure, the immense labor necessary to carry on the interior and vital operations of our bodies. In this connection, we call to mind the fanciful theories of the ancients in reference to the uses of the heart. They regarded it as the abode of the soul and the source of the nobler emotions—bravery, generosity, mercy, and love. The words *courage* and *cordiality* are derived from a Latin word signifying *heart*. Many other words and phrases, as *hearty, heart-felt, to learn by heart*, and *large-hearted*, show how tenaciously these exploded opinions have fastened themselves upon our language.

29. At the present time, the tendency is to ascribe purely mechanical functions to the heart. This view, like the older one, is inadequate; for it expresses only a small part of our knowledge of this organ. The heart is unlike a simple machine, because its motive power is not applied from without, but resides in its own substance. Moreover, it repairs its own waste, it lubricates its own action, and it modifies its movements according to the varying needs of the system. It is more than a mere force-pump, just as the stomach is something more than a crucible, and the eye something more than an optical instrument. (*Read Note* 9.)

---

tractions without the aid of our will and even without our knowledge. While you are asleep and while you are awake, from the first moment of your birth, even from *before* your birth, up to the present time, it has never for one moment stopped or flagged in its movements, for if it were to do so death would be the result."—*Dr. J. C. Dalton.*

9. The Heart.—"You all know where it is. It is the most wonderful little pump in the world. There is no steam-engine half so clever at its work, or so strong. There it is, in every one of us, beat, beating—all day and all night, year after year, never stopping, like a watch ticking; only it never needs to be wound up,—God winds it up once for all."—*Author of " Rab and His Friends."*

---

28. Amount of blood expelled? Theories of the ancients?
29. The tendency at the present time? Why is this view inadequate?

30. The Arteries.—The tube-like canals which carry the blood away from the heart are the arteries. Their walls are made of tough, fibrous materials, so that they sustain the mighty impulse of the heart, and are not ruptured. In common with the heart, the arteries have a delicately smooth lining membrane. They are also elastic, and thus re-enforce the action of the heart; they always remain open when cut across, and after death are usually found empty.

31. The early anatomists observed this condition, and supposing that it existed during life, came to the conclusion that these tubes were designed to act as air-vessels—hence the name *artery*, from Greek words which signify "containing air." This circumstance affords us an illustration of the mistaken notions of the ancients in reference to the internal operations of the body. Cicero speaks of the arteries as "conveying the breath to all parts of the body."

32. The arterial system springs from the heart by a single trunk, like a minute and hollow tree, with numberless branches. As these branches leave the heart, they divide and subdivide, continually growing smaller and smaller, until they can no longer be traced by the naked eye. If, then, we continue the examination by the aid of a microscope, we see these small branches sending off still smaller ones, until all the organs of the body are penetrated by arteries.

33. The Pulse.—With each contraction of the left side of the heart, the impulse causes a wave-like motion to traverse the entire arterial system. If the arteries were exposed to view, we might see successive waves speeding from the heart to the smallest of the branches, in about one-sixth part of a second. The general course of the arteries is as far as possible from the surface. This arrangement is certainly wise, as it renders them less liable to injury—the wounding of an artery being especially dangerous. It also protects the arteries from external and unequal pressure, by which the force of the heart would be counteracted and wasted. Accordingly, we

---

30. What are the arteries? Their walls? Their membrane?
31. Early anatomists? The service of the illustration?
32. The arterial system? The branches and sub-branches of the arteries?
33. Successive undulations from the heart? Course of the arteries? Protection of the arteries? General location of the arteries?

generally find these vessels close to the bones, or hiding behind the muscles and within the cavities of the body.

34. In a few situations, however, the arteries lie near the surface; and if we apply the finger to any of these parts, we shall distinctly feel a throbbing motion taking place in harmony with the heart-beat. This is part of the wave-motion just mentioned, and is known as the pulse. All are familiar with the pulse at the wrist, in the *radial* artery; but it is not peculiar to that position, for it may be felt in the *carotid* of the neck, in the *temporal* at the temple, and elsewhere, especially near the joints.

35. Since the heart-beat makes the pulse, whatever affects the former affects the latter also. Accordingly, the pulse is a good index of the state of the health, so far as the health depends upon the action of the heart. It informs the physician of the condition of the circulation in four particulars—its rate, regularity, force, and fullness; and nearly every disease modifies in some respect the condition of the pulse. A very ingenious instrument, known as the sphygmograph, or pulse-writer, has recently been invented, by the aid of which the pulse is made to write upon paper its own signature, or rather to sketch its own profile. This instrument shows

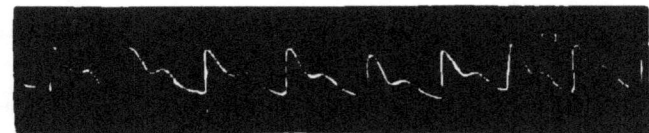

FIG. 37.—THE FORM OF THE PULSE.

with great accuracy the difference between the pulses of health and those of disease. In Fig. 37 is traced the form of the pulse in health, which should be read from left to right. That part of the trace which is nearly perpendicular coincides with the contraction of the ventricles, while the wavy portion marks their dilatation. (*Read Note* 10.)

---

10. The Beating of the Pulse.—"According to experiments made in Paris, the pulse of a lion beats forty times a minute; that of a tiger, ninety-

36. The Veins.—The vessels by which the blood returns to the heart are the veins. At first they are extremely small; but uniting together as they advance, they constantly increase in size, reminding us of the way in which the fine rootlets of the plant join together to form the large roots, or of the rills and rivulets that flow together to form the large streams and rivers. In structure, the veins resemble the arteries, but their walls are comparatively inelastic. They are more numerous, and communicate with each other freely in their course, by means of interlacing branches.

37. But the chief point of distinction is in the presence of the valves in the veins. These are little folds of membrane, disposed in such a way that they open only to receive the blood flowing toward the heart, and close against a current in the opposite direction. Their position in the veins on the back of the hand may be readily observed, if we first obstruct the return of blood by a cord tied around the forearm or wrist. In a few minutes the veins will appear swollen, and upon them will be seen certain prominences, about an inch apart. These latter indicate the location of the valves, or, rather, they show that the vessels in front of the valves are distended by the blood, which cannot force a passage back through them.

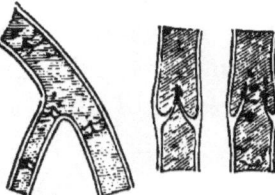

FIG. 38.—THE VALVES OF THE VEINS HIGHLY MAGNIFIED.

38. This simple experiment proves that the true direction of the venous blood is toward the heart. That the color of the blood is dark will be evident, if we compare the hand thus bound by a cord with the hand not so bound. It also proves that the veins lie near the surface, while the arteries are beneath the muscles, well pro-

---

six times; of a tapir, forty-four times; of a horse, forty times; of a wolf, forty-five times; of a fox, forty-three times; of a bear, thirty-eight times; of a monkey, forty-eight times; of an eagle, one hundred and sixty times. It was impossible to determine the beatings of the elephant's pulse. A butterfly, however, it was discovered, experienced sixty heart pulsations in a minute."

---

36. What are the veins? How do they form? What do they resemble?
37. Valves in the veins? What are they? Their position? Experiment with the cord?
38. What will be proved by the experiment? What inference is drawn?

tected from pressure; and that free communication exists from one vein to another. If now we test the temperature of the constricted member by means of a thermometer, we will find that it is colder than natural, although the amount of blood is larger than usual. From this fact we infer, that whatever impedes the venous circulation tends to diminish vitality; and hence, articles of clothing or constrained postures, that confine the body or limbs, and hinder the circulation of the blood, are to be avoided as injurious to the health.

39. The Capillaries.—A third set of vessels completes the list of the organs of circulation, namely, the *capillary* vessels, so called (from the Latin word *capillaris*, hair-like), because of their extreme fineness. They are, however, smaller than any hair, having a diameter of about $\frac{1}{3000}$ of an inch, and can only be observed by the use of the microscope. These vessels are the connecting link between the last of the arteries and the first of the veins. The existence of these vessels was unknown to Harvey, and was the one step wanting to complete his great discovery. The capillaries were not discovered until 1661, a short time after the invention of the microscope.

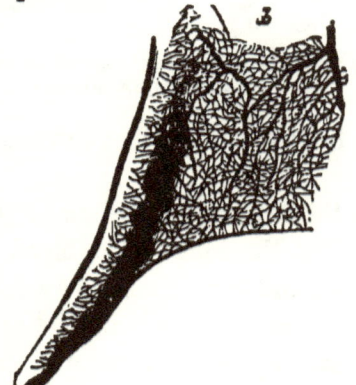 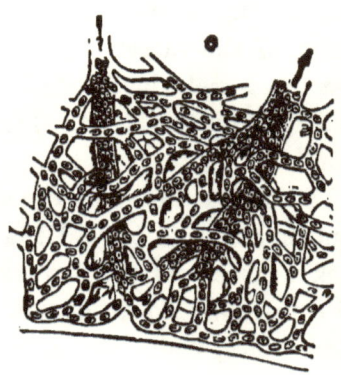

FIG. 39.—WEB OF A FROG'S FOOT, slightly magnified.

FIG. 40.—MARGIN OF FROG'S WEB, magnified thirty diameters.

40. The circulation of the blood, as seen under the microscope, in the transparent web of a frog's foot, is a beautiful sight, possessing more than ordinary interest, from the fact that something much grander is taking place in our own bodies. It is like opening a secret page in the history of our own frames. We there see distinctly the three classes of vessels with their moving contents; first, the artery, with its torrent of blood rushing down from the heart; secondly, the vein, with its slow, steady stream flowing in the opposite direction; and between them lies the network of capillaries, so fine that the corpuscles can pass through only "in single file.". The current of the capillaries has here an uncertain or swaying motion, hurrying first in one direction, then hesitating, and turning back in the opposite direction, and sometimes the capillaries contract so as to be entirely empty. Certain of the tissues are destitute of capillaries; such are cartilage, hair, and a few others on the exterior of the body. In all other structures, networks of these vessels are spread out in countless numbers; so abundant is the supply, that it is almost impossible to puncture any part with the point of a needle without lacerating tens, or even hundreds of these vessels. (*Read Note* II.)

41. The capillaries are elastic, and may so expand as to produce an effect visible to the naked eye. If a grain of sand, or

---

11. Course of the Blood in the Capillaries.—"The phenomena of the capillary circulation are only observable with the aid of the microscope. It was not granted to the discoverer of the circulation to see the blood moving through the capillaries, and he never knew the exact mode of communication between the arteries and veins. After it was pretty generally acknowledged that the blood did pass from the arteries to the veins, it was disputed whether it passed in an intermediate system of vessels, or became diffused in the substance of the tissues, like a river flowing between numberless little islands, to be collected by the venous radicles and conveyed to the heart. Accurate microscopic investigations have now demonstrated the existence, and given us a clear idea of the anatomy of the intermediate vessels. In 1661 the celebrated anatomist Malpighi first saw the movement of the blood in the capillaries, in the lungs of a frog. This spectacle has ever since been the delight of the physiologist. We see the great arterial rivers, in which the blood flows with wonderful rapidity, branching and subdividing, until the blood is brought to the superb network of fine capillaries, where the corpuscles dart along one by one, the fluid then being collected by the veins, and carried in great currents to the heart."—*Flint.*

---

41. Elasticity of the capillaries? Grain of sand in the eye? Blush? Other cases?

some other foreign particle, lodge in the eye, it will become irritated, and in a short time the white of the eye will be "blood-shot." This appearance is due to an increase in the size of these vessels. A blush is another example of this, but the excitement comes through the nervous system, and the cause is some transient emo- tion, either of pleasure or pain. Another example is sometimes seen in purplish faces of men addicted to drinking brandy; in them the condition is a congestion of the capillary circulation, and is per- manent, the vessels having lost their power of elastic contraction.

42. Rapidity of the Circulation.—That the blood moves with great rapidity is evident from the almost instant effects of certain poisons, as prussic acid, which act through the blood. Experi- ments upon the horse, dog, and other inferior animals, have been made to measure its velocity. If a substance which is capable of a distinct chemical reaction (as *potassium ferrocyanide*, or *barium ni- trate*) be introduced into a vein on one side of a horse, and at the end of twenty or thirty-two seconds, blood be taken from a distant vein on the other side, its presence may be detected. In man, the blood moves with greater speed, and the circuit is completed in twenty-four seconds.

43. What length of time is required for all the blood of the body to make a complete round of the circulation? This question cannot be answered with absolute accuracy, since the amount of the blood is subject to continual variations. But, if we assume this to be one-eighth of the weight of the body—about eighteen pounds—it will be sufficiently correct for our purpose. Now to complete the circuit, this blood must pass once through the left ventricle, the capacity of which is two ounces. Accordingly, we find that, under ordinary circumstances, all the blood makes one com- plete rotation every two minutes—passing successively through the heart, the capillaries of the lungs, the arteries, the capillaries of the extremities, and through the veins.

44. Assimilation.—The crowning act of the circulation—the furnishing of supplies to the different parts of the body—is

42. Show what time is required for a given portion of blood to travel once around the body.
43. Time required for all the blood to circulate completely around?
44. What is meant by assimilation? What can you say of its use, etc.? Time?

effected by means of the capillaries. The organs have been wasted by use; the blood has been enriched by the products of digestion. Here, within the meshes of the capillary network, the needy tissues and the needed nutriment are brought together. By some mysterious chemistry, each tissue selects and withdraws from the blood the materials it requires, and converts them into a substance like itself. This conversion of lifeless food into living tissue is called assimilation. The process probably takes place at all times, but the period especially favorable for it is during sleep. Then the circulation is slower, and more regular, and most of the functions are at rest. The body is then like some trusty ship, which, after a long voyage, is "hauled up for repairs." (*Read Note* 12.)

45. Injuries to the Blood-vessels.—It is important for us to be able to discriminate between an artery and a vein, in the case of a wound, and if we remember the physiology of the circulation we may readily do so. For, as we have already seen, hemorrhage from an artery is much more dangerous than that from a vein. The latter tends to cease spontaneously after a short time. The arterial blood flows away from the heart with considerable force, in jets, and its color is bright scarlet. The venous blood flows toward the heart from that side of the wound furthest from the heart, its stream being continuous and sluggish; its color is dark. In an

---

12. Assimilation in Repair.—"Most animals have the power to repair, to a greater or less extent, the mutilations they undergo. In man, if the skin is torn off, a new skin heals over the injury, and a broken bone is caused to re-unite by the deposit of bone tissue between the fragments. But among the lower animals this power is carried to a high degree. The tail of a lizard, if cut off, will quickly form anew, although of a complex structure; and spiders and crabs are able to develop new claws upon the stumps of broken ones. Observations made on salamanders, or water-lizards, show the still more remarkable fact that the eye and a part of the head may be entirely restored. Certain kinds of earth-worms can reproduce a large portion of their bodies, and any fragment of the hydra is able to restore itself, and become a complete creature after its kind. Assimilation is especially active in early years, while the body is growing; for this reason, among others, the perfect health of children requires that they shall give a greater number of hours to sleep—deep, regular, and undisturbed sleep—than is needed in later life."—*Milne Edwards.*

---

45. What is stated of the injuries to the blood-vessels?

injury to an artery, pressure should be made between the heart and the wound, while in the case of a vein that persistently bleeds, it should be made upon the vessel beyond its point of injury.

46. Effects of Alcohol upon the Heart.—The first symptoms after a moderate dose of alcohol is an increase of the heart's action, a flushing of the face, a sensation of warmth within, a general glow without, and some other appearances of increased vitality. The action has been that of a spur or goad. It has caused strength to be expended instead of increasing it, and, in fact, costs the system whatever amount of force is necessary to expel it; so that there is a loss of strength, and not a gain.

47. The late Dr. Parkes made a careful study of the amount of strain put upon the heart by alcohol. He found that it increased both the number and force of the heart's pulsations. The period of rest between the beats is reduced, and, consequently, the heart's nutrition must be interfered with. He estimates, in one set of experiments, that the extra work of the heart, induced by alcohol, was equivalent to the lifting of 15.8 tons one foot daily; and during two days, 24 tons in excess of the regular work. Another experimenter states that he has known a single glass of liquor to cause 8000 extra heart-beats, equivalent to the unnecessary lifting of 9 tons the distance of one foot. Estimated in another way, this amount of over-tax of the heart is equal to that which takes place, during one day, in a person having a fever that raises the pulse six to nine beats above the rate of health.

48. Alcohol as a Fat Producer.—Alcohol is said to diminish waste, and to make those "fleshy" who use it. This may well be the case in those—and the proportion is not small—who are rendered sluggish and sleepy by it. The fat which they acquire is the fat of inaction. If we may judge of the true influence of alcohol by experiments on the lower animals, that are compelled to take it pure, we will not grant it any fattening power.

49. There is a certain "fatty degeneration" in man—the result of alcohol drinking—that is very disastrous, namely, a deposit of

---

46. How does alcohol affect the heart's action?   48. How does alcohol make one fleshy?
47. Give Dr. Parkes' experiment.   49. What results?

fat in the muscles of the body. This is destructive or weakening to muscular power, and when it evinces itself in the heart, it creates a change that is to be dreaded as sapping the strength of the one particular organ that should be strong in drinkers. It attacks them at a vital spot. The blood also undergoes a fatty change which greatly impairs its work of nourishing the body.

50. Exhaustion Due to Alcohol.—The heart does not become habituated to the poison nor become tolerant of it. On the contrary, it is set moving, with this abnormal activity, with each renewal of the dose. This form of exertion is not exercise, it is overwork; it is not strengthening, it is exhausting. Very few persons who habitually use alcoholic stimulants are aware of the enormous strain that is imposed upon the heart, although to those who studiously consider the matter the wonder is that this organ is not more rapidly worn out than it is. If it were not for the fact that the heart is made of the strongest muscular tissue in the body, it would of necessity fail from overstrain long before it does.

51. The condition of the heart, mentioned in the last section, is known to physicians as "fatty heart," and in part explains why it is that drunkards are so little able to withstand the attack of those diseases which are attended by fever. It is a well known fact that they are among the first to succumb to cholera and other epidemic diseases. Sunstroke is another disorder peculiarly frequent in that class of persons; and to indicate that fact some physicians apply the term "drink-stroke" to that disease.

52. Action of Tobacco on the Heart.—Tobacco both quickens and enfeebles the heart. In some of those who habitually use it, it gives rise to a throbbing or heaving sensation in the region of the heart, an exaggerated kind of palpitation; at times, this is so tumultuous that the patient fears lest his last hour has come. In other cases, there is a weak and irregular heart-beat, caused by tobacco poisoning. This is not so alarming to the patient as the condition just mentioned, but is no less dangerous and much less easily cured. It is apt to injure a man's capacity for business affairs, being repressive of healthful energy and exertion.

---

49. What change in the blood due to alcohol?
50. Does the heart tolerate alcohol? Do users of it know the effects?
51. Can they withstand fever? 52. What two noticeable effects from tobacco?

TABLE OF THE PRINCIPAL ARTERIES.

(SEE PLATE OPPOSITE PAGE 129.)

The Head.

Internal Ca-rot'id,
Ver'te-bral, } Supply the brain.

Oph-thal'mic, supplies the eye.

External Ca-rot'id
gives off........... {
Lin'gual, supplies the tongue.
Fa'ci-al, supplies the lower part of the face.
Tem'po-ral, supplies the upper part of the head and face.

The Trunk.

The A or'ta, arising from the heart, is the main arterial trunk.

Cor'o-na-ry, supplies the walls of the heart

Bron'chi-al, supplies the lungs.

In-ter-cos'tals, supply the walls of the chest.

Gas'tric, supplies the stomach.

He-pat'ic, supplies the liver.

Splen'ic, supplies the spleen.

Re'nal, supplies the kidney.

Mes-en-ter'ics, supply the bowels.

Spi'nal, supplies the spinal cord.

The Upper Limb.

Branches of the Ax-il-la'ry, supply the shoulder.
   "   "   Bra'chi-al, supply the arm.
   "   "   Ra'di-al,
   "   "   Ul'nar, } supply the forearm and fingers.

The Lower Limb.

Branches of the Fem'o-ral, supply the hip and thigh.
   "   "   Pop-li-te'al,
   "   "   Tib'i-al, } supply the leg and foot.
   "   "   Per-o-ne'al,

QUESTIONS FOR TOPICAL REVIEW.

CHAPTER VIII.

RESPIRATION.

The Objects of Respiration—The Lungs—The Air-passages—The Movements of Respiration—Expiration and Inspiration—The Frequency of Respiration—Capacity of the Lungs—The Air we Breathe—Changes in the Air from Respiration—Changes in the Blood—Interchange of Gases in the Lungs—Comparison between Arterial and Venous Blood—Respiratory Labor—Impurities of the Air—Dust—Carbonic Acid—Effects of Impure Air—Nature's Provision for Purifying the Air—Ventilation—Animal Heat—Spontaneous Combustion.

1. The Object of Respiration.—In one set of capillaries, or hair-like vessels, the blood is impoverished in order to support the different members and organs of the body. In another capillary system the blood is refreshed and again made fit to sustain life. The former belongs to the greater or *systemic* circulation; the latter to the lesser or *pulmonary*, so called from *pulmo*, the lungs, in which organs it is situated. The blood, as sent from the right side of the heart to the lungs, is venous, dark, impure, and of a nature hurtful to the tissues. But, when the blood returns from the lungs to the left side of the heart, it has become arterial, bright, pure, and no longer injurious. This marvellous purifying change is effected by means of the very familiar act of respiration, or breathing.

2. The Lungs.—The lungs are the special organs of respiration. There are two of them, one on each side of the chest, which cavity they, with the heart, almost wholly fill. The lung-substance is soft, elastic, and sponge-like. Under pressure of the finger, it *crepitates*, or crackles, and floats when thrown into water; these properties being due to the presence of air in the minute air-cells of the lungs. To facilitate the movements necessary to these organs, each of them

---

1. Difference between the two sets of capillaries? Change effected by respiration or breathing?
2. What are the lungs? How many lungs are there? Lung-substance? Its properties? The pleura?

is provided with a double covering of an exceedingly smooth and delicate membrane, called the *pleura*. One layer of the pleura is

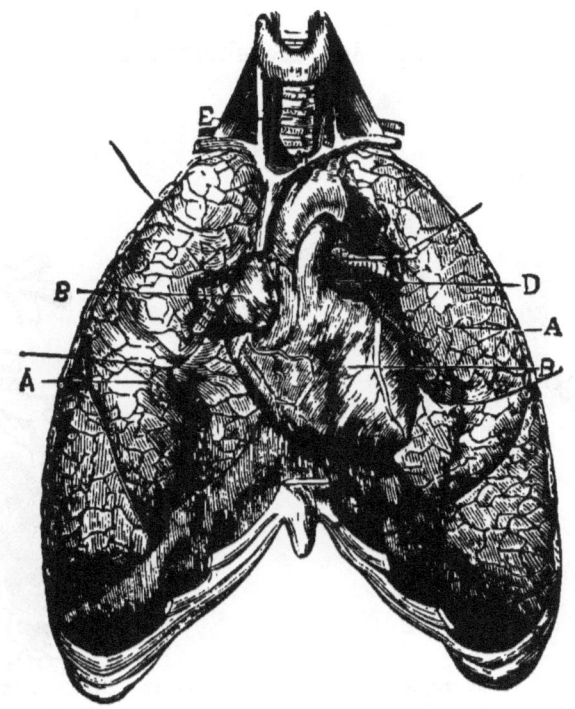

FIG. 41.—ORGANS OF THE CHEST.

A, Lungs.   D, Pulmonary Artery.
B, Heart.   E, Trachea.

attached to the walls of the chest, and the other to the lungs; and they glide, one upon the other, with utmost freedom. Like the membrane which envelops the heart, the pleura secretes its own lubricating fluid, in quantities sufficient to keep it always moist.

3. The Air-Passages.—The lungs communicate with the external air by means of certain air-tubes, the longest of which—the *trachea,* or windpipe—runs along the front of the neck (Fig. 41, E, and 42). Within the chest this tube is divided into two branches, one entering each lung; these in turn give rise to numerous branches, or bronchial tubes, as they are called, which gradually diminish in size until they are about one twenty-fifth of an inch in diameter. Each of these terminates in a cluster of little pouches, or "air-cells," having very thin walls, and covered with a capillary network, the most intricate in the body (Fig 43).

4. These tubes are somewhat flexible, sufficiently so to bend when the parts in which they are situated move; but they are

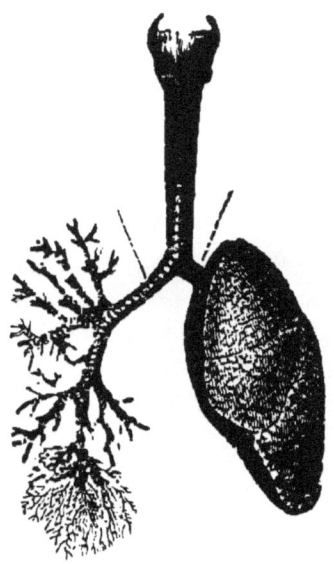

FIG. 42.—LARYNX, TRACHEA, AND BRONCHIAL TUBES.

FIG. 43.—DIAGRAM AND SECTION OF THE AIR-CELLS.

greatly strengthened by bands or rings of cartilage which keep the passages always open; otherwise there would be a constantly-recurring tendency to collapse after every breath. The lung-substance essentially consists of these bronchial tubes and terminal air-cells, with the blood-vessels ramifying about them (Fig. 44). At the top of the trachea is the larynx, a sort of box of cartilage, across which are stretched the vocal cords. Here the voice is produced chiefly by the passage of the respired air over these cords, causing them to vibrate.

5. Over the opening of the larynx is found the *epiglottis*, which fits like the lid of a box at the entrance to the lungs, and closes during the act of swallowing, so that food and drink shall pass

---

4. Office of the bronchial tubes? What further can you state of them?
5. The epiglottis? When it does not close in time, what is the consequence?

backward to the œsophagus, or gullet (Fig. 45). Occasionally it does not close in time, and some substance intrudes within the larynx, when we at once discover, by a choking sensation, that

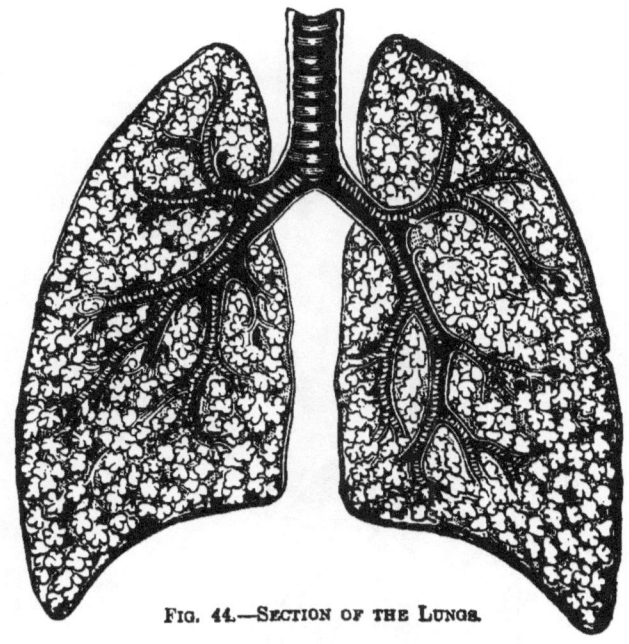

FIG. 44.—SECTION OF THE LUNGS.

"something has gone the wrong way," and, by coughing, we attempt to expel the unwelcome intruder. The epiglottis is one of the many safeguards furnished by nature for our security and comfort, and is planned and put in place long before these organs are brought into actual use in breathing and in taking food.

6. The air-passages are lined throughout almost their whole extent with mucous membrane, which keeps them in a constantly moist condition. This membrane has cells of a peculiar kind upon its outer surface. If examined under a powerful microscope, we may see, even for a considerable time after their removal from the body, that these cells have minute hair-like processes in motion, which wave like a field of grain under the influence of a breeze (Fig. 46). This is a truly beautiful sight; and since it is found that these little *cilia*, as they are called, always produce currents in one

<hr />

6. Lining of the air-passages? Ciliated cells? Their uses? The three diseases of the lungs?

direction—from within outward—it is probable that they serve a useful purpose in catching and carrying away from the lungs dust and other small particles drawn in with the breath (Fig. 46). The

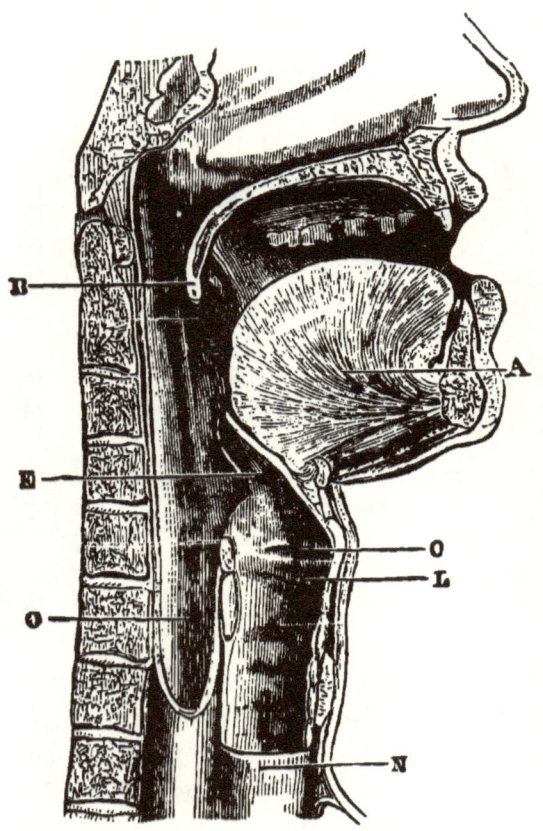

FIG. 45.--SECTION OF THE MOUTH AND THROAT,

A, The Tongue. C, Vocal Cord. N, Trachea.
B, The Uvula. E, Epiglottis. O, Œsophagus.
  L, Larynx.

three diseases which more commonly affect the lungs, as the result of exposure, are pneumonia, or inflammation of the lungs, affecting, principally, the air-cells; bronchitis, an inflammation of the large bronchial tubes; and pleurisy, an inflammation of the pleura, or outside wrapping of the lungs. Among the young, an inflammation of the trachea takes place, known as croup.

7. The Movements of Respiration.—The act of breathing has

7. The act of breathing? Extension of the chest by breathing?

two parts—(1), *inspiration*, or drawing air into the lungs, and (2), *expiration*, or driving it out again. In inspiration, the chest extends in its length, breadth, and height. The motion outward and upward can be observed every time we draw a full breath; and is caused by a lifting of the ribs. But the motion downward is not so apparent, as it is caused by a muscle within the body called the *diaphragm*. This is the thin partition which separates the chest from the abdomen, rising like a dome within the chest (Fig. 20).

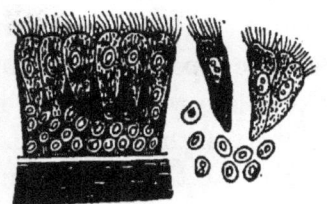

FIG. 46.—CILIATED CELLS HIGHLY MAGNIFIED.

8. With every inspiration the diaphragm contracts, and in so doing, approaches more nearly a level surface, and thus enlarges the capacity of the chest. Laughing, sobbing, and sneezing are due to sudden action of the diaphragm. On the proper acting of this muscle depends our power to breathe deeply; and like other muscles, its strength is increased by exercise. This gives that endurance, or "long wind," as it is commonly called, which is possessed in a marked degree by the mountaineer, the oarsman, and the trained singer. The habit of taking frequent and deep inspirations, in the erect position, with the shoulders thrown back, tends greatly to increase the capacity and power of the organs of respiration.

9. Expiration is a less powerful act than inspiration. The diaphragm relaxes, and ascends in the form of a dome; the ribs descend and contract the chest; while the lungs themselves, being elastic, assist to drive out the air. The latter passes out through the same channels by which it entered. At the end of each expiration there is a period of repose, lasting about as long as the period or action.

10. Frequency of Respiration.—It is usually estimated that we breathe once during every four beats of the heart, or about eighteen times in a minute. There is, of course, a close relation between the

8. Contraction of the diaphragm? Power of the diaphragm? Effects of extending t' ʔ walls of the chest? The habit of taking frequent and deep inspirations?
9. Expiration? The mechanism of expiration?
10. Frequency of respiration? Effect of hurried action of the heart?

heart and lungs, and whatever modifies the pulse, in like manner affects the breathing. When the action of the heart is hurried,
a larger amount of blood is sent to the lungs, and, as a consequence,
they must act more rapidly. Occasionally, the heart beats so very
forcibly that the lungs cannot keep pace with it, and then we experience a peculiar sense of distress from the want of air. This
takes place when we run until we are "out of breath." At the end
of every fifth or sixth breath, the inspiration is generally longer
than usual, the effect being to change more completely the air of the
lungs.

11. Although, as a general rule, the work of respiration goes on
unconsciously and without exertion on our part, it is, nevertheless,
under the control of the will. We can increase or diminish the
frequency of its acts at pleasure, and we can "hold the breath," or
arrest it altogether for a short time. From twenty to thirty seconds
is ordinarily the longest period in which the breath can be held;
but if we first expel all the impure air from the lungs, by taking
several very deep inspirations, the time may be extended to one and a
half or even two minutes. This should be remembered, and acted
upon, before passing through a burning building, or any place where
the air is very foul. The arrest of the respiration may be still
further prolonged by training and habit. It is said that the pearl-
fishers of India can remain three or four minutes under water without being compelled to breathe.

12. Capacity of the Lungs.—The lungs are not filled and
emptied by each respiration. For while their full capacity, in the
adult, is three hundred and twenty cubic inches, or more than a
gallon, the ordinary breathing air is only one-sixteenth part of that
volume, or twenty cubic inches—being two-thirds of a pint.
Accordingly, a complete renovation, or rotation, of the air of the
lungs does not take place more frequently than about once a minute;
and by the gradual introduction of the external air, its temperature
is considerably elevated before it reaches the delicate capillaries that
surround the air-cells. In tranquil respiration, less than two-thirds

---

11. Respiration controlled by the will? Advantage of the knowledge to us?
12. Capacity of the lungs? Time required to renovate the air in the lungs? In tranquil
respiration? Importance of the provision?

of the breathing power is called into exercise, leaving a reserve capacity of about one hundred and twenty cubic inches, equivalent to three and one-half pints. This provision is indispensable to the continuation of life; otherwise, a slight interference with respiration—by an ordinary cold, for instance—would suffice to cut off the necessary air, and the spark of life would be speedily extinguished.

13. The Air we Breathe.—The earth is enveloped on all sides by an invisible fluid, called the atmosphere. It forms a vast ocean of air, forty-five miles deep, encircling and pervading all objects on the earth's surface, and is absolutely essential for the preservation of all vegetable and animal life—in the sea, as well as on the land and in the air. At the bottom, or in the lower strata of this ocean of air, we move and have our being. Perfectly pure water will not support marine life, for a fish may be drowned in water from which the air has been exhausted, just as certainly as a mouse, or any other land animal will perish if held under water for a short time. The cause is the same in both cases—the animal is deprived of the requisite amount of air. It is also stated, that if the water-supply of the plant be deprived of air, its growth is checked. (*Read Note* I.)

---

1. The Atmosphere.—"It surrounds us on all sides, yet we see it not; it presses on us with a load of fifteen pounds to every square inch of surface of our bodies, or from seventy to one hundred tons on us in all, yet we do not so much as feel its weight. Softer than the softest down—more impalpable than the finest gossamer—it leaves the cobweb undisturbed, and scarcely stirs the lightest flower that feeds on the dew it supplies; yet it bears the fleets of nations on its wings around the world, and crushes the most refractory substances beneath its weight. When in motion, its force is sufficient to level the most stately forests with the earth; to raise the waters of the ocean into ridges like mountains, and dash the strongest ships to pieces like toys. It bends the rays of the sun from their path, to give us the twilight of evening and of dawn; it disperses and refracts their various tints, to beautify the approach and retreat of the orb of day. But for the atmosphere, sunshine would burst on us and fail us at once, and at once remove us from midnight darkness to the blaze of noon. We should have no twilight to soften and beautify the landscape, no clouds to shade us from the scorching heat; but the bald earth, as it revolved on its axis, would turn its tanned and weakened front to the full and unmitigated rays of the lord of day."—*Buish.*

---

13. The atmosphere? How high or deep? How essential to life? Marine life in perfectly pure water and air?

14. The air is not a simple element, as the ancients supposed, but is formed by the mingling of two gases, known to the chemist as oxygen and nitrogen, in the proportion of one part of the former to four parts of the latter. These gases are very unlike, being almost opposite in their properties : nitrogen is weak, inert, and cannot support life; while oxygen is powerful, and incessantly active, and is the essential element which gives to the atmosphere its power to support life and combustion. The discovery of this fact was made by the French chemist, Lavoisier, in 1778.

15. Changes in the Air from Respiration.—Air that has been once breathed is no longer fit for respiration. An animal confined within it will soon die ; so, also, a lighted candle placed in it will be at once extinguished. If we collect a quantity of expired air and analyze it, we shall find that its composition is not the same as that of the inspired air. When the air entered the lungs it was rich in oxygen ; now it contains twenty-five per cent. less of that gas. Its volume, however, remains nearly the same—its loss being made up by another and very different gas, which the lungs exhale, called *carbonic acid*, or, as the chemist terms it, *carbonic dioxide*.

16. The expired air has also gained moisture. This is noticed when we breathe upon a mirror or the window-pane, the surface being tarnished by the condensation of the watery vapor given off by the lungs. In cold weather, this causes the fine cloud which is seen issuing from the nostrils or mouth with each expiration, and contributes in forming the feathery crystals of ice which decorate our window-panes on a winter's morning.

17. This watery vapor contains a variable quantity of animal matter, the exact nature of which is unknown ; but when collected it speedily putrefies and becomes highly offensive. From the effects, upon small animals, of confinement in their own exhalations, having at the same time an abundant supply of fresh air, it is believed that the organic matters thrown off by the lungs and skin are direct and active poisons ; and that to such emanations from the body, more

14. Composition of the air? Properties of the two gases ?
15. Air once breathed? An animal in it? A candle? Analysis of expired air? Change in volume?
16. What else has the expired air gained? When and where noticed?
17. Nature of the watery vapor? Its effects upon animals?

than to any other cause, are due the depressing and even fatal results which follow the crowding of large numbers of persons into places of limited capacity. (*Read Note 2.*)

18. History furnishes many painful instances of the ill effects of overcrowding. In 1756, of one hundred and forty-six Englishmen imprisoned in the Black Hole of Calcutta, only twenty-three, at the end of eight hours, survived. After the battle of Austerlitz, three hundred prisoners were crowded into a cavern, where, in a few hours, two-thirds of their number died. On board a steamship, during a stormy night, one hundred and fifty passengers were con-

---

2. **The Two Breaths.**—"Every time you breathe, you breathe two different breaths : you take in one, you give out another. The composition of those two breaths is different. Their effects are different. The breath which has been breathed out must not be breathed in again. To tell you why it must not would lead me into anatomical details, not quite in place here as yet ; but this I may say : those who habitually take in fresh breath will probably grow up large, strong, ruddy, cheerful, active, clear-headed—fit for their work. Those who habitually take in the breath which has been breathed out by themselves, or any other living creature, will certainly grow up—if they grow up at all—small, weak, pale, nervous, depressed, unfit for work, and tempted continually to resort to stimulants and become drunkards.

"If you want to see how different the breath breathed out is from the breath taken in, you have only to try a somewhat cruel experiment, but one which people too often try upon themselves, their children, and their workpeople. If you take any small animal with lungs like your own—a mouse, for instance—and force it to breathe no air but what you have breathed already ; if you put it in a close box, and, while you take in breath from the outer air, send out your breath through a tube into that box, the animal will soon faint ; if you go on long with this process, he will die. * * * * What becomes of this breath which passes from your lips ? Is it merely harmful, merely waste ? God forbid ! God has forbidden that anything should be merely harmful or merely waste in this so wise and well-made world. The carbonic acid which passes from your lips at every breath is a precious boon to thousands of things of which you have daily need. For though you must not breathe your breath again, you may at least eat your breath, if you will allow the sun to transmute it for you into vegetables ; or you may enjoy its fragrance and its color in the shape of a lily or a rose. When you walk in a sunlit garden, every word you speak, every breath you breathe, is feeding the plants and flowers around."— *Rev. Charles Kingsley on the Two Breaths.*

---

18. Give some of the instances furnished by history.

fined in a small cabin, but when morning came, only eighty remained alive.

19. Changes in the Blood from Respiration.—The most striking change which the blood undergoes by its passage through the lungs, is the change of color from a dark blue to bright red. That this change is dependent upon respiration has been fully proved by experiment. If the trachea, or windpipe, of a living animal be so compressed as to exclude the air from the lungs, the blood in the arteries will gradually grow darker, until its color is the same as that of the venous blood. When the pressure is removed, the blood speedily resumes its bright hue. Again, if an animal breathes an atmosphere containing more oxygen than atmospheric air, the color changes from scarlet to vermilion, and becomes even brighter than arterial blood. This change of color is not of itself a very important matter, but it indicates a most important change of composition.

20. The air, as we have seen, by respiration loses oxygen and gains carbonic acid: the blood, on the contrary, gains oxygen and loses carbonic acid. Oxygen is the food of the blood corpuscles; while the articles we eat and drink go more directly to the plasma of the blood. The air, then, it is plain, is a sort of food, and we should undoubtedly so regard it, if it were not for the fact that we require it constantly, instead of taking it at stated intervals, as is the case with our articles of diet. Again, as the demand of the system for food is expressed by the sensation of hunger, so the demand for air is marked by a painful sensation called suffocation.

21. Interchange of Gases in the Lungs.—But the air and the blood are not in contact, as they are separated from each other by the walls of the air-cells and of the blood-vessels. How then do the two gases, oxygen and carbonic acid, exchange places? Moist animal membranes have a property which enables them to transmit gases through their substance, although they are impervious to liquids. This may be beautifully shown by suspending a bladder containing dark venous blood in a jar of oxygen. At the end of a

19. Change in the blood from blue to red. Upon what does the change depend? How shown?
20. What does the air lose and gain by respiration? What, the blood? Air as food?
21. Moist animal membranes? How shown with the bladder?

few hours the oxygen will have diminished, the blood will be brighter in color, and carbonic acid will be found in the jar.

22. If this interchange take place outside of the body, it must take place more perfectly within it, where it is favored by many additional circumstances. The walls of the vessels and the air-cells offer no obstacle to this process, which is known as gaseous diffusion. Both parts of this process of exchange are equally important. Without oxygen life ceases; if carbonic acid is not thrown off, it acts like a poison, producing unconsciousness, convulsions, and death.

23. Difference between Arterial and Venous Blood.—The following table presents the essential points of difference in the appearance and composition of the blood, before and after its passage through the lungs:

	Venous Blood.	*Arterial Blood.*
Color,	Dark blue,	Scarlet.
Oxygen,	8 per cent.,	18 per cent.
Carbonic Acid,	15 to 20 per cent.,	6 per cent., or less.
Water,	More.	Less.

The temperature of the blood varies considerably; but the arterial stream is generally warmer than the venous. The blood imparts heat to the air while passing through the lungs, and consequently the contents of the right side of the heart have a higher temperature than the contents of the left side.*

24. By means of the spectroscope, we learn that the change of color in the blood has its seat in the corpuscles; and that, according as they retain oxygen, or release it, they present the spectrum of arterial or of venous blood. There evidently exists, on the part of these little bodies, an affinity for this gas, and hence they have been called "carriers of oxygen." It was long ago thought that blue blood was peculiar to persons of princely or royal descent, and boastful allusions to the "*sang azure*" of kings and nobles are quite often met with. Physiology, however, informs us that blue blood flows in the veins of all—the low as well as the high—and that so far from being a mark of purity, it really indicates waste and decay.

* "Bernard has succeeded in establishing the following facts with regard to the temperature (of the blood) in various parts of the circulatory system in dogs and sheep: 1. The blood is warmer in the right than in the left cavities of the heart. 2. It is warmer in the arteries than in the veins, with a few exceptions."—*Physiology of Man, Flint.*

22. Gaseous diffusion? If oxygen be not received? If carbonic acid be retained?
23. Difference in the appearance and composition of the blood? Temperature of the blood? The blood while passing through the lungs? The consequence?
24. What do we learn by means of the spectroscope? "Carriers of oxygen"? Blue blood in the system?

25. Amount of Respiratory Labor.—During ordinary calm respiration, we breathe eighteen times in a minute; and twenty cubic inches of air pass in and out of the lungs with every breath. This is equivalent to the use of three hundred and sixty cubic inches, or more than ten pints of air each minute. From this we calculate that the quantity of air which hourly traverses the lungs is about thirteen cubic feet, or seventy-eight gallons; and daily, not less than three hundred cubic feet, an amount nearly equal to the contents of sixty barrels.

26. Of this large volume of air five per cent. is absorbed in its transit through the lungs. The loss thus sustained is almost wholly of oxygen, and amounts to fifteen cubic feet daily. The quantity of carbonic acid exhaled by the lungs during the day is somewhat less, being twelve cubic feet. Under the influence of excitement or exertion, the breathing becomes more frequent and more profound; and then the internal respiratory work increases proportionately, and may even be double that of the above estimate. It has been estimated that in drawing a full breath, a man exerts a muscular force equal to raising two hundred pounds placed upon the chest.

27. Impurities of the Air.—The oxygen in the atmosphere is of such prime importance, and its proportion is so nicely adjusted to the wants of man, that any gas or volatile substance which supplants it must be regarded as a hurtful impurity. All gases, however, are not alike injurious. Some, if inhaled, are necessarily fatal; *arsenuretted hydrogen* being one of these, a single bubble of which destroyed the life of its discoverer, Gehlen. Others are not directly dangerous, but because they take the place of oxygen, and exclude it from the lungs, they do harm, and become dangerous. To this latter class belongs carbonic acid.

28. Most of the actively poisonous gases have a pungent or offensive odor; and, as may be inferred, most repugnant odors indicate the presence of substances unfit for respiration. Accordingly, as we cannot see or taste these impurities, the sense of smell is our

25. The amount of air that passes in and out of the lungs?
26. Air absorbed in its transit through the lungs? The loss? Carbonic acid exhaled? Effect of excitement or exertion? What estimate?
27. Importance of the oxygen in the atmosphere? Injurious character of gases?
28. Pungency of gases? The inference? Our safeguard?

principal safeguard against them. In this we recognize the fore-thought which has stationed this sense, like a sentinel, at the proper entrance of the air-passages, to give us warning of approaching harm. Take, as an example, the ordinary illuminating gas of cities, from which so many accidents happen. How many more deaths would it cause if, when a leak occurs, we were not able to discover the escape of the gas by means of its disagreeable odor. (*Read Notes* 3 *and* 4.)

29. Organic matters exist in increased measure in the expired breath of sick persons, and impart to it, at times, a putrid odor. This is especially true in diseases which, like typhus and scarlet fever, are referable to a blood poison. In such cases the breath is one of the means by which nature seeks to expel the offending material from the system. Hence, those who visit or nurse fever-sick persons should obey the oft-repeated direction, "not to take the breath of the sick." At such times, if ever, fresh air is demanded, not alone for the sick, but also for those who take care of them (See Care of Sick-Room, Appendix).

---

3. Cleanliness the Sum Total of Hygiene.—"Disinfectants have the power of destroying the cause, and of arresting the spread of most epidemics and contagious diseases, but cleanliness is the best preventive of disease. Whenever practicable, the abundant use of water is better than disinfection. 'Let no one ever depend upon disinfectants, fumigations, and the like, for purifying the air. The offensive thing, not its smell, must be removed.' "—*Florence Nightingale, Notes on Nursing (in part).*

4. The True Prevention of Epidemics.—"It was in England that solution of the great problem of hygiene was first attempted. 'Preventive Medicine,' it is there called. Palmerston told a deputation which waited on him in order to ask him to order a fast on the approach of the second epidemic of cholera, to cleanse their sewers, and diligently visit the dwellings of the poor. And he did not confine himself to good advice, but, with his usual energy, he laid his hand on sanitary legislation, and purified the air of London and the large manufacturing towns. The result of the sanitary measures carried out was a reduction of the mortality of London from 26 to 23 per 1,000, and in some of the towns to 17 per 1,000—a low death-rate previously only equalled in the Isle of Wight. More than four thousand lives have been preserved yearly in London; and, assuming that the mortality among the sick is 1 in 20, this number represents a diminution in yearly sickness to the extent of eighty thousand."—*Dr. Joseph Seegen in the Vienna Medical Weekly.*

29. The air of rooms in which fever-sick persons are confined?

30. Dust in the Air.—Attention has lately been directed to the dust, or haze, that marks the ray of sunshine across a shaded room. Just as, many years ago, it was discovered that myriads of animalcules were found in the water we drank, so now the microscope reveals "the gay motes that dance along a sunbeam" to contain multitudes of animal and vegetable forms of a very low grade—the germs of fermentation and decay, and the probable sources of disease.

31. It is found that the best filter by which to separate this floating dust from the air is cotton wool, although a handkerchief will imperfectly answer the same purpose. In a lecture on this subject by Prof. Tyndall, he remarks that, "by breathing through a cotton wool respirator, the noxious air of the sick-room is restored to practical purity. Thus filtered, attendants may breathe the air unharmed. In all probability, the protection of the lungs will be the protection of the whole system. For it is exceedingly probable that the germs which lodge in the air-passages are those which sow epidemic disease in the body. If this be so, then disease can certainly be warded off by filters of cotton wool. By this means, so far as the germs are concerned, the air of the highest Alps may be brought into the chamber of the invalid."

32. Carbonic Acid in the Air.—We have already spoken of this gas as an exhalation from the lungs, and a source of impurity ; but it exists naturally in the atmosphere in the proportion of one-half part per thousand. In volcanic regions it is poured forth in enormous quantities from fissures in the earth's surface. Being heavier than air, it sometimes settles into caves and hollows in the surface. It is stated that in the island of Java, there is a place called the "Valley of Poison," where the ground is covered with the bones of birds, tigers, and other wild animals, which were suffocated by carbonic acid while passing over it. The Lake Avernus, the fabled entrance to the infernal regions, was, as its name implies, birdless, because the birds, while flying over it, were poisoned by the gas, and fell dead into its waters. In mines, carbonic acid

30. Animalcules in the water? Dust in the air ?
31. The best air filter ? The remarks of Prof. Tyndall ?
32. Carbonic acid in volcanic regions ? In Java ? At Lake Avernus ? In mines ?

forms the dreaded *choke-damp*, while carbureted hydrogen is the *fire-damp*.

33. In the open air, men seldom suffer from carbonic acid, for, as we shall see presently, nature provides for its rapid distribution, and even turns it to a good use. But its ill effects are painfully evident in our homes, schools, and churches, where it is liable to collect as the waste product of respiration, and of that combustion which is necessary for lighting and warming our homes. A man exhales, during repose, not less than one-half cubic foot of carbonic acid per hour. A single gas-burner liberates five cubic feet in the same time, therefore spoiling about as much air as ten men. A fire burning in a grate or stove emits some impure gases, and at the same time abstracts from the air as much oxygen as twelve men would consume in the same period, thus increasing the relative amount of carbonic acid in the air. From furnaces, as ordinarily constructed, this and other gases are constantly leaking and poisoning the air of tightly-closed apartments.

34. Effects of Impure Air.—Carbonic acid, in its pure form, is irrespirable, causing rapid death by suffocation. Air containing forty parts per thousand of this gas (the composition of the expired breath) extinguishes a lighted candle, and is fatal to birds; when containing one hundred parts, it no longer yields oxygen to man and other warm-blooded animals, and is, of course, speedily fatal to them. In smaller quantities, this gas causes headache, labored respiration, palpitation, unconsciousness, and convulsions.

35. In crowded and badly ventilated apartments, the air is breathed over until it contains from six to ten times the natural amount of carbonic acid. This contaminated air causes dullness, drowsiness, and faintness, because the dark, impure blood circulates through the brain, oppressing that organ, and causing it to act like a blunted tool. This is a condition not uncommon in our schools, churches, and court-rooms—the places of all others where it is desirable that the mind should be alert and free to act; but, unhappily,

---

33. In the open air? Amount of carbonic acid exhaled by a man? A gas-burner? A room fire? From furnaces?
34. Effects of inhaling carbonic acid alone? In small quantities?
35. Effects of the air in crowded and badly-ventilated rooms?

an unseen physiological cause is at work, dispensing weariness and stupor over pupils, audience, and juries. (*Read Notes 5 and 6.*)

---

5. The Ground-Atmosphere and its Relations to Dwellings.— "The soil, which naturally contains wholesome air, and gives facility to its every movement, is not less permeable by poisonous gases, which are often found to pervade and issue from it. It is easy to find illustrations of the fact that people are poisoned through the ground, since it is almost a daily occurrence. Here is one, related by an eminent authority, von Pettenkofer :—' In a residence at Augsburg, apparently endowed with every qualification for health and comfort, several priests lived together. On a certain morning, one of these, not the least zealous and prompt in the performance of his duties, was missed from his usual post at the matin service. His colleagues hurried back to their common dwelling in search of the missing priest, and found him lying prostrate and insensible upon the floor of his bed-chamber. A doctor was immediately called in, and at the first sight of his patient, declared him to be suffering from an attack of typhus fever. The Sisters of Charity, upon whom devolved the duty of nursing him, and those clerical associates who were active in their sympathy and prompt to visit him and give assistance, were, a few hours after, attacked in the same way. The doctor did not hesitate in his diagnosis, and pronounced the additional cases also typhus fever. A general alarm prevailed in the city, and many called at the house of the priest, who was greatly beloved. Among others was an old woman, who discovered a strong smell of gas, and believing this to be the cause of the sickness, obtained permission to remove the priest to her own house. The priest had no sooner breathed the fresh air than he began to revive, and during the very first evening of his removal to the new abode he became so much better as to make an importunate demand for food. He soon got entirely well. The old woman, thus confirmed in her gas theory, and eager to save the remaining patients, who had continued to increase in number in the priests' house, now had an interview with the manager of the gas-works which supplied the town, and prevailed upon him to investigate the condition of the gas-pipes in the vicinity of the priests' residence. This was done, and a leak from which the gas was escaping into the ground was found and stopped. The air of the house was perceived at once to improve, and with it the health of the patients that were not removed ; these finally completely recovered from what the doctor even was compelled to admit was not typhus fever, but poisoning by gas.' "—*The Book of Health.*

6. Pure Air and Good Morals.—"Cleanliness and self-respect go together, and it is no paradox to affirm that you tend to purify men's thoughts and feelings when you purify the air they breathe. * * * * With a low average of popular health you will have a low average of national morality, and probably also of national intellect. Drunkenness and vice of other kinds

36. Another unmistakable result of living in and breathing foul air is found in certain diseases of the lungs, especially consumption. For many years the barracks of the British army were constructed without any regard to ventilation; and during those years the statistics showed that consumption was the cause of a very large proportion of deaths. At last the government began to improve the condition of the buildings, giving larger space and air-supply; and as a consequence, the mortality from consumption has diminished more than one-third.

37. The lower animals confined in the impure atmosphere of menageries, contract the same diseases as man. Those brought from a tropical climate, and requiring to be closely housed, generally die of consumption. In the Zoological Gardens of Paris, this disease affected nearly all monkeys, until care was taken to introduce fresh air by ventilation, and then it almost wholly disappeared. The tendency of certain occupations to shorten life is well known, disease being occasioned by the fumes and dust which arise from the materials employed, in addition to the bad air of the workshop or factory, where many hours are passed daily. (*Read Note* 7.)

---

will flourish in such a soil, and you cannot get healthy brains to grow on unhealthy bodies."—*Lord Derby.*

7. Consumption is Lung Starvation.—" The practice of allowing the lungs only improper food, in the form of vitiated air, is one of the most prevalent habits of civilized life, and diseases of the lungs are its greatest bane and greatest dread. More persons die by consumption than by any other single disease. If there be added to those the large number that perish every year by inflammation of the lungs and bronchial tubes, disease and premature death may be well said to have in these organs their chief citadel. The leading cause of all this is, undoubtedly, the poor quality of the food on which the lungs are nurtured. The very best physicians, when their attention is directed to the subject, admit the full force of this conclusion, and that it has not received the attention it deserves. Professor Hartshorne remarks on this point, that ' the influence of impure air in promoting consumption has probably heretofore been underrated.' 'The vitiated air of the European barrack system for soldiers,' says Professor Parkes, 'is the only way in which the great prevalence of consumption in European armies can be accounted for.' This is the conclusion to which the Sanitary Commissioners for the army came,

---

36. A cause of consumption ? How was the fact illustrated ?
87. How, in the case of the lower animals ? Tendency of certain occupations ?

38. The following table shows the comparative amount of carbonic acid in the air under different conditions, and the effects sometimes produced:—

PROPORTION OF CARBONIC ACID.	In 1000 parts of Air
Air of country	.4
Air of city	.5
In hospital, well ventilated	.6
In school, church, etc., fairly ventilated	1.2 to 2.5
In court-house, factory, etc., without ventilation	4. to 40.
In bed-room, before being aired	4.5
In bed-room, after being aired	1.5
Constantly breathed, causing ill health	2.
Occasionally breathed, causing discomfort	8.
Occasionally breathed, causing distress	10.
Expired air	40.
Air no longer yielding oxygen	100.

39. Nature's Provision for Purifying the Air.

—We have seen that carbonic acid is heavier than air, and is poisonous. Why, then, does it not sink upon and overwhelm mankind with a silent, invisi-

---

in their celebrated report : 'A great amount of phthisis (consumption) has prevailed in the most varied stations of the army and in the most beautiful climates—in Gibraltar, Malta, Ionia, Jamaica, Trinidad, Bermuda, etc.—in all of which places the only common condition was the vitiated atmosphere which our barrack system everywhere produced. And, as if to clinch the argument, there has been of late years a most decided decline in phthisis in these stations, while the only circumstance which has notably changed in the time has been the condition of the air.' A very eminent authority, the late Dr. Marshall Hall, of England, said, in reference to pure air in the treatment of consumption, 'If I were seriously ill of consumption, I would live out doors day and night, except in rainy weather, or midwinter ; then I would sleep in an unplastered log house. Physic has no nutriment, gaspings for air cannot cure you, monkey capers in a gymnasium cannot cure you, and stimulants cannot cure you. What consumptives want is pure air, not physic—pure air, not medicated air—plenty of meat and bread.' Let it be remembered, in this connection, that every hygienic or health-promoting measure which tends to cure a disease is much more efficacious in preventing it."—*Black's Ten Laws of Health.*

---

38. Give the fact as set forth in the table?
39. What can you state of the diffusive power of gases ? The added influence of the winds?

ble wave of death? Among the gases there is a more potent force than gravity, which forever prevents such a tragedy. It is known as the diffusive power of gases. It acts according to a definite law, and with a resistless energy compelling these gases, when in contact, to mingle until they are thoroughly diffused. The added influence of the winds is useful, by insuring more rapid changes in the air, air in motion being perfectly wholesome. The rains also wash the air.

40. We have seen that the whole animal creation is constantly taking oxygen from the atmosphere, and as constantly adding to it vast volumes of a gas, which is, even in small quantities, injurious to both man and animals. How, then, does the air retain, unchanged, its life-giving properties? The uniform purity of the air is secured by means of the vegetable creation. Carbonic acid is the food of the plant, and oxygen is its waste product. The leaves are its lungs, and under the stimulus of sunlight a vegetable respiration is set in motion, the effects of which are just the reverse of that of animals. Thus nature purifies the air, and at the same time builds up beautiful and useful worlds—the life of each growing out of the decay of the other. (*Read Note* 8.)

---

8. Plants and the Air.—"Though the air is dependent for the renewal of its oxygen on the action of the green leaves of plants, it must not be forgotten that it is only in the presence and under the stimulus of light that these organisms decompose carbonic acid. All plants, irrespective of their kind or nature, absorb oxygen and exhale carbonic acid in the dark. The quantity of noxious gas thus eliminated is, however, exceedingly small when compared with the oxygen thrown out during the day. Aside from the highly deleterious action that plants may exert on the atmosphere of a sleeping-room, by increasing the proportion of carbonic acid during the night, there is another and more important objection to be urged against their presence in such apartments. Like animals, they exhale peculiar volatile organic principles, which in many instances render the air unfit for the purposes of respiration. Even in the days of Audronicus this fact was recognized, for he says, in speaking of Arabia Felix, that 'by reason of myrrh, frankincense, and hot spices there growing, the air was so obnoxious to their brains, that the very inhabitants at some times cannot avoid its influence.' What the influence on the brains of the inhabitants may have been does not at present interest us; we have only

---

40. How is the constant purity of the air secured? Explain the process?

41. In the sea, as in the air, the same circle of changes is observed. Marine animals consume oxygen and give off carbonic acid, while marine plants consume carbonic acid, and liberate oxygen. Taking advantage of this fact, we may so arrange aquaria with fishes and sea-plants, in their proper combinations, that each may supply the needs of the other, and the water may seldom require to be renewed. This affords us, on a small scale, an illustration of the grand circle of changes taking place in the air about us, and also of the harmonious dependence of the two great kingdoms of nature.

42. Ventilation.—Since the external atmosphere, as provided by nature, is always pure, and since the air in our dwellings and other buildings is almost always impure, it becomes imperative that there should be a free communication from the one to the other. This we aim to accomplish by ventilation. As our houses are ordinarily constructed, the theory of ventilation, " to make the internal as pure as the external air," is seldom carried out. Doors, windows, and flues, the natural means of replenishing the air, are too often closed, almost hermetically, against the precious element. Special means, or special attention, must therefore be used to secure even a fair supply of fresh air. This is still more true of those places of public resort, where large numbers of persons are crowded together. (See Drainage, Appendix.)

43. If there are two openings in a room, one as a vent for foul air, and the other an inlet for atmospheric air, and if the openings be large in proportion to the number of air consumers, the principal object will be attained. Thus, a door and window, each opening into the outer air, will ordinarily ventilate a small apartment ; or a window alone will answer, if it be open both above and below, and

---

quoted the statement to show that long ago the emanations from plants were regarded as having an influence on the condition of the air ; and, in view of our present ignorance, it would be wise to banish them from our sleeping apartments, at least until we are better informed regarding their true properties."—*Draper on Poisoned Air.*

---

41. What process occurs in the sea?   How is the fact illustrated?
42. Character of the external air? Of the air in our dwellings? What becomes impera-tive?   Imperfect ventilation of our dwellings?
43. What hints are given for the ventilation of our dwellings?

the open space at each end be not less than one inch for each occupant of the room, when the window is about a yard wide. The direction of the current is generally from below upward, since the foul, heated air tends to rise; but this is not essential.* Its rate need not be rapid; a "draught," or perceptible current, is never necessary to good ventilation. The temperature of the air admitted may be warm or cold. It is thought by many that if the air is cold, it is pure; but this is an error, since cold air will receive and retain the same impurities as warm air.

44. Shall we open our bed-rooms to the night air? Florence Nightingale says, in effect, that night air is the only air we can then breathe. "The choice is between pure air without and impure air within. Most people prefer the latter — an unaccountable choice. An open window, most nights in the year, can hurt no one. In great cities, night air is the best and purest to be had in twenty-four hours. I could better

Fig. 47.—Showing manner of ventilating by inserting strip of wood beneath lower sash of window.

* When the window is of the common sash kind, a good supply of fresh air may be obtained without a current, by placing a strip of board about four inches wide under the lower sash (Fig. 47). The window is thus closed against rain and snow, but allows of a supply of fresh air to enter between the sashes. If still more ventilation is needed to keep the air of the room sweet, the same arrangement may be made at the top of the window.

44. State what Florence Nightingale says about inhaling night air?

understand, in towns, shutting the windows during the day than during the night." (*Read Note* 9.)

45. Animal Heat.—Intimately connected with respiration is the production of animal heat, or the power of maintaining the temperature of the body above that of the medium in which the creature moves; thus, the bird is warmer than the air, and the fish than the water. This elevation of temperature is the result of the various chemical changes which are constantly taking place in the system. Although common to all animals, in a greater or less degree, heat is not peculiar to them, since plants also generate it, especially at the time of sprouting and flowering. If a thermometer be placed in a cluster of geranium flowers, it will indicate a temperature several degrees above that of the surrounding air.

46. Among animals great differences are noticed in this respect, but the degree of heat produced is always proportional to the activity of respiration and the amount of oxygen consumed. Accordingly, the birds, whose habits are extremely active, and whose breathing capacity is the greatest, have uniformly the highest temperature. Sluggish animals, on the contrary, as frogs, lizards, and snakes, have little need for oxygen, and have incompletely developed lungs; these animals are cold to the touch—that is, they have relatively a lower temperature than man, and their positive temperature

---

9. Pure Air in our Homes during Cold Weather.—"Fresh air is the great natural disinfectant, antiseptic, and purifier, and not to be compared for a moment with any of artificial contrivance. There is plenty of it in the world; yet, disguise the fact as we may, there is no getting over the unwelcome truth, that to provide it in abundance in our climate is expensive, since during seven months in the year it must be artificially warmed, in order that our homes may be comfortable. To take in air at the average winter temperature of 28°, raise it to 68°, and discharge it again from our houses even once in an hour, is a process which cannot be accomplished without paying roundly; yet on no other condition can we reasonably expect health and long life. The best way is to freely admit that it is expensive, but worth the money it costs. If Benjamin Franklin thought that 'a penny saved is a penny earned,' he is equally sure that 'health is wealth.'"—*George Derby on the Prevention of Disease.*

---

45. Warmth of the bird as compared with that of the air? Of the fish and the water? Heat in animals and plants? How illustrated with the thermometer?
46. Amount of heat in animals, how apportioned? As regards the birds Frogs, and other sluggish animals? Arrangement made by zoologists?

is but little above that of the external air. Accordingly, zoologists have so arranged the animal kingdom that *warm-blooded* animals, including man, the birds, and the quadrupeds, are classified together; while the *cold-blooded* animals, such as the fish, tortoise, frog, and all that have no vertebral column, are classed by themselves.

47. The temperature of the human body is about 100° Fahrenheit, and remains about the same through winter and summer—in the tropics as well as in the frozen regions of the north. It may change temporarily within the range of about twelve degrees; but any considerable, or long-continued elevation or diminution of the bodily heat is certain to result disastrously.

48. Man is able to adapt himself to all extremes of climate; and, in fact, by means of clothing, shelter, and food, is able to create for himself an artificial climate wherever he chooses to reside. The power to resist cold consists chiefly in preventing the heat which is generated by the vital processes of the body from being lost by radiation. Warm clothing, such as we wear in winter, has, in reality, the same temperature as that which is worn in summer; but, by reason of being thick and porous, it is a bad conductor of heat, and thus prevents the escape of that produced by the body. If woollen fabrics were intrinsically warm, no one would wrap a piece of flannel, or blanket, around a block of ice to prevent its melting in summer.

49. The faculty of generating heat explains how it is that we are enabled to resist the effects of cold; but how does the body withstand a temperature higher than its own? Men have been known to remain several minutes in an atmosphere heated above the boiling-point of water, and yet the temperature of their own bodies was not greatly increased. Those who labor in foundries and glass-works are habitually subjected to very high degrees of temperature, but they do not suffer in health more than those engaged in many other occupations.

50. The regulation of the temperature of the body is effected by

47. State what is said respecting the temperature of the human body.
48. Ability of man to adapt himself to different climates? In what does the power to resist cold consist? What is said about warm clothing?
49. Men in an atmosphere above the boiling-point? In foundries and glass-works?
50. The regulation of the temperature of the body. Give the explanation

means of perspiration, and by its evaporation. So long as the skin acts freely, and the air freely absorbs the moisture, the heat of the body does not increase, for whenever evaporation takes place, it is attended with the abstraction of heat—that is, the part becomes relatively colder. This may be tested by moistening some part of the surface with cologne, ether, or other volatile liquid, and then causing it to evaporate rapidly by fanning. The principle that evaporation produces cold has been ingeniously and practically employed, in the manufacture of ice by means of freezing machines.

51. Spontaneous Combustion—Alcohol the Indirect Cause.— Is it possible that the temperature of the living body can be so increased that its tissues will burn spontaneously? From time to time cases have been reported in which, by some mysterious means, considerable portions of the human body have been consumed, apparently by fire—the victim being found dead, or incapable of explaining the occurrence. Hence, the theory has been current that, under certain conditions, the tissues of the body might become self-ignited; and the fact that this so-called *spontaneous combustion* has ordinarily taken place in those who had been addicted to the use of alcoholic drinks, has given a color of probability to the opinion. It has been supposed that the flesh of these unfortunate persons, becoming saturated with alcohol thus taken into the system, took fire upon being exposed to a flame, as of a lighted candle, or, indeed, without any external cause. But, whether this be possible or not, one thing is certain—this strange kind of combustion has never been actually witnessed by any one competent to give a satisfactory account of it.

52. The results that have been observed may be satisfactorily explained by the accidental ignition of the clothes, or other articles near the body, and by the supposition that the individual was at the time too much stupefied by intoxication, to notice the source of danger and provide for his safety. The highest temperature that has been observed in the body—about 112° Fahrenheit—is too low to ignite the vapor of alcohol; much less will it cause the burning of animal tissues. It is undoubtedly true that when the tissues are filled with alcohol, combustion will more easily take

---

51. State what is said of spontaneous combustion.
52. How is the theory refuted?

place than when the body is in a normal state; but, under any condition, the combustion of the body requires a higher degree of heat than can be generated by the body itself, or the mere *proximity* of a lighted candle, or any cause, of similar character.

53. The Effect of Alcohol upon Respiration.—Whenever wine, or any other form of alcoholic drink, is taken into the stomach, it is quite rapidly absorbed into the blood-current, and in a few minutes it imparts to the breath a peculiar, offensive odor. This is due to the vapor of alcohol that, little by little, is expelled from the body, along with the carbonic acid gas exhaled through the lungs. If the quantity of drink taken has been considerable, this disagreeable odor may continue a day or more.

This condition is evidence that an unnatural labor has been thrown upon the lungs; namely, it is an effort on the part of the general system to get rid of a poison that is hurtful to every organ by which it is retained. While this exhalation of alcoholic vapor continues, the respiratory act is impaired, for not only can less carbonic acid gas be thrown off, but there is also a diminished inhalation of oxygen.

54. Respiratory Diseases among the Intemperate.— The structure of the respiratory organs is such that they are relatively tolerant of the presence of alcohol in the body.

Wheezy breathing and hoarseness of voice are noticeable among inebriates; but this class does not suffer greatly from severe attacks of lung diseases that can be said to be directly due to the liquor they drink. Indirectly, however, they suffer greatly, as a class, from those diseases, because they incur exposures of every imaginable variety, while under the intoxicant influence of this powerful drug, which can, according as it is taken in less or greater quantity, deprive a person of his sober self-management or bring him down to utter loss of consciousness. It is in this way that the users of alcohol fall a prey, especially in the winter season, to attacks of pneumonia, or lung fever, and other serious disease of the respiratory organs.

---

53. Does alcohol appear in the breath? Does it interfere with respiration?
54. What respiratory diseases among the intemperate?

QUESTIONS FOR TOPICAL REVIEW.

CHAPTER IX.

The Nervous System.

Animal and Vegetative Functions Sensation, Motion, and Volition—The Structure of the Nervous System—The White and Gray Substances— T?, Brain —Its Convolutions—The Cerebellum—The Spinal Cord and its System of Nerves—The Anterior and Posterior Roots—The Sympathetic System of Nerves—The Properties of Nervous Tissue—Excitability of Nervous Tissues—The Functions of the Spinal Nerves and Cord—The Direction of the Fibres of the Cord—Reflex Activity, and its Uses—The Functions of the Medulla Oblongata and the Cranial Ganglia—The Reflex Action of the Brain—Effects of Alcohol, Tobacco, Snuff, Narcotics, Opium, Chloral, Hasheesh, Chloroform.

1. Animal Functions.—The vital processes which we have been considering in the three previous chapters—of digestion, circulation, and respiration—belong to the class of functions known as *vegetative* functions. That is, they are common to vegetables as well as animals; for the plant, like the animal, can originate nothing, not even the smallest particle of matter; and yet it grows, blossoms, and bears fruit, by reason of obtaining and digesting the nutriment which the air and soil provide. The plant has its circulatory fluid and channels, by which the nutriment is distributed to all its parts. It has, also, a curious apparatus in its foliage, by which it abstracts from the air those gaseous elements so necessary to its support; and thus it accomplishes vegetable respiration. These vegetative functions have their beginning and end within the organism of the plant; and their object is the preservation of the plant itself, as well as of the entire species.

2. The animal, in addition to these vegetative functions, has another set of powers, by the use of which he becomes conscious of a world external to himself, and brings himself into active relations

---

1. What processes are known as the vegetative functions? Why so called? What properties and functions does the plant possess? Their object?
2. What second set of powers has the animal? What functions are mentioned? The advantage they give?

with it. By means of the vegetative processes, his life and species are maintained; while, by means of certain animal functions, he feels, acts, and thinks. These functions, among which are sensation, motion, and volition, not only distinguish the animal from the plant, but, in proportion to their development, elevate one creature above another; and it is by virtue of his pre-eminent endowment, in these respects, that man holds his position at the head of the animal creation.

3. Among animals whose structure is very simple—the hydra, or fresh-water polyp, being an example—no special organs are empowered to perform separate functions, but every part is endowed alike; so that, if the animal be cut into pieces, each portion has all the properties of the entire original; and, if the circumstances be favorable, each of the pieces will soon become a complete hydra. As we approach man, in the scale of beings, we find that the organs multiply, and the functions become more complete. The function of motion, the instruments of which—the muscles and bones—have been considered in former chapters, and all the other animal functions of man, depend upon the set of organs known as the nervous system.

4. The Nervous System.—The intimate structure of this system differs from any tissue which we have before examined. It is composed of a soft, pulpy substance, which early in life is almost fluid, but which gradually hardens with the growth of the body. When examined under the microscope, it is found to be composed of two distinct elements: (1) the white substance, composing the larger proportion of the nervous organs of the body, which is formed of delicate cylindrical filaments, about $\frac{1}{8000}$ of an inch in diameter, termed the nerve-fibres; and (2) the gray substance, composed of grayish-red, or ashen-colored cells, of various sizes, generally possessing one or more off-shoots, which are continuous with the nerve-fibres just mentioned.

5. The gray, cellular substance constitutes the larger portion of

3. Animals whose structure is simple? As we approach man? Dependence of the animal functions of man?
4. The nervous tissues, of what composed? When examined by the aid of the microscope? The white substance? The gray substance?
5. Nervous centres and ganglia? Nerves? What do they serve? Cerebro-spinal system?

those important masses which bear the name of *nervous centres* and *ganglia* (from *ganglion*, a knot), in which all the nerve-fibres unite. These white nerve-fibres are found combined together in long and dense cords, called *nerves* (from *neuron*, a cord), which serve to connect the nervous centres with each other, and to place them in communication with all the other parts of the body which have sensibility or power of motion. That part of the nervous system which is concerned in the animal functions comprises the brain, the spinal cord, and the nerves which are derived therefrom; these are, together, called the *cerebro-spinal* system (Fig. 48); while that other set of organs, which presides over and regulates the vegetative functions, is called the sympathetic system of nerves.

6. The Brain.—The brain is the great volume of nervous tissue that is lodged within the skull. It is the largest and most complex of the nervous centres; its weight, in the adult, being about fifty ounces, or one-fortieth of that of the whole body. The shape of the brain is oval, or egg-shaped, with one extremity larger than the other, which is placed posteriorly in the skull, to the concavity of which it very closely conforms. The brain consists chiefly of two parts; the *cerebrum*, or brain proper, and the *cerebellum*, or "little brain." In addition to these, there are several smaller organs at the base, among which is the commencement or expansion of the spinal cord, termed the *medulla oblongata*, or oblong marrow.

7. The tissue of the brain is soft and easily altered in shape by pressure; it therefore requires to be placed in a well-protected position, such as is afforded by the skull, or *cranium*, which is strong without being cumbrous. In the course of an ordinary lifetime, this bony box sustains many blows with little inconvenience; while, if they fell directly upon the brain, they would at once, and completely, disorganize that structure. Within the skull, the brain is enveloped by certain membranes, which at once protect it from friction and furnish it with a supply of nutrient vessels; they are called the *arachnoid*, or "spider's web," the *dura mater*, and the *pia mater*, or the "tough" and "delicate coverings." The supply of blood sent

---

6. Location of the brain? Its weight? Its shape? Of what it consists? What organs at the base?
7. The tissue of the brain? What, therefore, is required? Blows on the head? Membranes of the brain? Blood sent to the brain?

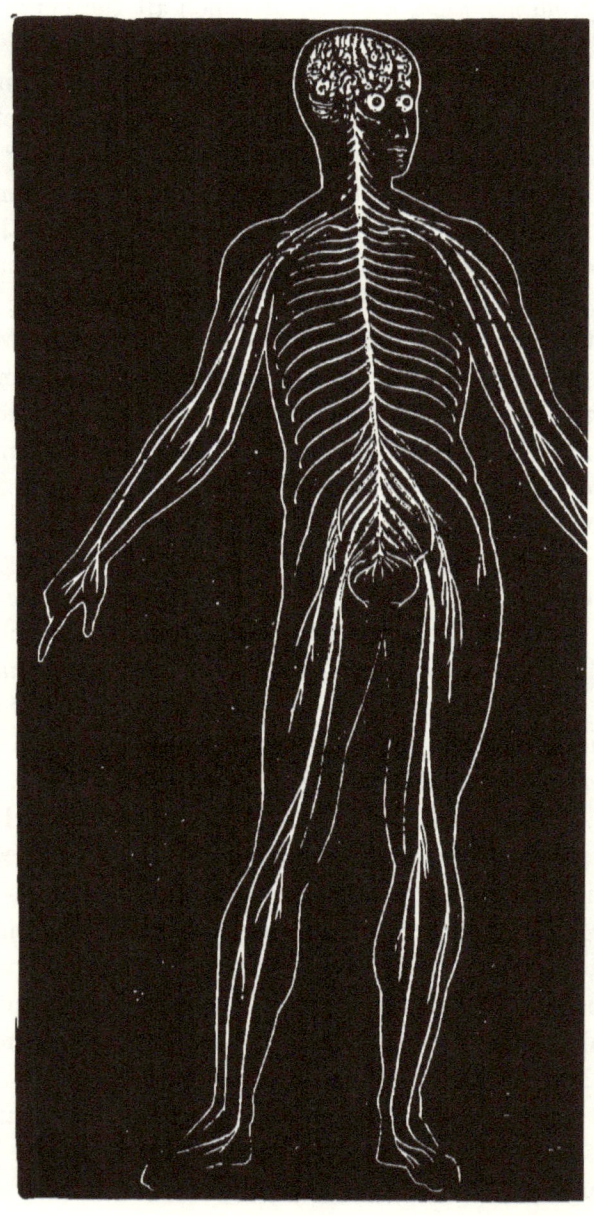

FIG. 48.—THE CEREBRO-SPINAL SYSTEM.

to the brain is very liberal, amounting to one-fifth of all that the entire body possesses. The brain of man is heavier than that of any other animal, except the elephant and whale.

8. The Cerebrum.—The brain proper, or *cerebrum*, is the largest of the intracranial organs, and occupies the entire upper and front portion of the skull. It is almost completely bisected by a fissure, or cleft, running through it lengthwise, into two equal parts called *hemispheres*. The exterior of these hemispheres is gray in color, consisting chiefly of nerve-cells, arranged so as to form a layer of gray matter one-fifth of an inch in thickness, and is abundantly supplied with blood-vessels. The interior of the brain, however, is composed almost wholly of white substance, or nerve-fibres.

9. The surface of the cerebrum is divided by a considerable number of winding and irregular furrows, about an inch deep, into "convolutions," as shown in Fig. 49. Into these furrows the gray matter of the surface is extended, and, in this manner, its quantity is vastly increased. The extent of the entire surface of the brain, with the convolutions unfolded, is computed to be equal to four square feet; and yet it is easily enclosed within the narrow limits of the skull. When it is stated that the gray matter is

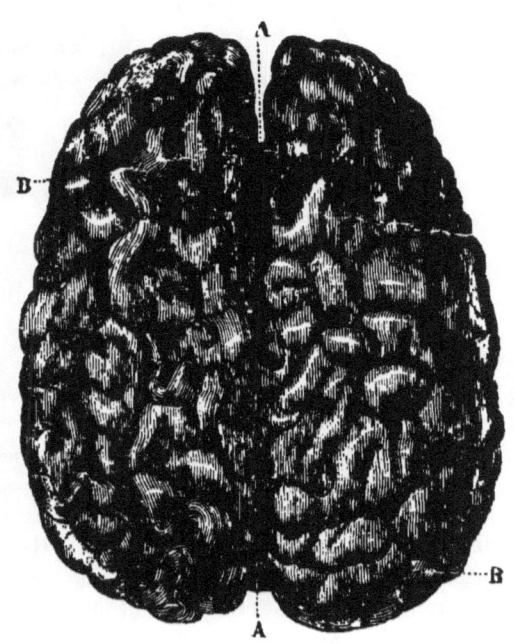

FIG. 49.—UPPER SURFACE OF THE CEREBRUM.
A, Longitudinal Fissure.
B, The Hemispheres.

the true source of nervous power, it becomes evident that this arrangement has an important bearing on the mental capacity of the individual. And it is noticed that in children, before the mind is brought into vigorous use, these markings or furrows on the surface are comparatively shallow and indistinct; the same fact is true of the brain in the less civilized races of mankind and in the lower animals. It is also noticeable that among animals, those are the most capable of being educated which have the best development of the cerebrum. (*Read Note* 1.)

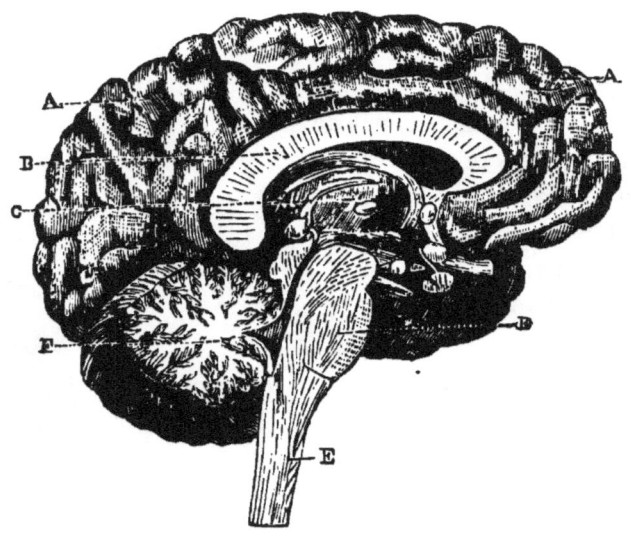

FIG. 50.—VERTICAL SECTION OF THE BRAIN.

A, Left Hemisphere of Cerebrum.   D, The Pons Varolii.
B, Corpus Callosum.   E, Upper extremity of the Spinal Cord.
C, Optic Thalamus.   F, The Arbor Vitæ.

1. The Brain.—"Our brains are seventy-year clocks. The Angel of Life winds them up once for all, then closes the case, and gives the key to the Angel of the Resurrection. Tic-tac! tic-tac! go the wheels of thought; our will cannot stop them; they cannot stop themselves; sleep cannot stop them; madness only makes them go faster; death alone can break into the case, and, seizing the ever-swinging pendulum, which we call the heart, silence at last the clicking of the terrible escapement we have carried so long beneath our wrinkled foreheads. * * * Now, when a gentleman's brain is ill-regulated or empty, it is, to a great extent, his own fault, and so it is simple retribution that, while he lies slothfully or aimlessly dreaming, the fatal habit settles on him like a vampire and sucks his blood, fanning him all the while with its hot wings into deeper slumber or idler dreams."—*Holmes' The Autocrat of the Breakfast-Table.*

10. The Cerebellum.—The " little brain" is placed beneath the posterior part of the cerebrum, and, like the latter, is divided into hemispheres.   Like it, also, the surface of the cerebellum is composed of gray matter, and its interior is chiefly white matter.   It has, however, no convolutions, but is subdivided by many parallel ridges, which, sending down gray matter deeply into the white, central portion, give the latter a somewhat branched appearance. This peculiar appearance has been called the *arbor vitæ*, or the "tree of life," from the fact that when a section of the organ is made, it bears some resemblance to the trunk and branches of a tree (Fig. 50, F).   In size, this cerebellum, or " little brain," is less than one-eighth of the cerebrum.

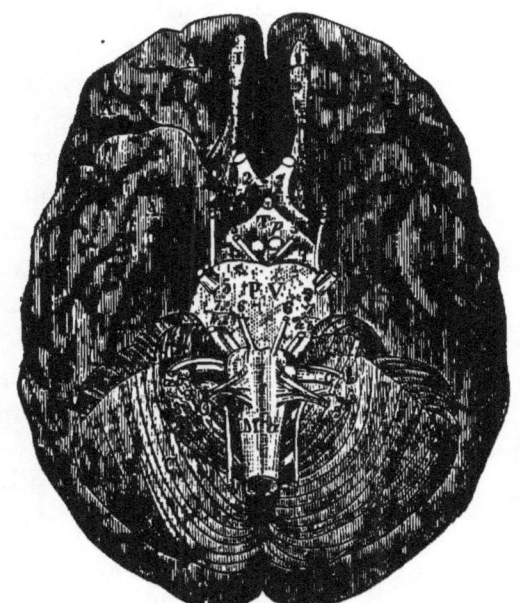

FIG. 51.—LOWER SURFACE OF THE BRAIN.
The numbers refer to the pairs of nerves.

11. From the under surface of the cerebrum, and from the front margin of the cerebellum, fibres collect together to form the *medulla oblongata* (Fig. 51, M*a*), which, on issuing from the skull, enters the spinal column, and then becomes known as the spinal cord.

10. Location of the "little brain?"   How divided?   Its surface and interior?   Its sub divisions?   Its size?
11. Medulla oblongata?   Cranial nerves?   Their shape and position?

From the base of the brain, and from the sides of the medulla originate, also, the *cranial nerves*, of which there are twelve pairs. These nerves are round cords of glistening white appearance, and, like the arteries, generally lie remote from the surface of the body, and are well protected from injury.

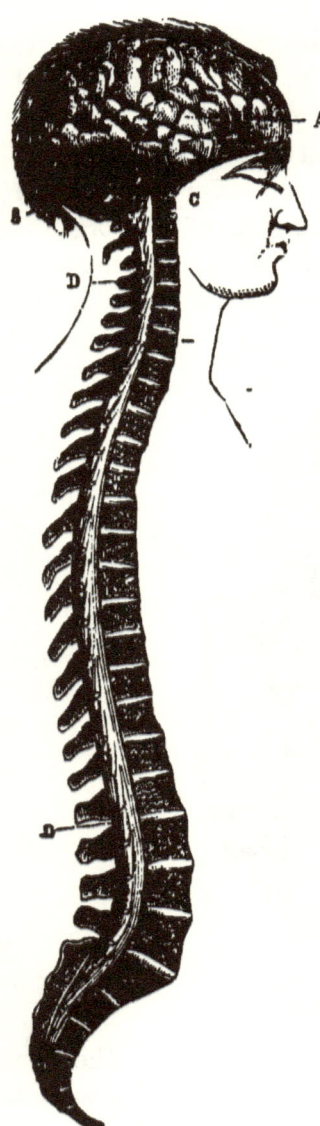

12. The Spinal Cord.—The spinal cord, or "marrow," is a cylindrical mass of soft nervous tissue, which occupies a chamber, or tunnel, fashioned for it in the spinal column (Figs. 52 and 53). It is composed of the same substances as the brain; but the arrangement is exactly reversed—the white matter encompassing or surrounding the gray matter, instead of being encompassed by it. The amount of the white substance is also greatly in excess of the other material. A vertical fissure partly separates the cord into two lateral halves, and each half is composed of two separate bundles of fibres, which are named the anterior and posterior columns.

13. These columns have entirely different uses, and each of them unites with a different portion of the nerves which have their origin in the spinal cord. The importance of this part of the nervous system is apparent from the extreme care taken to protect it from external injury. For, while a very slight disturbance of its structure suffices to disarm it of its power, yet so staunch is its bony enclosure, that only by very

Fig. 52.
A, Cerebrum, B, Cerebellum, D, D, Spinal Cord.

12. The spinal cord? Of what composed? How divided? Each half?
13. Uses of these columns? Importance of this part of the nervous system? How protected?

severe injuries is it put in peril. The three membranes that cover the brain are continued downward, so as to envelope and still further shield this delicate organism.

14. The Spinal Nerves.—The spinal nerves, thirty-one pairs in number, spring from each side of the cord by two roots, an anterior and a posterior root, which have the same functions as the columns bearing similar names. The posterior root is distinguished by possessing a ganglion of gray matter, and by a somewhat larger size.

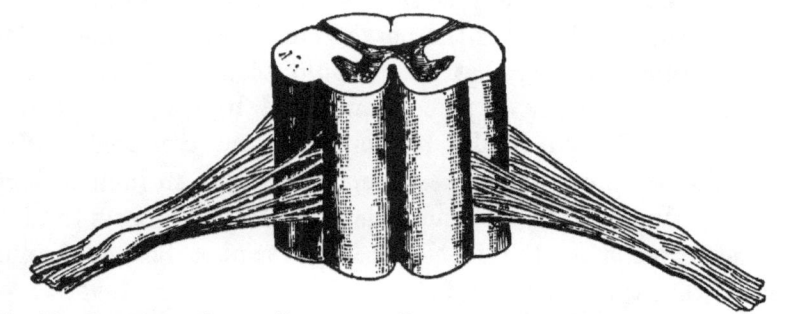

FIG. 53.—SECTION OF SPINAL CORD, WITH ROOTS OF SPINAL NERVES. FRONT VIEW.

The successive points of departure, or the off-shooting of these nerves, occur at short and nearly regular intervals along the course of the spinal cord. Soon after leaving these points, the anterior and posterior roots unite to form the trunk of a nerve, which is distributed, by means of branches, to the various organs of that part of the body which this nerve is designed to serve. The spinal nerves supply chiefly the muscles of the trunk and limbs and the external surface of the body.

15. The tissue composing the nerves is entirely of the white variety, or, in other words, the nerve-fibres; the same as we have observed forming a part of the brain. But the nerves, instead of being soft and pulpy, as in the case of the brain, are dense in structure, being hardened and strengthened by means of a fibrous tissue which surrounds each of these delicate fibres, and binds them together in glistening, silvery bundles. Delicate and minutely fine as are these nerve-fibres, it is probable that each of them pursues an unbroken, isolated course, from its origin, in the brain or elsewhere, to that particu'ar point which it is intended to serve. For although their extremities are often only a hair's breadth distant from each other, the impression which any one of them communicates is perfectly distinct, and is referred to the exact point whence it came.

16. This may be illustrated in a simple manner, thus: if two fingers be pressed closely together, and the point of a pin be carried lightly across from one to the other, the eyes may be closed, and yet we can easily note the precise instant when the pin passes from one finger to the other. If the nerve-fibres were less independent, and if it were necessary that they should blend with and support each other, all accuracy of perception would be lost, and all information thus afforded would be pointless and confused. These silvery threads must, therefore, be spun out with an infinite degree of nicety. Imagine, for instance, the fibre which connects the brain with some point on the foot—its length cannot be less than one hundred thousand times greater than its diameter, and yet it performs its work with as much precision as fibres that are comparatively much stronger, and less exposed. (*Read Note* 2.)

17. The Sympathetic System.—The *sympathetic system* of nerves remains to be described. It consists of a double chain

---

2. How Bodily Sensations are Located.—"A nervous fibre which ends in the skin forms, as far as its union with the brain or cord is concerned, one long, fine, unbroken thread. The fibres, thus ending in the skin, very soon join to form small branches, and finally in thick nerve trunks, but in no case do two nerve fibres coalesce so as to lose their identity. Every part of the skin has its own separate connections with the centre of the nervous system, which unite there just as telegraph wires unite at a terminus. The brain is the terminus of these lines of nerves, and, as it were, receives and explains the messages sent to it. It distinguishes very clearly by what particular fibre such a message has come, and just as the clerk in a telegraph office, where a great many wires meet from all sides, knows by experience from what direction each wire brings its message, so the brain also knows by experience what part of the skin is involved when a sensation reaches it along a certain nerve fibre. It is probable that the brain, by its imaginative faculty, has formed a complete picture of the surface of the body—a kind of chart

---

16. How may we illustrate the fact ?   The fibre connecting the brain with a point in the foot ?
17. The sympathetic system of nerves ?   Of what does it consist ?

of ganglia, situated on each side of the spinal column, and extending through the cavities of the trunk, and along the neck into the head. These ganglia are made up for the most part of small collections of gray nerve-cells, and are the nerve-centres of this system. From these, numerous small nerves are derived, which connect the ganglia together, send out branches to the cranial and spinal nerves, and form networks in the vicinity of the stomach and other large organs. A considerable portion of them also follows the distribution of the large and small blood-vessels, in which the muscular tunic appears. Branches also ascend into the head, and supply the muscles of the eye and ear, and other organs of sense.

18. In this manner the various regions of the body are associated with each other by a nervous apparatus, which is only indirectly connected with the brain and spinal cord, and thus it is arranged that the most widely separated organs of the body are brought into close and active sympathy with each other, so that "if one member suffers, all the other members suffer with it." From this fact, the name *sympathetic system,* or the *great sympathetic nerve,* has been given to the complicated apparatus we have briefly described. Blushing and pallor are caused by mental emotions, as modesty and fear, which produce opposite conditions of the capillaries of the face by means of these sympathetic nerves. (*Read Note* 3.)

---

slowly made, and always being more highly perfected, by means of which, with each impression from without, there arises in the brain a picture of the spot upon the skin where the irritation has taken place. Now, if an irritation were to pass from one nerve fibre to another, it is very plain, the brain could not tell the place from which it came, and could not localize impressions received from the world about us."—*Bernstein's Five Senses of Man.*

3. **The Wonderful Operations of the Sympathetic System.—Blushing or "Shame-redness."**—"A blow upon the head will knock a man senseless, but he still lives and survives; a blow of like violence upon the pit of the stomach is followed by instant death, because the great centre of the organic nerves lies there, and the vital actions are suspended by the blow, so that the system never lives to recover, but abolition of function and of life at once follows. Other actions also belong to this organic nervous system. It

---

18. Association of the various regions of the body? If one member suffers? Blushing?

19. The Properties of Nervous Tissue.—We have seen that in all parts of this system there are only two forms of nervous tissue, namely, the gray substance and the white substance, so called from their difference of color as seen by the naked eye; or the nerve-cell, and the nerve-fibre, so called from their microscopic appearance. Now these two tissues are not commonly mingled together, but either form separate organs or distinct parts of the same organs. This leads us to the conclusion that their respective uses are distinct. And this proves to be the simple fact; wherever we find the gray substance, we must look upon it as performing an active part in the system—that is, it originates nervous impulses; the white matter, on the contrary, is a passive agent, and serves merely as a conductor of nervous influences. Accordingly, the nervous centres, composed so largely of the gray cells, are the great centres of power, and the white fibres are simply the instruments by which the former communicate with the near and distant regions of the body under their control.

20. We may compare the brain, then, to the capital, or seat of government, while the various ganglia, including the gray matter of the cord, like so many subordinate official posts, are invested with authority over the outlying provinces; and the nerves, with the

---

controls the calibre of the blood-vessels, for which end filaments run along each of them. The body temperature is maintained by the production and dispersion of heat thus regulated, a continuous oscillation going on betwixt the internal vessels and those of the skin. It is connected with the emotions; and so the heart beats perceptibly with excitement, and the maiden's cheek blushes before words that should never be spoken, or thoughts that should never arise. The momentary dilatation of the vessels of the skin constitutes the blush (in the German, 'shame-redness'), which is not confined to the face, though, of course, it is only seen there—the body being hid by the clothes."—*Fothergill on the Maintenance of Health.*

"There is an old tradition that when the executioner of Charlotte Corday lifted her severed head high in air, and smote the face with his hand, the cheeks were seen to resent the insult with a blush. This reddening is not impossible, for a decapitated head certainly may exhibit, for a time, certain reflex movements. But whether sensibility is retained cannot be known."

19. Properties of nervous tissue? Office of the gray substance? Of the white? The nervous centres? White fibres?

20. What comparison is made between the brain and the nation's capital? The vital property, excitability? What example is given?

white matter of the cord, are the highways over which messages go and return between these provinces and the local or central govern- ments. But both forms of nervous tissue possess the same vital property called excitability, by which term is meant that, when a nerve-cell or fibre is stimulated by some external agent, it is capa- ble of receiving an impression, and of being by it excited into activity. A ray of light, for example, falling upon one extremity of a fibre in the eye, excites it throughout its whole length; and its other extremity within the brain, communicating with a nerve-cell, the latter in its turn is excited, and the sensation of sight is pro- duced. (*Read Note* 4.)

21. What sort of change takes place in the nervous tissue when its excitability is aroused, is not known; certainly none is visible. On this account, it has been thought by some that the nerve-fibre acts after the manner of a telegraph-wire; that is, it transmits its messages without undergoing any material change of form. But though the comparison is a convenient one, it is far from being strictly applicable, and the notion that nerve-force is identical with electricity has been fully proved to be incorrect.

---

4. The Relations of the Brain and Sympathetic Nerve.—" Buried in the hidden recesses of the body, between the spinal column and the great organs of nutrition, there is a double row of small knots of nervous sub- stance, bound together by a series of nerves running from one to another, in succession, from the neck to the base of the column. The whole appears like a long, fine cord, with knots at various distances—a collec- tion of little brains, if I may use a rather crude expression. It is, as the Swiss would say, the 'great council' of this federative republic, which counter- poises that cerebral royalty within us. It has been well named the great sympathetic nerve, and this it is which makes the laws by which our interior life is governed. The nutritive apparatus of a country, its com- merce, its industry, the incessant labor of its citizens, by which the public wealth is built up—and also let us add, the throbs of the national heart—all this the sympathetic system full plainly shows us should be left to itself. It would be a fine affair if the brain had to watch over the service of the stomach, or if, at its convenience, it regulated the movements of the master who disposes of its life. Besides, what would become of the poor body, if the least drowsiness attacked the universal centre ? Happy is it for us—and let us not be slow to own it—that nature has armed herself against these en- croachments of power."—*Macé's The Little Kingdom.*

21. Change in the nervous tissues ? Nerve force and electricity ?

9

22. The Functions of the Nerves.—The nerves are the in-strumeuts of the two grand functions of the nervous system—Sensation and Motion. They are not the true centres of either function, but they are the conductors of influences which occasion both. If the nerve in a limb of a living animal be laid bare, and irritated by pinching, galvanizing, or the like, two results follow, namely: the animal experiences a sensation, that of pain, in the part in which the nerve is distributed, and the limb is thrown into convulsive action. When a nerve in a human body is cut by accident, or destroyed by disease, the part in which it ramifies loses both sensation and power of motion; or, in other words, it is paralyzed. We accordingly say that the nerves have a two-fold use—a *sensory* and a *motor* function.

23. If a nerve that has been exposed be divided, and the inner end, or that still in connection with the nerve-centres be irritated, sensation is produced, but no movement takes place. But if the outer end, or that still connected with the limb, be irritated, then no pain is felt, but muscular contractions are produced. Thus we prove that there are two distinct sets of fibres in the nerves—one of which, the *sensory* fibres, conduct toward the brain, and another, the *motor* fibres, conduct to the muscles. The former may be said to begin in the skin and other organs and end in the brain, while the latter begin in the nervous centres and end in the muscles. They are like a double line of telegraph wires, one for inquiries, the other for responses.

24. We have already spoken of the two roots of the spinal nerves, called, from their points of origin in the spinal cord, the anterior and posterior roots. These have been separately cut and irritated in the living animal, and it has been found that the pos-terior root contains only sensory fibres, and the anterior root has only motor fibres. So that the nerves of a limb may be injured in such a way that it will retain power of motion and yet lose sensation; or the reverse condition, feeling without motion, may exist. Between

---

22. Functions of the nerves? In the case of the nerve of a living animal? Of the human body?
23. If an exposed nerve be divided? What is proved ? The course of the sensory set of fibres? Of the motor set? To what are they likened ?
24. The two roots of the spinal nerves ? What has been found? Difference of the two sorts of fibres ? Result of their union ?

these two sorts of fibres no difference of structure can be found; and where they have joined to form a nerve, it is impossible to distinguish one sort from the other.

25. Occasionally a nerve is so compressed as to be temporarily unable to perform its functions: a transient paralysis then takes place. · This is the case when the leg or arm " gets asleep," as it is expressed. When such is the condition with the leg, and the person suddenly attempts to walk, he is liable to fall, inasmuch as the motor fibres cannot convey orders to the muscles of the limb. Another fact is observed: there is no sensation in this nerve at the point of its compression; but the whole limb is numb, and tingling sensations are felt in the foot—the point from which the sensory fibres arise.

26. This illustrates the manner in which the brain interprets all injuries of the trunk of a nerve. Sensation or pain is not felt at the point of injury, but is referred to the outer extremities of the nerve, where impressions are habitually received. This is the reason why, after a limb has been amputated by the surgeon, the patient appears to suffer pain in the member that has been severed from the body; while some form of irritation at the end of the nerve in the wound, or stump, is the real source of his distress. Again, when the " funny-bone "—that is, the ulnar nerve at the elbow—is accidentally struck, the tingling sensations thus produced are referred to the outer side of the hand and the little finger, the parts to which that nerve is distributed.

27. All the spinal nerves, and two from the brain, are concerned in both sensation and motion. Of the remainder of the cranial nerves, some are exclusively motor, others exclusively sensory; and still others convey, not ordinary sensations, but special impressions, such as sight, hearing, and smell, which we have yet to consider. However much the functions of the nerves seem to vary, there is but little difference discoverable in the nerves themselves, when examined under the microscope. Whatever difference exists must

25. Transient paralysis? When such is the case with the leg? What other fact is observed?
26. What does this illustrate? Sensation? The feeling after a limb has been amputated? Striking of the "funny-bone?"
27. The spinal nerves, and two from the brain? Of the remainder? Difference in the nerves? How accounted for? The rate of conduction along a nerve? As compared with electricity?

be accounted for in consequence of the nerves communicating with different portions of the gray matter of the brain. The rate of motion of a message, to or from the brain along a nerve, has been measured by experiment upon the lower animals, and estimated in the case of man at about two hundred feet per second. As compared with that of electricity, this is a very slow rate, but, in·respect to the size of the human body, it is practically instantaneous. (*Read Note* 5.)

28. The Functions of the Spinal Cord.—As the anterior and posterior roots of the spinal nerves have separate functions, so the anterior and posterior columns of the cord are distinct in function. The former are concerned in the production of motion, the latter in sensation. If the cord be divided, as before in the case of the nerve, it is found that the parts below the point of injury are deprived of sensation and of the power of voluntary motion on both sides of the body—a form of paralysis which is called *paraplegia*.

29. This form of disease—paraplegia—is sometimes seen among men, generally as the result of a fall, or some other severe accident, by which the bones of the spine are broken, and the cord is crushed, or pierced by fragments of bone. The parts which are supplied by nerves from the cord above the point of injury are as sensitive and mobile as before. The results are similar, whether the division happens at a higher or lower portion of the spinal cord; but the danger to life increases proportionally as the injury approaches the brain. When it occurs in the neck, the muscles of inspiration are paralyzed, since they are supplied by nerves issuing from that

---

5. The Speed of Sensation and Thought.—"The rate of nervous and mental action is not the same in all individuals. In comparing the records made by astronomers, it has been found that an appreciable difference exists in the rapidity with which the same occurrence may be noted by different observers. This is known as the 'personal equation,' and is allowed for with the greatest nicety in the making up of astronomical reports. With very delicate apparatus for marking time, the various nervous impulses have been observed; from forty to a hundred feet in a second are the estimates of different experiments as to the speed of sensation; or, as it has been expressed, it would take a full-grown whale a second to feel the stroke of a harpoon in his tail."

---

28. Functions of the anterior and posterior columns of the cord? If the cord be divided?
29. Paraplegia? Result and danger to life? When the injury occurs in the neck?

region ; and as a result of this paralysis, the lungs are unable to act, and life is speedily brought to a close.

30. When the spinal cord of an animal has been cut, in experiment, it may be irritated in a manner similar to that alluded to when considering the nerves. If, then, the upper cut surface be excited, it is found that pain, referable to the parts below the cut, is produced ; but when the lower cut surface is irritated, no feeling is manifested. So we conclude that in respect to sensation, the spinal cord is not its true centre, but that it is merely a conductor, and is therefore the great sensory nerve of the body. When the lower surface of the cut is irritated, the muscles of the parts below the section are violently contracted. Hence we conclude that, in respect to the movements ordered by the will, the spinal cord is not their source, but that it acts only as a conductor, and is, accordingly, the great motor nerve of the body.

31. Direction of the Fibres of the Cord.—If one lateral half of the spinal cord be cut, or injured, a very singular fact is observed. All voluntary power over the muscles of the corresponding half of the body is lost, but the sensibility of that side remains undiminished. This result shows that the motor fibres of the cord pursue a direct course, while its sensory fibres are bent from their course. And this has been proved to be the fact ; for immediately after the posterior roots—the conductors of sensory impressions—join the posterior columns, they enter the gray matter of the cord, and passing over, ascend to the brain on the opposite side. Accordingly, the sensory fibres from the right and left sides interlace each other in the gray matter ; this arrangement has been termed the *decussation*, or crossing of these fibres. This condition serves to explain how a disease or injury of the cord may cause a paralysis of motion in one leg, and a loss of sensation in the other.

32. The direction of the anterior, or motor columns of the cord, is downward from the brain. In the cord itself, the course of the motor fibres is for the most part a direct one ; but in the medulla oblongata, or upper extremity of the cord, and therefore early in

---

30. Experiment of cutting the spinal cord of an animal? What inference is drawn?
31. What singular fact is noticed? What does the result show?
32. Direction of the anterior or motor columns? In the cord itself? In the medulla oblongata? The decussation?

their career, these fibres cross from side to side in a mass, and not separately, as in the case of the posterior fibres just mentioned. This arrangement is termed the *decussation* of the anterior columns of the medulla.

33. From this double interlacing of fibres results a cross action between the original and terminal extremity of all nerve-fibres which pass through the medulla—namely, those of all the spinal nerves. Consequently, if the right hand be hurt, the left side of the brain feels the pain ; and if the left foot move, it is the right hemisphere which dictates its movement. For the same reason, when a loss of sensation and power of motion affecting the right side of the body alone is observed, the physiologist understands that the brain has been invaded by disease upon its left side. This affection is termed *hemiplegia*, or the " half-stroke." The full-stroke, which often follows the rupture of a blood-vessel in the brain, is commonly called *paralysis*.

34. The Reflex Action of the Cord.—We have already considered the cord as the great motor and sensory nerve of the body, but it has another and extremely important use. By virtue of the gray matter, which occupies its central portion, it plays the part of an independent nerve centre. The spinal cord not only conducts some impressions to the brain, but it also arrests others ; and, as it is expressed, " reflects " them into movements by its own power. This mode of nervous activity is denominated the *reflex action* of the cord.

35. A familiar example of this power of the cord is found in the violent movements which agitate a fowl after its head has been cut off. The cold-blooded animals also exhibit reflex movements in an astonishing degree. A decapitated centipede will run rapidly forward, and will seemingly strive to overturn, or else climb over obstacles placed in its way. A frog similarly mutilated will sustain its headless body upon its feet, in the standing posture, just as it might do if it were still alive. If pushed over, it will regain its feet ; and if the feet are irritated, it will jump forward. There can

33. Result of the double interlacing of fibres? Where is the seat of pain when the right hand is hurt ? The moving of the foot? Loss of sensation in one side of the body ? 34. What other important use has the cord ? What is the activity denominated? 35. Example of the fowl? Centipede? Frog? What do they prove ?

be no doubt that, in the lower animals, movements may take place which are completely divorced from the will, sensation, and consciousness; for in those animals, as well as in man, these faculties have their principal seat within the brain.

36. An irritation is necessary, in most instances, to awaken reflex movements. In the case of the decapitated fowl, its muscles are excited to convulsive action by reason of its being thrown upon the hard ground and roughly handled. Let it be treated differently, and the convulsions will not take place : let it be laid gently upon soft cotton, and the body will remain comparatively quiet. It may comfort some people to know that the convulsions which follow decapitation are not attended with pain, nor are they a necessary part of the "act of death," as some suppose.

37. In the human body, likewise, actions are excited that are entirely distinct from the ordinary voluntary efforts. It is not permissible, desirable, nor even necessary to decapitate a man that the body may be disconnected from his brain, in order to test the effect of irritation upon the spinal cord—although the bodies of beheaded criminals have been experimented upon, and caused to move by powerful galvanic batteries. Such experiments are rendered unnecessary by the occurrence of certain deplorable cases of disease and injury, which effectually sever all communication between the brain and a large part of the body.

38. Thus, the cord by an accident may be so far injured as to terminate all sensation and voluntary motion in the lower half of the body, the patient seeming lifeless and powerless from the waist downward. And yet, by tickling or pinching either foot, the leg of the same side may be made to jerk, or even to kick with considerable force ; but, unless the patient is observing his limbs, he is wholly unconscious of these movements, which are, therefore, performed independently of the brain. And they are in no wise due to the muscles of the limb; for, if the cord itself become diseased below the point of injury, the muscles cease to contract.

39. For the production of this form of nervous action, three

---

36. What is necessary in most cases to awaken reflex movements? In the case of the fowl? Convulsions which follow decapitation?
37. Actions in the human body distinct from voluntary efforts?
38. Reflex action after injury of the cord? Why not due to the muscles?

things are requisite—(1) a nerve to conduct messages from the surface of the body, one of that variety formerly described as sensory, but which are now known to be incapable of awakening sensation ; (2) a portion of uninjured spinal cord, which shall reflect or convert impressions into impulses ; and (3) a motor nerve to conduct impulses outward to the muscles. The power of the cord to enforce reflex acts resides in the gray matter, into which the reflex nerves enter and from which they depart, by means of their posterior and anterior roots respectively.

40. The Uses of the Reflex Action.—The reflex activity of the cord is exhibited in the healthy body in many ways, but since it is never accompanied with sensation, we do not readily recognize it in our own bodies. Reflex movements are best studied in the cases of other persons, when the conditions enable us to distinguish between acts that are consciously, and those that are unconsciously performed. For example, if the foot of a person soundly asleep be tickled or pinched, it will be quickly withdrawn from the irritation.

41. Similar movements may be observed in cases where the consciousness and sensation are temporarily obliterated by disease, or by means of narcotic poisons. If the arm of a person who has been rendered insensible by chloroform be raised, and then allowed to fall, it will be noticed that the limb does not drop instantly, like a lifeless member, but a certain amount of rigidity remains in its muscles, which resists or breaks the force of its descent. Again, when a substance like melted sealing-wax, or a heated coin, falls upon the hand, the limb is snatched away at once, even before the feeling of pain has been recognized by the brain. When jolted in a rapidly moving car, we involuntarily step forward or backward, so as to preserve the centre of gravity of the body.

42. These and similar acts are executed by the same mechanism as that previously described in the case of paralysis from an injury of the spinal cord. The muscles thus called into play are those which are ordinarily under the sway of the will, but which in these

---

39. What are the requisites for the production of this form of nervous action?
40. Why do we not readily recognize the reflex activity of the cord in our own bodies? How best studied in others? Example?
41. Similar movements? Arm of a person? Melted wax or heated coin on the hand?
42. Result of healthful reflex activity? When may the reflex energy be deficient?

cases act through this reflex action of the cord, altogether independ-ently of the will. A healthful reflex activity produces an elasticity, or "tone," in the voluntary muscular system, which in a great measure explains the existence in the young and vigorous of a feeling of buoyancy and reserve power. Its possessor is restlessly active, and it may appropriately be said of him, " he rejoiceth as a strong man to run a race." But this reflex energy may be deficient. This is true when the blood is poor and wanting in its solid ingredients, or the circulation is feeble; the muscles, then, are flabby and weak, and the person himself is said to be "nerveless," or indisposed to exertion. Shivering from cold and trembling from fear may, in part, be referred to a temporary loss of tone, resulting from a powerful impression upon the brain. (*Read Note* 6.)

43. An excess of this activity may also be observed in disease. In this condition, the excitability of the cord is unnaturally aroused,

---

6. On Nervous Health, or Tone.—"That state of general vigor, which we call 'tone,' depends upon the healthy action of the nervous centres. It consists in the habitual moderate contraction of the muscles, due to a constant stimulus exerted on them by the cord, and is valuable less for itself than as a sign of a sound nervous balance. Tone is maintained partly by healthful impressions radiated upon the spinal cord through the nerves from all parts of the body, and partly by the stimulus poured down upon it from the brain. So it is disturbed by whatever conveys irritating or depressing influences in either direction. A single injudicious meal, a single sleepless night, a single passion or piece of bad news, will destroy it. On the other hand, a vivid hope, a cheerful resolve, an absorbing interest will restore it as if by magic. For in man, these lower officers in the nervous hierarchy draw their very breath according to the bidding of the higher powers. But the dependence of the higher on the lower is no less direct. The mutual action takes place in each line. A chief condition of keeping the brain healthy is to keep these unconscious nervous functions in full vigor, and in natural alternations of activity and repose. We see evidence of this law in the delightful effect of a cheerful walk after a depressed or irritated state of mind. Every part of the nervous system makes its influence felt by all the rest. A sort of constitutional monarchy exists within us; no power in this small state is absolute, or can escape the checks and limitations which the other powers impose. Doubtless the Brain is King, but Lords and Commons have their seats below and guard their privilege with jealous zeal. If the 'constitution' of your personal realm is to be preserved intact, it must be by the efforts of each part, lawfully directed to a common end."—*Hinton on Health and its Conditions.*

and frequent and violent movements of the limbs and body, called
convulsions, are the result.   The convulsions of young children,
and the nervous agitation of *chorea*, or St. Vitus's dance, are reflex
in character, as are also the symptoms attending poisoning by
strychnine, and those terrible diseases, *tetanus*, or "locked jaw,"
and *hydrophobia*.   The severity of the convulsions is not the same
in all cases of these disorders; but, in those last mentioned, the
most violent spasmodic movements are provoked by the slightest
form of irritation—such as the sound of pouring water, the sight of
any glittering object, the glancing of a mirror, the contact of cool
air, or even the touch of the bed-clothes.

44. Another variety of reflex motions takes place in certain involuntary muscles, and over these the cord exercises supreme control.   They are principally those movements which aid the performance of digestion and nutrition, the valve-action of the pylorus,
and other movements of the stomach and intestines.   In these
movements the mind shares no part.   And it is well that this is so;
for, since the mind is largely occupied with affairs external to the
body, it acts irregularly, becomes fatigued, and needs frequent rest.
The spinal cord, on the contrary, is well fitted for the form of work
on which depends the growth and support of the body, as it acts
uniformly, and with a machine-like regularity.

45. These operations are not accompanied by consciousness; for,
as a general rule, the attention is only called to them when they become disordered.   Many a person does not know where his stomach
is situated until he discovers its position by reason of a feeling of
distress within it, produced by giving that organ improper work to
perform.   In this manner the higher and nobler faculties of the
mind are liberated from the simply routine duties of the body, and
we are thus left to direct the attention, the reason, and the will to
the accomplishment of the great ends of our existence.   If it were
otherwise, we could only find time to attend to our ordinary physical
wants.

---

43. Excess of this activity in disease ? Hydrophobia, etc. ? The difference in severity of
the convulsions?
44. Another variety of reflex motions ? What are they ? What is stated of the mind in
connection with these movements ?
45. Consciousness in these operations ? Physical wants ?

46. The objects of the reflex activity of the cord are threefold. In the first place, it acts as the protector of man in his unconscious moments. It is his unseen guardian, always ready to act, never growing weary, and never requiring sleep. Nor does its faithful action wholly cease with the cessation of life in other parts. In the second place, it is the regulator of numerous involuntary motions that are necessary to the nutrition of the body. Here its actions are entirely independent of the brain, and are performed in a secret and automatic manner. And, thirdly, it acts as a substitute, and regulates involuntary movements in the muscles usually under the influence of the will. It thus takes the place of the higher faculties in performing habitual acts, and permits them to extend their operations more and more beyond the body and its material wants.

47. The Functions of the Medulla Oblongata.—The prolongation of the spinal cord within the skull has been previously spoken of as the medulla oblongata. It resembles the cord, in being composed of both white and gray matter, and in conducting sensory and motor influences. It likewise gives rise to certain nerves, which are here called cranial nerves (from *cranium*, the skull). All except two of these important nerves spring from the medulla, or the parts immediately adjoining it; the exceptions are the two nerves taking part in the special senses of sight and smell, which nerves have their origin at the base of the cerebrum.

48. The decussation, or crossing of the motor columns, has been previously described, when treating of the direction of the nerve-fibres of the cord; and the singular fact has been alluded to, that when one side of the brain is injured, its effects are limited to the opposite side of the body. One more fact remains to be observed in this connection, namely, this cross action does not usually take place in the cranial nerves. Accordingly, when apoplexy, or the rupture of a blood-vessel, occurs in the right hemisphere of the cerebrum, the left side of the body is paralyzed, but the right side of the face is affected; this is because that part of the body is supplied by the cranial nerves.

---

46. How many objects may the reflex activity be said to have? State the first. The second. The third.
47. How does the medulla oblongata resemble the cord?
48. What final fact is observed in the crossing of the motor columns?

49. A portion of the medulla presides over the important function of respiration, and from it arises the *pneumogastric* nerve, so called because its branches serve both the lungs and stomach. The feelings of hunger, thirst, and the desire for air are aroused by means of this nerve. The wounding of the gray matter of the medulla, even of a small portion of it, near the origin of the pneumogastric nerve, at once stops the action of the lungs and causes death. In consequence of the importance of this part, it has been termed the "vital knot." We find, also, that its location within the skull is exceedingly well protected, it being quite beyond the reach of any ordinary form of harm from without.

50. The Functions of the Cranial Ganglia.—The uses of the smaller gray masses lying at the base of the brain are not well ascertained; and, on account of their position, so remote from the surface, it would at first seem well-nigh impossible to study them. But, from the results following diseases in these parts, and from experiments upon inferior animals, they are becoming gradually better understood; and there is reason to believe that eventually the physiological office of each part will be clearly ascertained and defined. It is believed, however, but not absolutely proved, that the anterior masses, like the anterior roots of the spinal nerves and the anterior columns of the cord, are concerned in the production of motion; in fact, that they are the central organs of that function. The posterior gray masses are, on the contrary, supposed to be the seat of sensation.

51. The Function of the Cerebellum.—The function of the cerebellum, or "little brain," is the direction of the movements of the voluntary muscles. When this organ is the seat of disease or injury, it is usually observed that the person is unable to execute orderly and regular acts, but moves in a confused manner as if in a state of intoxication. Like the larger brain, or cerebrum, it appears to be devoid of feeling; but it takes no part in the operations of the mind.

52. The Function of the Cerebrum.—The cerebrum, or brain proper, is the seat of the mind; or, speaking more exactly, it is the

49. The pneumogastric nerve? The feelings aroused by it? The "vital knot?"
50. The uses of the smaller gray masses at the base of the brain?
51. Function of the cerebellum? When it is diseased?
52. Where is the seat of the mind? The subordination of the other organs? The gray matter?

material instrument by which the mind acts; and, as it occupies the highest position in the body, so it fulfills the loftiest uses. All the other organs are subordinate to it: the senses are its messengers, which bring it information from the outer world, and the organs of motion are its servants, which execute its commands. Here, as in the nervous apparatus of lower grade already considered, the gray matter is the element of power; and in proportion as this substance increases in extent, and in proportion to the number of convolutions in the hemispheres, do the mental faculties expand.

53. There have been a few, but only a few, men of distinguished ability whose brains have been comparatively small in size—the rule being that great men possess large brains. The relative weight of the brain of man, as compared with the weight of the body, does not, in all instances, exceed that of the inferior animals; the canary and other singing-birds have a greater relative amount of nervous matter than man; but man surpasses all other creatures in the size of the hemispheres of the cerebrum, and in the amount of gray substance which they contain.—(*Read Notes* 7 *and* 8.)

---

7. The Alliance of Mind and Body.—"The regular routine of our daily life is the counterpart of the mental routine. A healthy man wakens in the morning with a flush of spirits and energy; his first meal confirms and reinforces the state. The mental powers and susceptibilities are then at a maximum; as the nutrition is used up in the system they gradually fade, but may be renewed once and again by refreshment and brief remission of toil. Towards the end of the day lassitude sets in, and fades into the deep unconsciousness of healthy sleep. * * * The influences that affect the body extend not only to the grosser modes of feeling, and to such familiar exhibitions as after-dinner oratory, but also to the highest emotions—love, anger, æsthetic feeling, and moral sensibility. ' Health keeps an Atheist in the dark. Bodily affliction is often the cause of a total change in the moral nature."—*Bain's Mind and Body.*

8. Large Brains.—"As a rule the size of the brain is proportional to the mental development in human beings. The rule is not strictly maintained in every instance; occasionally a stupid man has a larger brain than a clever man. But these are only individual exceptions to a prevailing arrangement. The following are the brain weights of several distinguished men:

Cuvier	64.5 oz.	Lord Campbell	53.5 oz.
Abercrombie	63. "	Agassiz	53.4 "
Daniel Webster	53.5 "	De Morgan	52.7 "

---

53. What is stated of men in connection with the size of their brain? With the brains of other animals?

54. It is a singular fact that this cerebral substance is insensitive, and may be cut without causing pain. The removal of a consider-able quantity of the brain has taken place, as the result of accident, without causing death, and without even affecting seriously the intellect. A remarkable case of injury of the brain is recorded, in which, from the accidental explosion of gunpowder used in blasting a rock, the "tamping-iron" was driven directly through the skull of a man. This iron rod, three feet and seven inches long, an inch and a quarter in diameter, and weighing more than thirteen pounds, entered the head below the ear and passed out at the top of the skull, carrying with it portions of the brain and fragments of bone. The man sustained the loss of sight on one side, but otherwise re-covered his health and the use of his faculties. Moreover, disease has occurred, compromising a large portion of the brain, without impairing the faculties of the mind, when the disease was limited to one side only. (*Read Note* 9.)

"The average male brain in Europeans is 49.5 oz.; the female, 44 oz. Among idiots the weights have run from 27 to 8.5 oz. The brains of the insane are below the average of the sane. Tall men, as a rule, have larger brains than small men."—*Bain's Mind and Body*.

9. The Emotions Influence the Bodily Health.—"The exciting emotions which are pleasurable, such as joy and hope, are of a kind that seldom tend to a dangerous excess, and may be regarded as exercising generally an eminently healthful influence upon the body. Hilarity is a great refresher and strengthener of life. Laughter is a wholesome exercise, which, beginning at the lungs, diaphragm, and connected muscles, is continued to the whole body, 'shaking the sides,' and causing that jelly-like vibration of the frame of which we are so agreeably conscious when under its influence. The heart beats more briskly, but with a safe regularity of action, and sends the blood to the smallest and most distant vessel. The face glows with warmth and color, the eye brightens, and the temperature of the whole body is moderately raised. With the universal pleasurable sensation there comes a disposition of every organ to healthy action. When hilarity and its ordinary expression of laughter become habitual, the insensible perspiration of the skin is increased, the breathing quickened, the lungs and chest expanded, the appetite and digestion strengthened, and nutrition consequently increased. The old prov-erb, 'Laugh and grow fat,' states a scientific truth. The influence of laughter upon the body is recognized by Shakespeare, in his description of the

54. Sensitiveness of the brain substance? The removal of a portion of the brain? State the remarkable case mentioned.

55. Impressions conveyed to the hemispheres from the external world arouse the mental operations called thought, emotion, and the will. These are the godlike attributes which enable man to subjugate a world, and afterward cause him to "sigh for other worlds to conquer ;" which enable him to acquaint himself with the properties of planets millions of miles distant from him, and which give him that creative power by which he builds and peoples the new worlds of poetry and art.

56. All these mental acts, and many others, are developed through the action of the brain ; not that the brain and the mind are the same, or that the brain secretes memory, imagination, or the ideas of truth and justice, as the stomach secretes the gastric juice. But rather, as the nerve of the eye, stimulated by the subtile waves of light, occasions the notion of color, so the brain, called into action by the mysterious influences of the immaterial soul, gives rise to all intellectual, emotional, and voluntary activities.

57. The cerebrum, according to our present knowledge of it, must be regarded as a single organ, which produces different results, according as it is acted upon by the immaterial mind in different ways. Recent investigations, however, seem to prove that the faculty of language is dependent upon a small part of the left hemisphere of the cerebrum near the temple. At least, in almost every instance where this part is diseased, the patient can no longer express himself in speech and writing. (*Read Note* 10.)

'spare Cassius '—'Seldom he smiles.' 'To be free-minded and cheerfully disposed at hours of meat, and sleep, and exercise, is one of the best precepts of long-lasting.' Such is the testimony of Lord Bacon to the favorable influence of the pleasurable emotions upon the body. The depressing emotions, such as fear, anxiety, and grief, are always fatal to health, and frequent causes of death. There is an Eastern apologue which describes a stranger on the road meeting the Plague coming out of Bagdad.. 'You have been committing great havoc there,' said the traveler, pointing to the city. 'Not so great,' replied the Plague. 'I only killed one-third of those who died; the other two-thirds killed themselves with fright.' "—*The Book of Health.*

10. Mental Exercise Necessary to Perfect Health.—"The im-

---

55. Thought, emotion, and will ? What power do they give us ?
56. Are the brain and the mind identical ?
57. What do we know of the cerebrum and its powers ?

58. The Reflex Action of the Brain.—The reflex function of the organs within the skull is very active and important. Like that of the cord, it protects the body by involuntary movements, it regulates the so-called vegetative acts, and it takes the place of the will in controlling the voluntary muscles, when the attention is turned in other directions. The reflex power of the medulla governs the acts of respiration, which are absolutely and continuously essential to life. Respiration is, as we have seen, partly under the influence of the will; but this is due in part to the fact that respiration is indirectly concerned in one of the animal functions—that of speech.

59. Reflex action also occasions coughing and sneezing, whenever improper substances enter the air-passages. Winking is an act of the same sort, and serves both to shield the eyes from too great glare of light, and to preserve them by keeping the cornea moist. Looking at the sun or other strong light, causes sneezing by reflex action. Laughing, whether caused by tickling the feet or by some happy thought, and also sobbing, are reflex acts, taking place by means of the respiratory muscles.

60. Certain of the protective reflex movements call into play a large number of muscles, as in the balancing of the body when walk-

---

provement of the memory is a familiar instance of an increase of mental power produced by exercise; and the beating sense of fulness and quickened circulation in the head induced by intense study or thought, shows that an organic process goes on when the brain is in activity, similar to that which takes place in the muscular system under exercise. On the contrary, when the organ is little used, little expenditure of its power and substance takes place, little blood and little nervous energy are required for its support, and, therefore, little is sent; nutrition in consequence soon becomes languid, and strength impaired. To all these laws the brain is subject equally as the rest of the body. Frequent and regular exercise gives it increased susceptibility of action, with power to sustain it, the nervous energy acquiring strength as well as the vascular. Disuse of its functions, or, in other words, inactivity of intellect and of feeling, impairs its structure and weakens the several powers which it serves to manifest. The brain, therefore, in order to maintain its healthy state, requires to be duly exercised."—*Barlow on Physical Education.*

---

58. The reflex function of the organs within the skull? The reflex power of the medulla? Respiration?
59. What else does reflex action occasion? Winking? Other examples?
60. Muscles called into play by certain reflex movements? The somnambulist?

ing along a narrow ledge, or on a slippery pavement. The dodging motion of the recruit, when the first cannon ball passes over his head, is reflex and involuntary. The fact that these involuntary reflex acts are performed with great precision, will explain why it is that accidents seldom befall the somnambulist, or sleep-walker, although he often ventures in most perilous places.

61. Walking, sitting, and other acts of daily life, become automatic, or reflex, from habit : the mind is seldom directed to them, but delegates their control to the medulla and spinal cord. Thus a person in walking may traverse several miles while absorbed in thought, or in argument with a companion, and yet be conscious of scarcely one in a thousand of the acts that have been necessary to carry his body from one point to another. By this admirable and beautiful provision the mind is released from the charge of the ordinary mechanical acts of life, and may devote itself to the exercise of its nobler faculties. And it is worthy of notice, that the more these faculties are used, the more work does the reflex function assume and perform ; and thus the employment of the one insures the improvement of the other. (*Read Notes* 11 *and* 12.)

---

11. Automatic Action of the Brain.—"A large part of our mental activity consists of this unconscious work of the brain. There are many cases in which the mind has obviously worked more clearly and more successfully in this automatic condition, when left entirely to itself, than when we have been cudgeling our brains, so to speak, to get the solution. An instance, well authenticated, is related of a college student; he had been attending a class in mathematics, and the professor said to his students one day : 'A question of great difficulty has been referred to me by a banker—a very complicated question of accounts, which they have not themselves been able to bring to a satisfactory issue, and they have asked my assistance. I have been trying, and I cannot resolve it. I have covered whole sheets of paper with calculations, and have not been able to make it out. Will you try ?' He gave it to them as a sort of problem, and said he would be extremely obliged to any one who would bring him the solution by a certain day. This gentleman tried it over and over again ; he covered many slates with figures, but did not succeed. He was 'put on his mettle,' and determined to achieve the result. But he went to bed on the night before the solution was to be given in without having succeeded. In the morning, when he went to his desk, he found the whole

---

61. What is said of walking and other acts in connection with the office performed by the medulla and spinal cord ?

62. Effects of Alcohol upon the Brain.

—The brain under the influence of small and occasional doses of alcohol shows no serious changes other than an increased supply of blood to the head. Very serious changes, however, result from the habitual use of alcohol ; the brain becomes harder and tougher than is natural, and its cell elements show a wasting away, its substance appears shrunken, and an undue amount of watery fluid fills the cavities in the brain, in order to make up the diminished bulk. The blood-vessels of the brain are sometimes found to be in a weakened condition, and from this various diseased conditions may follow. (*Read Note* 13.)

problem worked out and in his own hand. He had risen in the night and unconsciously worked it out correctly, as the result proved ; and what is more curious still, the process was very much shorter than any of his previous trials."—*W. B. Carpenter on Unconscious Action.*

12. The Mind Should be Intelligently Cultivated.—"The cultivation of the mind should be carried on with judgment, and in due submission to the requirements of the body. If study be the duty of the youth, let him pursue it diligently, but with such intervals of rest and bodily exertion as may maintain good appetite and health.

"The proportion of hours of study and bodily exercise may vary with the degree of mental work, the healthfulness of the room and surrounding air, the natural strength of the body, and the degree of health ; but as a general rule it may be doubted whether any young person can sit at close study for more than two hours at a time without requiring bodily exertion to sustain vital action, and rest to recruit the mind. Two hours' mental work, and a quarter to half an hour's bodily exercise, will be quite compatible with the greatest progress in study.

"Moreover, it may be doubted whether such a student can work with advantage for more than eight hours a day, in addition to the intervals of rest, for the issue will not turn on the number of hours devoted to work, but the intensity of the attention given."—*Edward Smith on Health.*

13. Trembling due to Alcohol.—"Another condition is trembling due to alcohol. The hands are shaky, or unsteady, even when at rest, or if the hand is held out it is seen to vibrate slightly, or in more advanced condition, 'shakes like an aspen leaf.' I have seen this in a spirit-drinker, a barber, as almost the only symptom : he worked night and day, in shaving, and to 'steady his hand,' partook repeatedly of spirits—at first to relieve fatigue and then, because he saw that if he discontinued, his hand was too shaky to use the razor. Complete abstinence from alcohol and strong coffee quite removed his tremblings and his desire for spirits."—*Dr. W. S. Greenfield.*

<hr/>

62. How is the brain changed by alcohol ?

63. Effects of Alcohol on the Mind.—Alcohol produces an artificial insanity, in which, according to the quantity taken, the various types of mental diseases are distinctly manifest. The perceptions are bewildered, there is sleeplessness, loss of memory, delusion, clouded reasoning power, and benumbed moral sense following in the train of alcohol drinking. There is also a monomania caused by the prolonged use of alcohol—a craving for drink that knows no bounds, and but rarely a cure; this is dipsomania, or thirst-madness. (*Read Note* 14.)

64. The Impairment of the Will.—The direct result of the taking of alcohol is seen in the loss of self-control. "The worst estate of man is that wherein he loses the knowledge and government of himself." It is in the formation of the drinking habit that alcohol too often works the absolute ruin of its devotee, in both body and mind. It is apt to be a continuous habit, having for its sequel the dethronement of the will. It may be stated, as the rule, that after forty years of age, a man who has formed this habit is unequal by his own strength of will to abandon it. Many men of fine intellectual capacity and amiable qualities have become intemperate, and have so continued, as long as their efforts to get free again have not been supplemented by outside and enforced restraint.*

14. Alcohol a Poison of the Intellect.—"In the normal state of a man's mind, all the faculties, the imagination, the judgment, the memory, the association of ideas, are regulated by another superior faculty, viz., the attention. The attention of the will is the man himself; it is the *ego* which, being in the full possession of the resources of which it disposes, takes them where it will, when it will, to do whatever it pleases. Now in drunkenness, even at the very beginning, the will and the attention have disappeared. Nothing is left but the imagination and the memory, which, left to themselves, without regulation and without guides, produce the most irrational results."—*Charles Richet.*

* "Alcohol in small doses super-excites certain intellectual faculties—the imagination, the memory, and the association of ideas; but it paralyzes others, especially the will, the reflection, and judgment. Yet, with a stronger dose all trace of intelligence disappears. When old Sly is stretched on the ground insensible from drink and snoring in the mud, he excites compassion and disgust:

O monstrous beast! how like a swine he lies!
Grim death, how foul and loathsome is thine image!"

Charles Richet, in Revue des Deux Mondes.

63. What changes are noticed in the mind?
64. Give effect of alcohol upon the will.

It is for such as these that inebriate asylums have been built Other hard drinkers drift into violence and crime, and finally find a curative restraint within prison walls. The benumbing effects of drinking habits upon the moral being of man is universally known. "All delicacy, courtesy, and self-respect are gone; the sense of justice and of right is faint or quite extinct; there is no vice into which the victim of drunkenness does not easily slide, and no crime from which he can be expected to refrain. Between this condition and insanity there is but a single step," and death, in a worldly sense a deliverance, in spite of many an effort to rally, "terminates the miserable scene; one by one lights have been removed from the banquet of folly, and the last is now extinguished." (*Read Notes 15 and* 16.)

65. An illustration of the disadvantage of drunkenness to the moral tone of a community may be drawn from the results of the labors of Father Matthew, about forty years ago, as a temperance reformer. In the five years—1838–1842—the consumption of whiskey in Ireland fell 50 per cent.; the crimes of violence falling from 64,520 to

---

15. Drunkenness and Insanity.—"The connection between drunkenness and crime and drunkenness and poverty, is close and unvarying in its effect upon society. The remarkable increase of insanity in recent years may in part be traced to the use of intoxicating beverages. It has been asserted that at least seven-tenths of all the crime and poverty and calamity to the people of the United States spring from the abuse of liquors."—*Dr. J. E. Reeves.*

16. The Effects of Mild Stimulation.—"Words of caution to young men concerning the injurious effects of tobacco, as well as indulgence in wine or the pleasures of the table, elicit, in ninety-nine out of one hundred cases, the reply, 'It does not hurt me.' Does not hurt you! Wait and see. In years to come, when you ought to be in your prime, you will be a poor, nervous, irritable, nerve-dried creature. Your hands will tremble, your head will ache, your sleep be fitful and disturbed, your digestion impaired—in short, the unnatural and transient pleasure at one end of your life will be more than counterbalanced by the discomfort and misery at the other. It is a truth of the greatest moment, which ought to be so impressed upon the mind as to be always rising up within it, that *transgressions of the laws of health, not punished at one end of life, are sure to be at the other.*"—*J. R. Black on the Ten Laws of Health.*

47,027, and executions from 59 in the first year to 1 in the last year. (*Read Note* 17.)

66. The Poisonous Effects of Alcohol.—Alcohol is, in the main, a narcotic poison in its effects upon human beings, although the visible results vary immensely according to the quantity taken. If a sufficient quantity is taken to cause any visible result, a condition known as stimulation is observed.* If an extremely large dose is taken, a state of stupor follows, and death has been known to result in some cases. Between these two extremes there may be a variety of manifestations. As a stimulant, it appears to many to have a kindly action, to cause a glow and sense of warmth, to increase muscular activity, and to make the mind and organs of speech more nimble. Alcohol is not the only narcotic poison that exercises this influence, which is not kindly, but is in fact the first indica-

---

17. Alcohol and Crime.—"Thirty years of judicial experience have taught me that of the crimes which judges are called upon to try, and upon which sentences of the law are pronounced, more than eight-tenths of them involving any degree of violence in their character are directly traceable to the liquor shops. How often have I had young men look up at me when I asked them what they had to say why the sentence of the law should not be pronounced, declare, 'I should never have done this crime if it were not for drink. Rum was my ruin; rum struck the blow, and not my hand, that killed the man for whose death I am tried; rum has caused me to beat my wife, and injure my helpless child, and to do the act which now confines me to a prison.''—*Judge Noah Davis.*

* "Suppose, for instance, you measure your muscular strength with a 'health lift' or dynamometer (by which muscular exertion can be accurately measured), and then take some of the drink, in the strength-inspiring power of which you have most confidence, and when you are most exhilarated by it, and feel as if you could shoulder a large fragment of Mount Olympus, measure your strength again. The drink has fooled you, that is all. You *felt* that you were stronger than natural; you *find* that the narcotic has been true to its paralyzing nature, and that you are weaker. Then, after a time, when the drug has spent itself, and reaction (so called) comes on, and you feel weak and prostrated, measure your strength once more. Fooled again; the stuff has fooled you twice. When you felt yourself strong you were weak, and now when you feel yourself weak, you find yourself stronger—your natural strength is returning, and what you have called reaction is in reality recovery from the weakening effects of the narcotic."—*Dr. A. F. Kinne.*

---

66. Poisonous effects of alcohol?

tion of a paralysis of a portion of the nervous system. Most of the habitual takers of alcohol freely admit that they are injured by it in one way or another, and still they continue in their indulgence. In such cases the mental balance is already lost; for a person to covet that which he knows to be hurtful to him, is manifestly not the sign of a sound mind. (*Read Note* 18.)

67. Tobacco and its Effects.—Tobacco, familiarly known as "the weed," is an annual plant said to be a native of America. It grows to the height of several feet, with leaves of a pale green color. These leaves, when dried, are made into cigars, chewing-tobacco, and snuff, which are extensively used throughout the civilized world.

68. Tobacco as a Poison.—Tobacco is a poison to the young, and is far more hurtful to the adult than is generally supposed. It may be stated, as a rule, that there are few persons who use it habitually that do not suffer injury from it. The injury is mainly caused by what is known as "nicotine," one of the narcotic poisons, and particularly prominent in tobacco. Some of the effects of its limited use are nausea, vomiting, vertigo, and weakness; and its prolonged use, by those who are sensitive to it, often results in convulsions and other like symptoms, together with an irritability and weakened condition of the heart, known to physicians as the "tobacco-heart."

---

18. "Here is a company of 'jolly good fellows,' all standing on their feet, their faces red and radiant, and all swinging their arms and talking at once. These men have been taking alcohol, and, surely, you will say, it has stimulated them. But if you will attend for a moment to what they are saying, you will see that there is no true brain-stimulation about it. We shall be reminded rather of what Addison says of the difference between the mind of the wise man and that of the fool : 'There are infinite, numberless extravagancies, and a succession of vanities which pass through both. The great difference is that the first knows how to pick and cull his thoughts for conversation, by suppressing some and communicating others ; whereas the other lets them all indifferently fly out in words.' The case with these revelers is precisely this. The poison which they have taken has paralyzed their conservative faculties, and the talking propensity is running on without anything to hold it in check and regulate it."—*Dr. A. F. Kinne.*

---

67. Describe the tobacco plant.
68. What is its effect upon the nerves?

69. Effects on the Young.—Of the pernicious influence of the use of tobacco upon the young, the testimony of the Naval and Military Academies of the country is very decided. It has at times been allowed in both institutions, but at present it is forbidden, on the ground that its use is attended with serious damage to health. It is stated that its prohibition at the Naval Academy in 1881 was received with unanimous approval by the officers in charge, and with "great joy by many of the cadets." Tremor of the muscles, caused by smoking, was very noticeable in the drawings that form so important a part of the cadets' work. A teacher of drawing, of fourteen years experience, has said that he can always tell from the character of the lines in the drawings, whether or not the pupils used tobacco.* Its avoidance has resulted in the reduced number of minor ailments that swelled the sick-list in years when its use was unrestricted. Athletes and other persons who engage in running matches and the like, are commonly not allowed to use either alcohol or tobacco while they are "in training;" their use interferes with the fullest development of muscular strength. (*Read Note* 19.)

---

* "Prof. Mantegazza, of Florence, Italy, a distinguished sanitarian and physician, testifies that 'Tobacco is never necessary; it is always hurtful to boys and young men, to weak people, and those disposed to consumption. * * * * All good citizens should try to put a stop to the general invasion of tobacco, which threatens to involve the whole of Europe in a dense cloud of smoke, which poisons even those who do not smoke.'"

19. "The end of all science is to secure long life and good health to the individual and the race, and it ought to be a part of the rational creed of every good man and woman to abjure the use of tobacco, and keep others from falling into the vice."—*Dr. C. R. Drysdale.*

"Of tobacco, Franklin said that he could not think it had ever done much good in the world, since he never knew a person who used it habitually who would recommend another to do the same."

"Tobacco is certainly not a food for man, nor has it much value as a medicine. The tobacco-worm is the only animal known to thrive upon it."—*F. H. Hamilton.*

"An illustration of the depressing influence of tobacco is given by Dr. Jacob Bigelow, who states that soldiers, when wishing to shirk duty and get on the sick-list, sometimes succeed in bringing on the symptoms of alarming sickness by wearing a piece of tobacco under each arm-pit. The skin absorbs sufficient of the poison to affect the system to a marked degree."

70. Cigarette-Smoking.—This form of taking tobacco is injurious in two particulars that do not apply to the other forms. The smoker of cigarettes, either voluntarily or involuntarily, takes into his lungs a very large amount of smoke, and with it that hurtful element, carbonic oxide. Again, there is an excessive amount of adulteration of the tobacco in cigarettes; and one substance, opium, is largely so used and is extremely injurious.

71. Snuff-Taking.—In addition to the hurtful effects of tobacco generally, snuff-taking is notoriously injurious to the senses of smell and taste, and to the voice.

72. Narcotics.—The term narcotic is applied to different substances derived chiefly from the vegetable kingdom, which have the wonderful property of quieting pain and causing sleep. Next in importance to alcohol, which belongs to the narcotics, are opium (and its preparations), chloral hydrate, hasheesh and chloroform.

73. Opium.—Opium is the thickened juice of the poppy-plant of India, and is commonly regarded as the most important of the narcotics. Its active principle is morphine, which gives the soothing property to laudanum, paregoric, and Dover's powders. It is also used in nostrums to put infants to sleep: but unwisely used, often brings on a sleep that knows no waking.

74. Effects of Opium.—Opium is particularly injurious to the young, even small doses sometimes producing alarming symptoms. Upon adults the external effects are not as noticeable as are those of alcohol, but the mind is more deeply stirred and the flow of ideas more copious.

75. Danger from Opiates.—The use of opium for relieving pain has been known for hundreds of years. The enchanting sense of relief to suffering wrought by opiates leads to the morphine habit, commonly called opium-eating. It will be seen, therefore, why such great care is exercised by physicians in administering opiates, lest their patients afterward fall into the habit of taking them without medical advice. (*Read Note* 20.)

20. "The opium-eater loses none of his moral sensibilities or aspirations; he wishes and longs as earnestly as ever to realize what he believes possible,

70. What is said of cigarette-smoking ?
71. Snuff-taking?
72. What do you understand by narcotics ?

73. What is opium?
74. What are the effects of using opium ?
75. What the danger?

76. Physiological Effects of Opium.—The frequent use of opium disturbs and weakens the stomach as well as the other digestive organs; hence we invariably find the opium-eater to be a lean, yellow, sallow person. His muscular and mental powers are impaired, and his will is terribly enfeebled. This dreadful habit can be broken only with unspeakable suffering to its victim.

77. Chloral Hydrate. — Chloral hydrate, commonly called chloral, is produced from alcohol; but its power as a sedative was not generally known until within the past twenty years. It also is a destroyer of appetite as well as of digestion, unless prescribed in proper doses, and the unfortunates once given over to it find themselves unable to sleep without its continued use. It should never be taken except under the direction of a physician.

78. Hasheesh.—Hasheesh, the juice of Indian hemp, is said to be used by millions of the inhabitants of Asia. It is not much known in the western countries. In the East the excitement caused by its use takes the form of furious madness, leading its victim to commit acts of violence and murder. Hence the term " hasheeshers " in our language has come to be synonymous with assassins. (*Read Note* 21.)

79. Chloroform.—Chloroform, another product from alcohol, is

---

and feels to be exacted by duty; but his intellectual apprehensions of what is possible infinitely outruns his power, not of execution only, but even the power to attempt. He lies under the weight of incubus and nightmare; he lies in sight of all that he would fain perform, just as a man forcibly confined to his bed by the mortal languor of a relaxing disease, who is compelled to witness injury and outrage offered to some object of his tenderest love; he curses the spells which chain him down from motion; he would lay down his life if he might but get up and walk; but he is powerless as an infant, and cannot even attempt to rise."—*De Quincey's Confessions of an Opium-Eater.*

21. "As everybody knows, the intoxication caused by alcoholic liquors, by hasheesh, by opium, after a first period of excitement, brings about a notable impairment of the will. The individual is more or less conscious of this; other persons see it more clearly. Soon—especially under the influence of alcohol—the weakening of the will becomes excessive. The extravagances, violences, and crimes committed in this state are innumerable."—*Dr. T. Ribot.*

---

76. What effect upon the system ?
77. What do you know of chloral hydrate ?
78. What is hasheesh? Its use?
79. Chloroform? Its use?

used by inhalation when surgical operations are to be performed.
As it is very powerful and subtle in its action, the unskillful use
of it is dangerous in the extreme. The habit of taking chloroform
by those who are great physical sufferers, or whose constitutions
have been wrecked by the use of other narcotics, should be discouraged. It too often happens that the career of such is short,
for the drug may easily be taken in excess and so cause death.

80. Sleep Produced by Narcotics.—Opium and the opiates
have the power of quieting the activity of the brain, and of compelling sleep. This may be a blessed action if skilfully applied
by the physician, but not so applied it is the source of infinite peril.
The sleep so caused differs from natural, restful slumber, especially
in the fact that the after effects are commonly depressing and
disturbing to the brain to the extent of being harder to bear
than the wakefulness on account of which the drugs are taken.
Very young persons are especially subject to injury by sleep-
producing medicines; and many are the deaths that have been
caused among infants by the giving of " soothing syrups," " cordials,"
and "anodynes," that are so freely made and sold for the purpose of
compelling sleep.

81. Results of the Use of Narcotics.—The use of any of these
narcotics, without proper medical advice, is their abuse. In this
way they become powerful for harm. They are no longer remedies,
but poisons. Self-prescribed, they have a thousand times been the
instrument of unintentional suicide. (*Read Note* 22.)

---

22. The Narcotics and Digestion.—"The habitual use of opium and
other narcotic drugs is unfriendly to digestion, leading to nausea and a
distaste for wholesome food. The vigor of the organs of digestion is
impaired.

"The disturbing effects of tobacco, in producing nausea and vomiting, is
well known, and is almost the invariable experience of all beginners in the use
of that substance; loss of appetite is a very frequent result of the habitual
use of it."

---

80. What kind of sleep produced by narcotics?
81. What the results of the use of narcotics?

QUESTIONS FOR TOPICAL REVIEW.

CHAPTER X.

THE SPECIAL SENSES.

The Production of Sensations—Variety of Sensations—General Sensibility—Pain and its Function—Special Sensation, Touch, Taste, Smell, Sight, and Hearing—The Hand, the Organ of Touch—The Sense of Touch—Delicacy of Touch—Sensation of Temperature and Weight—The Tongue, the Organ of Taste—The Nerves of Taste—The Sense of Taste and its Relations with the other Senses—The Influence of Education on the Taste—The Nasal Cavities, or the Organs of Smell—The Olfactory Nerve—The Uses of the Sense of Smell—The Sense of Sight—Light—The Optic Nerve—The Eyeball and its Coverings—The Function of the Iris—The Sclerotic, Choroid, and Retina—The Tears and their Function—The Movements of the Eyeball—The Function of Accommodation—The Sense of Hearing and Sound—The Ear, or the Organ of Hearing—The External, Middle, and Internal Ear.

1. Production of Sensations.—We have already seen that the true centre of sensation is some organ within the skull, probably among the gray masses at the base of the brain; but the mind never perceives impressions at that point; on the contrary, it always refers them to the external organs of sensation. Hence, it is convenient to say that those outer parts possess the property of sensibility. For instance, we say that we hear with the ear, taste with the tongue, and feel with the fingers. That this is not the exact truth is proved by the fact that, whenever the nerve connecting one of these organs with the brain is severed, it at once loses its capacity for sensation.

2. Consciousness, another faculty of the brain, is necessary to complete a sensation. During sleep, and in other unconscious states, the usual impressions are presented to the ear, the nose, and

---

1. True centre of sensation? Place of the mind's impressions? What is it convenient to say? What further is stated?
2. Consciousness? During sleep? In profound insensibility?

the skin; but they fail to excite sensations, because the nerve-centres are inactive. In profound insensibility, from chloroform or ether, a limb may be removed without occasioning the least feeling.

3. Variety of Sensations.—All animals have some degree of sensibility. It is, of course, feeble and indistinct in the lower forms of life, but increases in power and variety as we ascend the scale. In the earth-worm, the nervous system is very simple, the sensibility being moderate and alike in all parts; hence, if its body be cut into two pieces, each piece will have the same degree of feeling as before. As we approach man, however, the sensations multiply and become more acute; the organs are more complex, and special parts are endowed with special gifts. These special organs cannot be separated from the rest of the body without the loss of the functions they are designed to exercise.

4. The lowest form of sensation—that of simple contact—is possessed by the lowest of the animal creation. The highest forms are those by which we are enabled to know the properties of external objects, such as shape, size, sound, and color. A variety of means of communicating with the outer world is the necessary possession of a high intelligence. Sensations are modified by use. They become more acute and powerful by moderate exercise, or they are dulled by undue excitement. The former is shown by the acute hearing of the Indian, by the sharp sight of the sailor, and by the delicate touch of the blind. The latter is exemplified by the impaired hearing of the boiler-maker, and the depraved taste of him who uses pungent condiments with his food. Again, impressions habitually presented may not be consciously felt, as is the case with the rumbling of carriages in a neighboring street, or the regular ticking of a clock. All sensations become less vivid with the advance of age, especially hearing and vision.

5. General Sensibility.—There is a property possessed by nearly all parts of the human body which we call general sensibility. We have recently seen that the brain is wholly insensitive, and may be cut or pinched without pain. The same is true of the nails, hair,

3. Sensibility in animals? In the earth-worm? In man?
4. The lowest form of sensation? The highest? Sensations, how modified? What further can you state as to habitual impressions?
5. General sensibility? What have we seen as regards the brain? Of what other structures is the same true?

the scarf-skin or external covering of the body, and a few other structures. In these parts no nerves are found. On the other hand, the sensibility of the true skin, and of mucous membranes, as of the eye and nose, is exquisite, these organs having a large supply of sensory nerve-fibres. The bones and tendons have less of these fibres, and are only moderately sensitive.

6. The sensibility of any part of the body, then, depends upon the number of nerves present; and, as a rule, the nervous supply is proportional to the importance of the part, and to its liability to injury. When, therefore, a surgical operation is performed, the most painful part of it is the incision through the skin—the muscles, cartilage, and bone being comparatively without sensation. Hence, if we could benumb the surface, certain of the lesser operations might be undergone without great inconvenience. This is, in fact, very successfully accomplished by means of the cold produced by throwing a spray of ether, or of some other rapidly evaporating liquid upon the part to be cut.

7. Tickling is a modification of general sensibility. At first it excites a pleasurable sensation, but this soon passes into pain. It is only present in those parts where the sense of touch is feeble. But all impressions are not received from without; there are, also, certain internal sensations, as they are called, which depend upon the condition of the internal organs, such as appetite, hunger, thirst, dizziness when looking down from some lofty position, drowsiness, fatigue, and other feelings of comfort or discomfort. General sensibility, whether of the internal or external organs of the body, chiefly depends upon the sensory fibres of the spinal nerve. The face, however, is supplied by the sensory cranial nerves. The sympathetic system has a low grade of feeling in health, but disease in the parts served by it arouses an intense degree of pain.

8. The Sensation of Pain.—What then is *pain?* Is it identical with ordinary sensibility? There seems to be some necessary connection between the two feelings, for they take place through

---

6. The cause of sensibility? Painful part in a surgical operation? Benumbing the surface? How done by ether?
7. Tickling? Internal sensations? The nerves of general sensibility?
8. Connection between pain and sensibility?

the same channels, and they are alike intense in the same situations. But sensibility habitually contributes to our sources of pleasure—the very opposite of pain; hence, these feelings cannot be identical.

9. Pain must, therefore, be a modification of the general sensibility which follows an excessive degree of excitement of the nerves, there being a natural limit to the amount of stimulation which they will sustain. So long as this limit is observed, the part excited may be said to be simply sensitive; but when it is exceeded, the impression becomes painful. This difference between sensibility and pain is well shown by the effects of sunlight upon the eye. The indirect illumination of the sun arouses only the former feeling, and is indispensable to our comfort and existence, while the direct ray received into the eye occasions great pain.

10. The Uses of Pain.—The dread of pain is a valuable monitor to the body. It puts us on our guard in the presence of danger, teaches moderation in the use of our powers, indicates the approach of disease, and calls attention to it when present. The word disease, in fact, according to its original use, had reference simply to the pain, or want of ease, which commonly attends disordered health. When we observe the serious mishaps which occur when sensibility and pain are absent, we cannot fail to appreciate its value. For example, a paralytic, in taking a foot-bath, forgets to test its temperature, and putting his limbs into water while it is too hot, is severely scalded without knowing it.

11. A traveler, overcome by cold and fatigue, lies down and falls asleep near a large fire, and when he is aroused in the morning, it is discovered that one of his feet has been insensibly destroyed. A grain of sand, lodging in an insensitive eye, may cause inflammation, and even the loss of sight. If intense light were not painful to the eye, many a child would innocently gaze upon the glories of the sun to the ruin of his sight.

12. Pain is, indeed, a present evil, but its relations with the future prove its mission merciful. Painful impressions cannot be

---

9. Explain the difference between pain and sensibility.
10. Dread of pain? How may its value be appreciated? Example?
11. The case of the traveler? Grain of sand? The sun and child?
12. Mission of pain? Painful impressions compared with those of pleasure?

recollected from past experience, and they cannot be called into existence by the fancy. Considered in the light of results, pain has a use above that of pleasure; for, while the immoderate pursuit of the latter leads to harm, the tendency of pain is to restrict the hurtful courses of life, and in this manner to protect the body.

13. The relations of pain to pleasure are thus described by the eminent physiologist, Magendie:—"By these sensations Nature induces us to concur in the order which she has established among organized beings. Though it may appear like sophistry to say that pain is the shadow of pleasure, yet it is certain that those who have exhausted the ordinary sources of pleasure have recourse to the causes of pain, and gratify themselves by their effects. Do we not see in all large cities, that men who are debauched and depraved find agreeable sensations where others experience only intolerable pain?" (*Read Note* 1.)

14. As to painful sensation among the inferior animals, the plan of Nature seems to be, that the higher the intelligence of the crea-

---

1. **Pain is "Nature's Harbinger of Mischief."**—"It must, therefore, be evident that pain is, under certain circumstances, really beneficial. It is often a great boon to have a sensitive stomach; for those who suffer pain after food are less apt habitually to err in diet, and thus to become dyspeptic or gouty, than those whose organs receive everything uncomplainingly. Pain in the stomach is frequently due (in well-to-do people) to the fact that they won't work and will eat; not that the stomach itself is weak (as they think), but that the supply of food being greater than the demand, the system becomes overstocked. In dyspepsia the cause is very often far away, and the stomach is no more the cause of the malady than the big toe is of the gout; but if the stomach gave no signs of perturbation, the evil would be allowed longer to exist unnoticed. We should always give early attention to pain, and discover its causes before they become too complex to be unraveled, and before the derangement which its presence indicates becomes permanent. The following incident well illustrates the extent to which pain may be dependent on fancy: 'A butcher was brought into a druggist's from the market-place opposite, laboring under a terrible accident. The man, on trying to hook up a heavy piece of meat above his head, slipped, and the sharp hook penetrated his arm so that he himself was suspended. On being examined, he was pale, almost pulseless, and expressed himself as suffering acute agony. The arm could not be moved without causing excessive pain, and in cutting off the

---

ture, and the more complete its power of defence, the more acute is its sensibility. We infer, therefore, that animals low in the scale of existence, and helpless, are not very liable to suffer pain.

15. Special Sensation.—The sensations of simple contact and pain are felt by nearly all parts of the system, whether external or internal, and are the necessary consequence of the general sensibility; but, so far as the objects which surround us are concerned, these impressions are vague and passive in character, and inform the mind of none of the properties or powers of these objects. Besides these feelings, therefore, man is endowed with certain special sensations, which are positive and distinct in character, and which he can call into exercise at will, and employ in the pursuit of knowledge. For reasons relating to the original constitution of the body, these sensations are to be regarded as modifications of the general sensibility already alluded to, constructed with special reference to the different forces of Nature of which we have any knowledge, such as heat, motion, gravity, sunlight, and the like. (*Read Note* 2.)

---

sleeve he frequently cried out; yet, when the arm was exposed, it was found quite uninjured, the hook having only traversed the sleeve of the coat!' The sensation here was perfectly real, but originated in a change of the brain and nerves, instead of in the external senses."—*Notes on Pain.*

2. **The Mutual Relations of the Special Senses.**—"A blind man attempting to express his notion of scarlet, said it resembled the sound of a trumpet. We are constantly reminded of the impressions of one sense by the operations of another. To my ear the bass note in music is what a dull black is to the eye. The reverberations of deep thunder seem like boulders with worn angles—with profiles blunt and irregular, as if drawn by the jerking pencil of the lightning; and one who never had the pleasure of seeing stars from a blow on the head, may get a tolerably correct idea of that kind of galaxy by snuffing at a bottle of volatile salts.

"Language is full of effort to report the impressions of one sense by the symbols of another. We say that an apple is sweet, that a rose is sweet, a face is sweet, a strain of music is sweet, and love is sweet, not to mention the saccharine reaction of the 'uses of adversity.' Here taste, smell, sight, hearing, and a social sentiment use the same word for that pleasurable sensation experienced by the mind through each distinctive organ. We assist the organ of one sense by that of another. We open the lips and part the teeth a little

---

15. The sensation of contact and pain? Special sensations of man? How regarded?

16. These distinct and active faculties are termed the special senses, and are five in number, viz., Touch, Taste, Smell, Sight, and Hearing. For the exercise of these senses, special organs are furnished, such as the hand, the tongue, the nose, the eye, and the ear. The manner in which the nerves of special sense terminate varies in the case of each organ, so that each is adapted to one set of sensations alone, and is incapable of perceiving any other. Thus the nerve of hearing is excited by the waves of sound, and not by those of light, while the reverse is true of the nerve of sight; and the nerve of smell can appreciate neither of them, being capable only of taking cognizance of the odorous properties of bodies. (*Read Note* 3.)

17. By some writers six senses are accorded to man, the addi-

---

when we are eager to hear; we listen and turn the eyes' attention inward when we would detect a delicate taste, or remember a faded impression.

"But this mutual accommodation of the senses is not so marvelous as it may seem, when we remember that the whole five, six, or seven, as you please, are but one power of nervous perception, specialized into a variety of functions, differentiated, as the learned say, that we may have more perfect work by a division of labor. The same necessity which developed nerve-contact into sight on the one hand and hearing on the other, might also express through one of these the sensations proper to the other, when the other was wanting. Seal up the eyes of a bat, say the naturalists, and let it loose in a room crossed with wires in every direction, and he will fly clear of them all, as if he had other means of perception as sensitive as the optic nerve.

"Laura Bridgman, with neither sight, hearing, nor smell, could detect the presence of a stranger in the room, without contact. Her mind then must have as distinct an image of every person as we have, yet not one of what we call our senses could go to the making up of that image. It could not be form as we know it, nor a voice, nor an odor, but it was itself other than all, exciting emotions of love, or hate, gratitude or repugnance, and the thought it excited must have had shape, though it is not easy to imagine how."—*The Schoolmaster.*

3. Variation in Structure in the Nerves of Special Sense.— "While in the more intellectual senses—Sight, Hearing, and Touch—the nerves have their protecting and isolating sheaths corresponding with the distinctness and separateness of the parts of the impression, in Smell, the nerves are a plexus of unsheathed fibres, corresponding with the fusion of the odorous impression into one whole, without distinction of parts."—*Herbert Spencer.*

---

16. What are the special senses? Special organs for them?
17. What is said in relation to one more than the five senses?

tional one being either the sense of temperature—for, as we shall presently see, this is not the same as touch—or, according to others, the muscular sense by which we are enabled to estimate the weights of bodies. The latter also differs in some respects from the sense of touch.

18. Organs of Touch.—The sense of touch is possessed by nearly all portions of the general surface of the body, but it finds its highest development in the hands. The human hand is properly regarded as the model organ of touch. The minute structure of the skin fits it admirably for this form of sensation; the cuticle, or scarf-skin, is fine and flexible, while the cutis, or true-skin, contains multitudes of nerve-filaments, arranged in rows of *papillæ* or cone-like projections, about one one-hundredth of an inch in length. It is estimated that there are 20,000 of these papillæ in a square-inch of the palmar surface of the hand. Now, although the nerves of the cutis are the instruments by which impressions are received and transmitted to the brain, yet the cuticle is essential to the sensation of touch. This is shown by the fact that whenever the true-skin is laid bare, as by a burn or blister, the only feeling that it experiences from contact is one of pain, not that of touch.

19. The office of the cuticle is thus made evident; it is to shield the nerve-filaments from direct contact with external objects. At the tips of the fingers, where touch is most delicate, the skin rests upon a cushion of elastic material, and receives firmness and permanence of shape by means of the nail placed upon the less sensitive side. Besides these favorable conditions, the form of the arm is such, and its motions are so easy and varied, that we are able to apply the test of touch in a great number of directions. The slender, tapering fingers, with their pliant joints, together with the strong opposing thumb, enable the hand to grasp a great variety of objects; so that, great as are the delicacy and grace of the hand, it is not wanting in the elements of power.

20. Its beauty and adaptation to the wants of man have made the hand an attractive theme for philosophers. They do not, however, always agree in their conclusions. One has the opinion that

18. The sense of touch, how prevalent? What is said of the hand?
19. Office of the cuticle? Tips of the fingers? The fingers with thumb?
20. What special importance is attributed to the hand?

man has acquired his intelligence and achieved his place as "lord of creation," because he has this organ. Buffon, in effect, declares that with fingers twice as numerous, and twice as long, we would become proportionally wiser; but Galen long ago took a more reasonable view, when he taught that "man is the wisest of animals, not because he possesses the hand, but because he is the wisest, and understands its use; for his mind, not his hand, has taught him the arts." Another has well said, that "no one can study carefully the human hand and fail to be convinced of the existence of the Deity."

21. The Sense of Touch.—Touch is the simplest of the senses. It is that which the child first calls into exercise in solving the early problems of existence, and it is that which is in the most constant use throughout life. We are brought by the touch into the most intimate relations with external objects, and by it we learn the greater number, if not the most important, of the properties of these objects, such as size, figure, solidity, motion, and smoothness or roughness of surface.

22. The sense of touch assists the other senses, especially that of sight, giving foundation and reality to their perceptions. Without it, the impressions received by the eye would be as vague and unreal as the figures that float through our dreams. A boy who had been blind from birth, at the age of twelve years received sight by means of a surgical operation; at first, he was unable to distinguish between a globe and a circular card of the same color before he had touched them. After that, he at once recognized the difference in their form. He knew the peculiarities of a dog and a cat by feeling, but not by sight, until one day, happening to take up the cat, he recognized the connection of the two sorts of impressions—those of touch and sight; and then, putting the cat down, he said: "So, puss, I shall know you next time."

23. Of all the senses, touch is considered the least liable to error; yet, if that part of the skin by which the sense is exercised is removed from its customary position, a false impression may be created in the mind. This is well illustrated by an experiment, which dates from

21. The simplicity of touch? What does it teach us?
22. Importance of the sense of touch to the development of the other senses?
23. Liability of touch to err? Describe the illustration.

the time of Aristotle. If we cross the middle finger behind the fore-finger, and then roll a marble or some small object upon the tips of the fingers (see Fig. 54), the impression will be that two marbles are felt. If the fingers, thus transposed, be applied to the end of the tongue, two tongues will be felt. When the nose is accidentally destroyed, the surgeon sometimes performs an operation for the purpose of forming a new one, by transplanting a partially removed

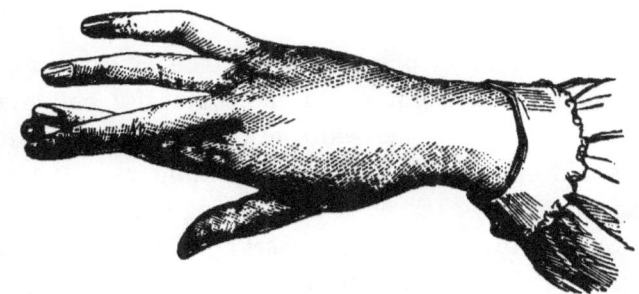

Fig. 54.

piece of the skin of the forehead upon the injured part; then, if the new nose be touched or pinched, the feeling is referred to the forehead. This fact illustrates one important truth—that the nerves will re-unite after they have been cut and feeling will be restored; if it were otherwise, a succession of slight cuts upon the fingers would seriously impair their tactile sensibility.

24. The Delicacy of Touch.—Although the hand is the proper organ of this sense, yet it is exercised by various parts of the body, their degree of sensibility being proportional to the number of papillæ they contain. The varying degrees of tactile delicacy of the different parts of the surface have been measured in an ingen-ious manner, by means of a pair of compasses, tipped with small pieces of cork. The two points of the compasses are touched at the same moment to the skin, the eyes being closed, and it is found that, in sensitive parts, the distance between the points may be quite slight, and yet each be plainly felt; while, in less sensitive parts, the points of the compasses are felt as a single point, although they are separated one or two inches.

25. At the tips of the fingers, the distance between the points being one-twentieth of an inch, a double impression is felt. The distance must be twice as great for the palm, four times as great for the lips, and, on the forehead, it must be twenty times greater. At the middle of the back, where the touch is least acute, the points must be separated more than two inches before they can be separately felt. Therefore, the sense of touch in the fingers is said to be fifty times more delicate than upon the posterior surface of the body.

26. Exquisite delicacy of touch is attained by practice. This is shown in many of the lighter and more graceful employments of daily life. Without it, the skill of the painter, sculptor, and musician would be rude indeed. By training, also, the physician acquires the *tactus eruditus*, or discriminating touch; but among the blind, delicacy of touch is most remarkable, and it there finds its highest value; for its possession, in a measure, compensates for the loss of sight by enabling them to read, by means of raised letters, to work with certain tools, and even to play upon musical instruments. A person born without sight, and without hearing or voice, may, by the education of the touch, be rescued from apparent imbecility, and be taught not only to read and write, but even to perform household and other useful labors.

27. Sensations of Temperature and Weight.—Each of these sensations has been described by the physiologists as a special sense, and they are rival candidates, so to speak, for the position and title of the sixth sense. In the sensation of temperature, or the thermal sense, touch bears a part, but the two feelings appear to be distinct. In proof of this, we observe, firstly, that they are not alike intense in the same situations; as, for example, the skin of the face and elbow, where the sense of touch is feeble, is very sensitive to impressions of heat and cold. Secondly, the ability to recognize temperature may be lost by paralysis, while the sensibility of touch remains unaffected. When the skin comes in contact with a very hot substance, the sensation felt is that of pain—not of touch. In like manner, a very cold substance causes pain, not the

---

25. Further experiments and results?
26. Exquisite delicacy of touch? The same among the blind?
27. Rival candidates for the sixth sense? Give the two reasons on the subject.

feeling of cold. So that a red-hot iron, and solid carbonic acid (the temperature of which is 108° below zero), feel alike; and each, if pressed slightly, will produce a blister. (*Read Note* 4.)

28. The *muscular sense*, by some considered distinct from touch, gives rise to the sensations of weight, and other forms of external resistance. That this feeling exists, is shown by the following simple experiment: If the hand be placed flat upon a table, and a somewhat heavy weight be put into it, touch alone is exercised, and a feeling of pressure results; but if the hand be raised, a certain amount of muscular effort must be put forth, and thus the sensation of weight is recognized. Through the muscular sense, precision of effort is rendered possible; for by it we learn to adjust the force exerted to the weight of the object to be lifted, moved, or carried. Without it all our movements would necessarily become ill-

---

4. Qualities Determined by the Sense of Touch.—"The eye, by the aid of certain signs, is often able to tell whether a body is hot—when, for instance, it is glowing or steaming—but a perception of warmth is not possessed by the eye. This is had by the skin alone, and it is of great importance to our preservation that this property is spread over the entire surface; for it surrounds the body like a protecting wall against its worst enemy—cold—which, if not thus guarded against at all points, would speedily destroy life. We are warned, however, of the approach of the enemy by a common sensation of the skin, and an inward chill, which is only caused by a coolness of the skin. The skin, in like manner, protects the body against the approach of a hurtful degree of heat. Thus, you see, the skin has certain *qualities* of sensation. Just as the eye, in looking at a wafer perceives that it is both red and circular, distinguishing both the color and form of bodies, so the sensitive skin by contact with an object distinguishes the qualities of form, firmness, hardness, liquidity, pressure, and temperature. * * * Weber has discovered the interesting fact that warm bodies feel lighter than cold ones: if a cold coin be placed upon the forehead of some person, whose eyes are shut, and then upon the same spot two warm coins, the weight would seem to him the same, whilst he could distinguish correctly in the case of cold weights. * * * If we place the elbow in hot water, we experience heat only in the part immersed, not in the whole arm, although the nerve just under the skin runs throughout the arm and hand. What we feel is a dull sense of pain in the whole arm if the water is too hot. So, too, if the elbow is placed in ice-water the pain is just the same in the arm; proving that the nerve-trunk can feel neither warmth nor cold."—*Bernstein's Five Senses of Man.*

---

28. The muscular sense? State what is said to illustrate the subject.

regulated and spasmodic.   In cases of disease, where the sensibility of the lower limbs is lost while power of motion remains, the patient is able to stand erect so long as he can see his limbs; but just as soon as his eyes are closed, he begins to waver, and will fall unless supported.

29. The Organ of Taste.—The *tongue* is the special organ of the sense of taste; but the back part of the mouth always possesses this faculty.   The tongue is a muscular organ, the muscles composing it being so numerous and interwoven as to give it the freedom and variety of motion which it possesses.   It can curve itself upward or downward; it can extend or contract itself; and, with its point, can sweep the cavity of the mouth, in all directions, in the search for scattered particles of food.

30. The upper surface of the tongue is peculiar, being marked by the presence of innumerable *papillæ*, some of which are of microscopic size, resembling those that abound in the fingers, and in other parts of the body that have the sense of touch.   Others are much larger, and give to the tongue its roughness of feeling and appearance.   Through the medium of these papillæ, the tongue receives impressions of touch and temperature, as well as taste: indeed, its extremity is fully as delicate, in respect to tactile sensations, as the tips of the fingers themselves.   It can recognize the two points of the compasses when separated not more than one twenty-fourth of an inch; the back of it is much less sensitive to touch, while at the same time it is more highly sensitive to impressions of taste.

31. Each lateral half of the tongue resembles the other in structure, and each receives the same number of nerves—three.   One of these regulates motion, the other two are nerves of special sense. One of the latter supplies the front half of the tongue, and is called the *gustatory* nerve.   This is a branch of the great cranial nerve, called the "fifth pair," which ramifies in all parts of the face.   The back of the tongue is endowed with the power of taste, through a nerve known as the *glosso-pharyngeal*, because it is distributed both to the tongue and throat.   This difference in the nervous supply of the tongue becomes significant, when we learn, as we shall

29. The organ of taste ?   The tongue?   Its powers of motion?
30. Peculiarities of the tongue?   Uses of the papillæ?
31. Resemblance in the parts of the tongue?   Powers and functions of the parts ?

presently, that each part of it perceives a different class of flavors.

32. The Sense of Taste.—Taste is the special sense by means of which we discover the savors, or flavoring properties of the substances which come in contact with the tongue. Mere contact with the surface of the tongue, however, is not sufficient, but contact with the extremities of the nerves of taste within the papillæ is required. In order that the substance to be tasted may penetrate the cells covering the nerves, it must either be liquid in form, or readily soluble in the watery secretion of the mouth—the saliva. The tongue must be moist also. If the substance be insoluble—as glass or sand—or the tongue dry, the sense of taste is not awakened. In sickness, when the tongue is heavily coated, the taste is very defective, or, as is frequently expressed, "nothing tastes aright."

33. All portions of the tongue are not alike endowed with the sense of taste, that function being limited to the posterior third, and to the margin and tip of this organ. The soft palate, also, possesses the sense of taste; hence, an article that has an agreeable flavor may very properly be spoken of as palatable, as is often done. All parts of the tongue do not perceive equally well the same flavors. Thus, the front extremity and margin, which is the portion supplied by the "fifth pair" of nerves, perceives more acutely sweet and sour tastes ; but the base of the tongue, supplied by the *glosso-pharyngeal* nerve, is especially sensitive to salt and bitter substances. The nerve of the front part of the tongue, as before stated, is in active sympathy with those of the face, while the relations of the other nerve are chiefly with the throat and stomach ; so that when an intensely sour taste is perceived, the countenance is involuntarily distorted, and is said to wear an acid expression. On the other hand, a very bitter taste affects certain internal organs, and occasions a sensation of nausea, or sickness of the stomach. (*Read Note* 5.)

---

5. Flavors and the Sense of Taste.—"The cause and intimate nature of tastes are no better understood than those of odors. Flavors

34. Relations of Taste with other Senses.—Taste is not a simple sense. Certain other sensations, as those of touch, temperature, smell, and pain, are blended and confused with it; and certain so-called tastes are really sensations of another kind. Thus an astringent taste, like that of alum, is more properly an astringent feeling, and results from an impression made upon the nerves of touch, that ramify in the tongue. In like manner, the qualities known as smooth, oily, watery, and mealy tastes, are dependent upon these same nerves of touch. A burning or pungent taste is a sensation of pain, having its seat in the tongue and throat. A cooling taste, like that of mint, pertains to that modification of touch called the sense of temperature.

35. Taste is largely dependent upon the sense of smell. A considerable number of substances, like vanilla, coffee, and garlic, which appear to possess a strong and distinct flavor, have in reality a powerful odor, but only a feeble taste. When the sense of smell

---

elude analysis and defy classification, even that which divides them into *agreeable* and *disagreeable*, for the taste of individuals and of nations singularly differs in this respect. The Laplander and the Esquimaux drink great quantities of train-oil, which for them is a greatly-esteemed article of food, and is most admirably adapted to the exigencies of a Polar climate; the Abyssinians eat raw flesh, and find its flavor excellent, while the inhabitant of the West partakes of it with the greatest repugnance and only as a medicine. Oysters, which are so generally esteemed in our country, are to some persons disagreeable and nauseous; and truffles, the delight of the gourmand, are rejected by the uninitiated on account of their flavor and their perfume. It is the same with almost all alimentary substances; they are eagerly sought after by some, and despised or abhorred by others. Let us remember the proverb ' *de gustibus non disputandum,*' and not dispute in regard to tastes; each is suited to its own country, and goodly numbers acclimatize themselves, to the great advantage of peoples among whom at first they seem exceedingly strange. Man should control his taste, and habituate it to all wholesome aliment; this neither excludes choice, nor blunts the delicacy of the sense; and while we resist its seductions, we should give timely heed to its instincts and its counsels, for they are often invaluable."—*The Wonders of the Human Body.*

---

34. What is stated of the relations of taste to other senses ?
35. Its dependence on smell ? on sight ?

is interfered with by holding the nose, it becomes difficult to distinguish between substances of this class. The same effect is frequently observed when smell is blunted during an ordinary cold in the head. Sight also contributes to taste. With the eyes closed, food appears comparatively insipid; and a person smoking tobacco in the dark is unable to determine by the taste whether his cigar is lighted or not. Accordingly, it is not a bad plan to close the nose and shut the eyes when about to swallow some disagreeable medicine.

36. Influence of Education on the Taste.—The chief use of the sense of taste appears to be to act as a guide in the selection of proper food. Hence its organs are properly placed at the entrance of the digestive canal. As a general rule, those articles which gratify the taste are wholesome; while the opposite is true of those which impress it disagreeably. This statement is more exact in reference to the early than to the later years of life, when, by reason of improper indulgence, the sense of taste has become dulled or perverted. The desires of a child are simple; he is fully satisfied with plain and wholesome articles of diet, and must usually " learn to like " those which have a strongly marked flavor. Accordingly, it is far easier at this age to encourage the preference for plain food, and thus establish healthful habits, than later in life to uproot habits of indulgence in stimulating substances, after their ill effects begin to manifest themselves.

37. The tastes of men present the most singular diversities, partly the result of necessity and partly of habit or education. The Esquimaux like the rank smell of whale-oil, which is a kind of food admirably suited to the requirements of their icy climate; and travelers who go from our climate to theirs are not slow to develop a liking for the same articles that the natives themselves enjoy. The sense of taste is rendered very acute by education, as is shown in an especial manner by those who become professional " tasters " of tea and wine.

38. The Sense of Smell—the Nasal Cavities.—The sense of

---

36. The chief use of the sense of taste ? The position of its organs ? The rule as regards wholesome and unwholesome food ? Remarks respecting the rule ?
37. Diversity in tastes of men ? How shown ? The education of the sense of taste ?
38. Location of the sense of smell ? The nose ? " Roof of the mouth ?"

smell is located in the delicate mucous membrane which lines the interior of the nose. That prominent feature of the face, the nose, which is merely the front boundary of the true nasal organ, is composed partly of bone and partly of cartilage. The upper part of it is united with the skull by means of a few small bones, to which circumstance is due its permanence of shape. The lower portion, or tip of the nose, contains several thin pieces of cartilage, which render it flexible and better able to resist the effects of blows and pressure. Behind the nose we find quite a spacious chamber, separated from the mouth by the hard palate, forming the "roof of the mouth," and also by the soft palate (see Fig. 55); and divided into two cavities by a central partition running from before backward.

39. These nasal cavities, constituting the true beginning of the air-passages, extend from the nose backward to the upper opening of the throat, and rise as high as the junction of the nose with the forehead. The inner wall of each cavity is straight and smooth; but from the outer wall there jut into each cavity three small scroll-like bones. The structure of these bones is very light, and hence they have been called the "spongy" bones of the nose. In this manner, while the extent of surface is greatly increased by the formation of these winding passages, the cavities are rendered extremely narrow; so much so, in fact, that a moderate swelling of the mucous membrane which lines them, as from a cold, is sufficient to obstruct the passage of air through them.

40. The Nerve of Smell.—The internal surface of the nasal passages is covered by a delicate and sensitive mucous membrane. Its surface is quite extensive, following as it does all the inequalities produced by the curved spongy bones of the nose. Only the upper portion of it is the seat of smell, since that part alone receives branches from the "first pair" of cranial nerves, or the olfactory nerve, which is the special nerve of smell (see Fig. 55). In Fig. 55 is shown the distribution of this nerve, in the form of an intricate network upon the two upper spongy bones. The nerve itself (1) does not issue from the skull, but rests upon a thin bone which separates it from the cavity of the nose; and the branches which proceed from it pass through this bone by means of numerous small openings. The engraving represents the outer surface of the right nasal cavity; the three wave-like inequalities, upon which the nervous network is spread out, are due to the spongy bones. The left cavity is supplied in the same manner.

41. The nerves which ramify over the lower part of the membrane, and which endow it with sensibility to touch and pain, are branches of the "fifth pair" of nerves. An irritation applied to the parts where this nerve is distributed occasions sneezing—that is, a spasmodic contraction of the diaphragm, the object of which

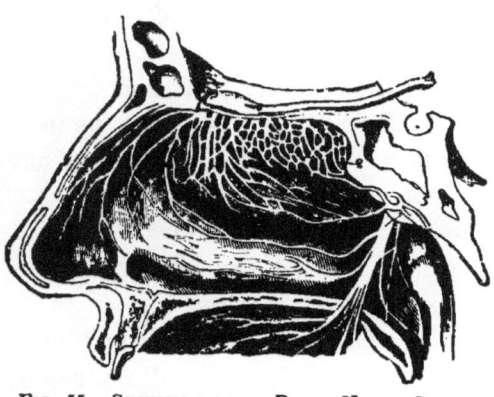

FIG. 55.—SECTION OF THE RIGHT NASAL CAVITY.

is the expulsion of the irritating cause. The manner in which the olfactory nerve-fibres terminate is peculiar. Unlike the extremities of other nerves, which are enclosed by a greater or less thickness of tissue, these come directly to the surface of the mucous membrane, and thus are in very close contact with the odorous particles that are carried along by the respired air. The surface is at all times kept in a moist condition by an abundant flow of nasal mucus; otherwise it would become dry, hard, and insensitive from the continual passage of air to and fro in breathing. Birds, which respire, more actively than men, have a special gland for secreting a lubricating fluid, located in the air-passages of the head.

42. The Uses of the Sense of Smell.—Smell is the special sense which enables us to appreciate odors. Touch, as we have seen, is largely concerned with solid bodies, and taste with fluids, or with solids in solution. Smell, on the other hand, is designed to afford us information in reference to substances in a volatile or gaseous form. Invisible particles issue from odorous bodies and are brought by the respired air in contact with the terminal fila-ments of the olfactory nerve, upon which an agreeable or disagree-able impression is produced. The fineness of the particles that constitute odors is often so extreme that they elude all attempts to measure or weigh them. A piece of musk, for instance, may be kept for several years, constantly emitting perfume without any appreciable loss of weight. In other cases, a loss of substance is perceptible, as in the essential oils, which enter into the composi-tion of the ordinary perfumes.

43. Smell, like taste, aids us in the choice of proper food, lead-ing us to reject such articles as have a rank or putrid odor, and which are, as a rule, unfit to be eaten. The highest usefulness of this sense, however, consists in the protection it affords to the organs of respiration. Stationed at the gateways of the air-passages, it examines the current of air as it enters, and warns us of the presence of noxious gases, and of other and generally invisible enemies to health. Not all dangerous vapors are offensive, but al-most all offensive vapors are unfit to be breathed. A number of small stiff hairs grow from the margin of the nostrils to prevent the entrance of dust and other atmospheric impurities, which would be alike injurious to the olfactory mucous membrane and to the lungs. The benevolent design of the Maker of our bodies may be observed in all parts of their mechanism ; but, probably, in none is it more clearly displayed than in connection with the sense of smell. (*Read Note* 6.)

---

6. The Protective Function of the Sense of Smell.—"Smell seems to be regarded as an endowment bestowed simply for pleasure, serving to promote no important or vital end. That its main use is to signal danger to internal parts is not duly appreciated. The detection of an offensive odor is thought to be the only bad thing about it, and which, to those habituated to it, is of no subsequent importance. Men even pride themselves, on becom-ing accustomed to offensive odors, and quite enjoy the sight of one whose nerve of smell is not benumbed like their own. Instead of seeking to blunt the sensibilities of this nerve, it should be a study to improve it, as the most deli-cate and available test of air impurity—far superior, under ordinary circum-stances, to the tests of science. In this way, all ordinary atmospheric impu-rities may be quickly detected ; and it is truly remarkable how, by a little attention, this sense can be so improved as to detect instantly even slight im-

---

44. The sense of smell is developed in a remarkable degree in certain of the inferior animals, and is especially acute in reference to the peculiar odors that characterize the different animals. The lion and other carnivorous beasts scent their prey from a great distance; and the fox-hound is able to track the fox through thickets and over open country for many miles; while the timid, helpless herbivora, such as the deer and sheep, find in the sense of smell a means of protection against their natural enemies, of whose approach they are in this manner warned. By training this sense in the dog, and making it subservient to his use, man is able to hunt with success certain shy and very fleet animals, which otherwise he could but seldom approach. Among men, individuals differ greatly in respect to the development of this sense; and especially in certain savage tribes it is found to be extremely delicate. Humboldt states that the natives of Peru can by it distinguish in the dark between persons of different races. (*Read Note 7.*)

---

purities to which it had before been insensible. In many houses, by the total neglect of this sense, there is an ever-present *family odor*, produced by some special kind of household impurity, and of which the inmates do not seem to be aware. To those accustomed to pure air, house odors are always perceptible and disagreeable. This ought to be accepted as sufficient evidence of their unhealthful tendencies; not perhaps of an instant or violent sort, yet enough so to give rise to many sensations of slight discomfort, and producing, when long continued, a state of the body very favorable to the beginning and growth of virulent diseases."—*Black's Ten Laws of Health.*

7. The Effects of Certain Odors.—" I have not seen it anywhere laid down as a general rule, but I believe it might be affirmed, that we are intended to be impressed only sparingly and transiently by odor. There is a provision for this in the fact that all odors are vapors or gases, or otherwise volatile substances; so that they touch but the inside of the nostril, and then pass away.

"In conformity with this fleeting character of odorous bodies, it is a law in reference to ourselves, to which, as far as I know, there is no exception, that there is not any substance having a powerful smell of which it is safe to take much internally. The most familiar poisonous vegetables, such as the poppy, hemlock, henbane, monk's-hood, and the plants containing prussic acid, have all a strong and peculiar smell. Nitric, muriatic, acetic, and other corrosive acids, have characteristic potent odors, and all are poisons. Even bodies with agreeable odors, like oil of roses, or cinnamon, or lavender, are wholesome only in very small quantities, and, when the odor is repulsive, only in the smallest

---

44. Sense of smell in the inferior animals? How, and in what cases, illustrated?

45. The Sense of Sight.—Sight, or vision, is the special sense by means of which we appreciate the color, form, size, distance, and other physical properties of the objects of external nature. Primarily, this sense furnishes us with information concerning the different shades of color and the different degrees of brightness : these are the simple sensations of sight, such as the yellowness and glitter of a gold coin. In addition to these, there are composite visual sensations, produced by the joint action of the other senses and by the use of the memory and judgment ; such as, in the case of the coin, its roundness, solidity, size, its distance and direction from us. So that many of our sensations, commonly considered as due to sight, are in reality the results of intellectual processes which take place instantaneously and unconsciously.

46. This faculty not only is valuable in the practical every-day affairs of life, but it contributes so largely to the culture of the intellect and to our higher forms of pleasure, that some writers are disposed to rate it as the first and most valuable of the senses. Others, however, maintain that the sense of hearing does not yield in importance to that of sight ; and they cite in support of their position the fact that the blind are commonly cheerful and gay, while the deaf are inclined to be morose and melancholy. In respect to the relative capacity for receiving education in the deaf and blind, it is found that the former learn more quickly, but their attainments are not profound ; while the blind acquire more slowly, but are able to study more thoroughly.

47. Light—The Optic Nerve.—Unlike the senses previously considered—touch, taste, and smell—sight does not bring us into

---

quantities. So far as health is concerned, the nostril should be but sparingly gratified with pleasing odors or distressed by ungrateful ones. No greater mistake can be made in sick-rooms than dealing largely in aromatic vinegar, eau de cologne, lavender water, and other perfumes. This hiding of one odor by another is like trying to put away the taste of bitter aloes by that of Epsom salts. Physical comfort is best secured by rarely permitting an infraction of the rule that the condition of health is no odor at all."—*Wilson on the Five Gateways of Knowledge.*

---

45. What is sight? What information does it furnish ? Composite visual sensations ?
46. Comparison between sight and hearing ? Relative capacity of deaf and blind.
47. Sight, unlike the other senses ? In the case of the stars ?

immediate contact with the bodies that are examined; but, by it, we perceive the existence and qualities of objects that are at a greater or less distance from us. In the case of the stars, the distance is incalculable, while the book we read is removed but a few inches. Light is the agent which gives to this sense its wide range. The nature of this mysterious force is not known, and it is not here to be discussed, since its study belongs more properly to the province of natural philosophy.

48. It is sufficient, in this connection, to state that the theory of light now generally accepted, and which best explains the facts of optics, is that known as the undulatory theory. This theory supposes that there exists an intangible, elastic medium, which fills all space, and penetrates all transparent substances, and which is thrown into exceedingly rapid undulations or waves, by the sun and every other luminous body—the undulations being propagated with extreme rapidity, and moving not less than 186,000 miles in a second.

49. These waves are thought to produce in the eye the sensation of light, in the same manner as the sonorous vibrations of the air produce in the ear the sensation of sound. That part of the eye which is sensitive to these waves is the expansion of the *optic nerve*. It is sensitive to no other impression than that of light, and it is the only nerve which is acted upon by this agent. The optic nerve, also called the "second pair" of cranial nerves, is the means of communication between the eye and the brain.

50. The two nerves constituting the pair arise from ganglia lying at the base of the cerebrum—one of them on each side—from which points they advance to the eyes, being united together in the middle of their course in the form of the letter X (Fig. 51-2). By this union the two eyes are enabled to act harmoniously, and in some respects to serve as a double organ. By reason of this same intimate nervous communication, when serious disease affects one eye, the fellow-eye is extremely liable to become the seat of *sympathetic* inflammation; and this, if neglected, almost certainly results in hopeless blindness.

---

48. The undulatory theory of light? What does the theory suppose?
49. The sensation of light? Optic nerve?
50. The two nerves constituting the pair of nerves?

11

51. The Organ of Sight—The Eye.—The proximity of the eye to the brain, and the important part it performs in giving expression to the emotions, have given it the name of "the window of the soul." The exceeding beauty of its external parts, and the high value of its function, have long made this organ the subject of enthusiastic study. It is chiefly within the last twenty years, however, that this study has been successful and fruitful of practical results. Several ingenious instruments have been invented for the examination of the eye in health and disease, and new operations have been devised for the relief of blindness and of impaired vision. As a result, it is now a well-marked fact that, in civilized lands, the number of those who suffer from loss of sight is proportionally much less than in countries where science is less known and cultivated.

52. The most obvious fact in respect to the apparatus of sight is that there are two eyes, which may either act together as one, and be fixed upon one object, or one eye may be used independently of the other. In consequence of this arrangement, the loss of one eye does not necessitate blindness, and, in fact, it not infrequently happens that the sight of one eye may be long impaired or lost before the fact is discovered. We next notice that it is placed at the most elevated part of the body, in front, and near the brain. It also commands a wide range of view, being itself moved with great rapidity, and being further aided by the free motion of the head and neck. The organ of vision consists essentially of two parts: the optical instrument itself—the eyeball—and its enveloping parts, or the case in which the instrument is kept free from harm. The latter, which are external, and which we shall first consider, are chiefly the *orbits*, the *eyelids*, and the apparatus for the *tears*.

53. The Orbits.—The eyeball, which is a delicate organ, is well defended against external injury within the orbits or bony sockets of the head. These are deep conical hollows, bounded in part by the bones of the skull, and in part by those of the nose and cheek. The orbit juts out beyond the most exposed portion of the

---

51. Why is the eye called the "window of the soul?" Why the subject of enthusiastic study?

52. The most obvious fact? The consequence? The next thing noticed? Its range of view? Of what does the organ of vision consist?

53. The protection of the eyeball against injury? The overhanging brow? The opening for the optic nerve?

eyeball, as may be seen by laying a book over the eye, when it will be found that no part of the eyeball, unless it be very prominent, will be touched by the book; so that the only direction in which an injury is liable to be received is immediately in front of the eye. The overhanging brow is itself covered by a layer of thick skin, studded with short, stout hairs, which are so bent as to prevent the perspiration from running into the eye and obscuring vision. Through a hole in the bottom of the orbit, the nerve of sight passes outward from the brain. The orbit also contains a considerable amount of a fatty tissue, upon which, as upon an elastic cushion, the eye rests.

54. The Eyelids.—The eyelids are two movable curtains, or folds, which, when shut, cover the front part of the orbit, and hide the eye from view. The upper lid is the larger, has a curved margin, and moves freely, while the lower lid is comparatively short and straight, and has but a slight degree of motion (Fig. 56). Skin covers the exterior of the lids, while a fine mucous membrane lines their inner surface, and is likewise spread out over the entire front of the eyeball. This membrane, which is called the *conjunctiva*, is highly sensitive, and thus plays an important part in protecting the eye against the lodgment of sand,

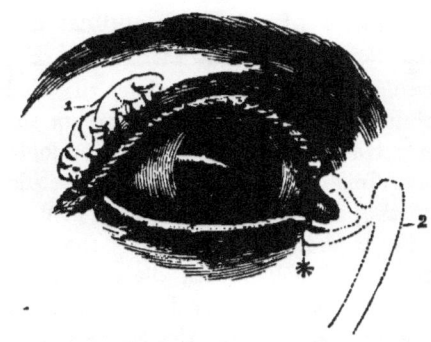

FIG. 56.— FRONT VIEW OF RIGHT EYE. (Natural Size.)
1. The Lachrymal, or tear gland, lying beneath the upper eyelid.
2. The Nasal Duct is shown by the dotted line. The * marks the orifice in the lower lid.
The central black spot is the *pupil;* surrounding it is the *iris;* and the triangular white spaces are the visible portion of the *sclerotic.*

ashes, chaff, and other foreign particles that are blown about in the air. This sensitive membrane will not endure the presence of these particles. If any find access, it causes a constant winking, a flow of tears, and other signs of irritation, until it is removed. *Read Note* 8.)

8. How to Remove Foreign Bodies from the Eye.—"Lay your finger on the cheek, and draw the lower lid gently down, while the

54. What are the eyelids? The upper lid? The lower one? The mucous membrane of the eye?

55. The long, silky eyelashes, which garnish the edges of the lids, act like a sieve to prevent the entry of dust and other irritants; and together with the lids, they regulate the amount of light which is permitted to enter the eye, so that it is shielded from a sudden flood or glare of light. The little points seen in the figure just within the line of the lashes, especially on the lower lid, represent the mouths of numerous little sebaceous glands (Fig. 57, D, D), such as are always found in the neighborhood of hairs. These glands supply a thick, oily material which greases the edges of the lids and prevents their adhering together, and likewise prevents the overflow of the tears upon the cheek.

56. The Lachrymal Fluid, or the Tears.—Just within the outer part of the bony arch of the brow, where the bone may be felt to be sharper than in other positions, is lodged a little organ called the lachrymal gland, the situation of which is indicated in

person looks as much upward as possible, and we shall see about the whole extent of the lower portion of the conjunctiva, and thus, if any foreign substance is there, it will be readily detected, and easily wiped away with a folded soft rag or handkerchief. Both lids have a piece of cartilage in them to stiffen them, like pasteboard, and keep them fitting close to the eyeball. The upper portion of this conjunctival sac can only be seen by turning over the upper lid. The way to do this is to let the person look down with the eyes closed. Taking hold of the lashes with one hand, and applying a pencil, or some small, round, smooth object, over the lid above the globe, we lift the lashes out and up, warning the person to still keep looking down. The lid will suddenly turn over with a little spring from the bending of the cartilage. In this way nearly the whole of the conjunctival sac will be exposed, and any foreign body wiped away, as above described. But suppose no friend or oculist is by us to do this. The next best thing is to take hold of the lashes of the upper lid, and draw it forward and downward over the lower one, blowing the nose violently with the other hand at the same time.

"If the foreign substance is on the cornea, take a strip of paper not stiffer than ordinary writing-paper, about a quarter of an inch wide, and roll it up as if you were going to make a candle-lighter. Look at the lower end, and you will see it comes to a point. With this point now you may safely attempt to remove any foreign substance from the corner. The tears which will flow soften the paper, and prevent injury to the delicate covering membrane of the cornea."—*Dr. B. Jay Jeffries.*

Fig. 56, 1. This is the gland whence flows the watery secretion, commonly called the *tears*, which is designed to perform an exceedingly important duty in lubricating the lids, and in keeping the exposed surface of the eyeball moist and transparent. For, without this or some similar liquid, the front of the eye would speedily become dry and lustreless, like that of a fish which has been removed from the water; the simple exposure of the eye to the air would then suffice to destroy vision.

57. This secretion of the tears takes place at all times, during the night as well as the day; but it is seldom noticed, unless when under the influence of some strong mental emotion—whether of sorrow or happiness—it is poured forth in excess, so as to overflow the lids. Strong light or a rapid breeze will, among many other causes, excite the flow of the tears. That portion of this secretion which is not used in moistening the eye is carried off into the nose by a canal situated near the inner angle of the eye, called the *nasal duct.* This duct is shown in Fig. 56, 2, and is connected with each lid by delicate tubes, which are indicated by dotted lines in the figure; the asterisk marks the little opening in the lower lid, by which the tears enter the nasal duct. By gently turning the inner part of that lid downward, and looking in a mirror, this small "lachrymal point" may be seen in your own eye. In old people, these points become turned outward, and do not conduct the tears to the nasal cavity, thus causing an overflow of tears upon the face.

58. Thus we observe that the gland which forms the tears is placed at the outer part of the eye, while their means of exit is at the inner angle of the eye; which fact renders it necessary that this watery fluid shall pass over the surface of the eyeball before it can escape. This arrangement cannot be accidental, but evinces design, as it thus secures the perfect lubrication of the surface of the eye, and cleanses it from the smaller particles of dust which may enter it, in spite of the vigilance of the lids and lashes. The act of winking, which is generally unconsciously performed, and which takes place six or more times in a minute, assists this passage of the

---

57. When does the secretion of the tears occur? The secretion not used for the eye? Location of the nasal duct? Its use? The overflow of tears in old people?
58. The watery fluid passing over the eyeball? Design of the arrangement? Winking?

tears across the eye, and is especially frequent when the secretion is most abundant.

59. The Eyeball.—The eyeball, or globe of the eye, upon which sight depends, is, as the name indicates, spherical in shape. It is not a perfect sphere, since the front part projects somewhat beyond the rest, and at the posterior part the optic nerve (Fig. 57, N) is united to it, resembling the junction of the stem with the fruit. In

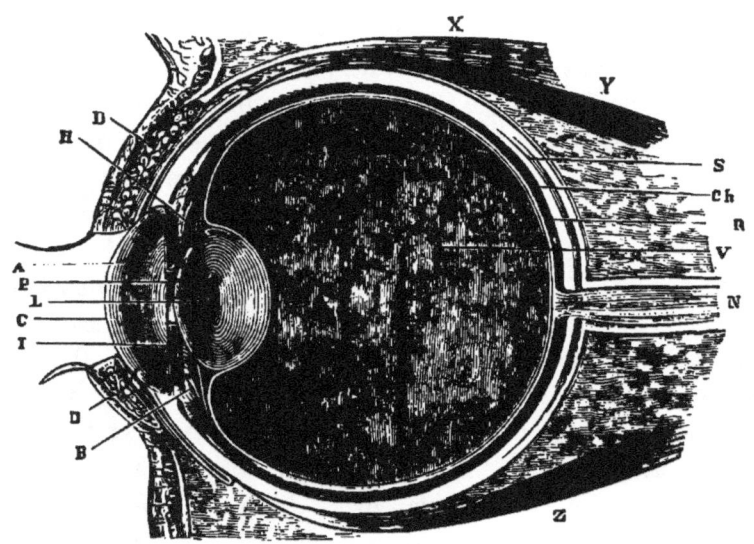

FIG. 57.—VERTICAL SECTION OF THE EYE. (Enlarged.)

C, The Cornea.	Ch, The Choroid.
A, The Aqueous Humor.	R, The Retina.
I, The Iris.	N, The Optic Nerve.
P, The Pupil.	DD, The Eyelids.
L, The Crystalline Lens.	X, The Levator Muscle of the Upper
H, The Ligament of the Lens.	Lid.
B, The Ciliary Process.	Y, The Upper Straight Muscle of the
V, The Cavity containing the Vitreous Humor.	Eye.
S, The Sclerotic.	Z, The Lower Straight Muscle.

its long diameter—that is, from side to side, it measures a little more than an inch; in other directions it is rather less than an inch. In structure the ball of the eye is firm, and its tense round contour may in part be felt by pressing the fingers over the closed lids.

60. The eyeball is composed chiefly of three internal, transparent media, called *humors*, and three investing coats, or *tunics*. The

59. Describe the shape of the eyeball. Its structure.
60. Of what is the eyeball composed? State how.

former are the *aqueous humor*, Fig. 57, A, the *crystalline lens* L, and the *vitreous humor* V. Of these the lens alone is solid. The three coats of the eyeball are called the *sclerotic* S, the *choroid* Ch, and the *retina* R. This arrangement exists in respect to five-sixths of the globe of the eye, but in the anterior one-sixth, these coats are replaced by the *cornea* C, which is thin and transparent, so that the rays of light pass freely through it, as through a clear window-pane.

61. In shape, the cornea is circular and prominent, resembling a miniature watch-glass, about $\frac{1}{25}$ of an inch thick. In structure, it resembles horn (as the name signifies), or the nail of the finger, and is destitute of blood-vessels. The *sclerotic* (from *scleros*, hard) is composed of dense, white fibrous tissue, and gives to the eyeball its firmness of figure and its white color; in front, it constitutes the part commonly called "the white of the eye." It is one of the strongest tissues in the body. It possesses very few vessels, and is not very sensitive. It affords protection to the extremely delicate interior parts of the eye, and the little muscles which effect its movements are inserted into the sclerotic a short distance behind the cornea (see Fig. 57, Y, Z). It is perforated posteriorly to admit the optic nerve.

62. The *choroid* is the second or middle coat of the eyeball, and lies closely attached to the inner surface of the sclerotic. Unlike the latter, its structure is soft and tender; it is dark in color, and possesses a great abundance of blood-vessels. Its dark color is due to a layer of dark brown or chocolate-colored cells spread out over its inner surface. This dark layer serves to absorb the rays of light after they have traversed the transparent structures in front of it. If the rays were reflected from side to side within the eye, instead of being thus absorbed, confused vision would result from the multitude of images which would be impressed upon the optic nerve.

63. This mechanism has been unconsciously imitated by the opticians, who, when they make a microscope or telescope, take care that the interior of its tube shall be coated with a thick layer of

61. The shape of the cornea? Its structure? The "white of the eye?"
62. The second or middle coat of the eyeball? Its dark color?
63. Similar mechanism in microscopes? The albinos? White rabbits?

black paint or lamp-black; for without it, a clear delineation of the object to be viewed is impossible. The Albinos, in whom these dark cells of the choroid are wanting, have imperfect vision, especially in the daytime and in strong lights. The dark cells are also wanting in white rabbits, and other animals that have red or pink eyes; their vision appears to be imperfect in the presence of a brightlight.

64. The Iris.—Continuous with the choroid, in the front part of the globe of the eye, is a thin, circular curtain, which occasions the brown, blue, or gray color of the eye in different individuals. On account of the varieties of its color, this membrane has received the

FIG. 58.—FRONT SECTION OF ITS EYEBALL, VIEWED FROM BEHIND, AND SHOWING SUSPENSORY LIGAMENT, IRIS, AND PUPIL.

name *Iris*, which is the Greek word for "rainbow" (see Fig. 57, 1). A front view of it is shown in Fig. 56. The iris is pierced in its centre by a round opening, called the *pupil* (P), which is constantly varying in size. In olden times it was spoken of as the "apple of the eye." The hinder surface of the iris, except in Albinos, has a layer of dark coloring matter resembling that of the choroid. The iris is a muscular organ, and contains two distinct sets of fibres, one of which is circular, while the other radiates outward from the pupil. Their action regulates the size of the pupil; for when the circular set acts, the opening contracts. Their action is involuntary, and depends on the reflex system of nerves, which causes the contraction of the pupil when a strong light falls upon the eye, and its expansion when the illumination is feeble. The suspensory ligament holds the crystalline lens in its place. Fig. 58.

65. The iris, accordingly, serves a very useful purpose in regulating the admission of light to the eye (see Fig. 58). It, however, does not act instantaneously; and hence, when we pass quickly from a dark room into the bright sunlight, the vision is at first confused by the glare of light, but as soon as the pupil contracts, the ability to see becomes perfect. On the other hand, when we enter a dark apartment, such as a cellar, for a short time we can see nothing clearly; but as soon as the pupil expands and admits more light, we are enabled to distinguish the surrounding objects. Animals of the cat species, and others which prowl around after nightfall, are enabled to see in the dark by having the iris very dilatable. The size of the pupil affects the lustre of the eye. When it is large, as it usually is during youth, the eye appears clear and brilliant; while in old age the pupil is small and the eye is dull. The brilliancy of the eye is in part, at least, dependent upon the reflection of light from the front surface of the crystalline lens.

66. Certain poisonous vegetables have the property of causing the pupil to dilate, and have been used in small doses to increase the beauty of the eye. One of these drugs has been so largely used by the ladies for this purpose, that it has received the name *belladonna*, from the Italian words meaning "beautiful lady." This hazardous practice has resulted more than once in the death of the person desiring thus to increase her personal attraction. The common English name for belladonna is "deadly nightshade." (In the diagram on page 257 the shape and relations of the iris are more accurately shown than in the figure referred to above.)

67. The Retina constitutes the third and inner coat of the globe of the eye. This, the important part of the eye that is sensitive to light, is a kind of nervous membrane, formed by the expansion of the optic nerve. Its texture is soft, smooth, and very thin; it is translucent and of an opaline, or grayish-white color. It is sensitive to light alone; and if any form of mechanical irritation be applied to it, the sensations of touch and pain are not experienced, but flashes of fire, sparks, and other luminous appearances are perceived. Thus an electric shock given to the eyeball occasions a flash of light; and a sudden fall, or a blow upon the eye, is often apparently accompanied by the vision of "stars."

---

66. Means used to increase the beauty of the eye? The injurious consequences?
67. What part does the retina constitute? How formed? Its texture? Color? Sensitiveness?

68. These phenomena are due to what is termed the "specific energy" of the optic nerve, which nerve, in common with the other nerves of the special sense, obeys a general law of nature, which requires that, whenever one of these nerves is stimulated, it shall respond with the sensation peculiar to itself. These flashes of retinal light have no power to illuminate external objects, although the opposite of this statement has been maintained. On the occasion of a remarkable trial in Germany, it was claimed by a person who had been severely assaulted on a very dark night, that the flashes of light caused by repeated blows upon the head enabled him to see with sufficient distinctness to recognize his assailant. But the evidence of scientific men entirely refuted this claim, by pronouncing that the eye, under the circumstances named, was incapacitated for vision. Too intense light occasions a feeling of pain, but it is of a peculiar kind, and is termed "dazzling."

69. All parts of the retina are not equally sensitive, and singularly enough, the point of entry of the nerve of sight in the back part of the eyeball is entirely insensible to light, and is called the "blind spot." The existence of this point may be proved by a simple experiment. Hold the accompanying figure, on page 250, directly in front of and parallel with the eyes. Close the left eye,

FIG. 59.

and fix the sight steadily on the left-hand circle; then, by gradually varying the distance of the figure from the eye, at a certain distance (about six inches), the right-hand circle will disappear, but nearer or further than that, it will be plainly seen. The other eye may be also tried, with a similar result: if the gaze be directed to the right-hand circle, the left one will seem to disappear. The experiment

68. Specific energy of the optic nerve? Trial in Germany?
69. Sensitiveness of all parts of the retina? Experiment to prove the existence of the "blind spot?"

may be repeated by using two black buttons on the marble top of a bureau, or on some other white surface. The blind spot does not practically interfere with vision, since the eye is seldom fixed immovably on an object, and the insensitive parts of the two eyes can never be directed upon the same object at the same time.

70. Impressions made upon the retina are not at once lost, but continue a measurable length of time, and then gradually fade away. Thus, a bright light or color, gazed at intently, cannot be immedi ately dismissed from sight by closing or turning away the eyes. A stick lighted at one end, if whirled around rapidly in the dark, presents the appearance of an unbroken luminous ring; and the spokes of a rapidly revolving carriage-wheel seem to be merged into a plane surface. If an object move too rapidly to produce this sort of lasting impression, it is invisible, as in the case of a cannon-ball passing through the air in front of us.

71. If a card, painted with two primary colors—as red and yellow —be made to rotate swiftly, the eye perceives neither of them distinctly; but the card appears painted with their secondary color— orange. The average duration of retinal images is estimated at one-eighth of a second; and it is because they thus endure, that the act of winking, which takes place so frequently, but so quickly, is not noticed and does not interrupt the vision. The retina is easily fatigued or deprived of its sensibility. After looking steadfastly at a bright light, or at a white object on a black ground, a dark spot, corresponding in shape to the bright object, presents itself in whatever direction we look. This spot passes away as the retina resumes its activity.

72. If a white color be gazed at intently, and the eyes then be turned to a white surface, a spot will appear; but its color will be the complement of that of the object. Fix the eye upon a red wafer upon a white ground, and on removing the wafer a greenish spot of the same shape takes its place. This result happens because a certain portion of the retina has exhausted its power to perceive the red ray, and perceives only its complementary ray, which is

---

70. Duration of impressions upon the retina? How illustrated?
71. What further illustration? Winking, why it is not noticed? Ease with which the retina is fatigued or deprived of sensibility? How shown?
72. How further shown? How is the result accounted for? "Color-blindness?"

green. The color thus substituted by the exhausted retina is called a physiological or accidental color. In some persons the retina is incapable of distinguishing different colors, when they are said to be affected with "color-blindness." Thus, red and green may appear alike, and then a cherry-tree, full of ripe fruit, will seem of the same color in every part. Railroad accidents have occurred because the engineer of the train, who was color-blind, has mistaken the color of a signal. (*Read Note* 9.)

73. The Crystalline Lens.—Across the front of the eye, just behind the iris, is situated the *crystalline lens*, enclosed within its own capsule. It is supported in its place partly by a delicate circular ligament, and partly by the pressure of adjacent structures. It is colorless and perfectly transparent, and has a firm but elastic texture. In shape, it is doubly convex, and may be rudely compared to a small lemon-drop. The front face of the lens is flatter than the other, and is in contact with the iris near its pupillary margin, as is represented in the diagram on page 257. It is only one-fourth of an inch thick.

74. When this little body becomes opaque, and no longer affords free passage to the rays of light, as often happens with the advance of age, an affection termed "cataract" is produced. Between the crystalline lens and the cornea is a small space which contains the

---

9. Color-blindness.—"Daltonism, or color-blindness, receives its name from the eminent English chemist, who described this infirmity as it existed in his own case. It arises from an unnatural condition of the organs of vision which prevents the discrimination of certain colors. Some persons will mistake red for green ; so that ripe cherries on a tree appear the same as the leaves ; others recognize only black and white. Persons thus affected are sometimes incapable of discriminating musical tones. The healthy eye ordinarily fails to discriminate between certain colors, blue and green especially, when viewed by artificial light. But even this may in a measure be overcome by training, so that an expert dealer in silk obtains a knowledge of the shades of blue, green, and violet, which is proof against the confusing influence of gaslight and tinted curtains. The eyes of persons who have much to do with colors are more liable to become overstrained than those dealing chiefly with rays of white light."—*Flint's Physiology (in part).*

73. The location of the crystalline lens ? How supported ? Its color and texture ? Shape ? Size ?
74. Cataract ? Aqueous humor ? Vitreous humor ?

aqueous humor (see Fig. 57, A). This humor consists of five or six drops of a clear, colorless liquid very much like water, as its name implies. That part of the globe of the eye lying behind the lens is occupied by the *vitreous humor*, so called from its fancied resemblance to melted glass (Fig. 57, v). This humor is a transparent, jelly-like mass, enclosed within an exceedingly thin membrane. It lies very closely applied to the retina, or nervous membrane of the eye, and constitutes fully two-thirds of the bulk of the eyeball.

75. The Uses of the Crystalline Lens.—A convex lens has

the property of converging the rays of light which pass through it; and the point at which it causes them to meet is termed its focus.

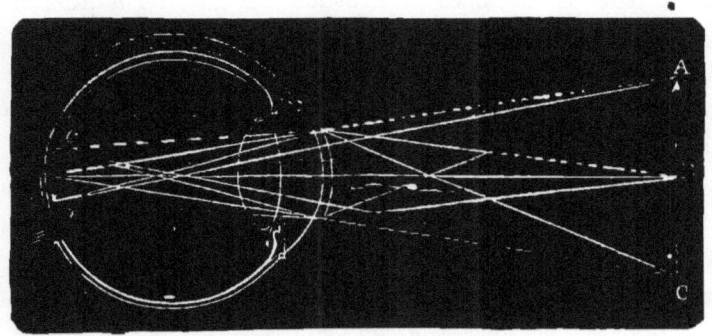

FIG. 60.—THE RETINAL IMAGE.

If a lens of this description, such as a magnifying or burning-glass, be held in front of an open window, in such a position as to allow its focus to fall upon a piece of paper, it will be found to depict upon the paper a miniature image of the scene outside of the window. It will be further noticed that the image is inverted, or upside down, and that the paper at the place upon which the image is thrown is much brighter than any other part.

76. Now all the transparent structures of the eye, but especially the crystalline lens, operate upon the retina, as the convex lens acts upon the paper—that is, they paint upon the retina a bright, inverted miniature of the objects that appear in front of the eye (Fig. 60). That this actually takes place may be proved by experiment. If the eyeball of a white rabbit, the walls of which are

75. What is a lens and its focus? The miniature image, how produced?
76. How are figures painted upon the retina? How proved?

transparent, be examined while a lighted candle is held before the cornea, an image of the candle-flame may be seen upon the retina.

77. The form and structure of the crystalline lens endow it with a remarkable degree of refractive power, and enable it to converge all the rays of light that enter it through the pupil, to a focus exactly at the surface of the retina. When this lens is removed from the eye, as is frequently done for the cure of cataract, it is found that the rays of light then have their focus three-eighths of an inch behind the retina; that the image is four times larger than in the healthy eye; that it is less brilliant, and that its outline is very indistinct. From this we learn that one of the uses of the crystalline lens is to make the retinal image bright and sharply-defined, at the same time that it reduces its size. Indeed, the small size of the image is a great advantage, as it enables the limited surface of the retina to receive, at a glance, impressions from a considerable field of vision.

78. As the image upon the retina is inverted, how does the mind perceive the object in its true, erect position? Many explanations have been advanced, but the simplest and most satisfactory appears to be found in the fact that the retina observes no difference, so to speak, between the right and left or the upper and lower positions of objects. In fact, the mind is never conscious of the formation of a retinal image, and until instructed, has no knowledge that it exists. Consequently, our knowledge of the relative location of external objects must be obtained from some other source than the retina. The probable source of this knowledge is the habitual comparison of those objects with the position of our own bodies; thus, to see an elevated object, we know we must raise the head and eyes; and to see one at our right hand, we must turn the head and eyes to the right.

79. Long-sight or Hyperopia, and Short-sight or Myopia.— The eye is not in all cases perfectly formed. For example, persons may from birth have the cornea too prominent or too flat, or the lens may be too thick or too thin. In either of these conditions sight will be more or less defective from the first, and the defect

77. What can be said in respect to the form and structure of the crystalline lens?
78. How is the inverted image upon the retina presented in its true position to the mind?
79. The uniform perfection of the eye? Examples? The most common imperfection?

will not tend to disappear as life advances. The most common imperfection, however, is in the shape of the globe; which may be short (Fig. 61, H), as compared with the natural eye, N, or it may be too long, M.

80. When the globe is short, only objects that are at a distance can be clearly seen, and the condition of the vision is known as "long-sight," or hyperopia. It will be observed, by reference to Fig. 61, that the focus of the rays of light would fall behind the retina of this eye. When the globe is too long, only objects that

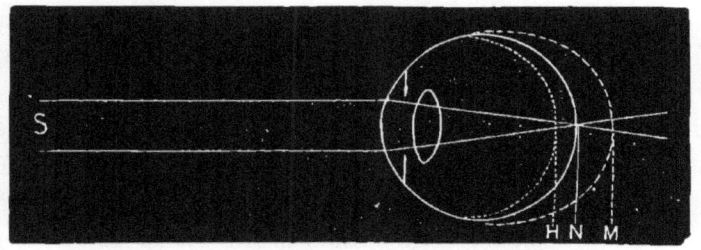

FIG. 61.—THE DIFFERENT SHAPES OF THE GLOBE OF THE EYE.

N, The Natural Eye.   M, The Short-sighted Eye.
H, The Long-sighted Eye.   S, Parallel Rays from the Sun.

are very near to the eye can be clearly seen, and the condition resulting from this defect is termed "short-sight," or myopia. The focus of the rays of light is, in this case, formed in the interior of the eye in front of the retina.

81. Long-sight, or hyperopia, is common among school-children, nearly as much so as short-sight, and must not be confounded with the defect known as the "far sight" of old people; although in both affections the sight is improved by the use of convex glasses. Children not infrequently discover that they see much better when they chance to put on the spectacles of old persons. For the relief of short-sight, concave glasses should be employed; as they so scatter the rays of light as to bring the focus to the retina, and thus cause the vision of remote objects to become at once distinct. That form of "squint," in which the eyes are turned inward, is generally

80. How is "long-sight' explained ? "Short-sight?"
81. Long-sight, how common? With what must it not be confounded ? Kind of glasses for short-sight? Why? Squint?

dependent upon long-sight, while that rarer form, when they turn outward, is due to short-sight. (*Read Note* 10.)

82. The Function of Accommodation.—If, after looking through an opera-glass at a very distant object, it is desired to view another nearer at hand, it will be found impossible to obtain a clear vision of the second object unless the adjustment of the instrument be altered, which is effected by means of the screw. If an object, like the end of a pencil, be held near the eye, in a line with another object at the other side of the room, or out of the window, and the eye be fixed first upon one and then upon the other, it will be found that when the pencil is clearly seen, the further object is indistinct; and when the latter is seen clearly, the pencil appears indistinct, and that it is impossible to see both clearly at the same time. Accordingly, the eye must have the capacity of adjusting itself to distances, which is in some manner comparable to the action of the screw of the opera-glass.

83. This, which has been called the function of accommodation, is one of the most admirable of all the powers of the eye, and is exercised by the crystalline lens. It consists essentially in a change in the curvature of the front surface of the lens, partly through its

---

10. On the Production of Short-Sight.—"The observations of Cohn in the schools and University of Breslau, of Kruger in Frankfort-on-the-Main, of Erismann in St. Petersburgh, of Von Hoffmann in Wiesbaden, and others abroad, prove most conclusively that one of the bad effects of school and college life is to produce diseases of the eyes. They have shown that near-sightedness increases rapidly in frequency as you go up in the scale of schools from the primaries of the rural districts to the universities. The gravity of this finding may be appreciated when we remember that near-sightedness is a disease, and that it very frequently descends from one generation to another, marked by such organic changes in the eyes as tend to the production of the worst forms of the malady, and to blindness. In 1867, Cohn, of Breslau, published the results of the examination of the eyes of 10,060 scholars. His examinations covered the entire range of school-life. He found that 1,750 of the 10,060 children had defective vision—about seventeen per cent. He also examined, without selection, 410 of the 964 students of the Breslau University, and found that not one-third had normal eyes."—*Dr. C. R. Agnew.*

---

82. What is stated in connection with the opera-glass? Experiment with pencil and distant object?
83. Function of accommodation? In what does it consist? How is the function explained?

own elasticity, and partly through the action of the ciliary muscle. When the eye is at rest—that is, when accommodated for a distant object—the lens is flatter and its curvature diminished (see Fig. 62) ; but when strongly accommodated for near vision, the lens becomes thicker, its curvature increases, and the image on the retina is made more sharp and distinct. Since a strong light is not required in

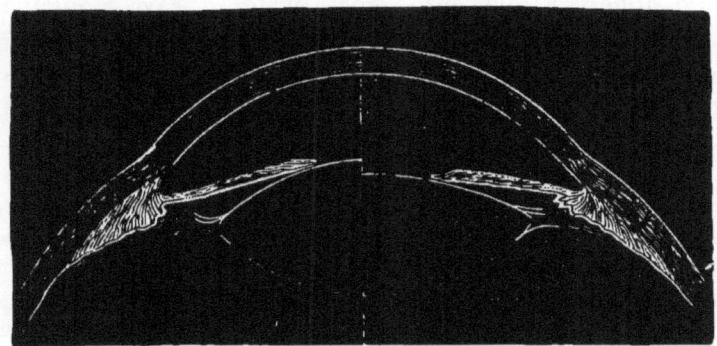

FIG. 62.—THE FUNCTION OF ACCOMMODATION.
The right half of the diagram shows the eye at rest. The left half shows the lens accommodated for near vision.

viewing near objects, the pupil contracts, as is shown in the left-hand half of the diagram.

84. Old-sight, or Presbyopia.—But this marvelously beautiful mechanism becomes worn with use; or, more strictly speaking, the lens, like other structures of the body, becomes harder with the approach of old age. The material composing the lens becomes less elastic, the power to increase its curvature is gradually lost, and as a consequence, the person is obliged to hold the book further away when reading, and to seek a stronger light. In a word, the function of accommodation begins to fail, and is about the first evidence that marks the decline of life. By looking at the last preceding diagram, and remembering that the increased curvature of the lens cannot take place, it will be at once understood why old-sight is benefited in near vision by the convex lens, such as the spectacles of old people contain. It acts as a substitute for the deficiency of the crystalline lens. (*Read Note* 11.)

11. **The Choice of Glasses.**—"The perfectly healthy, normal eye, begins to need a glass for ordinary work at between forty and forty-five years

84. Change of sight with the approach of old age? Explain the change?

85. The Sense of Hearing—Sound.—Hearing is the special sense by means of which we are made acquainted with *sound.* What is sound? It is an impression made upon the organs of hearing, by the vibrations of elastic bodies. This impression is commonly propagated by means of the air, which is thrown into delicate undulations in all directions from the vibrating substance. When a stone is thrown into smooth water, a wave of circular form is set in motion from the point where the stone struck, which, as it advances, constantly increases in size and diminishes in force.

86. Somewhat resembling this is the undulation, or sound-wave,

---

of age—of course, we here exclude all debilitated conditions of the body resulting from disease. Now, then, comes the question—shall we put on glasses, and of what strength? To answer some prevalent fallacies handed down from one generation to another, we cannot do better than quote from the highest authority, Prof. Donders, who says: 'The opinion is rather general that we should refrain as long as possible from the use of convex glasses. But, is it not folly to weary the eyes and the mind together, without necessarily condemning ourselves to guess, with much trouble, at the forms which we could see pretty well with glasses?'

"Strangely enough, people have fallen also into the opposite fault. Some have thought, by the early use of spectacles, to be able to preserve their power of vision, and have recommended and employed 'conservative glasses.' If I am not mistaken, self-interest had something to do with this recommendation. So long as the eye does not err, and remains free from fatigue in the work required of it, its own power is sufficient, and it is inexpedient to seek assistance in the use of convex glasses. Having made up their minds that they require glasses, how are they to know what glasses to procure, or what number is correct? Generally, people go to the nearest spectacle-vender, and purchase what they see best with at the time. We say distinctly, once for all, that the ophthalmic surgeon is the one to be consulted as to the wearing of glasses. He, by testing the eye, can alone decide whether any, and what glasses, should be worn. Opticians and spectacle-venders know nothing about the laws which govern the refraction and accommodation of the eye. It is not their business, any more than it is the apothecary's to know about disease. The advice of the ophthalmic surgeon will also be found invaluable as to how to wear glasses, whether springs or spectacles, so as not to fatigue the eyes by straining them from improper use of these invaluable aids to man's happiness. We conclude by saying, that all advice in this article applies to those having normal, healthy, strong eyes."—*Dr. B. Joy Jeffries.*

---

85. Hearing? What is sound? How propagated commonly? Stone thrown in water?
86. Sound-wave in the atmosphere? Its shape? Rate of motion? Sound, in water air and solid bodies?

which is imparted by a sonorous vibration to the surrounding atmosphere. Its shape, however, is spherical, rather than circular, since it radiates upward, downward, and obliquely, as well as horizontally, like the wave in water. The rate of motion of this spherical wave of air is about 1,050 feet per second, or one mile in five seconds. In water, sound travels four times as fast as in air, and still more rapidly through solid bodies; along an iron rod its velocity is equal to two miles per second.

87. The earth, likewise, is a good conductor of sound. It is said that the Indian of our western prairies can, by listening at the surface of the ground, hear the advance of a troop of cavalry while they are still out of sight, and can even discriminate between their tread and that of a herd of buffaloes. Solid substances also convey sounds with greater power than air. If the ear be pressed against one end of a long beam, the scratching of a pin at the other extremity may be distinctly heard, which will not be at all audible when the ear is removed from the beam. Although air is not the best medium for conveying sound, it is necessary for its production. Sound cannot be produced in a vacuum, as is shown by ringing a bell in the exhausted receiver of an air-pump, for it is then entirely inaudible. But let the air be re-admitted gradually, then the tones become more and more distinct, and when the receiver is again full of air, they will be as clear as usual.

88. All sonorous bodies do not vibrate with the same degree of rapidity, and upon this fact depends the *pitch* of the sounds that they respectively produce. The more frequent the number of vibrations within a given time, the higher will be the pitch; and the fewer their number, the lower or graver will it be. Now, the rate of the successive vibrations of different notes has been measured, and it has thus been found that if they are less than sixteen in a second, no sound is audible; while, if they exceed 60,000 per second, the sound is very faint, and is painful to the ear. The extreme limit of the capacity of the human ear may be considered as included between these points, but the sounds which we ordinarily hear are embraced between 700 and 3,000 vibrations per second.

87. The earth as a conductor of sound? What has the western Indian been taught? Solid substances as conductors? As regards sound, in what respect is air necessary? Sound in a vacuum?
88. Pitch. To what due? Capacity of ear?

89. The *ear*, which is the proper organ of hearing, is the most complicated of all the structures that are employed in the reception of external impressions. The parts of which it is composed are numerous, and some of them are extremely small and delicate. Nearly all these parts are located in an irregularly shaped cavity hollowed out in the temporal, or " temple " bone of each side of the head. That part of the bone in which the auditory cavity is placed has the densest structure of all bones of the body, and has, therefore, been called the " petrous," or rocky part of the temporal bone. In studying the ear, it is necessary to consider it as divided into

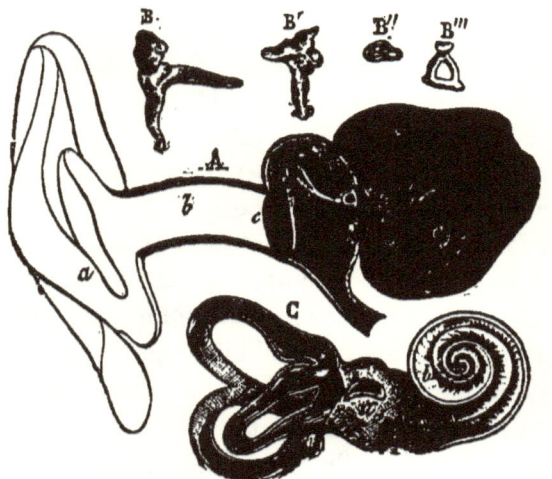

FIG. 63.—THE EAR AND ITS DIFFERENT PARTS.
A, Diagram of the Ear.
a, *b*, External Ear.   *d*, Middle Ear.
c, Membrana tympani.   *e*, Internal Ear.
B to B''', Bones of the Middle Ear (magnified).
C, The Labyrinths, or Internal Ear (highly magnified).

three portions, which are called, from their relative positions, the *external* ear, the *middle* ear, and the *internal* ear. (In the diagram, Fig. 63, A, the first is not shaded, the second is lightly shaded, and the last has a dark background.)

90. The External Ear.—The external portion of the organ of hearing, designated in Fig. 63, A, includes, first, that outer part (*a*), which is commonly spoken of as " the ear," but which in fact is only the portal of that organ ; and, secondly, the *auditory canal* (*b*). The former consists of a flat, flexible piece of cartilage, projecting slightly from the side of the head, attached to it by ligaments, and supplied with a few weak muscles. Its surface is uneven, and curiously curved, and from its resemblance to a shell, it has been called the *concha.* It probably serves to collect sounds, and to give them an inward direction, although its removal is said not to impair the acuteness of hearing more than a few days.

91. In those animals whose hearing is more delicate than that of man, the corresponding organ is of greater importance, it being larger, and supplied with muscles of greater power, so that it serves as a natural kind of ear-trumpet, which is easily movable in the direction of any sound that attracts the attention of the animal. Bold, preying animals generally have the concavity of this organ directed forward, while in timorous animals, like the rabbit, it is directed backward. Fishes have no outer ear, but sounds are transmitted directly through the solid bones of the head, to the internal organ of hearing.

92. The *auditory canal* (Fig. 63, A, *b*), which is continuous with the outer opening of the ear, is a passage an inch and a quarter in length, its inner extremity being bounded by a closely-fitting, circular membrane. This canal is of oval form, is directed forward and inward, and is slightly curved, so that the inner end is ordinarily concealed from view. The pouch of the skin which lines this passage is smooth and thin, especially at the lower end, where it covers the membrane just mentioned.

93. As in the case of the nostrils, a number of small, stiff hairs garnish the margin of the auditory canal, and guard it, to some extent, against the entrance of insects and other foreign objects. The skin, too, covering its outer half, is furnished with a belt of little glands which secrete a yellow, bitter substance, called " ear-wax," which is especially obnoxious to small insects. As the outer layer of this wax-like material loses its useful properties it becomes dry, and falls out of the ear in the form of minute, thin scales, a fresh supply being furnished from the little glands beneath. In its

91. The ear in the animals of delicate hearing? Rabbit? Fishes?
92. What is the auditory canal? Describe it?
93. How is it guarded and protected? Ear-wax?

form, the auditory canal resembles the tube of an ear-trumpet, and serves to convey the waves of sound to the middle portion of the ear.

94. The Middle Ear, or Tympanum.—The middle ear is a small cavity, or chamber, of irregular shape, about one-fourth of an inch across from side to side, and half an inch long (see Fig. 63, A, *d*). From the peculiar arrangment of its various parts it has

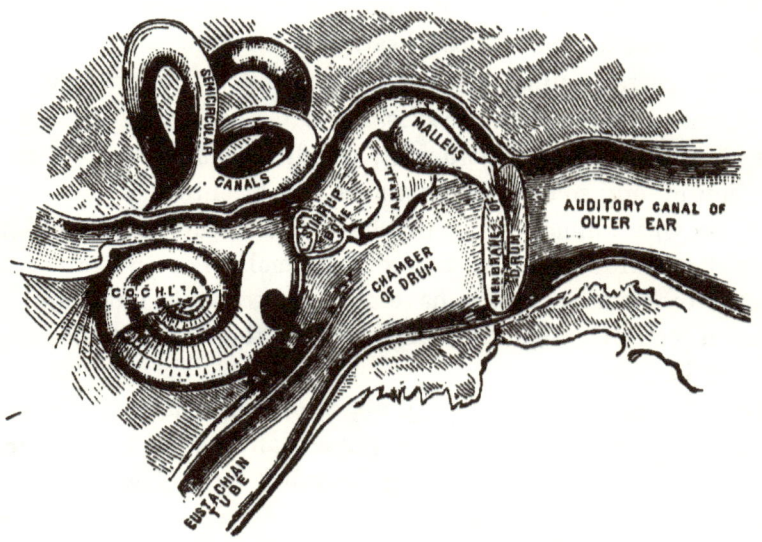

FIG. 64.—SHOWING THE INTERNAL MECHANISM OF THE EAR (GREATLY ENLARGED).

very properly been called the *tympanum*, or the "drum of the ear." The middle ear, like the external canal, contains air.

95. The circular membrane, already mentioned as closing the auditory canal, is the partition which separates the middle from the external ear, and is called the *membrana tympani* (*c*), and may be considered as the outer head of the drum of the ear. It is sometimes itself spoken of as the "drum," but this is incorrect, since a drum is not a membrane, but is the hollow space across which the membrane is stretched. This membranous drum-head is very tense and elastic, and so thin as to be almost transparent; its margin is fastened into a circular groove in the adjacent bone. Each wave of

---

94. What is the middle ear? Why called tympanum ?
95. What is the membrana tympani ? Describe it.

sound that touches this delicate membrane causes it to vibrate, and it, in turn, excites movements in the parts beyond.

96. Within the tympanum is arranged a chain of remarkable "little bones," or *ossicles*. They are chiefly three in number, and from their peculiar shapes bear the following names : *malleus*, or the mallet; *incus*, or the anvil; and *stapes*, or the stirrup. A fourth, the smallest bone in the body, in early life intervenes between the incus and stapes, but at a later period it becomes a part of the incus. It is called the *orbicular* bone. Small as are these ossicles —and they, together, weigh only a few grains—they have their little muscles, cartilages, and blood-vessels, as perfectly arranged as the larger bones of the body. One end of the chain of ossicles, the mallet, is attached to the membrane of the tympanum, or outer drum-head, while the other end, the stirrup, is firmly joined by its foot-piece to a membrane in the opposite side of the cavity. The chain, accordingly, hangs suspended across the drum between the two membranes; and when the outer one vibrates under the influence of the sound-wave, the chain swings inward and transmits the vibration to the entrance of the inner ear.

97. The musical instrument, the drum, is not complete if the air within be perfectly confined ; we therefore find in all instruments of this kind a small opening in the side, through which air may pass freely. By this means the pressure of the air upon the vellum which forms the head of the drum is made equal upon all sides, and the resonance of the drum remains unaffected by the varying density of the atmosphere. It will, therefore, emit its proper sound, whether it be struck in the rarefied air of the mountain-top, or in the condensed air of a mine. The tympanum, or drum of the ear, in like manner has an opening, by means of which it communicates freely with the external air. This opening is a narrow canal, about an inch and a half long, called the *Eustachian tube,* after the name of its discoverer, Eustachius.

98. The course of this passage is indicated in Fig. 64, directed downward and inward : its other extremity opens into the upper

---

96. What are the ossicles? Their number and names? Their arrangement?
97. The Eustachian tube? Describe it, and state its use.
98. What can you state of the action of the Eustachian tube?

part of the throat. The passage itself is ordinarily closed, but whenever the act of swallowing or gaping takes place, the orifice in the throat is stretched open, and the air of the cavity of the tympanum may then be renewed. Air may at will be made to enter through this tube, by closing the mouth and nose, and then trying

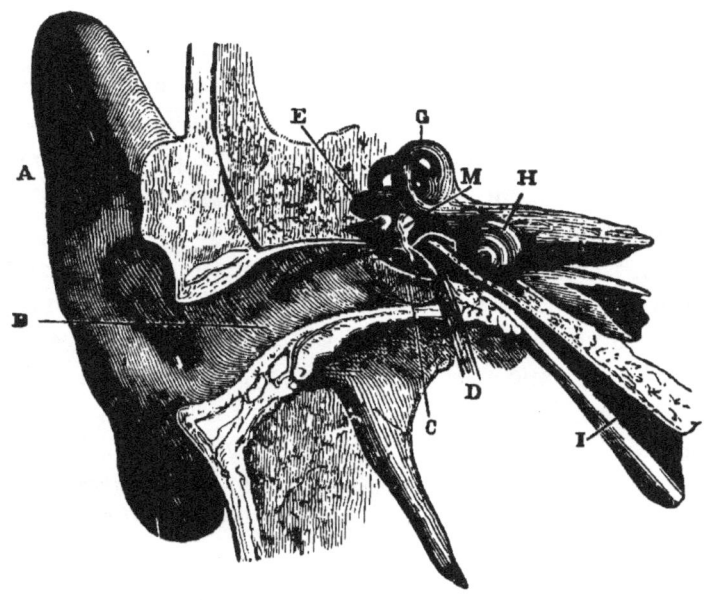

FIG. 65.—SECTION OF THE RIGHT EAR.

A, The Concha.
B, Auditory Canal.
C, Membrane of the Drum.
(the lower half.)
D, A Small Muscle.

E, Incus, or Anvil.
M, Malleus, or Mallet.
I, Eustachian Tube.
G, Semicircular Canals.
H, Cochlea, or Snail's Shell.

to force air through the latter. When this is done, a distinct crackle or clicking sound is perceived, due to the movement of the membranes, and of the little bones of the ear.

99. The Eustachian tube serves, also, as an escape-pipe for the fluids which form within the middle ear; and hence, when its lining membrane becomes thickened, in consequence of a cold or sore throat, and the passage is thus more or less choked up, the fluids are unable to escape as usual, and therefore accumulate within the ear. When this takes place, the vibrations of the membrane are interfered with; the sounds heard appear muffled and indistinct; and a temporary difficulty of hearing, which is known as "throat-deafness," is the result. This result resembles the effect produced by interrupting the vibrations of a sonorous body, such as all are familiar with; if the finger be placed upon a piano-string or bell when it is struck, the proper sound is no longer fully and clearly emitted. But the primary use of this tube is to afford a free com-munication between the middle ear and the external atmosphere, and thus secure an equal pressure upon both sides of the membrane of the drum of the ear, however the density of the atmosphere may vary. If, from undue tension of the membrane, pain is experienced in the ears, when ascending into a rare atmosphere, as in a balloon, or descending into a dense one, as in a diving-bell, it may be relieved by repeating the act of swallowing, from time to time, in order that the inner and outer pressure may thus be promptly equalized.

100. The Internal Ear, or Labyrinth.—The most essential part of the organ of hearing is the distribution of the *auditory nerve*. This is found within the cavity of the internal ear, which, from its exceedingly winding shape, has been termed the *labyrinth* (see Fig. 64, c). This cavity is hollowed out in dense bone, and consists of three parts—the *vestibule* (*a*), or ante-chamber, which is connected with the other two; the *cochlea* (*b*), or snail's shell; and the three *semicircular canals* (*c*). The manner in which the nerve of hearing is distributed is remarkable, and is peculiar to this nerve. In the vestibule and the canals its fibres are spread out over the inner surface, not of the bony cavity, but of a membranous bag, which conforms to and partially fills that cavity, and which floats in it, being both filled and surrounded with a clear, limpid fluid.

101. A singular addition to the mechanism of hearing is observed within this membranous bag of the labyrinth. This consists of two small oval ear-stones, and a quantity of fine powder of a calcareous nature, which is called " ear-sand." When examined under the

---

100. The essential part of the organ of hearing? Its location? Formation?
101. Where is the " ear-sand " found? Give the theory as to its use.

12

microscope, these sandy particles are seen to lie scattered upon and among the delicate filaments of the auditory nerve; and it is probable that, as the tremulous sound-wave traverses the fluid of the vestibule, the sand rises and falls upon the nerve-filaments, and thus intensifies the sonorous impression.

102. In the cochlea, or snail's shell, which contains the fluid, but no membrane, the nerve branches upon a spiral shelf, which, like the cochlea itself, takes two and a half turns, growing continuously smaller as it winds upward. As many as three thousand nerve-fibres of different lengths have been counted therein; these, it has been thought, form the grand, yet minutely small key-board, upon which strike all the musical tones that are destined to be conveyed to the brain. The vestibule, it is also supposed, takes notice of noise as distinguished from musical sounds; while the office of the semicircular canals is, in part at least, to prevent internal echoes, or reverberations.

103. The vestibule communicates with the chain of bones of the middle ear by means of a small opening, called the "oval window," or *fenestra ovalis*. Across this window is stretched the membrane, which has already been alluded to as being joined to the stirrup-bone of the middle ear. Through this window, then, the sound-wave, which traverses the external and middle ear, arrives at last at the labyrinth. The limpid fluid which the latter contains, and which bathes the terminal fibres of the nerve of hearing, is thus agitated, the nerve-fibres are excited, and a sonorous impression is conducted to the brain, or, as we say, a sound is heard.

104. Protection of the Sense of Hearing.—From what has been seen of the complicated parts which compose the organ of hearing, it is evident that while many of them possess an exquisite delicacy of structure, Nature has well and amply provided for their protection. We have observed the concealed situation of the most important parts of the mechanism of the ear—the length of its cavity, its partitions, the hardness of its walls, and its communication with

---

102. In the cochlea, or snail's shell? "Key-board" in the internal ear? The vestibules? Semicircular canals?
103. With what does the vestibule communicate? What is the theory by which sound is conducted to the brain?
104. The formation of the organ of hearing with a view to its protection?

the atmosphere; all these provisions rendering unnecessary any supervision or care on our part in reference to the interior of the ear. But in respect to its external parts, which are under our control and within the reach of harm, it is otherwise. We may both observe the dangers which threaten them, and learn the means necessary to protect them.

105. Caution.—One source of danger to the hearing consists in lowering the temperature of the ear, especially by the introduction of cold water into the auditory canal. Every one is familiar with the unpleasant sensation of distension, and the confusion of sounds which accompany the filling of the ear with water when bathing : the weight of the water within it really distends the membrane, and the cold chills the adjacent sensitive parts. It is not surprising, therefore, that the frequent introduction of cold water, and its continued presence in the ear, enfeebles the sense of hearing. Care should be taken to remove water from the ear after bathing, by holding the head on one side, and, at the same time, slightly expanding the outer orifice, so that the fluid may run out. For a like reason, the hair about the ears should not be allowed to remain wet, but should be thoroughly dried as soon as possible.

106. It may be stated as a general rule, to which there are but few exceptions, that no cold liquid should ever be allowed to enter the ear. When a wash or injection is rendered necessary, it should always be warmed before use. The introduction of cold air is likewise hurtful, especially when it pours through a crevice directly into the ear, as it may often do through the broken or partially closed window of a car. The avoidance of this evil gives rise to another almost as great, namely, the introduction of cotton or other soft substances into the ear to prevent it from " catching cold." This kind of protection tends to make the part unnaturally susceptible to changes of temperature, and its security seems to demand the continued presence of the " warm " covering. As a consequence of its presence, sounds are not naturally conveyed, and the sensitiveness of the nerve of hearing is gradually impaired.

---

105. Danger to which the hearing may be subjected? Advice?
106. The general rule as to the use of water for the ear?

107. The chief source of injury, however, to the ear is from the introduction of solid substances into the auditory canal, with the design of removing insects or other foreign objects that have found their way into the ear, or with the design of scraping out the ear-wax. For displacing a foreign object, it is usually sufficient to syringe the ear gently with warm water, the head being so held that the fluid easily escapes. If a live insect has gained entrance to the ear, it may first be suffocated by pouring a little oil upon it, and afterward removed by syringing the ear as just mentioned.

108. The removal of ear-wax is generally unnecessary; for, as we have before seen, Nature provides that the excess of it shall become dry, and then spontaneously fall out in the form of fine scales. The danger from the introduction of solid implements into the outer ear is chiefly found in the fact that the membrane which lies at the bottom of it is very fragile, and that any injury of it is liable to impair permanently the hearing of the injured ear. (*Read Note* 12.)

109. How Alcohol affects the Special Senses.—The narcotic or benumbing influence of alcohol is felt by all forms of nervous tissue, and among them the nerves of special sense. Vision is more susceptible of injury by this poison than any of the other senses, and it may be either slightly impaired or wholly lost. There is, in such cases, a progressive loss of power in the optic nerve that can only be remedied by a perpetual abandonment, on the part of the sufferer, of alcoholic drink; and even this must not be delayed too long after dimness of sight has commenced.

110. Alcohol and Color-Blindness.—Progressive loss of color-perception has been noticed by physicians in persons who use liquor habitually, though not to the extent of intoxication. This form of gradually growing "color-blindness" becomes a matter of highest importance, since it may occur in a railroad engineer, or pilot, who drinks, or in the case of some official responsible for the lives and limbs of travel by steam. No persons who indulge in alcoholic beverages can safely be allowed to occupy trusts of this nature.

---

107. Chief source of injury to the ear? Directions for removing foreign objects from the ear? Of a live insect?
109. Do those who drink alcohol have good vision?
110. What about their perception of color?

III. Effect of Alcohol on Other Senses.—Hearing and taste are dulled by alcohol. Touch is indirectly robbed of its efficiency in a certain proportion of cases, where a tremor of the muscles of the arm, or the "palsy of drunkards," occurs. Fine penmanship or drawing, and the use of keen-edged tools, depend upon a delicate employment of touch; but with a hand that shakes like the palsied limb of an aged man, this becomes an impossibility. In this way has alcohol deprived many a man of the means of his livelihood. This is said to be especially true of those who belong to the class of topers who drink little and often. (*Read Note* 13, *Page* 210.)

II2. False Apparitions due to Alcohol—Delirium Tremens.— In certain diseases the eyes appear to see objects that do not in reality exist within their view. High fever is one of these diseases; delirium tremens, or "the horrors," experienced by some hard drinkers, is another. The latter condition is marked by a variety of terrifying and loathsome creatures; if there be any form of reptile that is especially repulsive to the delirious person, this is the form that is most liable to haunt him. These false images may be dimly seen at first, but as the disease progresses they generally become perfectly distinct, and real, and torturing; many a victim has thrown himself down from a window, regardless of its height, in his eager haste to escape from his unreal visions. Alarming sounds, also, are heard in some cases of this disorder.

II3. The Effect of Tobacco upon Vision.—Oculists are nearly unanimous in the opinion that impairment of sight and even its utter loss may result from tobacco-smoking, the optic nerve being gradually impaired, as in the case of those who lose their sight by alcohol, as described in the foregoing paragraph of this Chapter, Section 109. There is a relief for this approaching blindness if the patient will consent to wholly abstain from tobacco; and yet, "there are those who would rather smoke than see," and persist in the injurious habit in spite of every proper medical caution.

II4. Certain narcotic substances have an injurious influence over the sense of hearing; among these are tobacco and coffee used in excess. The opium habit is injurious to the sense of sight.

111. Other senses?
112. Are unreal objects ever seen as real? How is delirium tremens described?
113. Has tobacco any influence over vision?
114. Have alcohol and tobacco together any influence? Other injuries?

QUESTIONS FOR TOPICAL REVIEW.

CHAPTER XI.

THE VOICE.

Voice and Speech—The Larynx, or the Organ of the Voice—The Vocal Cords— The Laryngoscope—The Production of the Voice—The Use of the Tongue— The Different Varieties of Voice—The Change of Voice—Its Compass— Purity of Tone—Ventriloquy.

1. Voice and Speech.—In common with the majority of the nobler animals, man possesses the power of uttering sounds, which are employed as a means of communication and expression. In man, these sounds constitute the voice ; in the animals they are designated as the cry. The song of the bird is a modification of its cry, which is rendered possible from the fact that its respiratory function is remarkably active. The sounds of the animals are generally produced by means of their breathing organs. Among the insects, they are sometimes produced by the extremely rapid vibrations of the wings in the act of flight, as in the case of the mosquito ; or by the rubbing together of hard portions of the external covering of the body, as in the cricket. Almost all kinds of marine animals are voiceless. The tambour-fish and a few others have, however, the power of making a sort of noise in the water. (*Read Note* 1.)

2. But man alone possesses the faculty of speech, or the power to use articulate sounds in the expression of ideas, and in the com-

---

1. Voice in Man and Animals.—"The human voice, taking male and female together, has a range of nearly four octaves. Man's power of speech, or the utterance of articulate sounds, is due to his intellectual development more than to any great structural difference between him and the Apes. Song is produced by the glottis, speech by the mouth. The parrot and mocking-bird use the tongue in imitating human sounds."—*Orton's Zoology.*

---

1. The uttering of sounds by animals? How produced?
2. The evidence of man's superior endowment? What is stated of the idiot? Parrot? Raven?

munication of mind with mind. Speech is thus an evidence of the superior endowment of man, and involves the culture of the intellect. An idiot, while he may have complete vocal organs and full power of uttering sounds or cries, is entirely incapable of speech; and, as a rule, the excellence of the language of any people will be found to be proportional to their development of brain. Man, however, is not the only being that has the power to form articulate sounds, for the parrot and the raven may also be taught to speak by rote; but man alone attaches meaning to the words and phrases he employs.

3. Relation to Hearing.—Speech is intimately related to the sense of hearing. A child born deaf is, of necessity, dumb also; not because the organs of speech are imperfect, for he can utter cries and may be taught to speak, and even to converse in a rude and harsh kind of language; but because he can form no accurate notion of sound. A person, whose hearing is not delicate, or as it is commonly expressed, who "has no ear for music," cannot sing correctly. A person who has impaired hearing commonly talks in an unnaturally loud and monotonous voice. These examples show the necessary relation of intelligence and the sense of hearing with that form of articulate voice, which is termed speech. (*Read Note* 2.)

---

2. Certain Peculiarities of the Voice.—"Voice is a sound produced in the throat by the passage of the air through the glottis, as it is expelled from the lungs. It is grave and strong in man, soft and higher in women; it varies according to age. It is alike in both sexes in infancy, but is modified in youth; then the voice is said to 'change.' In the young woman it descends a note or two, and becomes stronger. In the young man the change is much more strongly marked. At the fourteenth or fifteenth year the voice loses its regularity, becomes harsh and unequal; the high notes cannot be sounded, while the grave ones make their appearance. A year is generally sufficient for this change to be complete, and the voice of the child gives place to that of the man. Exercise of the voice in singing should be very moderate, if not entirely suspended, while this change is going on. Voice is divided into singing and speaking voice. One differs from the other almost as much as noises do from musical sounds. It is the short duration of speaking sounds which distinguishes them from those of singing. This is proved by the fact that if we prolong the intonation of a syllable, or utter it like a note, the musical

---

3. Speech and hearing? A deaf child? Person having "no ear for music?" Impaired hearing? What do the examples show?

4. The Organ of the Voice.—The essential organ of the voice is the Larynx. This has been previously alluded to in its relation to the function of respiration; and, in the chapter on that subject, are figured the front view of that organ (Fig. 42), and its connection with the trachea, tongue, and other neighboring parts (Fig. 45). It is situated at the upper part of the neck, at the top of the trachea, or tube by which air passes into and out of the lungs. The framework of the larynx is composed of four cartilages, which render it at once very strong and sufficiently flexible to enable it to move according to the requirements of the voice.

5. The names of the cartilages are (1) the *thyroid*, which is a broad, thin plate, bent in the middle and placed in the central line of the front part of the neck, where it is known as the *pomum Adami*, or Adam's apple (Fig. 66, B), and where it may be felt moving up and down with each act of swallowing; (2) the *cricoid*, which is shaped like a seal ring, with the broad part placed posteriorly (Fig. 66, E). At the top of the cricoid cartilage are situated the two small *arytenoid* cartilages, the right one of which is shown in Fig. 66, C. These latter little organs are much more movable

---

sound becomes evident. And if we pronounce all the syllables of a phrase in the same tone, the speaking voice closely resembles psalm-singing. Every one must have noticed this in hearing school-boys recite or read in a monotone, and the analogy is complete when the last two or three syllables are pronounced in a different tone. Spoken voice is moreover always a chant more or less marked, according to the individual and the sentiment expressed. The accentuation peculiar to certain languages also gives the speech the character of a chant; to a French ear an Italian preacher seems always to sing. A chant also is caused by those inflections of the voice, which express our emotions and our passions. They extend from the feeble murmur, which the ear scarcely perceives, to the piercing cry of pain. Affectionate, sympathetic, imperious, or hostile, they sometimes charm, sometimes irritate, and always move us. It is related of Grétry, that he amused himself by noting as exactly as possible the 'Bonjour, monsieur!' of the persons who visited him; and these words expressed by their intonation, in fact, the most opposite sentiments, although literally the same. Baron, the comedian, moved his audience to tears by his recitation of the stanzas of the song, '*Si le roi m'avait donné Paris sa grand'ville.*'—If the king had given me Paris his great city."—*Le Pileur on Wonders of the Human Body.*

4. Organ of the voice? Where situated? Of what is its framework composed?
5. Names, formation, and situation of the cartilages?

than the other two, and are very important in the production of the voice. They have a true ball-and-socket joint, and several small muscles which contract and relax with as perfect regularity and accuracy as any of the larger muscles of the body.

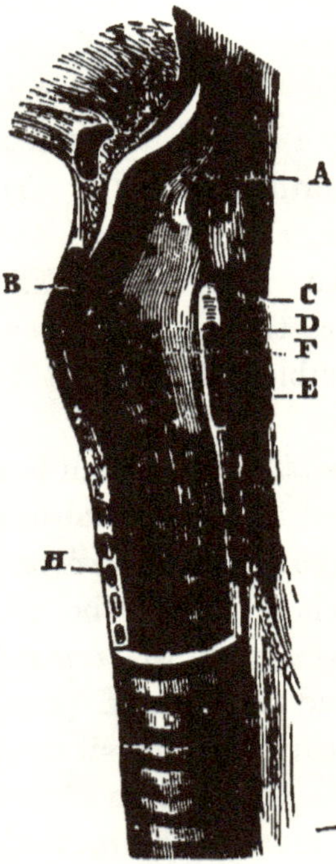

6. The interior of the larynx is lined with a very sensitive mucous membrane, which is much more closely adherent to the parts beneath than is usually the case with membranes of this description. The epiglottis (A), consisting of a single leaf-shaped piece of cartilage, is attached to the front part of the larynx. It is elastic, easily moved, and fits accurately over the entrance to the air-passages below it. Its office is to guard these delicate passages and the lungs against the intrusion of food and other foreign articles, when the act of swallowing takes place. It also assists in modifying the voice.

7. **The Vocal Cords.**—Within the larynx, and stretched across it from the thyroid cartilage in front to the arytenoid cartilages behind, are placed the two sets of folds called the vocal cords. The upper of these, one on each side, are the false cords, which are comparatively fixed and inflexible. These are not at all essential to the formation of vocal sounds, for they have been injured, in those lower animals whose larynx resembles that of man, without materially affecting their characteristic cries. Below these, one on each side, are the two vocal cords (Fig. 66, F), which pursue a similar direction to the false cords—namely, from before backward. They are composed of a highly· elastic, though strong tissue, and are covered with a thin, tightly-fitting layer of mucous membrane. Their edges are smooth and sharply-defined, and when they meet,

FIG. 66. — SECTION OF THE LARYNX AND TRACHEA.
A, The Epiglottis.
B, The Thyroid Cartilage.
C, Arytenoid Cartilage.
D, Ventricle of the Larynx
E, Cricoid Cartilage. ·
F, Right Vocal Cord.
H, The Trachea.

6. Lining of the interior of the larynx? The epiglottis?
7. Where are the vocal cords? The false cords? The true cords?

as they do in the formation of sounds, they exactly match each other.

8. Between the true and false vocal cords is a depression on each side, which is termed the ventricle of the larynx (Fig. 66, D). The integrity of these true cords, and their free vibration, are essential to the formation of the tones and the modulation of the natural voice This is shown by the fact that, if one or both of these cords are injured or become diseased, voice and speech are weakened ; or when the mucous membrane covering them becomes thickened, in consequence of a cold, the vocal sounds are rendered husky and indistinct. When an opening is made in the throat below the cords—as not infrequently occurs in consequence of an attempt to commit suicide—voice is impossible except when the opening is closed by external pressure.

9. The interval or space between the true cords of the voice is constantly varying, not only when their vocal function is in exercise, but also during the act of respiration. Every time the lungs are inflated, the space increases to make wide the entrance for the air, and diminishes slightly during expiration. So that these little cords move gently to and fro in rhythm with the expansion and contraction of the chest in breathing. These movements and others may be seen to take place, if a small mir-

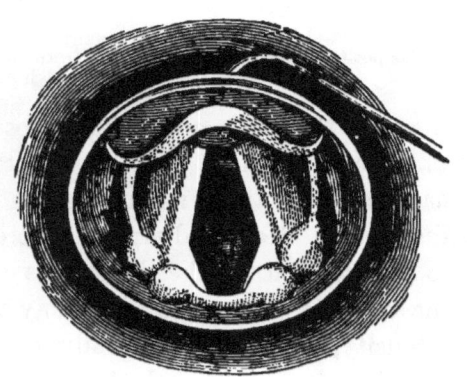

FIG. 67.—A VIEW OF THE VOCAL CORDS BY MEANS OF THE LARYNGOSCOPE.

ror attached to a long handle be placed back into the upper part of the throat ; the handle near the mirror must be bent at an angle of 45°, so that we may look "around the corner," so to speak, behind the tongue. The position which the mirror must assume will be understood by reference in Fig. 45. A view of what may be seen under

8. Where is the ventricle of the larynx? The essentials to the formation of the tones and modulation of the voice?
9. Variation in the interval between the true cords of the voice? Experiment with the mirror?

favorable circumstances, during tranquil inspiration, is represented in Fig. 67. The vocal cords are there shown as narrow, white bands, on each side of the central opening, and since the image is inverted, the epiglottis appears uppermost. The rings partly seen through the opening belong to the trachea. This little mirror is the essential part of an instrument, which is called the laryngoscope, and simple as it may seem, it is accounted one of the most valuable of the recently-invented appliances of the medical art.

10. The Production of the Voice.—During ordinary tranquil breathing, no sound is produced in the larynx, true vocal tones being formed only during forcible expiration, when, by an effort of

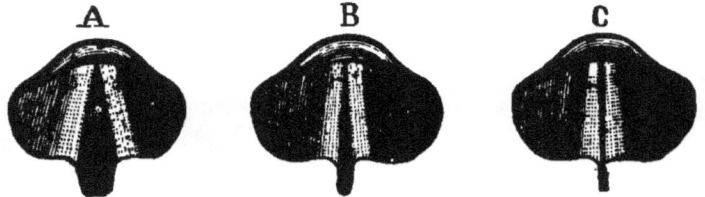

FIG. 68.—THE DIFFERENT POSITIONS OF THE VOCAL CORDS.
A, The position during inspiration. B, In the formation of low notes. C, In the formation of high notes.

the will, the cords are brought close together, and are stretched so as to be very tense. The space between them is then reduced to a narrow slit, at times not more than $\frac{1}{100}$ of an inch in width ; and the column of expired air being forced through it, causes the cords to vibrate rapidly, like the strings of a musical instrument. Thus the voice is produced in its many varieties of tone and pitch ; its intensity, or loudness, depending chiefly upon the power exerted in expelling the air from the lungs. When the note is high, the space is diminished both in length and width ; but when it is low, the space is wider and longer (Fig. 68, B, c), and the number of vibrations is fewer within the same period of time.

11. The personal quality of the voice, or that which enables us to recognize a person by his speech, is mainly due to the peculiar shape of the throat, nose, and mouth, and the resonance of the air contained within those cavities. The walls of the chest and the trachea take part in the resonance of the voice, the air within

10. The formation of true vocal tones?
11. To what is the personal quality of the voice mainly due ? What aids are there ?

them vibrating at the same time with the parts above them. This may be tested by touching the throat or breast-bone, when a strong vocal effort is made. The teeth and the lips also are important, as is shown by the unnatural tones emitted by a person who has lost the former, or by one who is affected with the deformity known as "hare-lip." The tongue is useful, but not indispensable to speech; the case of a woman is reported, from whom nearly the whole tongue had been torn out, but who could, nevertheless, speak distinctly and even sing.

12. The Varieties of voice are said to be four in number; two, the bass and tenor, belonging to the male sex; and two, the contralto or alto, and soprano, peculiar to the female. The baritone voice is the name given to a variety intervening between the bass and tenor. In man, the voice is strong and heavy; in woman, soft and high. In infancy and early youth, the voice is the same in both sexes, being of the soprano variety: that of boys is both clear and loud, and being susceptible of considerable training, is highly prized in the choral services of the church and cathedral. At about fourteen years of age the voice is said to change—that is, it becomes hoarse and unsteady by reason of the rapid growth of the larynx. In the case of the girl, the change is not very marked, except that the voice becomes stronger and has a wider compass; but in the boy, the larynx nearly doubles its size in a single year, the vocal cords grow thicker, longer, and coarser, and the voice becomes masculine in character. During the progress of this change, the use of the voice in singing is injudicious.

13. The ordinary range of each of the four varieties of the voice is about two octaves; but this is exceeded in the case of several celebrated vocalists. Madame Parepa Rosa has a compass of three full octaves. When the vocal organs have been subjected to careful training, and are brought under complete control of the will, the tension of the cords becomes exact, and their vibrations become exceedingly precise and true. Under these circumstances the voice is said to possess "purity" of tone, and can be heard at a great distance, and above a multitude of other sounds. The power of a

pure voice to make itself heard was recently exemplified in a striking manner at a musical festival held in an audience-room of
extraordinary size, and amid an orchestra of a thousand instruments
and a chorus of twelve thousand voices, the artist named above also
sang; yet such was the purity and strength of her voice that its
notes could be clearly heard rising above the vast waves of sound
produced by the full accompaniment of chorus and orchestra.
(*Read Note* 3.)

14. In the production of the articulate sounds of speech, the
larynx is not directly concerned, but those sounds really depend
upon alterations in the shape of the air-passages above that organ.
That speech is not necessarily due to the action of the larynx is
proved by the following simple experiment. Let an elastic tube
be passed through the nostril to the back of the mouth. Then,
while the breath is held, cause the tongue, teeth, and lips to go
through the form of pronouncing words, and at the same time, let a
second person blow through the tube into the mouth. Speech, pure

---

3. The Benefits of Vocal Exercise.—" Reading aloud and recitation are
more useful and invigorating musical exercises than is generally imagined, at least
when managed with due regard to the natural powers of the individual, so as
to avoid effort and fatigue. Both require the varied activity of most of the
muscles of the trunk to a degree of which few are conscious, till their attention
is turned to it. In forming and undulating the voice, not only the chest, but
also the diaphragm and abdominal muscles are in constant action, and communicate to the stomach and bowels a healthy and agreeable stimulus ; and
consequently, where the voice is raised and elocution rapid, as in many kinds
of public speaking, the muscular effort comes to be even more fatiguing than
the mental. When care is taken, however, not to carry reading aloud so far
at one time as to excite the least sensation of soreness or fatigue in the chest,
and it is duly repeated, it is extremely useful in developing and giving tone to
the organs of respiration, and to the general system. To the invigorating
effects of this kind of exercise, the celebrated Cuvier was in the habit of ascrib-
ing his own exemption from consumption, to which, at the time of his appoint-
ment to a professorship, it was believed he would otherwise have fallen a sacri-
fice. The exercise of lecturing gradually strengthened his lungs and improved
his health so much that he was never afterward threatened with any serious
pulmonary disease. But, of course, this happy result followed because the
exertion of lecturing was not too great for the then existing condition of his
lungs."—*Combe's Physiology.*

---

14. The production of the articulate sounds ? What experiment is mentioned ?

and simple, or, in other words, a whisper is produced. Still further continue the experiment, while permitting vocal sounds to be made, and there will be produced a loud and whispering speech at the same moment; thus showing that voice and speech are the result of two distinct acts. Sighing, in like manner, is produced in the mouth and throat; if, however, a vocal sound be added, the sigh is changed into a groan.

15. Ventriloquism is a peculiar modification of natural speech, which consists in so managing the voice that words and sounds appear to issue, not from the person, but from some distant place, as from the chimney, the cellar, or the interior of a chest. The original meaning of the word ventriloquism (that is, speaking from the belly) indicates the early belief that this mode of speech was dependent upon the possession and use of some special organ besides the larynx and mouth; but at the present time it is known that it is produced by these organs alone, and that the sources of deception consist, on the part of the performer, in the dexterous management of the voice, together with a talent for mimicry; and, on the part of the auditory, in the liability of the sense of hearing to error in respect to the direction of sounds. The ventriloquist not only seems to " throw his voice," as it is said, or simulates the sound as it usually appears at a distance with but little motion of the lips and face, but he imitates the voices of an infant and of a feeble old man, of a drunken man disputing with an exasperated wife, the broken language of a foreigner, the cry of an animal in distress, demonstrating that the performer must be proficient in the art of mimicry. Ventriloquism was known to the ancient Romans and Greeks; and it is thought that the mysterious responses that were said to issue from the sacred trees and shrines of the oracles at Dodona and Delphi were really uttered by priests who had the power of producing this form of speech. (*Read Notes* 4 *and* 5.)

---

4. Improvement of Conversation by Vocal Training.—" For years I had fallen into a low, drawling, lazy tone of voice in my ordinary conversation; my utterance came forth in a cloud, and had its dwelling there. From divers experiments and observations I had long ago assured myself that

---

15. What is ventriloquism? Indication of the original meaning of the word? How are the ventriloquous sounds produced?

this was a capital defect; but this assurance had brought with it no reform. Now, at last, I attempted it in good earnest. I studied to bring myself out of my listlessness, to acquire a rapid, distinct, and articulate enunciation. No man can miss this acquisition unless from some organic infirmity, provided only that he pursue it steadily and earnestly. I employed a variety of exercises for the voice, as recitation, the frequent repetition of the same passage, slowly at first, and then more quickly, up to my highest pitch of rapidity, the pronunciation of foreign languages, Greek for the sake of fullness, and French for distinctness and despatch. As a result, I became comparatively a clear and satisfactory speaker; and as my talk was more distinct my thoughts were all the more pointed and precise. I acquired an evenness of tone, a confidence, a complacency; my conversation, as the French say of their language, went of itself; I had leisure to look chiefly to my direction, to march on to my object."
—*Self-Formation, by Capel Lofft.*

5. Ventriloquism and Sound-Painting.—"Ventriloquism bears the same relation to other phenomena of sound that perspective does to optical phenomena. The art of perspective consists in portraying upon a flat surface the appearance of objects at a distance from it, so that the same effect shall be produced upon the eye by the picture as would be produced by the objects themselves. In order to do this, the form, tints, and shades are reproduced, not as they really are, but as they are modified by position and distance. Or it may be said to consist in making and arranging a group of objects so that when *viewed* at a given distance they shall produce the same optical effect produced by another set of objects arranged in different positions and at different distances.

"Ventriloquism consists in making and arranging sounds so that when *heard* at a given distance they shall produce the same effect upon the ear that another set of sounds produce arranged in different positions and at different distances.

"Sounds from a distance are of course weakened, and they also have another quality which may be compared to the indistinctness or outline in objects seen at a distance. In proportion as the fine ear of the ventriloquist can appreciate these modifications will be his success in imitating distant sounds. For as to see correctly is the first essential to success in drawing, so is hearing correctly the first essential in ventriloquism.

"There are many sounds which cannot be imitated by voice merely, such as the singing of birds, the strident noise of a saw, the whistling of a plane, etc. Such and similar unmusical sounds are imitated by means of the teeth, the lips, or the soft parts of the mouth. Thus, the noise of a saw is like that produced by hawking, only much prolonged, and modified by the cheeks; singing of birds may be imitated by whistling through the teeth; the foaming of soda-water by breathing with open lips into a tumbler, etc. To persons having a fine ear this amusing art is not difficult, but we object to the name applied to it. It ought to be called *sound-painting.*"

QUESTIONS FOR TOPICAL REVIEW.

CHAPTER XII.

THE USE OF THE MICROSCOPE IN THE STUDY OF PHYSIOLOGY.

I. The Law of the Tissues.—The will of an infinite Creator is obeyed by atoms as well as by worlds. He has seen fit to commit all the functions of life to structures or tissues so small as to be invisible to the naked eye. A muscle, for example, as we have already learned, is composed of innumerable filaments, visible only by the aid of the microscope ; and the power of the muscular mass is but the sum of the contractile power of the filaments which enter into its composition. Again, each cell of the liver, invisible to unassisted sight, is a secreting organ, and the liver performs as much duty as the sum of these minute organs renders possible.

2. The Necessity of the Microscope.—If, therefore, we would know the real structure of the human body, we *must* make use of the microscope. Our eyes are constructed for the common offices of life, to provide for our wants and guard us from the ordinary sources of danger ; but by arming them with *lenses*, the real structure of plants and animals is revealed to our intelligence ; and enemies, otherwise invisible, that lie in wait in the air we breathe, and in our daily food and drink, to destroy life, are guarded against.

3. Convex Lenses, or magnifying glasses, are disks of glass or other transparent substances, which have the property of picturing upon the retina of the eye an image of an object larger than the image produced there without their aid. The glasses used in microscopes are either double convex lenses (*a*) or plano-convex lenses (*b*). If either of these lenses be placed over a hole in the shutter of a darkened room, or over the key-hole of a door, and a piece of paper be held at a proper distance, a picure of all objects in

---

1. The will of the Creator, by what obeyed? The power of a muscle? Amount of duty performed by the liver?
2. Necessity for using the microscope? The advantages gained by its use?
3. What are convex lenses? Kind of lenses used in microscopes? Experiment? Picture thrown upon the eye? Derivation of the word microscope?

front of the lens will be thrown on the paper, as in the camera-obscura or the magic-lantern. Now, in the same manner, a lens throws a picture of objects to which it is directed on the retina of

a   b

Fig. 69.

the eye, and when that picture is larger than the image made in the eye by the object without the aid of the lens, it is magnified, or the lens has served as a *microscope*, so called from its use in seeing small objects, from *mikros*, small, and *skopeo*, to see.

4. Different Kinds of Microscopes.—Microscopes are either *simple* or *compound.* The glasses of magnifying spectacles, like those commonly used by aged persons, are simple microscopes. Magnifying glasses, mounted in frames, such as are for sale by opticians and others for the detection of counterfeit money, are simple microscopes, and are useful in studying the coarser structure of plants and animals.

5. The most powerful simple microscopes are made by melting in a flame a thread of spun glass, so as to form a minute globule or bead, which, when set in a piece of metal and used to examine objects on a plate of glass held up to the light, gives a high magnifying power. In practice, however, it is found better to use several magnifying glasses of moderate power than a simple lens alone of high power. A combination of two lenses is called a *doublet*—of three, a *triplet.* All *simple* microscopes throw an enlarged image of the object upon the retina. *Compound* microscopes are so constructed that the enlarged image of an object is again magnified by a second lens, and hence their magnifying power is vastly superior to that of simple microscopes.

6. The accompanying diagrams will explain the action of the

---

4. Kinds of microscope? What are simple microscopes?
5. Construction of the most powerful simple microscopes? In practice? A doublet? Triplet? Why are compound microscopes superior to simple ones?
6. Explain, by means of the diagram. the action of the compound microscope.

compound microscope compared with that of the simple microscope. In Fig. 70, which represents the working of the simple microscope, the rays from the object (*a b*), passing through the lens (L), form an image (*a' b'*) in the retina of the eye (E), and as all images are inverted in the eye, the object is seen as all other objects are, and appears erect. In Fig. 71 is seen the action of the compound microscope. An inverted image (*a' b'*) of the object (*a b*) is magnified by the second lens (L'), and an erect image is thrown upon

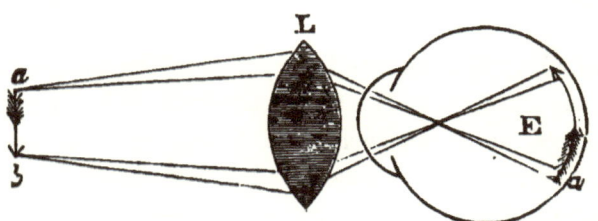

FIG. 70. —SIMPLE MICROSCOPE.

the retina, which, as all other objects seen erect with the naked eye are inverted, gives to the image a contrary direction, or inverts it to the mind.

7. A Compound Microscope consists of two portions: the optical portion, or the lenses, and the mechanical portion, or the instrument which bears the lenses. The glasses of a compound microscope are two: the *object-glass* and the lower lens of Fig. 71, and the *ocular* or *eye-piece* and the upper piece of Fig. 71. Both the object-glass and the eye-piece may, and usually do, consist of more than one lens, for, as has been previously mentioned, better results are obtained by a combination of lenses of moderate power than by single lenses of high power and great curvature.

8. How to Choose and Use a Microscope.—No attractiveness in the mechanical part of a microscope can compensate for inferior lenses; and the very first consideration in the choice of an instrument should be the excellence of the optical part of the instrument. In the use of the instrument, care should be exercised to keep the lenses clean, free from dust, not to press the object-glass upon the object under observation, and not to wet it in the water in which most objects are examined. A good microscope requires its own table; and when not in use, should be covered by a bell glass, or a clean linen cloth.

9. The mechanical portion of the instrument varies greatly in different instruments. That one is the best which is the simplest, the most solid and most easily managed. Most objects in human anatomy are examined in water or in other liquids, or they are themselves liquids; hence an oblique stage is often inconvenient.

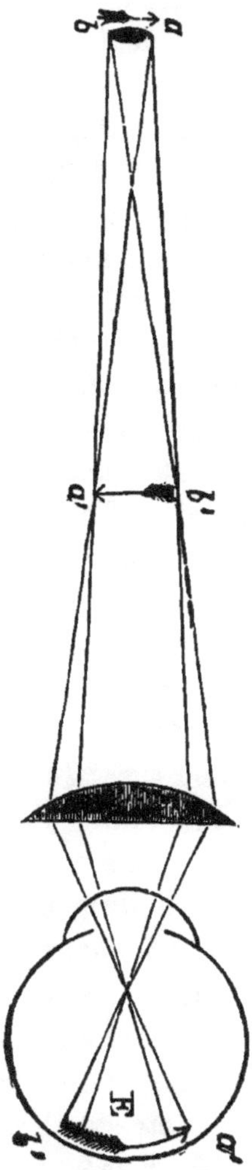

10. Additional Apparatus.—As almost all objects in human anatomy are examined by transmitted light thrown up from the mirror beneath the stage through the object to the eye, they must be placed upon strips of clear glass about three inches long and one inch wide, commonly called "slides." These should be procured with the microscope. Again, most objects seen with high powers require to be covered with a thin plate of glass, very properly called a "cover," that the moisture of the specimen may not tarnish the object-glass. Square or circular covers of very thin glass are therefore provided; and a good supply of these should be always on hand. These glasses should be kept in a covered dish filled with a mixture of alcohol and water. Simple water will not remove the fatty matter which exists in all animal tissues, and, therefore, the glasses cannot be thoroughly cleaned with it alone.

11. When glasses are required for use, they should be removed from the liquid and wiped clean and dry with a soft linen handkerchief. Delicate knives, scissors, needles mounted in handles, forceps, pipettes or little tubes for taking up water, should be ob-

Fig. 71.—Compound Microscope.

9. The characteristics of the best instrument? What special requisites should be insisted upon? Why, as to a horizontal stage?
10. Slides? Covers, square and circular? How kept?
11. Cleaning the glasses? Knives, scissors, etc.? Various liquids?

tained; these are essential to all microscopical study. The table should be supplied with glass-stoppered bottles containing the various liquids ordinarily used in the study of physiology. Thus, tincture of iodine is indispensable in studying vegetable structure, acetic acid in the study of animal tissues; and other articles will have to be added from time to time, as your progress in study demands them.

12. Preliminary Studies.—In order to prepare the way for the study of any department of science with the aid of the microscope —for the microscope is but an eye, and can be turned in almost any direction for purposes of investigation—it is necessary to become acquainted with the many objects which are liable to complicate the examination of particular structures. Both air and water are full of floating bodies, and the most common of these should first occupy the attention. In the city, particles of starch are alway floating in the air. Take a very minute portion of wheat flour, place it in the middle of a clean glass "slide," drop upon it a drop of pure water, cover it with a plate of thin glass, and examine it with a power of from one hundred to six hundred diameters. It will be found to be composed of minute grains or granules, the largest of which are made up of coats or layers, like an onion, arranged around a central spot called the *hilum.*

13. Make another preparation in the same manner, and, after adding the water and before covering with the thin glass cover, add a small drop of a solution of iodine. Now, upon examining the specimen, every grain will be seen to be of a beautiful deep blue color. After thus studying wheat starch, the starch of Indian corn, of arrow-root, and of various grains should be examined in like manner, and their resemblances and differences noted. The granules of potato-starch are as distinctly marked as any.

14. Fibres of cotton, lint, and wool are liable to be found in every specimen prepared for microscopical examination. In order to study these, any cotton, woolen, or linen fabric, or garment, may be scraped, and the scrapings placed on a piece of glass moistened with

---

12. Bodies, in air and water? The examination of starch?
13. The examination with solution of iodine? Advice respecting other articles?
14. Directions for examining cotton and other fibres? Vegetable hairs?

water, covered with the thin glass plate or cover as before, and examined with the same magnifying power, namely, from one hundred to six hundred diameters. Vegetable hairs or down are constantly floating in air and water. These are of very various forms, are simple or grouped, and form very interesting objects of study. They are readily procured from the epidermis or outer membrane of the leaves or stems of plants, by cutting with a delicate knife.

15. The tissues of plants, epidermis, ducts, and woody fibres are constantly found in microscopic preparations. They may be studied in delicate sections made with a sharp knife, or by tearing vegetable tissues apart with needles. The down of moths, the hairs of different animals, the fibres of paper, the most common animalcules in water, the dust of shelves, and generally the structures found in all vegetable and animal substances by which we are surrounded, should be studied as a preliminary to any special line of microscopical investigation.

16. **The Study of Human Tissues.**—When this has been done and familiarity with the use of the instrument has been obtained, proceed to the study of the human body, for human physiology is our subject. If the end of the finger be pricked with a pin, a drop of blood may be procured for examination. Place this on one of the glass slides, cover it with a thin piece of glass, press down the cover so as to make a thin layer, and then examine with the magnifying power just mentioned. Do not add water, for that will cause the blood corpuscles to disappear. If the drop of blood is placed under the microscope at once after being drawn from the finger, most interesting phenomena will be observed. The red corpuscles will be seen to arrange themselves in rows, like piles of coin, while the blood is coagulating. The spherical, white corpuscles will be left out of the rows of red disks, and, if the highest power be used, will be seen to change their shape constantly.

17. If you scrape with a dull knife the inside of the cheek, the flattened scales of " pavement epithelium," or of the insensible cov-

---

15. Directions for examining various tissues?   Down of moths and other structures?
16. Directions for examining a drop of blood?
17. Examination of the scales of the mouth?   Dandruff?

ering which, analogous to the scarf-skin on the outer surface of the body, lines the cavities of its interior, may be readily studied. They have the appearance of transparent tiles, each enclosing a round or oval body, called its nucleus. Dandruff and the scrapings from the skin of the body are composed of scales like those of the mouth, but they differ somewhat in being hardened by horny matter, and in having a very faint central body or nucleus.

18. The Tissues of the Inferior Animals.—The warm-blooded animals do not differ in the tissues or microscopic structures that compose them, but only in the amount and arrangement of these tissues. Milne-Edwards says these tissues "do not differ much in different animals, but their mode of association varies, and it is chiefly by reason of the differences in the combination of these associations in various degrees, that each species possesses the anatomical properties and characters which are peculiar to it."

19. Hence the butcher's stall will furnish all the materials for the study of the microscopic tissues. The structure of the heart, lungs, liver, brain, and muscle, may all be studied, and well studied, by using minute pieces of the flesh of the lower animals, especially of the quadrupeds. Such portions of these animals as are not exposed for sale can be readily obtained by order from the slaughter-house. To examine with the powers of which we have been speaking, it is only necessary to cut off exceedingly small pieces, tear them apart with needles, or make very delicate sections with a sharp knife.

20. Incentives to Study.—A complete knowledge of all minute structures is not to be expected at once, for you are here introduced into a new realm of Nature, a world of little things as vast, as wonderful, and as carefully constructed as the starry firmanent—that other realm of grand objects which the astronomer nightly scans with the telescope. It will not appear singular, therefore, if, at first, you feel strange and awkward in this new creation. With a little perseverance, however, and with the attention directed toward simple objects at the outset, it will not be long before an increasing experience will engender confidence.

21. If to all this there be added an enthusiastic study of the

---

18. In what, as respects the tissues, do the warm-blooded animals differ? Statement of Milne-Edwards?
19. How to procure materials for the study of the tissues of man?

standard authorities on the subject, the rate of progress will be much more rapid. As compared with similar studies, few possess more interest than microscopy, and to the one who pursues it with fondness, it constantly affords sources of pleasure and agreeable surprises; and in the end often leads to new and valuable additions to the sum of human knowledge. The depths which the microscope is employed to fathom are no more completely known than are the heights above us explored and comprehended by the astronomer.

QUESTIONS FOR TOPICAL REVIEW.

APPENDIX.

Poisons and their Antidotes.

ACCIDENTS from poisoning are of such frequent occurrence, that every one should be able to administer the more common antidotes, until the *services of a physician can be obtained.* As many poisons bear a close resemblance to articles in common use, no dangerous substance should be brought into the household without having the word *poison* plainly written or printed on the label ; and any package, box, or vial, without a label, should be at once destroyed, if the contents are not positively known.

When a healthy person is taken severely and *suddenly* ill *soon after some substance has been swallowed,* we may suspect that he has been poisoned. In all cases where poison has been taken into the stomach, it should be quickly and thoroughly expelled by some active emetic, which can be speedily obtained. This may be accomplished by drinking a tumblerful of warm water, containing either a tablespoonful of powdered mustard or of common salt, or two teaspoonfuls of powdered alum in two tablespoonfuls of syrup. When vomiting has already taken place, it should be continued by copious draughts of warm water or mucilaginous drinks, such as gum-water or flaxseed tea, and tickling the throat with the finger until there is reason to believe that all of the poisonous substance has been expelled from the stomach.

The following list embraces only the more common poisons, together with such antidotes as are usually at hand, to be used until the physician arrives.

Poisons.

Acids.—*Hydrochloric acid ; muriatic acid* (spirits of salt); *nitric acid* (aqua fortis); *sulphuric acid* (oil of vitriol).

ANTIDOTE.—An antidote should be given at once to neutralize the acid. Strong soapsuds is an efficient remedy, and can always be obtained. It should be followed by copious draughts of warm water or flaxseed tea. Chalk, magnesia, soda, or saleratus (with water), or lime-water, are the best remedies. When sulphuric acid has been taken, water should be given sparingly, because, when water unites with this acid, intense heat is produced.

Oxalic acid.

ANTIDOTE.—Oxalic acid resembles Epsom salts in appearance, and may easily be mistaken for it. The antidotes are magnesia, or chalk mixed with water.

Prussic Acid; *oil of bitter almonds; laurel water; cyanide of potassium* (used in electrotyping).

ANTIDOTE.—Cold douche to the spine. Chlorine water, or water of ammonia largely diluted, should be given, and the vapor arising from them may be inhaled.

Alkalies and their Salts.—AMMONIA (hartshorn), *liquor or water of ammonia.* POTASSA :—*caustic potash, strong lye, carbonate of potassa* (pearlash), *nitrate of potassa* (saltpetre).

ANTIDOTE.—Give the vegetable acids diluted, as weak vinegar, acetic, citric, or tartaric acids dissolved in water. Castor oil, linseed oil, and sweet oil may also be used ; they form soaps when mixed with the free alkalies, which they thus render harmless. The poisonous effects of saltpetre must be counteracted by taking mucilaginous drinks freely, so as to produce vomiting.

Alcohol.—*Brandy, wine ; all spirituous liquors.*

ANTIDOTE.—Give as an emetic ground mustard or tartar emetic. If the patient cannot swallow, introduce a stomach pump ; pour cold water on the head.

Gases.—*Chlorine, carbonic acid gas, carbonic oxide, fumes of burning charcoal, sulphuretted hydrogen, illuminating or coal-gas.*

ANTIDOTE.—For poisoning by chlorine, inhale, cautiously, ammonia (hartshorn). For the other gases, cold water should be poured upon the head, and stimulants cautiously administered; artificial respiration. (See *Marshall Hall's Ready Method*, page 293.)

Metals.—*Antimony, tartar emetic, wine of antimony*, etc.

ANTIDOTE.—If vomiting has not occurred, it should be produced by tickling the throat with the finger or a feather, and the abundant use of warm water. Astringent infusions, such as common tea, oak bark, and solution of tannin, act as antidotes.

Arsenic.—*White arsenic, Fowler's solution, fly-powder, cobalt, Paris green,* etc.

ANTIDOTE.—Produce vomiting at once with a tablespoonful or two of powdered mustard in a glass of warm water, or with ipecac. The antidote is hydrated peroxide of iron. If Fowler's solution has been taken, lime-water must be given.

Copper.—*Acetate of copper* (verdigris), *sulphate of copper* (blue vitriol), food cooked in dirty *copper vessels*, or pickles made green by *copper.*

ANTIDOTE.—Milk or white of eggs, with mucilaginous drinks (flaxseed tea, etc.), should be freely given.

Iron.—*Sulphate of iron* (copperas), etc.

ANTIDOTE.—Carbonate of soda in some mucilaginous drink, or in water, is an excellent antidote.

Lead.—*Acetate of lead* (sugar of lead), *carbonate of lead,* (white lead), water kept in *leaden pipes* or *vessels*, food cooked in *vessels* glazed with *lead.*

ANTIDOTE.—Induce vomiting with ground mustard or common salt in warm water. The antidote for soluble preparations of lead is Epsom salts; for the insoluble forms, sulphuric acid largely diluted.

Mercury.—*Bi-chloride of mercury* (corrosive sublimate), *ammoniated mercury* (white precipitate), *red oxide of mercury* (red precipitate), *red sulphuret of mercury* (vermillion).

ANTIDOTE.—The white of eggs, or wheat flour beaten up with water and milk, are the best antidotes.

Silver.—*Nitrate of silver* (lunar caustic).

ANTIDOTE.—Give a teaspoonful of common salt in a tumbler of water. It decomposes the salts of silver and destroys their activity.

Zinc.—*Sulphate of zinc,* etc. (white vitriol).

ANTIDOTE.—The vomiting may be relieved by copious draughts of warm water. The antidote is carbonate of soda administered in water.

Narcotic Poisons.—*Opium* (laudanum, paregoric, salts of morphia, Godfrey's cordial, Dalby's carminative, soothing syrup, cholera mixtures), *aconite, belladonna, hemlock, stramonium, digitalis, tobacco, hyosciamus, nux vomica, strychnine.*

ANTIDOTE.—Evacuate the stomach by the most active emetics, as mustard, alum, or sulphate of zinc. The patient should be kept in motion, and cold water dashed on the head and shoulders. Strong coffee must be given. The physician will use the stomach pump and electricity. In poisoning by nux vomica or strychnine, etc., chloroform or ether should be inhaled to quiet the spasms.

Irritant Vegetable Poisons.—*Croton oil, oil of savine, poke, oil of tansy,* etc.

ANTIDOTE.—If vomiting has taken place, it may be rendered easier by copious draughts of warm water. But if symptoms of insensibility have come on without vomiting, it ought to be immediately excited by ground mustard mixed with warm water, or some other active emetic, and after its operation an active purgative should be given. After evacuating as much of the poison as possible, strong coffee or vinegar and water may be given with advantage.

Poisonous Fish.—*Conger eel, mussels, crabs,* etc.

ANTIDOTE.—Evacuate, as soon as possible, the contents of the stomach and bowels by emetics (ground mustard mixed with warm water or powdered alum), and castor oil, drinking freely at the same time of vinegar and water. Ether, with a few drops of laudanum mixed with sugar and water, may afterward be taken freely.

Poisonous Serpents.—ANTIDOTE.—A ligature or handkerchief should be applied moderately tight above the bite, and a cupping-glass over the wound. The patient should drink freely of alcoholic stimulants containing a small quantity of ammonia. The physician may inject ammonia into the veins.

Poisonous Insects.—*Stings of scorpion, hornet, wasp, bee,* etc.

ANTIDOTE.—A piece of rag moistened with a solution of carbolic acid may be kept on the affected part until the pain is relieved; and a few drops of carbolic acid may be given frequently in a little water. The sting may be removed by making strong pressure around it with the barrel of a small watch-key.

Drowning.

MARSHALL HALL'S "READY METHOD" of treatment in asphyxia from drowning, chloroform, coal-gas, etc.

1st. Treat the patient *instantly on the spot*, in the *open air*, freely exposing the face, neck, and chest to the breeze, except in severe weather.

2d. In order *to clear the throat*, place the patient gently on the face, with one wrist under the forehead, that all fluid, and the tongue itself, may fall forward, and leave the entrance into the windpipe free.

3d. *To excite respiration*, turn the patient slightly on his side, and apply some irritating or stimulating agent to the nostrils, as *veratrine, dilute ammonia*, etc.

4th. Make the face warm by brisk friction; then dash cold water upon it.

5th. If not successful, lose no time; but, *to imitate respiration*, place the patient on his face, and turn the body gently, but completely *on the side, and a little beyond;* then again on the face, and so on, alternately. Repeat these movements deliberately and perseveringly, *fifteen times only* in a minute. (When the patient lies on the thorax, this cavity is *compressed* by the weight of the body, and *ex*piration takes place. When he is turned on the side, this pressure is removed, and *in*spiration occurs.)

6th. When the prone position is resumed, make a uniform and efficient pressure *along the spine*, removing the pressure immediately, before rotation on the side. (The pressure augments the *ex*piration, the rotation commences *in*spiration.) Continue these measures.

7th. Rub the limbs *upward*, with *firm pressure* and with *energy*. (The object being to aid the return of venous blood to the heart.)

8th. Substitute for the patient's wet clothing, if possible, such other covering as can be instantly procured, each bystander supplying a coat or cloak, etc. Meantime, and from time to time, *to excite inspiration*, let the surface of the body be *slapped* briskly with the hand.

9th. Rub the body briskly until it is dry and warm, then dash *cold* water upon it, and repeat the rubbing.

Avoid the immediate removal of the patient, as it involves a *dangerous loss of time;* also, the use of bellows, or any *forcing* instrument; also, the *warm bath*, and *all rough treatment.*

The Care of the Sick-Room.

The sick-room should be bright and airy, and "Sweetness and light" its motto. Other things being equal, it is best on one of the upper floors—in the case of some "catching" disease on the top floor. Let it be on the sunny side of the house. If for any reason the light of the sun is temporarily to be avoided—as when the eyes are sensitive or have been operated upon—let the light be shut out by a proper arrangement of blinds or curtains. The air-supply to be breathed by the sick person should be pure. Those who, in health, find themselves in an impure air can quit it; they are not compelled to suffer from it; but a sick person may be incapable of recognizing the bad quality of the air, as well as helpless to free himself from it.

To keep the air pure, the windows should be opened as often as three times a day, care being taken to protect the patient from being chilled, while the room is being aired.

Unless the physician shall direct differently, one window—that most remote from the bed—should be open an inch or more both day and night, and in all seasons. The extent to which the sash shall be lowered must be governed largely by the weather and the direction of the wind.

A fire, in an open fireplace, except in summer weather, will be a great help towards keeping the air pure. The upward current through a chimney-flue, if unobstructed, is equal to or not far below 20,000 cubic feet per hour; an outlet sufficient for a room occupied by ten persons.

The inlet of air, however, must not be forgotten, otherwise the air of the room tends to become both impure and too thin. As our houses are generally constructed, the inlet of air is best secured by a window-sash being lowered from the top.

Take special care that no stationary wash-basin or other sewer-connected convenience is improperly plumbed, and that sewer gas cannot by any possibility escape into the sick-room.

The swinging of doors to create a current is not an efficient means of ventilation, as it agitates the air of the room without purifying it, and often disturbs the patient.

A draught of air is to be avoided; it will seldom occur that the air of the room requires to be so speedily changed that the patient need be exposed to a draught; never, when care has been taken to provide continuous and gradual ventilation.

It should be borne in mind that cold air is not necessarily pure air, and that ventilation is not less needed in winter than in warm weather.

Sleep is a great necessity to the sick. If a well person slumbers in the day-time, it will interfere with his sound repose at night, but with the sick this is generally not the case. The more they sleep the more favorable are the chances for their recovery: so that it will be readily seen how important it is to avoid noise and jar in the sick-room, especially if the disease is acute.

Bear in mind that even slight noises, as the rustling of garments, the creaking of doors, whispering, or noisy footfalls, may be sufficient to disturb a brain that is rendered sensitive by pain or wakefulness.

The clothing next the skin should be changed more frequently in sickness than in health. These changes must be quickly and deftly made, and with as little disturbance as possible.

Under some conditions of disease, the best welfare of the patient is accomplished by having two beds in the room instead of one.

The temperature of the room must be watched. To that end a thermometer should always be present, and easily approached. It is better not to have it directly in the view of the patient. The temperature should not be allowed to vary much from 65° F., unless the doctor otherwise directs.

Let the furniture be as plain and as free from upholstery as possible; not many pieces are required. Movable carpets or rugs are better than those that are permanently laid. Curtains about the windows are out of place in a sickroom: so are flowering plants and birds, as a general rule. Florence Nightingale, however, makes an exception in the case of chronic invalids, and consents to the comforting influence of a pet bird or two.

In regard to the admission of visitors and conversation, much will depend upon the strength of the patient and the kind of sickness: at many times these are to be forbidden, as having a disquieting influence. When contagious disease is in the house, the sick-room must be avoided by all except those who have the care of the patient, and those having this care should avoid coming in contact with the other members of the household, especially the children.

Bear in mind that everything brought in contact with the sick is liable to endanger the health of the well.

No articles in use by the invalid should be removed or used by others until thoroughly disinfected; the dishes and spoons should be put in boiling water before being taken from the room. The room itself should be fumigated with sulphur when the person is removed from it.

Old pieces of muslin, etc., may be used instead of handkerchiefs to receive the poisonous discharges from the nose, mouth, and throat. These can be destroyed by fire, and thus prevent the danger of conveying the disease to others.

"Taking the breath" and kissing should be avoided by those in attendance upon the case.

The bottles of medicine and other reminders of illness should, as far as convenient, be withdrawn from the view of the sick.

Such as are to be kept always at hand, should be arranged in an orderly way upon a tidily-covered bed-side table. The sight of a siphon bottle of aërated water is agreeable to most patients; that may be kept in the room, but the vessels containing milk, drinking-water, etc., should be kept elsewhere.

Disinfection.

Filth fosters or produces certain diseases; it should, therefore, be removed as soon as possible. When it is difficult to remove it, disinfectants come into play, as they have the power to rob it of some of its disease-making force. But let it be remembered that disinfection is not cure ; it is not a substitute for cleanliness and pure air. The true cure is the removal of filth ; and when our homes are concerned in some question of drainage where the filth is out of our sight, it may be necessary to consult and employ the plumber or some other artisan.

In times gone by, it was the custom to mask bad smells by burning pastiles, coffee, cascarilla, and the like. These are not now much used, for most persons have come to understand that the fumes thus created do not remove, but simply overpower the evil odors.

Chemistry has advanced to such a point that various pungent chemical substances, formerly not well known, can be furnished at small cost, and these substances have the power, in varying degrees, to check vile odors. Carbolic acid, chloride of lime, and Labarraque's solution are among the best known of these, but there are also certain of the salts of iron, and zinc, and the permanganate of potash that may be used. Sulphur is much used for the fumigation of rooms that have been infected.

Another cheap disinfectant is a solution of chloride of lead. It is inodorous, effective, and the cost is small. Take half a drachm of the nitrate and dissolve it in a pint or more of boiling water. Dissolve two drachms of common salt in a pail or bucket of water ; pour the two solutions together, and allow the sediment to sink. A cloth dipped in this solution, and hung up in a room, will correct a bad odor promptly, or if the solution be thrown down a drain, or upon foul-smelling refuse, it will have the same effect.

The room to be purified with sulphur should be made as tight as possible, so that no fumes can escape, either by window, door, or chimney. Put three pounds of sulphur in an iron pot, which should not stand upon woodwork or carpet, lest they be burned, but in a large pan of ashes, or upon a layer of bricks ; on this sulphur pour a tablespoonful of alcohol. This is then set on fire, and everybody immediately withdraws from the room. The room should remain closed ten hours, after which it should be thoroughly aired before it is occupied, for the fumes of the sulphur are irritating to the lungs.

The chemicals above mentioned should be known and labeled as poisons. Many persons have been injured, if not killed, by incautiously or ignorantly drinking those that are of a liquid form.

Heat is one of the best, if not the best disinfecting agent. Articles of bedding and furniture that cannot well be treated otherwise, can be purified by a long exposure to a temperature of 240° F. In some cities, especially in England, furnaces are made for the reception of bulky articles that have become infected.

Fresh pure air is another powerful agent. If woven fabrics, clothing, and the like are for a long time aired out of doors, they cease to be infective ; probably by the enormous dilution, if not destruction, of the elements of danger.

Certain diseases are "catching;" they have the power of spreading from one person to another, chiefly by the particles that pass off from the body of the patient. Among these diseases are small-pox, measles, scarlet-fever, and diphtheria. The articles that are worn or used by the patient become "infected," and they should be disinfected before they are used by others. As a rule, of course, a doctor will be called in to attend to these diseases. When that is so, follow his directions as to disinfection, as well as every other part of the treatment of the case. For substances that are not injured by being washed, a good and cheap disinfectant is sulphate of zinc ("white vitriol") and common salt dissolved in water, boiling hot if possible, using eight tablespoonfuls of the zinc and four of salt to the gallon of water. This is useful for clothing, bed-linen, towels, handkerchiefs, etc. After these articles have lain for an hour or two in this solution, they should be allowed to stand in boiling water before being washed. Infected articles that are of little value should, of course, be destroyed by fire.

The United States Treasury Department has published the following formula for the disinfection of the rags coming from Egypt: "1. Boiling in water for two hours under a pressure of fifty pounds per square inch; 2. Boiling in water for four hours without pressure; or, 3. Subjection to the action of sulphur fumes for six hours, burning one and one-half to two pounds of roll-brimstone in each 1,000 cubic feet of space, with the rags well scattered upon racks." Either of these three methods is accepted as sufficiently thorough to prevent the spreading of cholera by means of rags.

Emergencies.

"The readiness is all."—Hamlet.

The life of many a child has been saved by the fire-drill in schools, and great good has been done on shipboard by a drilling of the crews.

If in a building filled with smoke, get down on hands and knees and crawl to door or window.

In a cellar, well, or vat, where carbonic acid can collect, the true posture is to stand erect. If a candle, on being lowered into a suspected place, is put out, you may know that there is danger to human life.

Burns and Scalds.—The secret of the best treatment of these injuries is to exclude the air from the wounded surfaces. When they are slight, and the skin is not destroyed but merely blistered, prevent the displacement of the skin as much as possible. Let the blisters be punctured, if necessary, to let out the liquid, and then keep the skin in place by cotton cloth or lint, wet with a solution of one teaspoonful of carbolic acid in a quart of water, or a strong solution of baking soda. The cloth should be kept wet constantly, but do not irritate the wound by taking off the dressing too often.

Extensive burns are much worse than deep burns. In the former case, the outlook is grave, and the patient will probably require the best aid, both medical and surgical, of some physician.

Scars after Burns.—If a burn be on the face, neck, or near a joint, it is not well to hasten the healing process, on account of the contraction that always takes place as the scar is formed.

" **Fire** is a source of danger, and is very destructive to life at times. Spontaneous combustion of the human body when saturated with alcohol is a myth, though perhaps the alcoholized body does burn more readily than one free from inflammable fluid. When a lady is on fire, she should not, and ought not to be permitted to run ; that fans the flames amazingly. She must be laid down and rolled up in the nearest woolen article,—rug, coat or blanket. Such wrapping up in a non-inflammable article is a most effective method of extinguishing the flames. Immersion in water is, unfortunately, rarely practicable."—*Fothergill.*

Illuminating Gas is dangerous in two ways. If it escapes into a tightly-closed room in sufficient quantities, it causes the death of the inmates by suffocation, unless some one from without discovers the perilous situation. If not too late, remove the patient into fresh air, undo the clothing, dash cold water on the face and neck, and employ artificial respiration, as in drowning (see p. 293). Again : If it escapes freely into an apartment, it forms an explosive compound by mixing with the air. If then a light is unguardedly taken into the place, an explosion that may be destructive to life will result. Always thoroughly air any room that has the odor of escaping gas before a light is taken in.

Kerosene is the cause of even more "accidents" than gas. Too much care cannot be taken in its use. Buy only that which has been tested, but remember that not all that are marked as "safe" are truly so. If a responsible oil-man certifies that the oil will not "flash" under 140 degrees, it may be regarded as safe if properly used. Lamps should be filled only in the daytime. Never attempt to fill a lamp that is lighted, and never put kerosene in the stove for the purpose of kindling a fire. Very small lamps are dangerous, as also is a lamp that has burned a long time, and has but very little oil in it.

Frost-bites.—Keep away from the fire and in a cool room. Rub the nose or other part that has been "bitten" with snow or ice-water until the blood again is warmed and circulating in the part. Chilblains should not be brought to the fire ; if the skin is unbroken, it should be hardened by brushing it over with alcohol having tannin in it.

Cuts.—These, if severe, should be promptly attended by a physician, but every one should know how to treat small wounds. Learn the difference between the two kinds of bleeding, called "arterial" and "venous." Arterial is bright red and comes in jets (or with throbs corresponding to the pulse) ; venous is dark-colored and flows continuously. In the former, press on that side of the wound nearer to the heart ; in the latter, on the further side. Or, pressure may be made over the wound itself with the fingers ; this may stop the loss of blood from small arteries as well as from veins. Loss of blood from arteries is apt to be more rapid and dangerous than that from veins, and when the cut vessel is a large one, the skill of the surgeon will ordinarily be required in order to close the bleeding artery permanently and securely.

It is well, in every household, to have, in some handy and well-known place, some strips of old muslin and some lint, or oakum, a bandage or two and some adhesive plaster, a soft sponge, and needles and thread in a basket or box by themselves. In this way, valuable time may be saved in the staunching of blood, flowing in consequence of some accidental cut or other injury.

Fits or Convulsions.—These may be trivial or grave. If it is a young woman, the attack is probably hysterical and, as a rule, not dangerous, and a sprinkle of cold water will bring relief. If the patient struggles with regularity of movement, and there is bloody froth on the lips, it is a case of epilepsy, and requires a physician's attendance. Meanwhile, protect the head from injury by putting a pillow or some soft article beneath it; a cork introduced between the teeth will prevent the biting of the tongue. Prevent the person from falling or injuring himself, but do not attempt to forcibly hold him quiet.

In children, apply cloths dipped in water to the head; disturb the child as little as possible; do not use a warm bath until directed by the doctor.

Fainting.—This occurs when the blood is deficient in the brain. The proper position, therefore, is upon the back. Let the window be opened to admit fresh air; fanning, and the sprinkling of water are useful. If the clothing about the chest is tight, let it be loosened. If the faint occurs at church or some public gathering, remove the person promptly to the outer air; for foul air is frequently the cause of the trouble.

Vertigo.—This is "a rush of blood to the brain." The body should be placed in a sitting posture, with the head erect. If the blood escapes into the brain by reason of the rupture of a blood-vessel within it, the case is very grave, and the physician should be summoned at once. Meanwhile, let the position of the body be as above stated. Apoplexy is known, in very many cases, by the helpless condition of an arm or leg, or both.

Sunstroke is seldom produced in this climate in persons who have not labored too hard. Fatigue and sun-heat are commonly the joint causes of sudden prostration in summer; although "heat-stroke" may occur in an artificially-heated atmosphere, without exposure to the sun. In the tropics, the least possible exertion is by the natives put forth during the midday hours. On very hot days, therefore, avoid fatigue and labor in the open air as much as possible. Keep the head cool. If any unusual, dizzy feeling comes on, apply cold water to the head and neck. If a person falls unconscious, and the skin is decidedly hot and dry, he should be taken to a cool place. If the face and head are red and hot, apply ice-water on cloths. If pale, give stimulants gradually, and use cold water sparingly.

Shock may be caused by a fall or a blow upon the head or the pit of the stomach. It is known by slowing of the pulse and respiration; the face is pale and the skin becomes cool. The head should be placed low, some ammonia in water be given, and warmth applied to the surface of the body.

The Home and Health.

The location of the house should be airy, dry, and sunny.

A certain amount of elevation is necessary, in order to secure proper drainage. Too much shade must not fall upon the house, as sunlight is very necessary to a proper degree of animal vigor. Young children, as is well known, especially profit by the tonic influence of sunlight.

The cellar is an important part of the dwelling; therefore, unless care be taken for its ample ventilation, it will be the source from which is supplied much of the air breathed in the upper chambers of the house. If the cellar is damp the house is liable to become so, and if vegetables are stored in the cellar, an especial degree of care is needed to ventilate it thoroughly and constantly.

House Drainage.—An English writer has stated that "the most important part of the house is the drains." This, no doubt, sounds strangely to the ears of many, who have been brought up to view the parlor or drawing-room as the true centre of the house, and yet it is no foolish saying, when we reflect that with a bad system of drainage to a house every dweller therein stands in peril of several forms of disease that, mild as the cases may be, are a source of anxiety, and when severe, too often have a fatal termination. Drain-diseases, such as typhoid fever, dysentery, diphtheria, and scarlet fever, often destroy entire families. These diseases do not always spring upon a home through defective drainage, but when they do, they frequently show themselves in a very violent form.

Drainage (as applied to dwellings) consists in conveying away from the house the liquid and solid impurities that would otherwise accumulate in or near the dwelling. Waste is a necessary accompaniment of all animal life, to the preparation and the taking of food, to the clothing of the body, to bathing and other simple acts of daily life. The waste material of houses tends to decay and to become offensive. It must, therefore, not only be put out of sight and smell, but must be removed so far away that it cannot return in the form of dangerous, invisible gases of decomposition.

The best house-drains are made of iron or glazed earthenware, carefully selected and well laid. The joints of the pipes should be gas-tight. The soil-pipe should be carried up to and through the roof. All the waste-pipes from basins, etc., in the rooms should be joined in a gas-tight manner to the soil-pipe, and each and every basin and other fixture should have a separate trap. What is a trap? It is a device that is designed to retain a certain portion of the water running through it—called the "water-seal"—so that the ascent of air or gas, from the drain back into the room, is prevented. It "traps" the sewer gas away from us. Whenever a fixture has been used and there is not, beyond all doubt, a sufficiency of water to fill the trap, additional water should be poured in. Traps are of various sizes, and of an infinite variety of patterns and patents, and must vary greatly according to their situation ; but one thing should be made sure of in their use—namely, that they hold not less than two inches of water as a "seal."

There is at almost all seasons of the year an upward, because warmer, current of air through the main pipes. It is therefore better to have a fresh-air inlet pipe near the point where the drain leaves the house-wall. This helps to prevent the unsealing of traps. It also brings about a purer condition of the air in the interior of the system of pipes—so useful is this air-current through the soil-pipe that if applied there is little danger of the escape of sewer gas into the living rooms.

What is sewer gas or sewer air? It varies greatly in different places and at different times. It is not a definite gas, like oxygen, nitrogen, etc., but varies in composition, and what is still more worthy of note, it varies in its dangerous qualities. It is not always offensive, although it is generally so ; its odor has been described as being "sweetish and sickish." Its dangerous qualities have not yet been determined by chemistry or the microscope, but one practical point may be borne in mind—namely, that when a case or cases of contagious disease occur in any house along any given line of sewer pipes, it is best to use disinfectants in the drainage of the other dwellings along the same line of sewer. Children should avoid playing over or around the sewer-gratings in the streets at all times, and especially when scarlet fever and like contagious diseases are known to be in the neighborhood ; for the exit of sewer air at these points is always very free, unless it be directly after rainfall.

One other point must be remembered—that the best-laid system of house-plumbing is not indestructible. In the course of time, defects will arise, breaks will occur ; for this reason it would be well for every householder to have an examination made at intervals of every joint and along the whole line of the house connection with the sewer or drain.

It is thought by many that sewer gas is not found in the country because there are no sewers—they have been misled by the word. If the words "drain air" or "filth gas" had been adopted, the universal production of this injurious substance, in close connection with every abode of man, wherever located, might have been better understood. In country houses there are, perhaps, fewer dangers of contamination of the air we breathe by waste products, because there are fewer water-closets, wash-basins, sinks, etc., and the rooms are less exposed to impure air.

But in the country danger is apt to come by or through the pollution of the water supply. The well, which furnishes that cool and refreshing draught, is the point to be watched. It is convenient to have the well near the house, because when snow is on the ground and the weather is cold, the distance to the well from the house is a matter of no small moment. Near the house must be the stable and pens for animals—the waste from the house goes upon the ground, and not very far away from the house—the chamber slops and the more offensive matters go into a pit, which must not be too distant. The result of all these conditions is a pollution of the soil at all these points—a pollution which spreads with every rainfall, and which, sooner or later, reaches the well ; yet the water may appear as pure as ever. It only remains to have the suitable disease-germ lodged in this polluted territory to bring down the whole household with a fever. This is the kind of soil-pollution which is hard to cure, and which, in long-settled countries, causes laws to be enacted requiring all vaults for the reception of house and human waste to be made water-tight, so as to save the soil from its poisoning influence.

This is the kind of poisoning which, in the Dark Ages, caused so much unrighteous persecution of the innocent. In those days, no care whatever was taken in the towns, high-walled, crowded, and unsewered, to protect the water supply from pollution—as a result, some terrible epidemic of fever would arise. Then the angry populace would, in their ignorance, cry out : "The Jews have poisoned the wells." The wells were poisoned, no doubt, but the Jew was no more worthy of blame than were his accusers. Nevertheless, the Jews were not spared—they were robbed, imprisoned, executed.

Drainage in the city is a comparatively easy problem when the city's sewers are laid in the streets. In the country it is more difficult, and on this account the fewer fixtures or "modern improvements" there are in the house the better it will be. There should be no less care within the country house, where waste-pipes are put in, than in the city house. The material should be well selected, tightly joined, and properly ventilated. The water-closet should be remote from the house. Earth-closets are better than the ordinary vaults—house-waste from kitchen and laundry should be taken to a considerable distance from the house, and far away from the well, and either deposited in a water-tight cesspool or conveyed away, by a system of subsoil drainage tiles, arranged so as to fertilize some unoccupied plot of ground.

On Going into the Country.

To spend the summer in the country would be the choice of all city-dwellers, whenever their purses will permit of it. And there are not a few advantages in such a course ; the change of scene is good, the mountains and the seaside give a purer and cooler air—an air that invigorates and aids in restful sleep at night, so different from the midsummer atmosphere in hot cities. There are fewer excitements in the country ; we do not "live so fast," and there is full scope for healthful life and activity in the open air, with the green and blue of nature all about us, instead of the monotonous walls of towering houses.

But this course, pleasant and helpful to so many, is not without its danger.

Many who "go away" on vacation are brought home sick on account of fever or other sickness caused by defects and faults of drainage existing in these temporary summer homes. Scarcely a year goes by that one or more summer resorts have not gained the ill name of being the hotbeds of typhoid fever, dysentery, and the like.

In view of this, how important it becomes that we exercise judgment, and seek skilled advice in the selection of our summering places.

Again, there is another danger that must not be overlooked. Let us suppose that the summer vacation has passed by without accident; that we return invigorated by the experience, and that the home in the city has been empty and closed during our absence; what has happened that the air in the rooms newly reopened should be foul and stifling? This has taken place; the water that stands in the traps of house pipes, and shuts off gases from the sewer, when the rooms are in use and water is daily entering the different wash-basins, etc., has during our absence been evaporated. For weeks, perhaps, there has been no "water-seal" in the traps, and the ascent of sewer air has been going on continuously, so that not only is the air utterly unfit to live in, but all the curtains, carpets, and other absorbing materials have become saturated with the pollution thus allowed to enter. Let it be remembered that when a sink, etc., is not in use, it is gradually losing the trap-water by the evaporation.

What is the remedy, you will ask, for the condition of things caused by closing up the house, as above stated? To this the reply is, that the house should from time to time be opened and aired, and water should be poured down each and every sanitary fixture, in sufficient quantity to renew the supply of water in the trap of each.

EXERCISES FOR HOME GYMNASTICS.

(See Page 43.)

Fig. 1.—Position for Exercising.

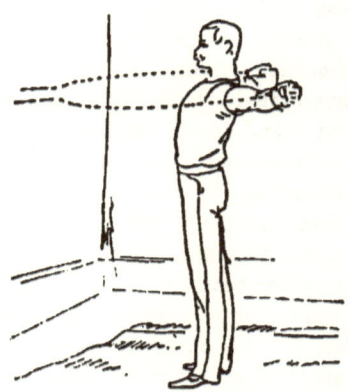

Fig. 2.—To develop Muscles across the Upper Back.

Fig. 3.—To develop Front Arm, Chest, Abdomen, Front Leg.

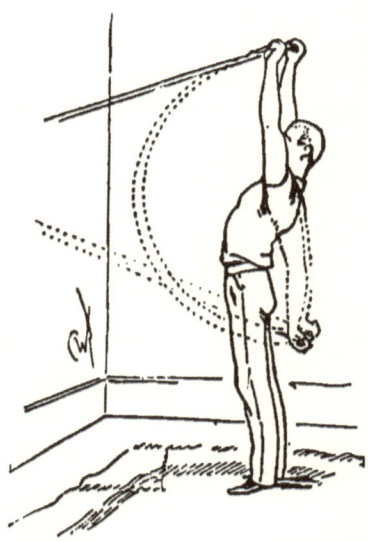

Fig. 4.—To develop Lower Back and Middle Back.

Note.—The cuts of the above illustrations were kindly furnished by the Narragansett Machine Company, manufacturers of the apparatus, Providence, R. L

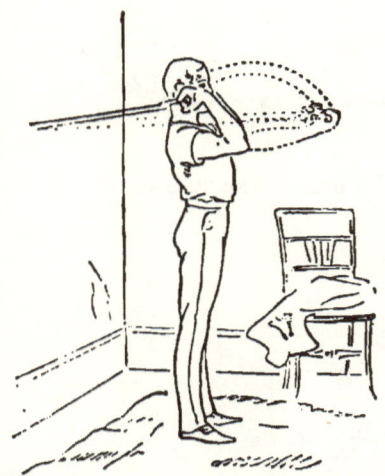

Fig. 5.—To develop Back Upper Arm.

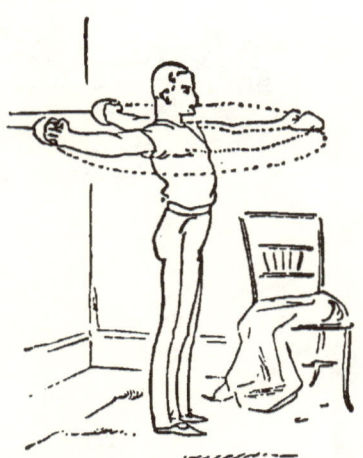

Fig. 6.—To develop Chest Muscles and Front Arm.

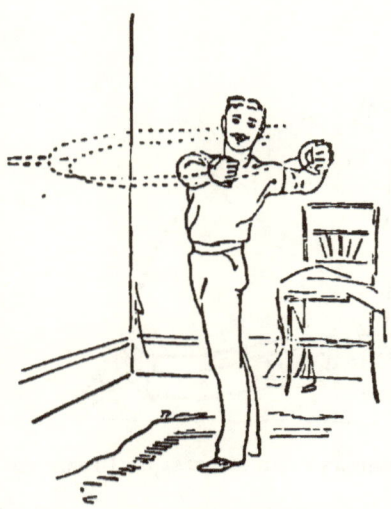

Fig. 7.—To develop Side-waist Muscles.

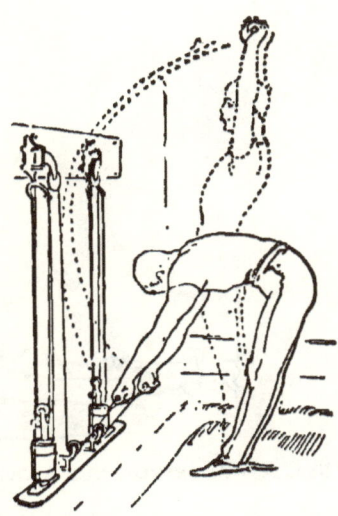

Fig. 8.—To develop Upper and Lower Back, Shoulder, Back Arm and Back Leg.

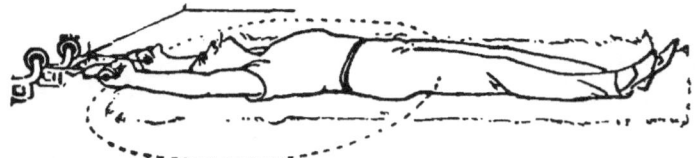

FIG. 9.—TO DEVELOP ABDOMEN; TO DEEPEN THE THORAX.

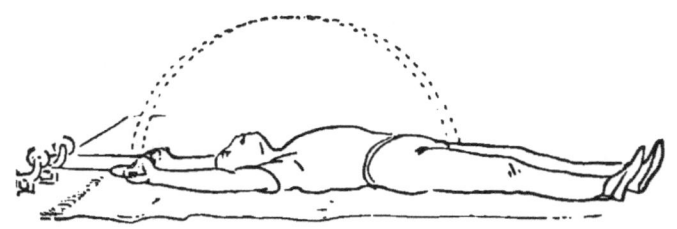

FIG. 10.—TO WIDEN THE THORAX AND DEVELOP THE SIDES OF WAIST.

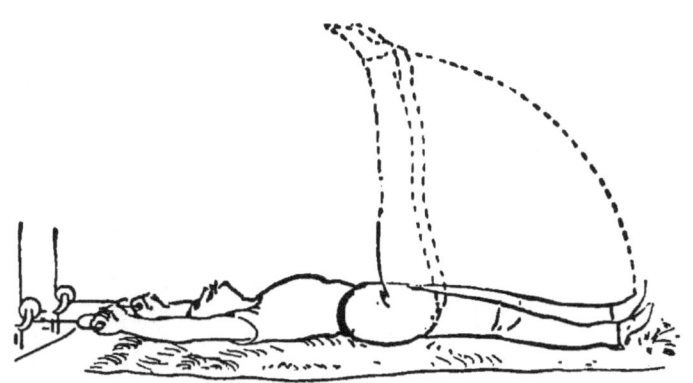

FIG. 11.—TO DEVELOP THE ABDOMINAL MUSCLES AND THE MUSCLES OF UPPER LEG.

GLOSSARY.

Ab-do'men (Latin *abdo*, to conceal). The largest cavity of the body, containing the liver, stomach, intestines, etc.; the belly.

Ab-sor'bents (L. *ab* and *sorbeo*, to suck up). The vessels which take part in the process of absorption.

Ab-sorp'tion. The process of sucking up fluids by means of an animal membrane.

Ac-com-mo-da'tion of the Eye. The alteration in the shape of the crystalline lens, which accommodates or adjusts the eye for near and remote vision.

Ac'id, Lactic (L. *lac*, milk). The acid ingredient of sour milk; the gastric juice also contains it.

Al-bu'men, or Albumin (L. *albus*, white). An animal substance resembling white of egg.

Al-bu'mi-nose (from *albumen*). A soluble animal substance produced in the stomach by the digestion of the albuminoid substances.

Al-bu'min-oid substances. A class of proximate principles resembling albumen; they may be derived from either the animal or vegetable kingdoms.

Al'i-ment (L. *alo*, to nourish). That which affords nourishment; food.

Al-i-ment'ary Ca-nal (from *aliment*). A long tube in which the food is digested, or prepared for reception into the system.

An-æs-thet'ics (Greek, *av, an*, without, αἰσθησία, *aisthesia*, feeling). Those medicinal agents which prevent the feeling of pain, such as chloroform, laughing-gas, etc.

An-i-mal'cule (L. *animal'culum*, a small animal). Applied to animals which can only be seen with the aid of the microscope. Animalculum (plural, animalcula) is used with the same meaning.

A-or'ta (Gr. ἀορτέομαι, *aortcomai*, to be lifted up). The largest artery of the body, and main trunk of all the arteries. It arises from the left ventricle of the heart. The name was first applied to the two large branches of the trachea, which appear to be lifted up by the heart.

A'que-ous Humor (L. *aqua*, water). A few drops of watery colorless fluid occupying the space between the cornea and crystalline lens.

A-rach'noid Mem'brane (Gr. ἀράχνη, *arachne*, a cobweb, and εἶδος, *eidos*, like). An extremely thin covering of the brain and spinal cord. It lies between the *dura mater* and the *pia mater*.

AR'BOR VI'TÆ (L.). Literally, "the tree of life;" a name given to the peculiar appearance presented by a section of the cerebellum.

AR'TER-Y (Gr. ἀήρ, *aer*, air, and τηρειν, *terein*, to contain). A vessel by which blood is conveyed away from the heart. It was supposed by the ancients to contain air; hence, the name.

AR-TIC-U-LA'TION (L. *articulo*, to form a joint). The more or less movable union of bones, etc.; a joint.

A-RYT'E-NOID CAR'TI-LA-GES (Gr. ἀρύταινα, *arutaina*, a pitcher). Two small cartilages of the larynx, resembling the mouth of a pitcher.

AS-SIM-I-LA'TION (L. *ad*, to, and *similis*, like). The conversion of food into living tissue.

AU-DI'TION (L. *audio*, to hear). The act of hearing sounds.

AU'DI-TO-RY NERVE. One of the cranial nerves; it is the special nerve of hearing.

AU'RI-CLE (L. *auris*, the ear). A cavity of the heart.

BAR'I-TONE (Gr. βαρύς, *barus*, heavy, and τόνος, *tonos*, tone). A variety of male voice between the bass and tenor.

BEL-LA-DON'NA (It. beautiful lady). A vegetable narcotic poison. It has the property of enlarging the pupil, and thus increasing the brilliancy of the eye; so called from its use by Italian ladies.

BI-CUS'PID (L. *bi*, two, and *cuspis*, prominence). The name of the fourth and fifth teeth on each side of the jaw; possessing two prominences.

BILE. The gall, or peculiar secretion of the liver; a viscid, yellowish fluid, and very bitter to the taste.

BRONCH'I (Gr. βρόγχος, *brogchos*, the windpipe). The two first divisions or branches of the trachea; one enters each lung.

BRONCH'I-AL TUBES. The smaller branches of the trachea within the substance of the lungs, terminating in the air-cells.

BRONCH-I'TIS (from *bronchia*, and *itis*, a suffix signifying inflammation). An inflammation of the larger bronchial tubes; a "cold" affecting the lungs.

CAL-CA'RE-OUS (L. *calx*, lime). Containing lime.

CA-NAL' (L.). In the body, any tube or passage.

CA-NINE' (L. *canis*, a dog). Name given to the third tooth on each side of the jaw; in the upper jaw it is also known as the eye-tooth, pointed like the tusks of a dog.

CAP'IL-LA-RY (L. *capil'lus*, a hair, *capilla'ris*, hair-like). The name of the extremely minute blood-vessels which connect the arteries with the veins.

CAR'BON DIOX-IDE (CO_2). Chemical name for carbonic acid gas.

CAR-BON'IC A'CID. The gas which is present in the air expired from the lungs; a waste product of the animal kingdom, and a food of the vegetable kingdom.

CAR'DI-AC (Gr. καρδια, *cardia*, the heart). The cardiac orifice of the stomach is the upper one, and is near the heart; hence its name.

CAR-NIV'O-ROUS (L. *ca'ro*, flesh, and *vo'ro*, to devour). Subsisting upon flesh.

CA-ROT'ID AR-TE-RY. The large artery of the neck, supplying the head and brain.

CAR'TI-LAGE. A solid but flexible material, forming a part of the joints, air-passages, nostrils, etc.; gristle.

CA'SE-INE (L. *ca'seus*, cheese). The albuminoid substance of milk, it forms the basis of cheese.

CER-E-BEL'LUM (diminutive for *cer'ebrum*, the brain). The little brain, situated beneath the posterior third of the cerebrum.

CER'E-BRUM (L.). The brain proper, occupying the entire upper portion of the skull. It is nearly divided into two equal parts, called "hemispheres," by a cleft extending from before backward.

CHO'ROID (Gr. χόριον, *chorion*, a membrane or covering). The middle tunic or coat of the eyeball.

CHYLE (Gr. χυλός, *chulos*, juice). The milk-like fluid formed by the digestion of fatty articles of food in the intestines.

CHYME (Gr. χυμός, *chumos*, juice). The pulpy liquid formed by digestion within the stomach.

CIL'I-A (pl. of *cil'i-um*, an eyelash). Minute, vibratile, hair-like processes found upon the cells of the air-passages, and other parts that are habitually moist.

CIR-CU-LA'TION (L. *cir'culus*, a ring). The circuit, or course of the blood through the blood-vessels of the body, from the heart to the arteries, through the capillaries into the veins, and from the veins back to the heart.

CO-AG-U-LA'TION (L. *coag'ulo*, to curdle). Applied to the process by which the blood clots or solidifies.

COCH'LE-A (L. *coch'lea*, a snail-shell). The spiral cavity of the internal ear.

CONCH'A (Gr. κόγχη, (*konche*, a mussel-shell). The external shell-shaped portion of the external ear.

CON-JUNC-TI'VA (L. *con* and *jun'go*, to join together. A thin layer of mucous membrane which lines the eyelids and covers the front of the eyeball; thus joining the latter to the lids.

CON-TRAC-TIL'I-TY (*L. con* and *tra'ho*, to draw together). The property of muscle which enables it to contract, or draw its extremities closer together.

CON-VO-LU'TIONS (L. *con* and *vol'vo*, to roll together). The tortuous foldings of the external surface of the brain.

CON-VUL'SION (L. *convel'lo*, to pull together). A more or less violent agitation of the limbs or body.

COR'NE-A (L. *cor'nu*, a horn). The transparent, horn-like substance which covers the anterior fifth of the eyeball.

COR'PUS-CLES, BLOOD (L. dim. of *cor'pus*, a body). The small bi-concave disks which give to the blood its red color; the *white* corpuscles are globular and larger.

Cos-met′ic (Gr. *κοσμέω, kosmeo,* to adorn). Beautifying; applied to articles which are supposed to increase the beauty of the skin, etc.

Cra′ni-al (L. *cra′ nium,* the skull). Pertaining to the skull. The nerves which arise from the brain are called cranial nerves.

Cri′coid (Gr. *κρίκος, kri′kos,* a ring). A cartilage of the larynx resembling a seal-ring in shape.

Crys′tal-line Lens (L. *crystal′lum,* a crystal). One of the so-called humors of the eye; a double convex body situated in the front part of the eyeball.

Cu′ti-cle (L. dim. of *cu′tis,* the skin). The scarf-skin; also called the *epider′mis.*

Cu′tis (L., skin or hide). The true skin, lying beneath the cuticle; also called the *der′mis.*

De-cus-sa′tion (L. *decus′sis,* the Roman numeral ten, X). A reciprocal cross-ing of fibres from side to side.

Di′a-phragm (Gr. *διαφράσσω, diaphrasso,* to divide by a partition). A large, thin muscle which separates the cavity of the chest from the abdomen; a muscle of respiration.

Dif-fus′ion of Gases. The power of gases to become intimately mingled, without reference to the force of gravity.

Duct (L. *du′co,* to lead). A narrow tube; the *thoracic duct* is the main trunk of the absorbent vessels.

Du-o-de′num (L. *duode′ni,* twelve). The first division of the small intestines, about twelve fingers-breadth long.

Du′ra Ma′ter (L.). Literally, the hard mother; the tough membrane which envelops the brain.

Dys-pep′si-a (Gr. *δυς, dus,* difficult, and *πεπτω, pepto,* to digest). Difficult or painful digestion; a disordered condition of the stomach.

E-mul′sion (L. *emul′geo,* to milk). Oil in a finely divided state suspended in water.

En-am′el (Fr. *email*). The dense material which covers the crown of the tooth.

Endocardium (Gr. *ένδο, endo,* within, and *κάρδια, kardia,* the heart. The lining membrane of the heart.

En′er-gy, Specific, of a Nerve. When a nerve of special sense is excited, whatever be the cause, the sensation experienced is that peculiar to the nerve; this is said to be the law of the specific energy of the nerves.

Ep-i-glot′tis (Gr. *έπί, epi,* upon, and *γλῶττις, glottis,* the entrance to the windpipe). A leaf-shaped piece of cartilage which covers the top of the larynx during the act of swallowing.

Ex-cre′tion (L. *excer′no,* to separate). The separation from the blood of the waste particles of the body; also the materials excreted.

Ex-pi-ra′tion (L. *expi′ro,* to breathe out). The act of forcing air out of the lungs.

Ex-ten'sion (L. *ex,* out, and *ten'do,* to stretch). The act of restoring a limb, etc., to its natural position after it has been flexed, or bent; the opposite of *Flexion.*

Fe-nes'tra (L.). Literally, a window; the opening between the middle and internal ear.

Fi'brine (L. *fi'bra,* a fibre). An albuminoid substance found in the blood; in coagulating it assumes a fibrous form.

Flex'ion (L. *flecto,* to bend). The act of bending a limb, etc.

Fol'li-cle (L. dim. of *fol'lis,* a bag). A little pouch or depression in a membrane ; it has generally a secretory function.

Fun'gous Growths (L. *fun'gus,* a mushroom). A low grade of vegetable life.

Gan'gli-on (Gr. γάνγλιον, *ganglion,* a knot). A knot-like swelling in the course of a nerve ; a smaller nerve-centre.

Gas'tric (Gr. γαστήρ, *gaster,* stomach). Pertaining to the stomach.

Gland (L. *glans,* an acorn). An organ consisting of follicles and ducts, with numerous blood-vessels interwoven ; it separates some particular fluid from the blood.

Glos'so-phar-yn-ge'al Nerve (Gr. γλῶσσα, *glossa,* the tongue, and φαρυγξ, *pharugx,* the throat). The nerve of taste supplying the posterior third of the tongue ; it also supplies the throat.

Glu'ten (L.). Literally, glue ; the glutinous albuminoid ingredient of wheat.

Gran'ule (L. dim. of *gra'num,* a grain). A little grain ; a microscopic object.

Gus-ta'tion (L. *gusto,* to taste). The sense of taste.

Gus'ta-to-ry Nerve. The nerve of taste supplying the front part of the tongue, a branch of the "fifth" pair.

Hem'or-rhage (Gr. αἷμα, *hai'ma,* blood, and ῥήγνυμι, *regnumi,* to burst). Bleeding, or the loss of blood.

Hem-i-ple'gia (Gr. ἥμισυς, *hemisus,* half, and πλήσσω, *plesso,* to strike). Paralysis, or loss of power, affecting one side of the body.

Hem'i-spheres (Gr. σφαῖρα, *sphaira,* a sphere). Half a sphere, the latera halves of the cerebrum, or brain proper.

He-pat'ic (Gr. ἧπαρ, *hepar,* the liver). Pertaining to the liver.

Her-biv'o-rous (L. *her'ba,* an herb, and *vo'ro,* to devour). Applied to animals that subsist upon vegetable food.

Hu'mor (L.). Moisture : the humors are transparent contents of the eyeball.

Hy-dro-pho'bi-a (Gr. ὕδωρ, *hudor,* water, and φοβέω, *phobeo,* to fear). A disease caused by the bite of a rabid dog or other animal. In a person affected with it, convulsions are occasioned by the sight of a glittering object, like water, by the sound of running water, and by almost any external impression.

Hy'gi-ene (Gr. ὑγίεια, *hugieia,* health). The art of preserving health and preventing disease.

Hy'per-o'pi-a. Abbreviated from Hy'per-met-ro'pi-a (Gr. ὑπέρ, *huper,* beyond, μέτρον, *metron,* the measure, and ὤψ, *ops,* the eye). A defect of vision dependent upon a too short eyeball ; so called because the rays of light are brought to a focus at a point behind the retina ; the true "far sight."

IN-CI'SOR (L. *inci'do*, to cut). Applied to the four front teeth of both jaws, which have sharp cutting edges.

IN'CUS (L.). An anvil ; the name of one of the bones of the middle ear.

IN-SAL-I-VA'TION (L. *in*, and *sali'va*, the fluid of the mouth). The mingling of the saliva with the food during the act of chewing.

IN-SPI-RA'TION (L. *in*, and *spi'ro*, to breathe). The act of drawing in the breath.

IN-TEG'U-MENT (L. *in*, and *te'go*, to cover). The skin, or outer covering of the body.

IN-TES'TINE (L. *in'tus*, within). The part of the alimentary canal which is continuous with the lower end of the stomach ; also called the intestines, or the bowels.

I'RIS (L. *i'ris*, the rainbow). The thin muscular ring which lies between the cornea and crystalline lens, and which gives the eye its brown, blue, or other color.

JU'GU-LAR (L. *ju'gulum*, the throat). The name of the large veins which run along the front of the neck.

LAB'Y-RINTH (Gr. λαβύρινθος, *laburin'thos*, a building with many winding passages). The very tortuous cavity of the inner ear, comprising the vestibule, semicircular canals, and the cochlea.

LACH'RY-MAL APPARATUS (L. *lach'ryma*, a tear). The organs for forming and conveying away the tears.

LAC'TE-ALS (L. *lac*, *lac'tis*, milk). The absorbent vessels of the small intestines ; during digestion they are filled with chyle, which has a milky appearance.

LA-RYN'GO-SCOPE (Gr. λάρυγξ, *larunx*, the larynx, and σκοπέω, *skopeo*, to look at). The instrument by which the larynx may be examined in the living subject.

LAR'YNX (Gr.). The cartilaginous tube situated at the top of the windpipe, or trachea ; the organ of the voice.

LENS (L.) Literally, a lentil ; a piece of transparent glass or other substance so shaped as either to converge or disperse the rays of light.

LIG'A-MENT (L. *li'go*, to bind). A strong, fibrous material binding bones or other solid parts together ; it is especially necessary to give strength to joints.

LIG'A-TURE. A thread of silk or other material used in tying around an artery.

LYMPH (L. *lym'pha*, spring-water). The colorless, watery fluid conveyed by the lymphatic vessels.

LYM-PHAT'IC VESSELS. A system of absorbent vessels.

MAL'LE-US (L.). Literally, the mallet ; one of the small bones of the middle ear.

Mar'row. The soft, fatty substance contained in the central cavities of the bones : the spinal marrow, however, is composed of nervous tissue.

Mas-ti-ca'tion (L. *mas'tico*, to chew). The act of cutting and grinding the food to pieces by means of the teeth.

Me-dul'la Ob-lon-ga'ta. The "oblong marrow," or nervous cord, which is continuous with the spinal cord within the skull.

Mem-bra'na Tym'pan-i (L.). Literally, the membrane of the drum ; a delicate partition separating the outer from the middle ear ; it is sometimes incorrectly called the drum of the ear.

Mem'brane. A thin layer of tissue serving to cover some part of the body.

Mi'cro-scope (Gr. μικρός, *mikros*, small, and σκοπέω, *skopeo*, to look at). An optical instrument which assists in the examination of minute objects.

Mo'lar (L. *mo'la*, a mill). The name applied to the three back teeth of each side of the jaw; the grinders, or mill-like teeth.

Mo'tor (L. *mo'veo*, *mo'tum*, to move). Causing motion ; the name of those nerves which conduct to the muscles the stimulus which causes them to contract.

Mu'cous Mem'brane. The thin layer of tissue which covers those internal cavities or passages which communicate with the external air.

Mu'cus. The glairy fluid which is secreted by mucous membranes, and which serves to keep them in a moist condition.

My-o'pi-a (Gr. μύω, *muo*, to contract, and ὤψ, *ops*, the eye). A defect of vision dependent upon an eyeball that is too long, rendering distant objects indistinct ; near sight.

Na'sal (L. *na'sus*, the nose). Pertaining to the nose ; the *nasal cavities* contain the distribution of the special nerve of smell.

Nerve (Gr. νεῦρον, *neuron*, a cord or string). A glistening, white cord of cylindrical shape, connecting the brain or spinal cord with some other organ of the body.

Nerve Cell. A minute, round and ashen-gray cell found in the brain and other nervous centres.

Nerve Fi'bre. An exceedingly slender thread of nervous tissue found in the various nervous organs, but especially in the nerves ; it is of a white color.

Nu-tri'tion (L. *nu'trio*, to nourish). The processes by which the nourishment of the body is accomplished.

Œ-soph'a-gus (Gr.). Literally, that which carries food ; the tube leading from the throat to the stomach ; the gullet.

O-le-ag'i-nous (L. *o'leum*, oil). Of the nature of oil : applied to an important group of food principles—the fats.

Ol-fac'to-ry (L. *olfa'cio*, to smell). Pertaining to the sense of smell.

Oph-thal'mo-scope (Gr. ὀφθαλμός, *ophthalmos*, the eye, and σκοπέω, *skopeo*, to look at). An instrument devised for examining the interior of the globe of the eye.

Op'tic (Gr. ὁράω, ὄψομαι, *fut*, *opsomai*, to see). Pertaining to the sense of sight.

Or'bit (L. *or'bis*, the socket). The bony socket or cavity in which the eye-ball is situated.

Os'mose (Gr. ὠσμός, *osmos*, a thrusting or impulsion). The process by which liquids are impelled through a moist membrane.

Os'se-ous (L. *os*, a bone). Consisting of, or resembling bone.

Pal'ate (L. *pala'tum*, (the palate). The roof of the mouth, consisting of the hard and soft palate.

Pal'mar. Relating to the palm of the hand.

Pan'cre-as (Gr. παν, *pan*, all, and κρέας, *kreas*, flesh). A long, flat gland situated near the stomach; in the lower animals the analogous organ is called the sweet-bread.

Pa-pil'læ (L. *papil'la*). The minute prominences in which terminate the ultimate fibres of the nerves of touch and taste.

Pa-ral'y-sis. A disease of the nervous system marked by the loss of sensation, or voluntary motion, or both; palsy.

Par-a-ple'gi-a (Gr. παραπλήσσω, *paraplesso*, to strike amiss). A form of paralysis affecting the lower half of the body.

Pa-tel'la (L. dim. of *pat'ina*, a pan). The knee-pan; a small bone.

Pel'vis (L.). Literally a basin; the bony cavity at the lower part of the trunk.

Pep'sin (Gr. πέπτω, *pepto*, to digest). The organic principle of the gastric juice.

Per-i-car'di-um (Gr. περί, *peri*, and κάρδια, *kardia*, the heart). A porous membrane enclosing the heart, and secreting a lubricating fluid.

Per-i-stal'tic Move'ments (Gr. περιστέλλω, *peristello*, to contract). The slow, wave-like movements of the stomach and intestines.

Per-i-to-ne'um (Gr. περιτείνω, *periteino*, to stretch around). The investing membrane of the stomach, intestines, and other abdominal organs.

Per-spi-ra'tion (L. *perspi'ro*, to breathe through). The sweat, or watery exhalation of the skin; when visible, it is called *sensible* perspiration, when invisible, it is called *insensible* perspiration.

Pe'trous (Gr. πέτρα, *petra*, a rock). The name of the hard portion of the temporal bone, in which is situated the drum of the ear and labyrinth.

Phar'ynx (Gr. φάρυγξ, *pharugx*, the throat). The cavity between the back of the mouth and gullet.

Phys-i-ol'o-gy (Gr. φύσις, *phusis*, nature, and λόγος, *logos*, a discourse). The science of the functions of living, organized beings.

Pi'a Ma'ter (L.). Literally, the tender mother; the innermost of the three coverings of the brain. It is thin and delicate; hence the name.

Pleu'ra (Gr. πλευρά, a rib). A membrane covering the lung and lining the chest. There is one for each lung.

Pleu'ri-sy. An inflammation affecting the pleura.

Pneu-mo-gas'tric (Gr. πνεύμων, *pneumon*, the lungs, and γαστήρ, *gaster*, the stomach). The name of a nerve distributed to the lungs and stomach; it is the principal nerve of respiration.

Pneu-mo'ni-a (Gr.). An inflammation affecting the air-cells of the lungs.

PRES-BY-O'PI-A (Gr. πρέσβυς, *presbus*, old, and ὤψ, *ops*, the eye). A defect of the accommodation of the eye, caused by the hardening of the crystalline lens ; the "far-sight" of adults and aged persons.

PROC'ESS (L. *proce'do, proces'sus*, to proceed, to go forth). Any projection from a surface. Also, a method of performance ; a procedure.

PTY'A·LIN (Gr. πτύαλον, *ptualon*, saliva). The peculiar organic ingredient of the saliva.

PUL'MO-NA-RY (L. *pul'mo, pulmo'nis*, the lungs). Pertaining to the lungs.

PULSE (L. *pel'lo, pul'sum*, to beat). The striking of an artery against the finger, occasioned by the contraction of the heart, commonly felt at the wrist.

PU'PIL (L. *pupil'la*). The central, round opening in the iris, through which light passes into the depths of the eye.

PY-LO'RUS (L. πυλωρός, *puloros*, a gate-keeper). The lower opening of the stomach, at the beginning of the small intestine.

RE'FLEX ACTION. An involuntary action of the nervous system, by which an external impression conducted by a sensory nerve is reflected, or converted into a motor impulse.

RES-PI-RA'TION (L. *res'piro*, to breathe frequently). The function of breathing, comprising two acts: *inspiration*, or breathing in, and *expiration*, or breathing out.

RET'I-NA (L. *re'te*, a net). The innermost of the three tunics or coats of the eyeball, being an expansion of the optic nerve.

SAC'CHA-RINE (L. *sac'charum*, sugar). Of the nature of sugar; applied to the important group of food substances which embraces the different varieties of sugar, starch, and gum.

SA-LI'VA (L.). The moisture or fluids of the mouth, secreted by the salivary glands, etc.

SCLE-ROT'IC (Gr. σκληρός, *skleros*, hard). The tough, fibrous outer tunic of the eyeball.

SE-BA'CEOUS (L. *se'bum*, fat). Resembling fat; the name of the oily secretion by which the skin is kept flexible and soft.

SE-CRE'TION (L. *secer'no, secre'tum*, to separate). The process of separating from the blood some essential important fluid; which fluid is also called a secretion.

SEM-I-CIR'CU-LAR CANALS. A portion of the internal ear.

SEN-SA'TION. The perception of an external impression by the nervous system; a function of the brain.

SEN-SI-BIL'I-TY, GENERAL. The power possessed by nearly all parts of the human body of recognizing the presence of foreign objects that come in contact with them.

SE'RUM (L.). The watery constituent of the blood, which separates from the clot during the process of coagulation.

SKEL'E-TON (Gr.). The bony framework of an animal, the different parts of which are maintained in their proper relative positions.

Spec'tro-scope (from *spec'trum* and σκοπέω, *scopeo*, to examine the spectrum). An instrument employed in the examination of the spectrum of the sun or any other luminous body.

Sphyg'mo-graph (Gr. σφυγμός, *sphugmos*, the pulse, and γράφω, *grapho*, to write). An ingenious instrument by means of which the pulse is delineated upon paper.

Sta'pes (L.). Literally, a stirrup; one of the small bones of the tympanum, or middle ear, resembling somewhat a stirrup in shape.

Sym-pa-thet'ic System of Nerves. A double chain of nervous ganglia, connected together by numerous small nerves, situated chiefly in front of and on each side of the spinal column.

Syn-o'vi-a (Gr. σύν, *sun*, and ώόν, *oon*, egg, resembling an egg). The lubricating fluid of joints, so called because it resembles the white of egg.

Sys'to-le (Gr. συστέλλω, *sustello*, to contract). The contraction of the heart, by which the blood is expelled from that organ.

Tac-tile (L. *tac'tus*, touch). Relating to the sense of touch.

Tem'po-ral (L. *tem'pus*, time, and *tem'pora*, the temples). Pertaining to the temples; the name of an artery; so called, because the hair begins to turn white with age in that portion of the scalp.

Ten'don (L. *ten'do*, to stretch). The white, fibrous cord or band by which a muscle is attached to a bone; a sinew.

Tet'a-nus (Gr. τείνω, *teino*, to stretch). A disease marked by persistent contractions of all or some of the voluntary muscles; those of the jaw are sometimes solely affected; the disorder is then termed locked-jaw.

Tho'rax (Gr. θώραξ, *thorax*, a breast-plate). The upper cavity of the trunk of the body, containing the lungs, heart, etc.; the chest.

Thy'roid (Gr. θυρεός, *thureos*, a shield). The largest of the cartilages of the larynx; its angular projection in the front of the neck is called "Adam's apple."

Tra'che-a (Gr. τραχύς, *trachus*, rough). The windpipe, or the largest of the air-passages; composed in part of cartilaginous rings, which render its surface rough and uneven.

Trans-fu'sion (L. *transfun'do*, to pour from one vessel to another). The operation of injecting blood taken from one person into the veins of another; other fluids than blood are sometimes used.

Trich-i'na Spi-ra'lis (L.). A minute species of parasite or worm, which infests the flesh of the hog, and which may be introduced into the human system by eating pork not thoroughly cooked.

Tym'pa-num (Gr. τύμπανον, *tumpanon*, a drum). The cavity of the middle ear, resembling a drum in being closed by two membranes, and in having communication with the atmosphere.

U're-a (Gr.). A substance secreted from the blood by the kidneys.

U'vu-la (L. *uva*, a grape). The small pendulous body attached to the back part of the palate.

VAS'CU-LAR (L. *vas'culum*, a little vessel). Pertaining to, or containing blood-vessels.

VE'NOUS (L. *ve'na*, a vein). Pertaining to, or contained within a vein.

VEN-TI-LA'TION. The introduction of fresh air into a room or building in such a manner as to keep the air within it in a pure condition.

VEN-TRIL'O-QUISM (L. *ven'ter*, the belly, and *lo'quor*, to speak). A modification of natural speech by which the voice is made to appear to come from a distance. The ancients supposed that the voice was formed in the belly; hence the name.

VEN'TRI-CLES of the heart. The two largest cavities of the heart, situated at its apex or point.

VER'TE-BRAL COLUMN (L. *ver'te-bra*, a joint). The back-bone, consisting of twenty-six separate bones, called vertebræ, firmly jointed together; also called the spinal column and spine.

VES'TI-BULE. A portion of the internal ear, communicating with the semicircular canals and the cochlea; so called from its fancied resemblance to the vestibule or porch of a house.

VIL'LI (L. *vil'lus*, the nap of cloth). Minute thread-like projections found upon the internal surface of the small intestine, giving it a velvety appearance.

VIT'RE-OUS (L. *vi'trum*, glass). Having the appearance of glass, applied to the humor occupying the largest part of the cavity of the eyeball.

VIV-I-SEC'TION (L. *vi'vus*, alive, and *se'co*, to cut). The practice of operating upon living animals, for the purpose of studying some physiological process.

VOCAL CORDS. Two elastic bands or ridges situated in the larynx; they are the essential parts of the organs of the voice.

INDEX.

www.ingramcontent.com/pod-product-compliance
Lightning Source LLC
Chambersburg PA
CBHW020943030726
47496CB00005B/1332